T0208701

White Chocolate

M. Angela Lynch-Clare

iUniverse, Inc.
Bloomington

iUniverse books may be ordered through booksellers or by contacting:

iUniverse
1663 Liberty Drive
Bloomington, IN 47403
www.iuniverse.com
1-800-Authors (1-800-288-4677)

ISBN: 978-1-4502-4543-2 (sc)

Printed in the United States of America

iUniverse rev. date: 4/12/11

To my father who showed me the way.

making
with their

rhythms some-
thing torn

and new

Kamau Brathwaite
Islands

Thanks to my friends, Philippa Perry, Betty-Anne Jackson, Alexis Hutchinson and Lorna Kirven-Smith, who believed in me and my book and sustained me through the vicissitudes of the book's creation and final publication. Thanks to Claudette Anderson for your input and to Cheryl Woodruff who helped shape the book. Finally, thanks to my family: my daughters, Jasmine, Christina and Amanda and my husband Fred, who lived through the creative process with me and helped with the emergence of this final product. I am grateful for the love and support of all of you.

Contents

1

Housewarming

Charlie leapt and spun around. She waved her hands in the air. The calypso music was in her blood. She was its avatar. She shrieked as she shook her backside.

"Work it girl!" came a nearby shout."

Charlie licked her smooth, apricot-flavored lips and grinned as she executed intricate movements involving long dormant muscles. Bring on the liniment tomorrow(!)she decided, as hand on her belly she wriggled her waist and rotated in a circle. The scent of barbecuing meat mingled with night-blooming jasmine came with the breeze that cooled the party as they all danced with abandonment on the wooden dance floor in Charlie's backyard. Some of the white guests bounced up and down in tune with their own inner rhythms, instead of the calypso rhythm. This contrasted starkly with many of African descent sensuously cavorting to a familiar music.

Fire fire!

In she wire Papa

Ai yay yay,

O yo yo

Then she saw Lennie. Her husband, beer bottle in hand, was vigorously 'working up' on a white woman. He held her firmly by the waist as she screamed with delight and exuberantly accepted his every pelvic thrust with one of her own-all set to music. Charlie bit her lip 'til she tasted blood. He was a good father. He was tall, handsome, light-skinned, part East Indian with straight hair and he was a doctor. He had lightened her darkness. She gritted her teeth as she tossed her hair, shook her ass and finished her rotation. God damn it! She could bear it.

"Great party, Charlie," her friend Rose called out, shimmying past and laughing with her husband, Grantley.

"Charlie, there you are!" A large woman, face shining as if someone had just fried chicken on it; elbowed her way towards Charlie. "Meet some friends of mine." She grabbed Charlie's hand tugging her off the dance floor as Charlie looked back apologetically at her abandoned dance partner.

"Don't worry about me; go do your hostess thing," he said and leapt into the center of a group of gyrating hips and bouncing breasts..

"Girrrl, I'm so proud of you. And don't you look cute? Is it a Gallanos darling? How much did it cost?" The woman leaned forward, pecked Charlie on the cheek, and groped the back of her dress checking for the label with the garment's 'credentials'.

Charlie evaded the anticipated, seeking fingers. "Glad you made it, Rebbie." She eyed the six strangers. "Who are your friends and where's Scott?"

Rebbie rubbed her thumb and middle finger together. "Gotta make the money, honey; he's still seeing patients. He'll be along later. I was bragging on you to these ladies, talking up this mansion and your restaurants. You know how we love to see our black folks doing well. They just had to see for themselves, so I brought them along-knew you wouldn't mind. This is some housewarming. Meet Vera, Ruby, Jacquetta, Eliza, M'War and Shaniqua."

The strangers smiled at Charlie as a nearby reveler noted;

"This melanin thing is serious. The melanin challenged arrived first, and now the others are rolling in. Haw, haw!"

"Asshole!" said Rebbie. "Girl, how much did this place cost? Come, show it to us." She looped arms with Charlie.

"Charlie, is it true that you're the only black family living here in Angloville?" asked one of the strangers-a lively looking black blonde, in tiny clothes.

"That's not important," chimed in another one. "Charlie, Rebbie promised you'd show us the house. I'll bet its pretty, just like you. Let's go see it."

A tension headache was setting up shop above Charlie's right eyebrow.

"Come on; let's get on with the tour. I brought my video camera," Rebbie gently tugged Charlie's arm as the group closed in around them and they all advanced toward the house. "We'll have the next Delta meeting here and the Jack and Jill installation tea of course. It'll impress the hell out of the new mothers and show them that they're entering a quality organization. Uumhmm."The headache started to sell its wares as Charlie, fighting the urge to whirl on the bitch, arms akimbo, and invite her to fuck herself instead followed her proper West Indian upbringing and merely said, "Excuse me; I must get back to my guests."

"What, honey?" said Rebbie absently propelling Charlie ever more insistently toward the large, brightly illuminated house.

Charlie jerked her arm away. "Rebbie; go find a table for yourself and your friends. I'll have the caterer put out more food – nice meeting all of you." She pressed Rebbie back toward the party and the uninvited satellites fell in behind her. Then Charlie headed for her house, alone. She gave an annoyed West Indian chupse, audibly forcing air out through her teeth. "Uncouth big bitch," she muttered. Vowing that Rebbie would tour her house the day white cops stopped using black men for target practice; Charlie let herself into her bustling kitchen.

A few minutes later Charlie emerged from her kitchen behind a pair of waiters headed for the buffet table with laden trays. She paused for a moment to admire it all. Tikki torches flared dramatically and in the distance votive candles floated in the swimming pool. A slight breeze stirred colorful, balloon table centerpieces and laughter and snatches of desultory conversation punctuated the night air.

"What do you and your husband do?"

"He's a lawyer," came the quick response.

"So am I! Corporate law." The speaker examined a non existent speck on her perfectly manicured nails as the light played dazzlingly on the diamond eternity ring and tennis bracelet being so advantageously displayed.

Her conversational partner relaxed visibly and smiled before rummaging through her Byblos bag. She produced a purse size spray and spritzed herself. "I had this scent made for me while I was in France last month, but it's such a bother! It wears off so quickly ... Maybe I won't carry it in my store." She pouted.

They heard: "There's such a crush of people here. I hope no one scratches our car. Every time that Rolls goes to be repaired . . ."

"... the bathrooms by the pool were always wet. He couldn't deal with it, and he saw dirt in the folds of his tent! We're trying a new camp this year."

A sympathetic cluck presaged, "That's awful. My daughter was at a sleepaway last summer-for the gifted of course. She qualified for the Johns Hopkins program; her brother did too but he never went. Well, the white people expected the child to wash her own clothes, for Crissake! We had to drive to Pennsylvania to sort it out."

"…son's at Merril Lynch. He wants to leave but they keep promoting him!"

"...You really must try Chez Marc; my wife buys all her furs there."

"I can't do that. We have a moratorium on spending in our family right now. The baby starts Harvard this Fall. You know how kids are; she wanted to attend her sisters' alma mater. These Ivy League kids…Harrumph." The speaker gave a choking laugh.

"Did you go to Harvard too? Pat's formed a club for children of black Harvard graduates-along the lines of Jack and Jill. You know, so they can meet the right sort."

"High yella people can look frightening! My son brought home a big-lipped, big butt girl the color of shit and butter, and then had the nerve to tell me she was beautiful. I said, 'Boy, don't you ever again bring home anything that looks like it should have a tail'."

The summer Sag Harbor crowd was trying to gain converts to the good life.

"The ice cream in those waffle cones should be banned. I sniffed it and gained ten pounds on my backside last summer."

"...hard to get a decent pool man out there. Algae lined the entire pool and the bastard had to be coaxed to come take care of it."

"Bet he charged the 'black tax' too. You know how they always charge us more."

"You'd love Sag! Black folks have some houses out there, uumh, uumh, ooom!"

"Nooo! " A blood-curdling scream presaged the eruption of two Abercrombie clad pre-adolescent girls onto the lawn, one frantically clutching a hamster.

"You give him back to me right now. I'll kill you!" The pursuing child screamed and lunged at the animal.

A large woman in flowing robes hurried to the children. "Honey," she said firmly to the hamster-clutching child, "Give it to Mommy."

Charlie rushed to the scene. "What's going on?" she demanded.

The pursuer yelled. "Mommy, I told her she couldn't play with Cash. She wouldn't listen. He doesn't like strangers. She's scaring him. Gimme!" She lunged at her pet.

The girl, Frances, held on tightly and gave the animal a world class squeezing in its belly. The animal made a strange strangulated sound as it vomited, urinated, defecated and departed this vale of tears, pronto.

"No," whispered Charlie, "What did that little bitch do!"

Charlie's daughter, Germaine, slapped the hamster killer. Whap!

The hamster killer's mother, Effie slapped Germaine. Pow! Charlie rolled her fist to floor the woman, but couldn't. Lennie was holding her arm.

"No! Allow me," he said, as only too happy to step in and do this job for his wife; he made a preparatory fist.

This snapped Charlie back to reality. "No, Lennie! Stop! Someone help me!" she shrieked hanging onto his arm as she threw herself between him and the woman."

"Out of my way, woman! This pissing-tail, drunken fool come to my home, hit my child, and you telling me to stop before I roll her ass up with blows? But what drug you taking at all?"

Charlie clung even tighter. Men rushed to her aid and guests rubbernecked the donnybrook.

"Stop, man. That woman must be seeing green now."

"She wants you to hit her so she can collect."

"For God's sake, don't bring Jerry Springer to Angloville!"

They held him. Charlie commanded the DJ to "Play Music!" and Arrow's soka hit, Hot Hot Hot, blasted from the speakers. Guests hurried to the dance floor checking out the little tableau in transit. When Arrow screamed, "How you feelin'?" They yelled as one, "Hot, hot, hot," and danced in a sweaty frenzy.

Lennie dispatched the mother and child. The shamefaced father joined them and they departed to Lennie's "...and if I wasn't a gentleman I would kick all-you asses. But you better never ever come 'round here again." He held his daughter in his arms and gently smoothed the curly hair so like his own as he crooned, "Don't cry, doux doux darling. Papa will get you another one-a bigger, better one. Tomorrow!" They went inside. Charlie stored the body for later burial and returned to her hostess duties.

"Rev, how goes it?" she called sailing past his table.

"Fine, my child, lovely party." Reverend Lee burped softly and returned his attention to two pleasingly pneumatic church sisters, pillars of his Baptist church.

"You'd think she didn't have a care in the world," hissed one of them."

"She doesn't," said the Reverend. "She is truly blessed. I've known her since she was a little tyke in Harlem attending church every Sunday with her poor mother, bless her dear departed soul. Now see what she has achieved." He waved at their surroundings

"But she can't hold her man," said a sister with satisfaction.

Someone chimed in, "All this didn't help her when Lennie was in the closet at Harlem Hospital, getting to know that scrawny, little, doctor in the biblical sense. These black men and their white women; they will go after scraps." She chupsed.

"Oh God, yes!" guffawed a man. "I heard about that. His penis got caught in her IUD and they had to be surgically separated or something so?"

"Yes, the Medical Journals and the Amsterdam News both wrote it up. I hear they panicked and bawled and behaved like dogs fighting in a crocus sack, these West Indians can carry on; had to give her Valium to relax the muscles so she'd release him."

"Bless my soul!" sputtered the Reverend. "The good Lord beats his children without even a stick, that poor child." He shook his large head sorrowfully while in the background the calypso went,

I don' know an I don' know

Why nigger people is bad-minded so

"Charlie, over here," called out, a round, shiny, little, much-married physician sporting driving gloves and summer whites.

"Hey, having fun yet, big guy?" She playfully jabbed his belly.

"You surpassed yourself, lady, buying a spread like this, right here in Angloville, of all places. Did you buy under an assumed color?" He whooped loudly at his own wit, and his soft belly shook with mirth.

"Good to see you too," said Charlie.

He continued, "Now if Lennie would only pass his boards. But I guess he doesn't have to. He's got a Sugar Momma of a wife."

A struggling, East Indian perinatologist shook her finger at Charlie and advised. "Listen, Charlie, you need to get on Lennie's case and make him pass his specialty boards. Then he can work someplace like Lenox Hill in the city or even your local Lawrence Hospital; not El whatever-the-hell-the-name-of-that-place-in-the-Bronx- is. He could speak Spanish? Or Haitian for that matter?"

Charlie forced a laugh. "Lighten up, you guys, this is a party! By the way, some of you still owe me money from your poverty stricken residency days. Remember you used to eat and run up those pitiful, still unpaid tabs at my first Charlie's Chicken?""Uh-oh! You folks better behave 'cause Charlie gon' kick some ass and take some *names* and money too," said 'big guy' throwing his arm around her shoulder.

"Aw, Charlie, you sexy thing, we're just kidding around," said a psychiatrist. He bussed her soundly on the lips and pulled her to him. "Love your new place, hon; enjoying it? I saw in last month's Ebony that you've opened your eighth restaurant on the East Coast and plan to expand down South next-way to go!"

"So? All the more reason to want my money, and with interest too!"

"Dang, Charlie! don't hold your breath. Remember we graduated with MDs not MBAs; we're not rich like you. HMOs are running us out of town. I studied thirteen years post high school and now some high school dropout decides not only what I can do but also how much I should get paid for doing it. My earnings nose-dived seventy five percent. I need a loan-from you!"

His colleagues laughed uneasily.

"Yeah, Charlie, get loose with that pocketbook," urged an oncologist.

"You doctors are pathetic. I can't abide poverty. Let me get away from the pack of you in case it's contagious," Charlie laughed and moved on.

"Charlie! Oh my God this is fabulous! The setting. . .the food. . . the music. . ." Sophie threw her arms around Charlie in a congratulatory hug.

"Rotate, but don' win'."

Sophie sang along with the music, then flung her hands in the air and rocked her pelvis. "Out of my way and lemme show these Americans how to do it!" She sashayed past Charlie in precarious high heels, a knock-me-down-and-fuck-me Betsy Johnson summer dress and dancing attitude. Her husband behind her, hung on for dear life to her rocking hips.

She has 'West Indianized' me, so watch me now-you might learn a thing or two." He winked at Charlie then bounded onto the dance floor behind his wife.

I say to bend down low
and mek yuh bumsie
Oscillate

Charlie laughed and continued her peregrinations. She smiled as she saw Phoebe, her psychologist/sex therapist friend besieged by a large, white woman with lots of frizzy, strawberry-blonde hair and heard: "You gotta tell me if this is okay. My husband has wonderful erections but-"

"Honey, please don't," pleaded a pale, gangly, white man by her side whose sexual shortcomings were apparently being discussed.

The woman kept a restraining hand on his shoulder and confided, "He just stays hard and he keeps going on and on and on."

"Is it a problem for you?" asked Phoebe.

"Oh no, it's just great, but still I was wondering. You know... I'm Jewish and I like a lot of everything. A lot of hair." She tossed her wild mane, "a lot of food," a pat to the belly, "a lot of sex." She disappointed her audience with no demonstration for this one. "I just love everything in abundance," she caroled.

"Then you're just fine," stated Phoebe.

"How Jewish," cut in a bystander, "This love of excess. Is this why your noses are bigger, so you can breathe more air than the rest of us?"

Charlie decided to circulate further afield.

"The Republican Party is the logical choice for black advancement…"

"Hi Homer", she called out. "Up on your soapbox at my party I see. You politicians! I should charge you for providing a captive audience."

"Charlie, the hostess with the mostest," Homer said as he hugged her.

"Hi, Marguerite," Charlie acknowledged Homer's pretty, elegantly decked out wife, hovering on the outskirts of the group with a bored, fixed smile. "How're the kiddies?"

"Great," Marguerite responded unenthusiastically. "How're yours?"

"Same as yours, great!" replied Charlie. "By the way, Homer, I'm with you guys. I'm interested in three things money, money and more money. If the Republicans can deliver again, sign me on!"

"Yay for money!" cheered a black, Republican stockbroker.

A short, wide, butter-colored woman intercepted Charlie as she wended her way between the tables. "So what's the story on your kid's education?

There's no black kids in the Angloville schools," she said with a malicious smile.

"Jemima, I'm so happy to see you," said Charlie, "And it's plain wonderful of you to be concerned. What you said is true; but we haven't moved in here yet. Germaine's still finishing out the school year in Mamaroneck. This is the only date my fabulous caterer had available until late October, so we grabbed it since outdoor parties are such fun." Charlie smiled then played her trump card.

"We handled the school matter by joining Jack and Jill."

"Where's your best-friend, Maxi, I haven't seen her all evening?"

"She'll be here soon, she had business to take care of," Charlie lied as she too wondered where her best friend was.

"Oh," said Jemima. She looked around morosely then brightened up. "Nice party!"

Charlie saw the sight that cheered Jemima, Lennie now 'working up' exuberantly on a pretty, woman, whose dark skin was set off by a flaming red dress. His hands were all over her.

"Charlie, sit and eat, that's an order," Her friend, Rose reached out from a nearby table and pulled Charlie down into an empty chair.

Charlie complied gratefully. "Yes, ma'am."

"I'll bet you haven't eaten yet. Grantley, go fix a plate for Charlie," Rose ordered.

"Yes, ma'am," he rose with alacrity and a grin.

Everyone laughed and Rose continued, "Charlie, isn't it great, you and Lola are both coming into Jack and Jill in September. Rebbie's sponsoring Lola for membership."

"What's this?" asked Leroy, Lola's husband. "My wife and kids are joining a snooty organization for light-skinned blacks that wouldn't have accepted me when I was a child because I was too dark and too poor?"

"Honey, I'm sorry, I meant to tell you," his pale, sandy-haired wife said nervously. "But it's not like that anymore. Rebbie's bringing us in and she's very dark."

"Yes, that old field nigger stuff is passé," said Phoebe. "Kaput!" She tapped Leroy on the shoulder. "I saw you in Black Enterprise looking mighty handsome 'one of the hottest young black contractors around' I quote, uh huh, and with that big Manhattan project coming up... Brother's got it going on! Congrats!

"Thanks, Phoebe." Leroy laughed.

"Darling, you know the kids need to meet other suitable black kids," said Lola.

"Suitable," Leroy muttered and shook his head.

"Your kids are elementary school age. This is the perfect time for them to join the organization and make friends for life," Phoebe said firmly.

"Women!" a man snorted in disgust. "Good Lord! Where did that great looking piece of dark meat come from?" He stood up and stared at a woman on the dance floor. "She's fiery and wiry and win'ing like a corkscrew. Lord have mercy! And look at that backside! Who is she?"

"Man she could wuk up she waist in truth!" corroborated a West Indian male, seduced into the vernacular at the sight of the woman in the red dress 'getting on bad' with Lennie to the strains of that year's Trinidad Carnival Road March.

"That's Colette, Raymondo's ex-wife. She's such a-no I won't say it." The woman clammed up.

"Rose, I glimpsed your little chess champion, Sydney, earlier, is Buddy here too?"

"He's at a Beach Club in New Rochelle, attending his thirtieth Bat Mitzvah this year. He says the Rabbi told him last week that because he's met him at so many of these things he now considers him an honorary Jew. Over my dead body he is!"

Grantley, trailed by a waiter with drinks, showed up with Charlie's plate. She thanked them and looked up, as the DJ, in a sweat-soaked, red, baby tee, legs apart and pelvis thrust out, became particularly loud. He rolled his hips lasciviously and growled along with the music:

If you wan' to kiss an' caress
Rub down ev'ry strand o'hair
'Pon me ches'

A knot of white women, gathered close by, approvingly eyed the conspicuous bulge at his crotch. Yes, the party was a success. Charlie relaxed and ate her food. Charlie became aware of a strong, sickly-sweet scent on the evening air. She excused herself and followed her nose past the swimming pool and the koi pond to the secluded lower lawn. She found a group of pot smokers; among them was Mumtaz, Lennie's young, East Indian cousin from Trinidad. The girl was deep in conversation with a neighborhood WASP. She heard:

"Why the British accent? Surely the average Trinidadian doesn't speak that way."

"How astute of you," responded Mumtaz in her clipped proper speech. "I speak this way, precisely for that reason; so that some white ass-hole won't come up to me, compliment me on my 'picturesque' accent and say that it reminds him of his cook, or the girl who works for him. I speak like the English teachers who educated me, back home."

Charlie frowned in annoyance. Then reasoned that Mumtaz probably got her fill of drugs and lesbian sex too, if she so desired, as an undergraduate at nearby artsy, Sarah Lawrence College. It was not her responsibility to police Lennie's young relatives. She clapped her hands and yelled, "Everybody, on the floor, now-Last lap. Move it!"

"Aaaww! Don't throw us out, Charlie?" begged a blissed-out voice."

"Have to, it's my bedtime!" She strode back up the hill and yelled to the DJ. "Hit it! Give me one for the road!"

One of the good Baptist sisters, danced with an Italian real estate developer clad in white polyester pants, white moccasins, and a blue, open neck camp shirt that revealed a Virgin Mary medallion nestling on his hairy chest. He was a great bear of a man and his bulk fought her mudcloth robe encased bulk, seeking a common rhythm.

I bawling.

Suck me, Soucouya.

Bite, bite, bite me all over. . .

"Mama Mia!" the man breathed; dancing to the words rather than the music, he complied. He dropped to his knees, hugged the woman tightly around the hips and proceeded to nip at her thighs.

"What the-" exclaimed that good woman. Words failed her. Earnestly, she begged her God to look away for five minutes. Then she raised her powerful right arm and with all the power and glory of her Lord behind it, crashed it into the man's chin. She knocked him clean off his knees onto the crowded dance floor and then stalked off-nose in the air, in a high dudgeon.

"That's how I like my women; all sapphire!" approved a nearby man.

"Party hearty!" yelled Charlie, dancing past the supine figure.

Win', win'" yelled her husband. "Shake up your body line!" He did a few belly rolls that aroused lecherous female thoughts.

The music died and the party broke up. Charlie's headache that dimmed into the background suddenly turned up the wattage. She kneaded her temples and approached Lennie. "You'll have to see our guests off, my head is killing me. I'm going to sit in the gazebo for a few minutes. Have Maria bring me some Tylenol please."

"Sure. You can go to bed, I can make your excuses and manage for us."

"Thanks, but I can't. I just need to sit somewhere cool for a while then I can supervise the caterer. If I don't give everything a final look-see, there's bound to be screw-ups, which I'll pay for later. God, my head is killing me!" She moaned and walked away pressing her temples.

Lennie then said goodbye, his style. He hugged a young woman and rubbed her bottom in a lingering good night before moving on to other suitable candidates.

The guests reluctantly straggled out and snatches of their conversations filled the air, as people parted from their friends.

"Girl, the black, ugly, son of a monkey has hair like a shoe brush, but the child insists that she loves him."

"No! And your daughter's a good-looking, fair skin girl."

"Lennie, where's Charlie?"

"She's nursing a headache, I'll tell her good-bye for you."

"...moved in next door with the tackiest furniture – obviously we won't be going over to introduce ourselves."

"... that boy in Jack and Jill all his life, yet he still turned around and married a white woman-met her right at Harvard."

"You should've sent him to Howard."

"...blue-eyed bitch comes to the house to fuck my son and doesn't have the decency to say 'hello' or 'good afternoon' when she walks past me in the hallway!"

"Why can't these white girls leave our sons alone? They're all little Hottentots with one thing on their minds. They wear make-up at nine and their mothers loose them wild on the boys when they turn ten. We don't go for that slackness."

"Neither do they – it's just the loose ones. I have decent white friends that I'd trust my children with any day before I'd put them with some black folks that I know."

"Damn liberal! I told my boy child, and he's a teenager now; 'if you bring home mongrel puppies to me I'll throw them in the garbage where they belong-with the rest of the trash."

"I beg your pardon," said a cold voice behind the speaker, who, turning around, met a pair of outraged eyes, hazel, without benefit of contact lenses.

"Sorry, Monica, I don't mean people like you. Your father is a foreign white. But our American white folks are something else. That's who I mean."

"Crass fool," said Monica audibly. She tossed her sleek, pale hair and swept out, creamy yellow hand on her husband's barely brown arm.

Rebbie and her friends found Charlie slouched on the top step of the gazebo, pressing a large, cold glass of water to her forehead.

Rebbie exclaimed, "Girl, I was searching for you! I had to say goodbye personally. This was some house-warming; you Gopilals sure know how to throw a party. I managed to sneak out some peas and rice and a bag of the cod fish balls to take home and it wasn't easy. That caterer's one mean, suspicious dude."

"Sneak?" said Charlie. "So how'd you get a container for them?"

"Oh, I always bring my own ziplock bags to parties. You never can tell when you're gonna need 'em. These things sure are dynamite!" She pulled a cod fish ball from her Vuitton bag and was on it in a nanosecond."

Charlie looked fatigued as she agreed. "I can see that you're enjoying it,"

"Anyway, doll, tomorrow morning I'll be over around eleven to see the house. I'll pick up some bagels and cream cheese. Of course I'll bring the camera." Rebbie paused to swallow in a camel-like fashion, extending her neck.

Fascinated, Charlie watched the food ripple down.

"We'll have a nice breakfast," Rebbie said, loudly masticating another massive mouthful. "You won't have to do anything-God this is good!" She smacked her lips.

"Gimme one, Rebbie," one of her friends requested, with outthrust hand.

"No." Rebbie slapped the hand away and continued. "I'll let the ladies see the house." She gave a distressingly loud belch. "Mercy! That gas was stuck in my rib cage all night." She beat on her chest like a gorilla and executed three more short, sharp belches before cramming in another greasy mouthful.

Charlie flinched and avoided looking at the repugnant, open-mouthed chewing, now accompanied by belching. Waves of nausea overtook her and she groaned.

"What's it?" asked Rebbie advancing in concern.

"Ooooh my-" Charlie rose. She stumbled as her heel caught in her dress hem. Her glass flew out of her hand and caught Rebbie on the nose. Its cold contents dripped down her dress front. The woman shouted and her eyes teared.

"I'm so sorry," Charlie said in consternation.

Rebbie and her friends beat a hasty retreat with wails from their leader and much sympathetic clucking and hopes that Charlie would soon feel better.

Alone at last, Charlie wearily collapsed onto the seat in the gazebo. She sat dull-eyed, in the dark, feeling sick and empty. A breeze stirred the light fabric of her now torn dress and cooled her slightly. In the distance she heard Lennie's voice; she saw a dark figure that looked like Colette press against him. He reached for her but she ran off laughing. He followed, singing. The breeze carried the calypso words to Charlie,

Now we only supposin' doux-doux

Suppose you was a shoe brush

An' I was a dirty shoe

Then his handsome face appeared around the laurel bush, "Charlie, gotta take some people home, they missed their rides; don't wait up for me."

She nodded from the darkness and her eyes followed his white shirt until it was out of sight.

2

Afternoon Delight

"Oh! Oh! Oh! Oh! Ohhhh!" Maxi flexed her toes and had her first climax of the day, that Sunday afternoon. She clutched her husband to her and he nuzzled her neck affectionately.

"What will your best friend say about you missing her party yesterday?" he whispered,

"Grrrr" she growled deep in her throat. "Give me more reasons-again."

Afterward Maxi soaked in her Jacuzzi, and mused about Charlie. How could she explain to her best friend that last night her dress had fit just right? It perfectly set off a body with just the right amount of curve and give to it-thanks to regular pilates classes. She smiled as she remembered her hair with that tousled just-been-laid look and her sexy high heels. Who could blame her husband or her for that matter, for agreeing with him, that she was a matter that demanded immediate attention?

She blushed and did neck exercises. Concluding that last night's steamy sex was worth Charlie's wrath, Maxi finished her bath, donned her kimono, and entered her room.

Jordan looked up from the newspaper. "That was quick. Ran out of water?"

"No, I missed you," she said in a sexy voice then flashed him and laughed.

He panted and opened his arms to her.

"Kidding aside," she said sitting on the edge of the bed. "Jordan, I really feel bad about Charlie," she started lotioning her legs. "We should've gone to her party last night."

"No, we should've stayed home and made love which was what we wanted to do. You don't let people run your life," he said reaching for her.

"Jordan, stop, I'm serious. Tatiana slept over at Charlie's last night, I have to pick her up and I don't know what to say to Charlie."

"You'll think of something," he mumbled untying her kimono.

"No I won't, help me!" she pushed him off and retied her sash.

"Hey! You almost knocked me off the bed," he said, righting himself. "Okay, let's have it. You're afraid to speak to your friend because you missed her house-warming party last night. Big deal! You're not her only friend, or guest I should add. Tell her something came up." He picked up his newspaper. "Will you look at this! They're-"

"Jordan!" Maxi grabbed the paper from him. "Charlie and I are best friends, and she's always been there for me. The night I met her at Howard, I was in the library crying because Stats 101 was kicking my butt. She helped me, and I was a total stranger."

"Seems to me you've repaid the debt many times over; Germaine's always going somewhere with you and Tatiana because Charlie's too busy to take her. And you seem to have single-handedly supervised the decorating of her new house."

"Jordan, I'm an artist! I love doing that stuff. Anyway she had a decorator and-"

Okay, okay, I get it. Now why was this party so important again? Wasn't it just to showcase her new house? People do that all the time and they don't drop their friends if they miss the shebang. Anyway you know what her house looks like."

"I think it was more than that," Maxi said thoughtfully. "She was so driven about this party; she spared no expense and she's never been a party person."

"Like I said, she wanted to showboat in front of her friends and you missed it. Come to Poppa, let me comfort you," Jordan said opening his arms wide.

"You want to get laid."

"And what's wrong with that, wife? Come back here." He reached for her.

"No, we've got to eat," she said, heading for the door. "I'm going downstairs to make brunch. Later, Lover-boy." She blew him a kiss and left the room.

Maxi assembled the ingredients for Kedgeree and called Charlie.

Charlie blasted her. "Maxi, Don't lie to me, okay. When will you and Jordan stop skipping functions and staying home to make like rabbits? You two are the horniest, most anti-social couple I know!"

"I'm sorry. But you know how it is. One thing led to another." Maxi blushed and quickly changed the subject. "I bet it was the party of the year and everyone was impressed."

"Everyone except my best friend who couldn't even bother to attend."

"Honey, you know I'd have been there if you really needed me," Maxi protested as images of the previous night's epicurean banquet of the flesh flashed through her mind. Her knees went weak and she almost cut herself as she chopped the hard-boiled eggs. "Now tell me everything."

"Oh, Charlie!" Maxi commiserated at the end of her friend's recital, "Are you speaking to Lennie now?" she asked as she stirred rice into the curry and tasted it.

"No less than usual. You know there hasn't been anything between us for a long time. I haven't trusted him since that Harlem Hospital stunt and that was ages ago."

"That was the worse," agreed Maxi.

"And it's not the only thing he's done, but I pretend ignorance. What's that saying? 'Half a man is better than none at all'? Lennie's good window-dressing, he looks the part, and he's a good father when he's around. He's a barrel of laughs in social situations but a morose tight-lipped son of a bitch at home around me. Anyway, all that wifey-poo stuff would be bad for my business – I've got to keep that chicken frying, so this relationship suits me just fine."

"Charlie, don't give up. A good marriage could help you, keep you centered."

"Maybe, but I married tall, handsome and lazy with an M.D. behind its name to boot! I got my eye-candy but it's not an entree so it wore off real quick."

"Please try counseling. It's not too late."

"I don't want a relationship with him, he's like a l dip stick-in and out of every available cunt in Westchester; he's nasty! And I won't be publicly embarrassed again. This was it! I make the real money in this family and I'm calling the shots. I told him so."

"Hope it works."

"I'll make it work. He'll toe the line because he's lazy and enjoys the lifestyle I provide. I won't give his Mother the satisfaction of seeing us break up. She didn't want him to marry me because my skin is dark and I'm American to boot, on my Dad's side, and of course my hair is not naturally straight like theirs. She's some kind of weird, light-skinned, Trinidadian mixture with Black in it and she's married to an East Indian. Those mongrels despise American Blacks."

"I know how that goes," said Maxi. "West Indian men tend to be incorrigible and pretty much untrainable. I remember my own Dad's harem. But Mom stuck it out. People say she used obeah-the equivalent to your voodoo, with some bush tea –"

"Hey! Hey! No can do the pharmaceuticals, island girl. Anyway, your Dad was rich. Wasn't he a plantation owner or something?"

"He was. He was white and of British descent. He'd impregnate the pretty black girls who worked on the plantation. When their sisters came to help them postpartum, he'd knock them up too if they were lookers. Mom was the last in the line because she knew her 'roots' and I don't mean mathematics."

"You've got a lot of family," Charlie observed.

"I do. I have twenty-three half brothers and eighteen half-sisters."

"Sheesh! Sure you guys weren't Black Mormons?"

Maxi ignored the barb. "Of course I have my full sister Felicity who lives in the Bahamas."

"She's a lawyer, right?"

"Uh huh. You met her here a few years ago; remember that party I had for her?"

"Oh yeah, her husband was quite the stud."

"Was he? Oh well. Anyway, in his own way my Dad was sort of decent. He college-educated all his kids who wanted it, and settled money on all of us all at his death. Mom, my little sister Felicity and I lived in the 'great house', you call it the plantation house here-from as far back as I can remember."

"She just moved out the competition and moved on in." Charlie laughed.

"You can say that. He never married her, but she died happy in the great house and he was an okay father to Felicity and me; we were his major heirs. He left us well provided for."

"Don't knock that. My Dad tried to do the same for us, but Mom, bless her departed soul, got herself a boy-toy after Dad died-a hot young insurance salesman. He soon ran through all the money my Daddy left. He 'invested' it. That's why we had to move to Harlem. I had to drop out of Jack and Jill, and her boy-toy dropped out of sight."

"You never told me you were in Jack and Jill as a child."

"Yeah, I was. When Daddy was alive and we lived in St. Albans, Queens-stronghold of the black bourgeoisie then; things were great. Daddy had this huge dental practice and made tons of money. He was light-skinned and rich. So J and J turned a blind eye to my dark skin and let me in. We were far too rich to be ignored. Yeah, life was good."

"That's so sad!" Maxi put fan-folded cloth napkins at each place setting. She cocked her head to study the effect. "Your poor Mom must've been devastated by the change."

"We survived."

"But how? Didn't Jack and Jill offer some kind of financial support so you could keep on attending the club and maintain your friendships?"

"Not them. They probably enjoyed us getting our comeuppance it, gave them something to gossip about. "

"Come on, Charlie, they should've offered to help."

"Maxi, I don't accept charity, never have, never will. Anyway, I couldn't have come to meetings dressed in the cheap clothes I had to wear and I certainly couldn't invite those privileged kids to our place in Harlem. We weren't living in the Striver's Row or Sugar Hill section you know."

"Charlie, maybe you're misjudging them."

"Come off it Maxi. Anyway, last night I was the HNIC-"

"What?"

"HNIC, head nigger in charge. I showed them that I was back on the block-a bigger, better block than the one I left years ago."

"And how!" Maxi said measuring liqueur and fruit juice into two champagne flutes then topping them with chilled Taittinger. She placed the Sparkling Apricots at the place settings. "By the way, did Rebbie show up this morning?"

"No, I think she'd had enough by the time she left."

"I take it your Angloville estate impressed the hell out of her."

"She couldn't get enough of it, even brought her friends to show off to and a video camera to capture my house for posterity."

"You're lying!" Maxi laughed. "She's incorrigible,"

"And ubiquitous," added Charlie, "wherever there's free food she'll be there."

"Isn't it sad," Maxi chuckled. "Charlie, I'm going to have brunch with Jordan now; then I'll come pick up Tatiana." She topped the Kedgeree with chopped egg and parsley and set it on the warming tray on the table. "See you later, okay?"

"Sure," said Charlie. "Just remember, brunch is downstairs in the kitchen, not upstairs in that overworked bed."

"Bye, Charlie." Maxi smiled and hung up the phone.

3

Slumming

Charlie looked around furtively. The coast was clear. She ducked into Bob's Stores. If anyone she knew saw her, they'd have a field day. They'd delight in passing it on that Charlie might live in Angloville but she shops at Bob's Stores in Yonkers. That's her natural habitat. Well to hell with them! The children's sleepwear sale was dynamite. The stuff looked great and no one would ever know. Germaine couldn't wear them for sleepovers but for sleeping alone, you couldn't beat this bargain with a stick. She strode into the store; the stuff had her name on it.

Charlie held her Mischka bag so that it was prominently displayed, then she remembered where she was and relaxed. None of these shoppers would recognize a Mischka, not even if it jumped up and bit them in the ass. She shuddered as she looked at the shoppers from the Bronx and Mt. Vernon, and at the surrounding cheap and cheerful clothes. She gave the low-class white girl behind the counter a look that said, "Watch it bitch, I'm your better, and I don't shop Bob's Stores." Then said in polite and cultured tones, "I'll take these please"; while her well manicured, expensively beringed, brown fingers pulled out money from a matching Mischka wallet. Suddenly, she heard a familiar voice and the hairs on her neck rose.

"The hussies are always calling the boys, so I told her, 'all these fourteen year-old boys want to do is play their video games. They're not chasing no damn girls! And he definitely can't come to your house anymore; there are too many females there'. So help me! If another girl calls my house for my son, I'm gonna blast her then call her mother and complain-young hoes!"

Charlie held her breath but the voice soon boomed, "Charlie! Whazzup girl?"

With sinking heart Charlie looked around and met LaToya-Marie's amused eyes. She said a defiant hi then completed her transaction. Why did that big, bull bitch have to be here? Now she'd make trouble. She should be home worshipping that son of hers whom she kept from all female society except her own. Odd attitude she had towards that boy; you never could tell with people these days. Jerry Springer's people were real and the woman *was* crazy; poor kid. Then she caught sight of LaToya-Marie's friend, Heather. This big bitch was systematically pulling to pieces a pair of Bob's sixty-nine cent panties, practically destroying them in her search for any irregularities.

"I didn't know you Afro-Saxons shopped Bob's Stores," boomed LaToya-Marie.

Charlie ignored her and completed her transaction. When she turned around again, two pairs of eyes topping twin malicious grins, on two faces-one dark black, the other yellow, both ugly; skewered her.

Large, dark LaToya-Marie, with graying temples, and hair tightly scraped up into a bun on the top of her head, regarded her with amusement. Nostrils, large enough to drive a bus up, topping a quantity of chins that surely exceeded the legal limit, almost inhaled Charlie. LaToya-Marie laughed and clapped Charlie on the back. "I don't blame you. You can't have that girl of yours sleeping in pjs from Neiman Marcus when there's stuff like this around. She'd be out of her element."

Charlie bit her lip, temporarily at a loss for words. She bided her time. She saw short, broad-based, yellow Heather, hair in a no-nonsense mannish cut; furtively drop the large size panties back into a basket on the counter. She assumed an air of studied nonchalance and turned her attention to Charlie with a look that said "Gotcha!"

Charlie knew the pair couldn't wait to get home and tell their friends what they had seen. Let them! So what if she chose to shop here today she thought fiercely. She was above the snipes of low-level, black people who lived paycheck to paycheck; her financial issue was not whether she could afford something, but whether she could write it off. She had a massive house in Angloville, a handsome MD husband, a brilliant, pretty daughter, and she herself was no slouch in the looks department. Plus she was a size six; these heifers were prize bull size.

Charlie smiled. "Hi, LaToya-Marie, Heather, fancy seeing you here. My maid's going back to Jamaica tomorrow. She's been terrific, what with all the extra work involved in moving I just don't know what I would've done without her, I swear! I'm picking up some stuff for her to take for her children. These things are pretty and so reasonably priced, they'll love them. Are you picking up some for your girls? These things look just like them." Good looks alone hadn't got her where she was today, she thought complacently. Take that, fart-stoppers! You're messing with a superior mind. She gave a satisfied little smirk.

"Yeah right!" said Heather cackling nastily. "I see you found your level, no fancy Neiman Marcus–"

Charlie interrupted, "Heather, was Monifa in the musical revue that the kids in the Talented and Gifted Program put on last week? I didn't see her name in the paper. Oh, I forgot – your daughter didn't qualify for the program did she? "

"Enjoy the rest of your shopping, they've got good bargains?" thundered big LaToya-Marie glaring at Charlie while putting a restraining arm around the more diminutive Heather. The latter was now red-faced and resembled some large gravid animal straining to give birth to something wicked.

What the hell is going on between those two, wondered Charlie, surprised at the protectiveness she was seeing. Talk about your alternative lifestyles. God help them all because man surely couldn't!

"Don't let us hold you up. Like I said, they've got cute little pajamas on sale that would suit Germaine right down to the ground," said LaToya-Marie. She tugged on Heather's arm, and they walked off in animated discussion, no doubt about what they had seen. Heather, the smaller woman looked back and threw Charlie a baleful look then waddled on behind her friend on short, chunky legs,.

Charlie called to her. "Heather, my maid mentioned that K Mart's having a sale on oversize panties. She's going to pick some up for her mother this afternoon. The price is more reasonable than these that I saw you admiring." She reached into the basket and gingerly picked up a pair of the big things and let them fall. "My goodness! These have got to be Size All! Shall I have her pick up a packet for you when she goes?"

Heather turned and started to speak. "Why don't-"

"Gotta run," said Charlie. "I wish I could stay and chat longer, but I'm not comfortable leaving my car parked in this kind of mall." She smiled at the women, gathered up her packages and adjusted her Mischka bag on her shoulder. "Bye," she said and clicked off towards the exit, tossing her hair and her Hermes scarf over her shoulder.

Charlie got into her car, rested her head on the steering wheel and sat trembling. Damn, damn, damn! She smacked the steering wheel. Why did she still care what they thought of her? Then, with tears soundlessly rolling down her cheeks she headed for Angloville.

4

Westchester Love

Rose's creamy, tapioca flesh flowed lava-like over Grantley's strong, mahogany body. They were making Westchester love.

Oooooh Dindi

If I only had words

I would say...

Joabim crooned from the CD player. The music stoked their fires as it mingled with a soft summer breeze stealing into the bedroom of the large, house on the Sound. She sat astride him cresting the waves, knees firmly anchored on crisp, fresh, Ralph Lauren sheets. Her powerful, golden thighs gripped his body in a vice. The huge four poster bed rocked in rhythm and the heavy, highly polished furniture gleamed approvingly at black Westchester lovers, charmingly frolicking in their stylish bedroom on a Sunday afternoon. As the grandfather clock struck three in the distance, Rose slowly dabbed at her warm brow with a tissue and anxiously regarded her husband before saying, "Do you think our friends can make love as expertly as we do?"

Grantley looked at his wife incredulously.

"I mean, do they have orgasms like us? Do they even make love?" She stopped the action to ask this one, then smoothly resumed. "They don't seem close like us. I hear that Colette says Lennie, Charlie's Lennie, is good in bed." Again she stopped the back and forth rocking movement. She studied him, and then smoothly segued into an intricate circular motion that demanded acute concentration along with strong abdominals.

Damn! She'd broken his stride. "Woman, you'd better never ever find that out first hand." The grip of his dark hand tightened on her pale gold skin.

Grantley put his sexual self on cruise control and let his mind roam. He considered buying more dental equipment for his new office in White Plains. No wonder the suicide rate among dentists was so high; costs were prohibitive, being black didn't help either. Thank God for the liquor stores and apartment buildings the old man had left him down South. If it weren't for them he could never afford this woman and their children; expensive kids who punctuated his tale of financial woe. Maybe he'd float another loan and buy that fifteen thousand-dollar Pelton Crane dental unit. It was impressive. Hell! He'd get the chair as well. It was a ball-breaker. He had to be twice as good as a white dentist, and his office had to be the last word in luxury to lure his own people away from the white competition. It was the shit practicing dentistry while black.

Now Rose seemed to be coming unglued. He'd speak to Phoebe about her. Phoebe had impressed him on that panel discussing health problems in the black community. She had a handle on women's psychological problems. Rose needed her. It was a sin for a bright, former social worker to get her only intellectual stimulation from decorating magazines, daily aerobics classes at the Westchester Health Club-and of course, tennis followed by lengthy lunches and visits to homes of similarly idle women, while he was out there busting his butt.

Suddenly, Rose began to buck like a bronco. He firmly grasped her large muscular buttocks. What was she doing, trying to bust his balls literally? She was in imminent danger of becoming unseated, and would have them both on the floor if she didn't tone it down a bit. She was so athletic! It was that wild, Texan cowboy streak in her. He hung onto her for dear life.

Rose stroked her husband automatically. She wondered if she should spend the two hundred and fifty dollars on that beautiful, swimsuit she had seen at Bloomies. Sydney could wear it at Germaine's pool party later this summer. She hoped none of the other mothers was willing to shell out that much money for a swimsuit. Sydney had to be the best, most beautifully dressed twelve-year old in her group. This befitted her little princess, chess prodigy and future president of us all. Pity the other girls couldn't swim at her high level or play chess half as well as she did. But what could you expect? She had produced a superior product.

Her son, Buddy; now that was a m*an*- just fourteen and already as tall as his Daddy and more handsome than the law allowed, definitely needed new clothes. He was growing so fast. But boys just weren't like girls; there was only so much you could do with them. Her brow wrinkled as she thought of the awful, fast, little heifers calling her poor son round the clock. They were like bitches in heat, but she'd put a stop to them. They weren't going to get her son! They'd give him a disease – the dirty, little girls! and they'd pull him right off the high honor roll. Well that'd happen over his mother's dead body. She flexed her pubococcygal muscles viciously to keep Grantley alert, and with feigned interest altered her rhythm slightly. He really liked basketball. Maybe her housekeeper could help her find a black kid from the ghetto whom she could pay to teach Buddy to trash talk like a real black man. He'd be cute if she shaved his head. Living in Westchester shouldn't make him forget who he was. Tomorrow she'd buy him a thick gold necklace. He was a black man, her authentic little black man.

Rose stroked Grantley's chest and moaned slightly. Again she altered her rhythm and tried to appear interested. Baby Midian was such a charmer. It was a shame she couldn't dress him as fancy as a girl. Heaven knows she tried, but you could only do so much with little boys. She started to sigh then caught herself in time, arranged her lips in a smile and kept right on counting her blessings and screwing her husband.

Rose allowed herself to be fondled as she planned her children's wardrobes in detail and automatically kept the action going. Suddenly she remembered the current edition of Architectural Digest on the credenza downstairs. There had been a wonderful living room that she definitely had to copy. Bingo! She would redo her living room English Country style! This was exciting. She had always had a weakness for chintz. She had to go and look at that magazine. Now! This sex thing was taking too long. Resolutely Rose reached into the night-table drawer and pulled out her trusty vibrator. She applied it to the action site-her clitoris and his groin area shared the electrical charge.

Grantley's eyes were closed and he was grunting with satisfaction at the thought of the next day's problem resolution. Yes, Rose could definitely use some help. Suddenly electricity zapped him in the groin area-fast. It jolted him right back to the here and now as Rose contracted around him like a crazy person. Heart pounding and breath coming in gasps he kept up with her as the electricity shot through them both.

Bzzzzzzz.

Bzzzzzzzzz.

Aaaaaiiiiieeee!

Glory be
To technologeeeeeeeeeee!

They screamed as they spent loudly and were soon free to get on with their lives.

.

5

A Woman Today

Germaine slowly opened her eyes. Chiaroscuro light seeped between her eyelashes. She touched her hair and giggled. Today, she was a woman and her weird curly hair was finally straight. She leapt out of bed, and hurried to her closet. Soon, she'd be in Angloville with a closet almost as big as this bedroom. She pulled out the outfit she was going to wear that day. It was fierce!

She rushed to the mirror and removed the silk scarf and long clips that held her hair wrapped around her head. Then she combed out the glossy, brown hair that cascaded to just below her shoulders. "Yes! Yes!" she crowed and leapt into the air. She watched with pure pleasure as the hair rose and fell gracefully. Just then the 'phone rang.

"Hello? Granny? Yes, I'm thirteen today. It feels great. Guess what? Yesterday Mom let me get my hair straightened."

"I sent you a little something in the mail. Did you get it yet?"

"No, Granny."

"Well, put it in your bank account when you get it, you hear me child."

"Yes, Granny, and thank you," said Germaine, a smile in her voice.

"Now what is this foolishness you're telling me about putting chemicals in your hair? Your mother should know better. You don't need that. You have nice hair like your father and me. You're not black like her. "

"But, Granny, my hair's not straight. I needed a mild straightener."

"You're not Black, you don't need it. That Tiger Woods person is Black American and he's not admitting to it, so why should you pretend to be something you're not; calls himself Cablinasian or some foolishness so. "

"Cablinasian? What's that?"

"I don't know. Some nonsense he made up. But back to you-you have Caribbean heritage and mixed-race blood on your Daddy's side. You're not Black and you don't need a straightener. You have good hair. When you have to fill in those forms that ask for race, make sure you check the box that says 'other'. Hadra says that's what her granddaughter does-and she's black-skinned-not even a pretty gold like you!"

"Granny, I already do that.

"Good. Now give your Daddy a big kiss from me and you go and get ready for school and enjoy your birthday, honey-lamb. I'll see you this summer if not before, mmmwah." She made a kissing sound.

"Bye, Granny," said Germaine happily.

Germaine clicked on her TV. Destiny's Child was performing with Beyonce flinging her blonde tresses around. Germaine studied her. Maybe next time Mom would let her go a few shades lighter? Maybe get some light colored contact lenses? Then, move over Bionce, Germaine Gopilal has entered the building! Germaine gyrated her slight body, flung her own brown tresses around and belted out with Bionce,

My body's too bootylicious
For you, Babe.

There was a peremptory knock on the door and Charlie walked in. "Happy birthday, dar-Germaine, what on earth are you doing? Look at the time. You're not even dressed yet." Charlie looked annoyed.

"Oh, hi, Mommy," Germaine said, embarrassed. Why didn't Mommy ever wait for her to say 'come in' before she came barging into a room? Of course saying this to a West Indian mother was a good way to get slapped in the mouth.

"Must you be late for school on your birthday? You've only got a few weeks left in that school; can't you go in early?"

"Sorry, Mommy,"

Charlie sighed, "You'll miss the bus now; Daddy will have to drive you. I hope he didn't plan to go in early too." Charlie looked at her watch.

"Sorry," Germaine said again, with annoyance in her voice.

"I suppose it can't be helped now." Charlie sighed. "We'll work it out-by the way, nice pajamas. I'm glad I bought them for you. They probably won't stand up to too much washing, but what the hell? They're cute. Remember, don't wear them around your friends, children can be such snobs."

"Um hm," Germaine mumbled through clenched teeth.

"Happy Birthday, darling, you can open your presents after school. Have a great day." Charlie pecked Germaine's cheek; then left, trailing the scent of narcissus behind her.

"Germaine, doux-doux, come have breakfast with your Poppa," called Lennie. He rapped on her door on his way downstairs.

"Coming, Daddy," she yelled.

Soon showered and dressed she joined Lennie at the breakfast table.

"Wow! You look special. Happy birthday, kitten," Lennie said, rising to give her a hug. "Love your hair."

"Thanks, Daddy." She shook her head and her hair moved gloriously.

"Nice," he said and they beamed at each other.

Later as they pulled up to Germaine's school she wheedled: "Daddy, would you come in and give an excuse for me? That old beast O'Shaughnessy never shows any kind of sense when you give excuses for being late. But she'll be nice to a parent. She has to. Please." She grasped her father's arm and looked into his eyes entreatingly.

"Sure, why not," Lennie said. He reached out to ruffle her hair. Just in time he noticed the new glowing, swinging silk his hand would encounter and the forbidding look in his daughter's eyes. "I don't dare, Princess," he said laughing and withdrawing his arm. He threw it instead around her thin shoulders as they walked into the building.

"Excuse me."

"Mrs. O'Shaughnessy looked up from the computer keyboard where she was typing in information on that day's miscreants.

"Yes?" Her smile froze. It would have been wasted on what must've been a Spic man because the kid with him looked Spic. Those people were such mongrels, you never could tell what racial group they belonged to. The kid was kind of dark for the man. Didn't they have enough problems of their own without marrying crazy and confusing decent people about racial origins? Nigger? Spic? You couldn't tell with this one.

"Can I help you?" she said severely opening her gold eyes wide, up into the generously spread blue mascara.

"Yes, my daughter's late. We had a transportation problem this morning. My car wouldn't start so we had to wait for Triple A."

"A likely story! Doesn't she usually come by bus? I've seen her when the bus was delayed, and children had to come to me for late passes."

"Excuse me?" said Lennie, surprised.

"You heard me," she said firmly. "This child's late and will be punished for it. Here, girl, take this slip to your teacher. You're in detention this afternoon. Join Mr. Cooper in room 104." She waved them away.

"You're saying you won't accept my excuse," said Lennie incredulously.

"Yes." She jutted out her chin and flashed those Irish eyes.

"What kind of craziness is this? Where's the principal?"

"Out of the building attending a meeting'," she said, head down, eyes on the computer screen as she typed rapidly; "won't be back 'til lunchtime. Sit and wait."

There was a timid cough and the woman glanced up.

"Yes," she said pleasantly to a plump, golden-haired white boy. "Now, David, did we oversleep again?" She smiled conspiratorially at him.

David smiled back confidently.

"Let me get out of here before I do or say the wrong thing," Lennie said loudly to his daughter. He glared at O'Shaughnessy. "Woman, this won't end here. I'm going to report you to your boss. I don't waste my time with underlings like you."

"Underlings! Underlings!" she shouted, rising. "*You* dare call *me* underlings?" Her face turned bright red. It contrasted with her vivid, blue eye shadow and bulging eye whites. "Get out!" She snapped. Her Irish was now truly up and there was no telling what could happen. "And close the door behind you."

"Go to hell", Lennie muttered as he and Germaine left the office. David closed the door behind them.

"I hate that mean, old hag," Germaine hissed between gritted teeth. Bright, unshed tears glittered in her eyes.

"Come, doux-doux, don't go into conniptions. She's not worth it. Gotta run-I'm late for work already. Here take this. Buy yourself a nice lunch. You'll-"

"Daddy, this is a fifty! School lunch costs a dollar sixty," Germaine squealed.

"So you'll have change. Think of all the fun you'll have opening your presents later, okay? Now give me a smile." He tilted her chin upwards and bathed her in the warm brown light from his eyes.

Germaine pocketed the money and grinned. "Okay, Daddy," she said.

Lennie bent and pecked his daughter on the cheek then she walked away from him down the corridors of her school.

The new Germaine created a sensation. Everyone stared when she entered the classroom. Germaine blushed, preened and dropped her books. Four boys jumped to their feet and raced to pick them up. Two of them crashed into each other and the classroom exploded into laughter despite the teacher's demands for silence.

Books restored to her; Germaine strolled triumphantly to her seat. Had the pants been a tad tighter she could have started a riot. She sat, tossed her hair behind her and looked expectantly around the classroom. This was going to be a good day.

Germaine kept her neck in motion as much as possible, and the newly straightened hair whipped about her face as she scurried down the corridors with her white girlfriends. They all spun their heads, agitating their hair like prairie grass in the wind. They laughed animatedly and gestured often, displaying slim wrists that bore the mandatory Tiffany bracelets. Germaine always gave her hair an extra toss for good measure; she was now truly a part of it all.

"Well, will you look at Miss Thang," declared a big, black girl, crossing her arms on her chest and planting herself firmly in Germaine's path, behind her stood her posse.

Germaine had seen these girls on the bus. They were not from her neighborhood or in any of her classes. She was in the top groups with the white kids, and the one other black, kid, Kwesi – daughter of an African diplomat.

"Excuse me, please," said Germaine. She flicked her hair behind one ear with the hand wearing the Tiffany bracelet then swung it forward over the opposite shoulder. The posse girls imitated this action. They too pushed back imaginary long hair and laughed.

Germaine colored.

"'Excuse me, please'. Miss White Bitch is going to break her fuckin' neck with all that long straight hair. 'Please let me pass,'" the leader mocked Germaine in a high, artificial, supposedly 'white', voice.

"Germaine, ignore them. This is like, so childish," said her friend Paige, braces flashing indignantly. She grabbed Germaine and pulled her past the group of girls.

But the posse moved too. They blocked her path and chanted.

Oreo Oreo,
You hate your skin
The more eo."

"Go to class," shouted a large black woman, suddenly lumbering onto the scene. She was Mrs. Brown, the hall monitor.

"Why you bein' like that? We goin' to the bathroom with LaShawna, she's not well," said one of the posse girls.

"Now why does LaShawna need so much bathroom help?" said Mrs. Brown with an indulgent smile.

"You know, female thing-you know... "

Germaine flung her hair defiantly behind her ear and stalked off, with her white friends. She left the posse behind, arguing amiably with the hall monitor. They ran into a group of white boys from their Latin class. Kevin, the class clown was saying:

"What do you do if you see a black kid riding past you on a bicycle?"

"Wave to him?" asked someone.

"No, run behind him – it's probably your bike!"

The boys guffawed loudly. Then, seeing the girls they started scuffling, trying to bump each other into the attractive group of giggling girls. Germaine was getting a lot of attention and her girlfriends noticed it.

"David, you like Germaine. You've been watching her all day," giggled Paige.

"Yeah, he likes her."

"Look at 'im blush."

A chorus went up and David did blush deep red.

"Hey, stop guys. How can you say that? She's black! I don't have no jungle fever," the beleaguered David exclaimed.

Germaine felt enraged and cheapened as she stalked off with her white girl friends, who remained silent.

On line in the lunchroom, a black boy in gangsta apparel approached Germaine. He looked her over approvingly and said, "Yo, money, wha's y'name? I'm Kofi. This here's m'dog, Abdulla. Sit with us." He gestured toward a group of unfamiliar black teenagers at a nearby table.

"Do I know you from somewhere?" asked Germaine.

"Sure, baby. We take gym together."

"Well, with only gym and lunch in common, what would we talk about?"

"I'll show yuh. Come, Baby Girl, bring y' tray."

"No, thank you," Germaine said. She sighed and lifted her hair, then shook it out down her back like a mermaid in the presence of a mere mortal.

"Well, gimme y' digits so I can holler atcha later."

"You don't need that," Germaine assured him. She pushed her hair behind one ear and tossed it over the opposite shoulder. "Obviously friendship's not in our future."

"Fine, *be* that way," said Kofi. He turned and left with his friends, all of them with backside cleavage erupting from low slung boxers and jeans.

"Ugh!" Germaine wrinkled her nose and shuddered delicately while her white girlfriends giggled.

Later, alone in the halls, Germaine again encountered the posse from earlier that day. She gave a tight little smile and looked down. She felt herself walking like a wooden soldier as their eyes bored into her. Her heart raced.

"Hey, you, make-shift, white bitch!"

Germaine ignored them and kept on walking.

"I said you, Miss Oreo bitch." The girl intercepted Germaine and again the group surrounded her. "M' girl here don't like your hair." She moved her neck back and forth like a snake getting ready to strike.

"Yeah, I don' like it," said m'girl, LaSandra.

"Or y' freaky clothes. You want a piece o' me?" The girl flung tightly braided, synthetic extensions over her shoulder then raised her fists like a pugilist and danced around Germaine feinting and jabbing at the air.

Where was everyone, Germaine thought in a panic?

"Lord, LaSandra look at her. She scared!" General laughter and high-pitched voices urged on the would-be boxer.

"I said-"

"Break it up. Break it up," said Mrs. Brown. "What! You girls again! This isn't the time or place to chat. Now move it or you'll be late for class. Shoo!"

Germaine ran.

"You, girl, no running in the hall!" shouted Mrs. Brown.

"That's right, give her a detention."

"Yes, she breakin' the rules-she and that hair." Raucous laughter erupted at this.

Germaine's heart raced double time until she reached the safety of her accelerated math class. There in familiar territory she calmed down. The enemy was outside.

By seventh period, gym, Germaine had stopped shaking her hair. It seemed as if whenever she went into a hallway there was a group of black girls with short hair or braided extensions shaking their heads in imitation of her, and mouthing "Oreo" or "Bitch." So she held her head stiffly and stayed in the middle of the group when she walked the halls with her friends.

Gym was a mess. Germaine had to run, and her hair bounced naturally with the motion of her body. Most of the black girls booed her and made nasty comments with each bounce of her hair. They continually crashed into her as if by accident. She became nervous and kept dropping the ball. Finally the teacher made her sit on the sidelines. She sat and watched sullenly.

"Yo, Brown Sugar! What's y' flavor?" An unfamiliar black boy greeted her.

"Not you," she said giving him a dirty look.

"Don't be that way, gimme y' digits."

"B-A-C-K- O-F-F-, now leave me alone, okay?" she said between clenched teeth.

"Screw you," he said and gave her the finger. He turned to the boy next to him to discuss the stuck up black bitch who "acts like a fuckin' Jap, an' thinks she's the shit." While Germaine stared stonily ahead, eyes bright with tears.

6

The Visitor

"Girl, what food you have?" Rebbie pushed past Lola and entered her house.

Lola laughed, closed her front door and followed Rebbie to the kitchen. "Rebbie, you're too much. Glad you stopped by; I'm baking; come keep me company."

"I came to pick up the ticket money. You and Leroy are coming to our Fund-raiser aren't you?" Rebbie paused in the living room. "Well, you sure get it together early in the morning. This place is spotless. Where're the kiddies?"

"At Bible-Study camp, I try to keep them out as much as possible now that the house is on the market. Mary-Katherine can call anytime and say she wants to show it. So this place has to stay clean. Come, let's go into the kitchen."

"Wait a minute, what happened to your pictures?" Rebbie pointed to the sofa table that held a solitary vase of fresh-cut flowers." I remember you had the boopsies here, looking so cute. Where are they?"

"Hidden, I want to get this place sold so I've removed all 'ethnic markers:' family photos, ethnic art, anything that suggests that *we* live here. You know how they are. They hardly want us in their neighborhoods-forget about living in a house behind one of us."

"Ain't it the truth," Rebbie followed Lola into the kitchen. "But they can't be so picky in your case because this is Mt. Vernon. They know who lives here. This is Westchester's Harlem. Do I see baked Ham!? In June! Gimme some bread, girl, lemme make a sandwich. I'm so hungry; I played two sets of tennis already this morning."

"Sorry, Rebbie, I can't, that's tonight's dinner. We have a houseguest, my brother-in-law, Jimmy; he's visiting from Pennsylvania. Mom and Dad have a farm there and they cured and baked this ham for us, isn't it pretty. I'm saving it for dinner tonight-"

But Rebbie was already breaking off stray pieces of the meat and stuffing them into her mouth. "Girl, this is good." She made wild hand gestures. "Where's the-you know –" she made sawing motions with her hand. "You know..."

"Knife?" said Lola.

"Yeah, knife. Child, I'm going to graduate with my CRS soon, you know Can't-Remember-Shit. This falling estrogen level, peri menopause thing is kicking my ass. Anyway this'll go good with some tea. Got any iced tea, Hon?"

Lola bit her lip and got a knife. "I'll cut you a tiny piece. It's so pretty with the pineapple... and I wanted to save it for dinner tonight with Jimmy-"

"Girl, whatcha talkin' bout; cut the ham! Cut some for Scott too. I won't have to cook tonight. I'll pick up some peas n' rice from Charlie's Chicken, her Mt. Vernon restaurant is right around the corner from you- and some vegetables and I'll be set."

Lola cut the ham and said, "I'm really looking forward to coming into Jack and Jill this fall. Thanks for sponsoring me; the kids will love it. There aren't too many nice black kids around here. It'll be a relief when they can make friends whose parents have the same values-"

"What's this, you have potato salad?"

Lola turned around and saw Rebbie's big butt sticking out of her 'fridge as its owner bent forward, all the better to peruse the fridge's contents. Little ripples of cellulite larded the fat legs visible beneath the brief, white, tennis skirt.

"Rebbie, I told you. We're having company tonight, Jimmy-"

"Ah, come on, just a little. It's just Scott and me. I love me some homemade potato salad, uumhh, uummhh, uuummm!"

Lola bit her lip and reached down a plate from a nearby cabinet.

"What's this?" Rebbie removed a tub of raisin sauce and dipped in her finger. "It's good," she said licking her finger. She took another taste.

Lola flinched. "It's raisin sauce for the ham. You can have it all." She sliced bread and speeded up her sandwich preparation.

"I need to come to your house more often, girl. You folks are some eating people. She removed potato salad next then stuck her head back into the 'fridge, forcing it to reveal its secrets. "Lemme see what else you have in here. What, nothing good to drink? Hon, where's the iced tea mix? I'll fix us some," she said, finally emerging from the 'fridge.

"I'm not thirsty," Lola said dully. "But I'll mix some for you. You sit and rest. You must be tired after all that tennis." She had to keep Rebbie out of her pantry cabinet. God only knew what she'd take a shine to in there.

"I am a bit tired," Rebbie admitted bearing her spoils to the kitchen table. She sat and rifled through a stack of mail as Lola packed up the food for her and mixed iced tea.

"Thanks, Doll." Rebbie took the proffered sandwich and bit into it. "This is good." I always say there's nothing like a honey-cured ham. It is honey-cured right?"

"Yes", said Lola. She wiped crumbs off the counter and put away the bread knife. "Mom sent the bread too, it's homemade."

Rebbie returned to Lola's mail. "Too many catalogs, Lord! What's this? You're invited to the Delta's luncheon? Now that's a nice affair. The best food, great setting. You go girl! That's another organization you should join. I can get you in."

"Thanks, I want to join. When I was in college Moms couldn't afford the extra money for things like that. Then I had to drop out because there just wasn't enough money, period."

"Well you're sure makin' up for it now. Mr. Gorgeous is just pulling in that cash. When you get your big, old house girl, you won't have to speak to anybody!"

Lola laughed nervously. "Don't be silly. It is kind of exciting to be moving, but I wish I'd finished college. I read a lot and I'm studying from a vocabulary-building book. But all the black women I meet are so educated and they're in book clubs and read-"

"Girl, you don't need college you've got a BMW! I need a tad more mustard for this ham, Babes."

"I don't have a BMW, Rebbie; you know Leroy just got me an Escalade SUV," Lola said as she complied."

"Girl, that's why you got the Escalade, because you *have* a BMW – a black man working!" said Rebbie. She spread the mustard and chewed with a rapt expression. She slurped iced tea then asked, "How much money you guys plan to spend on the house?"

"That depends on the market; we looked in Angloville on Sunday-in Charlie's neighborhood. Gosh! It's expensive there. She has a lovely home."

"That Charlie, she's too cute. She's one of my best friends. Just the other day, I went by her for breakfast. She's really fixed up that house." Rebbie pulled a piece of ham from between her teeth, examined it, and then popped it back into her mouth.

"I really admire her," said Lola. "She's so strong, and beautiful. She can tell any man to go to Hell-"

"Tell me about this Jimmy, your brother-in-law who's visiting. Is he married? And is he cute like that Mr. Gorgeous you're married to?"

Lola resumed her cookie making and replied, "There is a family resemblance. And no, he's not married-he's a college kid. He's studying engineering at Temple."

"No kidding! We must get him together with my twins. They're in Nairobi now. That's their high-school graduation present. But they're starting U Penn in the fall, and he'll be right in Philly with them. This is perfect."

"We could introduce them," said Lola doubtfully. She envisioned her handsome, outgoing brother-in-law squiring around Michaela and McKenzie, or rather Mikki and Makki, as they preferred to be called – supersize, phlegmatic girls who said little and always looked bored and lethargic.

"He'll be working at his big brother's construction company when he graduates, won't he?" said Rebbie through a mouthful of food.

"I guess." Lola cut out cookies and placed them on a cookie sheet. She set the timer and slid them into the oven.

"It's so important for these young people to get to know each other. Next thing you know, that fine young brother will be marrying some White girl unless sensible older women steer him in the right direction."

Lola cleaned up the kitchen and tuned out Rebbie. Soon she would have her own big house in an exclusive Westchester suburb. She'd go back to college, maybe even have a career when the kids got older. She and her children would have the right friends; they'd be invited to all the best affairs...

"I swear you're not listening to me. I said can I borrow your punch bowl for the little gathering I'm having for the girls when they get back from Africa next week?"

"Of course," said Lola, flustered

"Lola, Lola, where are you Honeychil'?" Leroy strode into the kitchen. He looked boyish in his tight jeans and tee shirt. He grabbed his wife, kissed her soundly on the lips, and slid his hands down to her butt. "I just-"

She stiffened and gently pushed him off. He followed the direction of her eyes and saw Rebbie.

"Don't mind me, I was just leaving." Rebbie grabbed the bag with her food. "See you kids later," she said on her way out.

"Bye," said Lola.

"Baby, let's go!" said Leroy, tugging her toward the back stairs leading up to the bedrooms.

Red-faced, Lola giggled and followed.

7

After School Activities

Germaine entered room 104 and was confronted by a sea of black and brown faces. A thin, dark, African American man sat at a desk at the front of the room. He looked at a list and said loudly:

"Germaine Gopilal, I presume. You're new here. Join the others."

Germaine bit her lip and silently regarded the hostile dark faces in front of her.

"Go sit in the fourth row, in that middle seat."

Germaine stumbled through an obstacle course of stuck out feet and whispers of, "Oreo, Miss White Girl," and "Makeshift White Bitch," all the way to her seat

"Is everyone here?" said Mr. Cooper, looking at his list. "Timbuktu Allen, Offeibeia? Brown," he looked up and a girl raised her hand and corrected his pronunciation. He read on, "DeVaughn Charles, Duke Earl, Tyrek Gilkes, Germaine Gopilal, Lakeisha Greene, Adama Hall-nice name," he observed. "Adama means beautiful one; it's what I named my daughter."

A fat, dark girl with thick lips and a wide nose preened while the children around her tittered. Germaine looked at the clock. She could swear the hands weren't moving. The monotonous voice continued,

"...Tarik Jones, Shaquille Kendrik, Sir King." Germaine's head reeled. Was she in America, she didn't know people with names like this. Were their mothers drunk when they named them? "Koloshushu Price, Natachi Perry, Akeem Williams," all the way to Ramses X. She looked at her fellow detainees and felt no kinship.

During detention any girl who caught Germaine's eye tossed make-believe hair, or mouthed something nasty to her. The boys ogled her. Many of them displayed colorful Tommy Hilfiger boxers bunched up over their low-slung pants. Germaine tried to keep her eyes on her book. This was truly the worst day of her life.

Eventually it was over, and everyone headed for the late bus. Germaine self consciously kept her back and neck ramrod stiff so that her hair would not move as she walked. She avoided all eye contact and ignored nasty comments from the others.

The detention group had the late bus to themselves today. For a moment Germaine considered calling a cab. Then she remembered that the building was already locked and her cell 'phone was at home, forgotten in this morning's mad, late dash to school. She had no choice but to ride this bus. So chin tilted upward, expectations adjusted downward she squared her shoulders and mounted the bus steps.

There were no seats near the driver so heart pounding, Germaine slid into an empty middle row. She dropped her backpack onto the outer seat and scooted over to the inside and looked out the window. Someone dropped her backpack onto the floor and slid in beside her. She smelt a wild animal odor and turned around. A large, black boy sat beside her. Hadn't he heard about deodorant? Silently she cursed her fate and settled in for a long journey.

"Hey, sugar dumpling. You're new on this bus, huh?" the boy said, turning his fat body around in the seat to face her and squashing her up against the side of the bus. Germaine ignored him as her heart sank further. The big lard ass expected her to talk him, and she had to smell him all the way home. She looked down and surreptitiously slipped her hand into the pocket that held the fifty dollar bill Daddy had given her this morning. She'd had lunch money; this was hers to keep. The bill's crisp newness comforted her. She held it. Daddy should have picked her up; it was his fault that she was in detention. He should've fought that old witch this morning? Mommy would've.

"I said, 'hey, you're new on this bus'," he repeated aggressively.

"Leave the bitch alone. She think she the shit. She think she White," advised the high pitched voice of a girl sitting behind them.

"Yeah?" said Germaine's seatmate.

"Word," chimed in another high pitched, female voice from the front. "She think she better than me and you. She don' talk to people like us. They had to drag her to the detention room. Ain't that so Miss Thang?"

"Now ain't that somethin'?" said the large boy. He turned to her. "Gimme ya number, baby. We can discuss this here issue on the phone. You black like me, right?" He grabbed her by the shoulders and forced her to face him.

"Get off me!" said Germaine with panic rising. She hadn't expected anyone to actually touch her.

"T'ings hokay?" asked the driver in a thick Puerto-Rican accent.

"Hokay, Manuel. You just drive, vroom vroom," shouted a boy.

"Hokaaay! I drive," he responded happily.

"Anyway, Baby, I'm the Man," the fat boy said with a leer. "M'name's Tushaun Briggs, AKA Big Digger. I gets in your oven an' gives you good lovin', 'cause Baby, I'm a ten-an' it's not m' shoe size." He winked at her and stuck his hand down the front of his pants and wiggled it obscenely. "You know what I mean, now gimme somethin'."

Horrified, Germaine recoiled but Big Digger grabbed her and pulled her to him. She struggled as she clutched the fifty dollar bill even more desperately.

"She's a BAP, she too good for you," said a girl who stood in the aisle. "See that hair? She been shakin' it all day all over the school-she an' her white JAP friens!"

"Wooo ooooo watch us shake our hair." A group of girls advanced, shaking their heads, and clustered around Germaine's seat.

"This feels good," said a girl, grabbing a hank of Germaine's hair. "Girl, what shampoo you use?" She aggressively thrust her neck back and forth a few times as if cranking up to let fly with her head. "Tell me so I can buy some for my dog."

Uproarious laughter greeted this.

Germaine struggled to free her hair and felt chewing gum in it. Incredulous, she leapt up and shrieked, "What did you do? You put gum in my hair?"

General laughter and cheering greeted this. Some kids started the chant "Go fight! Go fight!" and they beat it out rhythmically on the back of the bus seats.

Big Digger pulled her back down onto the seat." Sit, sister, we've got work to do."

"I'm not your damn sister!" Germaine sobbed. "Leave me alone and stop the bus! Driver! Driver!" she screamed.

"Ees hokay mees?" said the driver. In the mirror he caught the eye of a large boy, who made a neck slitting gesture so he smiled helpfully and kept on driving.

"Let me off," screamed Germaine.

"Gimme some lovin' first," said Big Digger.

"Give us that hair," laughed the girls.

Someone grabbed a handful of Germaine's hair and yanked it again. "Miss Thang," she said with a laugh.

Suddenly Germaine felt wetness on her forehead. She screamed and looked up in time to see a pale girl with hair in an intricate, cornrow hairstyle, wiping spittle from the sides of her mouth.

"Eeew! You pig! Get away from me! Help!" Germaine shrieked.

"Eees hokay?" asked Manuel the driver. He now sounded a bit uneasy. But two large, muscular, black teenage boys got up and stood behind him, this ensured that he continued to mind his own business.

"Well, Miss high-and-mighty-hair-swingin'-wit'-her- white-frien's-black-bitch how does it feel to get down wid de niggahs? How does it feel, sistuh," a large girl demanded, sticking her face right in front of Germaine's.

"Get out of my face! It feels like shit, just the way you look," sobbed Germaine. "Let me off this bus!" She screamed then whimpered and put her hand back into her pocket and clutched her fifty. She massaged the bill as her tears flowed.

"Miss Thang, we's takin' you home, chicken-head; we knows where you lives. You'll get off there. Door to door service babeee".

This caused a fresh eruption of laughter.

"Skank hoe, why don't y' follow the yellow brick road to kiss-my-ass then do it!" added another girl.

I want m'lovin'," growled Big Digger. He grabbed her face and kissed her hard on the mouth to the accompaniment of cheers from the girls.

Germaine, trying to push him off with both hands, dropped the fifty.

"Look she's rich; now I'm rich!" a girl squealed triumphantly, pocketing the bill.

"No, no!" Germaine whimpered. "Give it back. It's mine!" She tried to lunge at the girl but Big Digger held her down.

"I shoulda had that money," he said with annoyance. "Now, Bitch, get ready we's goin' for part two."

"Ooooh," screamed the girls.

"They's gonna make babies right here!" shrieked a girl, jumping up and down and trembling with excitement.

"Ees hokay, Manuel," one of the guarding boys assured the driver with a wink.

"Yeah, mind yuh li'l, fuckin', beans 'n rice business," said the other one.

"Hokay," said little Manuel. "I drive. Vroom vroom?" He smiled ingratiatingly.

Germaine screamed and struggled. A girl said, "Maybe this is going too far."

"Shut yuh fuckin' mouth. She your frien'?" came a quick response.

"Help, help!" yelled Germaine.

"Go Digger! Go Digger!" chanted a chorus of boys and girls, beating out the rhythm on the bus seats.

"Shoot, this 'ho' sure is wild," the big boy said with a grin.

"True dat," agreed a watching boy, sticking his hands down the front of his pants and hefting his genitals into a more comfortable configuration.

Germaine paused for a second to catch her breath. Big Digger grabbed her hand and pressed it down on his hard crotch area, moving it rhythmically, with the chant.

"Ooooooh!" said the girls.

"Aaaaaah!" said Big with a wide smile.

"Heeeelp!" Germaine screamed. Someone pulled her hair; she turned quickly and bit them then lashed out viciously with her free hand. The blow found a mark because there was a yell followed by a punch to her shoulder. But she was too busy struggling to free her hand from the obnoxious crotch it was massaging, to see who had done this.

"It's the bitch's stop," announced a girl by the window.

The big boy gave an exaggerated aaaahh of satisfaction and allowed Germaine to snatch her hand away. She leapt up and stamped on his foot as she stumbled past him. He pinched her skinny behind. She turned and spat full in his face then fled pushing people to the side willy-nilly as she sped off the bus.

"Stop the bitch, I'll kill 'er," yelled Big Digger wiping spit from his eye.

"The ho' spat in his face," said a girl with a laugh.

Germaine heard thunderous footsteps behind her but she reached the door and flung herself out onto the grassy sidewalk. She fell hard and felt a shooting pain in her ankle. As she lay on the grass holding her ankle the bus door slammed.

"Bye, White bitch,"

"Bye, Oreo,"

"Bye, Stuck-up fuck."

"Hey, the bitch left her backpack!"

"Here, Miss Thang."

The door flew open and Germaine's heavy backpack whizzed out narrowly missing her head. Then the bus drove off to the sound of hoots and laughter.

Slowly and painfully Germaine pushed herself up from the ground. She abandoned the backpack and limped up her driveway. Her shoulder and ankle throbbed as she dragged herself upstairs to her bedroom and slammed the door. The sound reverberated in the empty house.

When Charlie and Lennie returned home, Germaine was still in her room. They knocked softly on her door, and entered, laden with gaily wrapped birthday gifts.

"Germaine, what's wrong honey? Are you tired? Wake up Birthday Girl, we've got presents for you," said Charlie.

"Happy Birthday to you," sang Lennie in a pleasant baritone as Charlie snapped on the light and they approached the bed where their daughter lay.

"What!" Charlie stopped in her tracks and dropped the presents.

Hunks of her daughter's beautiful, long, shiny, hair lay on the bed, on the floor, on the bedside table. A cropped head like that of a badly plucked fowl rose up from the bedclothes. Red, tear-swollen eyes seared them before the child threw herself back down on the bed and cried with great juddering sobs. Her body shook in paroxysms of sorrow as she burrowed into the pillows and moaned,

"I don't want to be black! I don't want to be black!"

8

The Parental Unit

This is entirely your fault. You always try to make the girl feel she's better than everyone else. Well guess what? Other people don't like that," Lennie said to Charlie.

"Well, maybe she is better than 'everyone else'! But that doesn't give them the right to practically rape her on a school bus-"

"Damn it woman! I didn't say it did. Anyway what the hell is 'better'?" Lennie chupsed and glared at his wife.

"You wouldn't know because you didn't grow up in this country, you stupid son of a bitch," Charlie retorted. "How the hell would you know what it's like to always have people try to pull you down into the gutter with them just because you share the same skin color? Do you know what it feels like to be hated by people who look like you, just because you appear to be going somewhere?"

"Spare me the lecture on African-American sociology. All you black Americans ever talk about is how downtrodden you were. For Crissake get a life!"

"You stupid jerk! I'm a West Indian! I grew up as a West Indian in this country and I was better than my surroundings. Knowing I was 'better' kept me focused as a teenager. I was better than the girls who let the boys score on the rooftops in the summer and later became unwed mothers, better than the kids who drank and did drugs-"

"Oh, God," Lennie groaned, "I understand, you're better than everybody."

"Better than the high school dropouts-so you go to hell, I am better than and she is better than!" Charlie screamed, breathing hard with rage.

"You could save the blasted speeches you know. She's not growing up poor in Harlem. She's in a rich, white suburb in Westchester. So you don't know what the hell you're talking about because you didn't grow up in her world."

"And who did it to her, ass-hole?"

"Look, you can call me all the names you want, but all I'm pointing out to you is that you screwed up the girl. Look at her now-she won't go back to school. She wants to go to the Caribbean, for God's sake! What kind of a mother are you that your daughter wants her grandmother at a time like this?"

"A hard-working mother whose money enables you to screw around, if you want to talk about screwing-"

"Fuck you! I'm talking about my daughter and your failure as a mother, to hell with all the rest of that."

"Well I'm talking about your failure as a father and a human being. Look at you- completely useless! You don't make enough to support our lifestyle for one month," she said scornfully. "I work twelve-hour days too many times to provide for us when I should be home with my daughter. You, lazy ass-hole, should have picked up my daughter on her birthday and brought her home from school in your car-which I paid for."

"Fuck you! You could have quit busting your balls, which I know you've got and done it yourself. You're some kind of mother-"

"You're nothing but window dressing. You don't care about your child-"

Bullshit!" yelled Lennie. "I was working, okay! I love my kid!"

"Yeah, when it's convenient," snorted Charlie.

Lennie stood menacingly in front of Charlie. "Watch it, okay? Mind your mouth before it gets you in trouble. You got what you wanted. You wanted me-I'm your window dressing? Fine! You can show the world you've got it all. Well Baby, you got me. So shut up and pay for me!"

"You're no trophy; you can't even pass your god-damn boards!"

"Aha! But I was what you could get. You don't like me. You fucked up everything including our child because you want it all. You're a cold, calculating bitch, and you like what I represent. I had no problem with that because I don't like you. But you fucked up my child and I take issue with that-"

"You sponging-"

"No, stop," Lennie held up his hand. "Hear me out. I might be all kinds of things, but I love my kid and-"

"That's why you left her to get into trouble," Charlie yelled.

"You bitch!" Lennie roared, and face flushed he rushed toward Charlie.

"Hah! What're you going to do, hit me because you're a poor excuse for a man and an inadequate father?" Charlie stood her ground and glared at him.

"Look, woman, don't push me-"

"Da – Da " Germaine, wearing pajamas and a baseball cap, stumbled into the room; gulping for air as she struggled to articulate, she clutched at her throat and wheezed.

"Sweetheart, where's your pump?" Charlie said sharply, running to her daughter even as she wondered how long she had been outside the door.

Germaine pointed to the stairs.

"Honey, is there one on the night table next to your bed?"

The child nodded.

"Lennie, get her pump-fast!" Charlie said sharply.

"No, you handle it like you handle everything else; you don't need me. I'm out of here so I can stay on the right side of a jail cell."

"Is that the new way to announce that you're going to get laid?" screamed Charlie helping her daughter onto the nearby sofa. She looked down at the child. "Baby, I'm here, calm down and try to breathe slowly. I'll get your pump?"

The front door slammed. Germaine clutched her mother with panic in her eyes and looked in the direction of the sound and wheezed. Tight-lipped, Charlie propped her daughter up on the sofa and pried herself free of the fingers. "It's okay, Baby. Daddy and I were just talking and we got a bit upset, but everything's alright. Really it is." She gave Germaine a quick kiss then flew up the stairs for the pump. The lousy son of a bitch! If he killed her daughter…

9

Buddy

"Buddy!"

The fans in the Garden howled as he dribbled skillfully past his opponents. He boxed out a vicious player. He was going to make it. Yes! Yes! Almost there! He made a quick feint, then crashed his elbow into the face of a would be interceptor. Sweat slicked his young, muscular body. He snapped it out of his eyes and cut a dazzling path through the pack. He was really rocking. He stood at the baseline and set up for a bank shot. Aiming... aiming. Yes! Slam dunk! The ball caromed into the basket. Yeeaaeah! He raised his shiny, wet, brown arm in the air in a power salute

"Buddy! I've been calling you for the last five minutes. Come at once, and put your clothes into the hamper and not on my floor," Rose yelled from her kitchen window.

Madison Square Garden became a driveway fronting a stately Tudor in Mamaroneck, Westchester and this basketball hoop stood near a wrought iron love seat on which rested a picture hat with a trailing, pink and lilac ribbon.

"Aaaw, Ma! I'm busy. I'm in awesome form today. Didja see that pass? Didja see that dunk? Cut me some slack Ma! Christ!"

"Buddy!" Rose's amber eyes flashed dangerously. "You come here right now or I'll ground you and stop your allowance." She stalked away from the window overlooking the site of his basketball fame. Suddenly she was back. "And furthermore young man, don't you dare take the Lord's name in vain while you're living under my roof." Like a guerilla warrior she was gone again, either to harass his sister to practice more chess or to stretch out on the sofa and look at decorating magazines.

She was always doing something to the house. Right now she was making everyone crazy constantly talking about a new living room. "Shit!" He muttered, but carefully under his breath; for he'd already developed a healthy love of mammon and his mother knew it.

Buddy loped into the house then quickly returned to Madison Square Garden. Again he baffled the opposing team with false passes and impressed his teammates with his slick moves. Yeah, man, this was da bomb! The crowd roared even louder.

They were calling his name.

"Hi, Buddy."

But he was oblivious to it all because they were paying him twenty-five million a year to play basketball.

"Buddy, tee-hee. We said hi."

"What?"

Buddy came abruptly out of his reverie. Two girls from school were in his front yard. Uh huh! He liked the way the blonde one, Jamie, was looking at him. Oh, God he'd been trying to make a sly move on her for weeks. He liked her flavor. The girl was hot! Hell no! She was all that and more! She ruled!

"Buddy."

Damn, they were still calling him. He'd better say something. "What's up," he said, and dribbled the ball past them. A big popular jock like him couldn't diss himself by putting moves on a girl. Shoot! They all came to him eventually. It was definitely stop, drop and drool time when he hit the hallways looking fly in his FUBUs and Oakleys. They knew he was the shit. Who could blame girls for intercepting passes before he even made them? They were only human!

"Oooh, Buddy, you're so sweaty. Do you want us to dab the sweat off you?"

That was Paige. She was such a slut. Once he got Jamie under control he'd stop her chillin' with Paige. Oh shit, not now! His basketball shorts were tenting over what promised to be a massive erection. He was rising as rapidly as Michael Jordan's income.

Buddy dribbled the ball precipitately away from the girls and toward the basket. He concentrated and muttered the name, team and salary of highly paid, professional athletes. "Mark Davis, Kansas City Royals, three ... no, thirteen million over five years. What a salary!" He bounced the ball. His

Dad, the dentist with all those years of schooling would never be a seven-figga nigga like these guys.

"A Rod, Texas Rangers." He leaped into the air just like the athletes in the ads. The girls could see the leverage power on his new Nikes. "$252 million. Oh God! What a package! Basketball salaries just weren't like this. Of course there were always the endorsements... Down! Down! He focused. Troy Aikman, football. Dallas Cowboys. What was it? 5 something... $5.87 million. Yeah, that was it. What was that freaky salary? Oh yeah, hockey. Mo Vaughn, Anaheim Angels. $ 13, 333, 333" Oh, God, it was working. He was deflating, detumescing to quote his old faggot science teacher.

He turned his head and gave the girls his special movie star grin. "Watch this," he commanded, setting himself up for a shot. Boy, was he ever lucky that his older cousin Jason had taught him this neat trick to get his erection down fast. It sure took a lot of concentration to come up with these crazy salaries. They were like unreal.

He changed his mind about shooting for the hoop; instead he tossed the ball in the air and deftly caught it behind his back.

"Ooooh!"

"Wow!"

He smiled and tried hard not to think about Jamie's hard little breasts jutting out in the tank top. Oh God! He'd hold one of them, squeeze it hard, and roll the nipple between his fingers. He groaned in anticipation. Hell! She might even let him... Fuck! The erection! "Kevin Brown, Dodgers. $15 million over 7 years." he muttered doggedly. "Shawn Green, LA Dodgers. $14, 000, 000. Shaquille Oneal, $17.14 million. Kick-ass salary! Go Shack!"

Maybe he should dribble the ball away from the girls. Down, son-of-a-bitch! Down! Goddamn bionic erection. One thousand six-hundred and fifty, one thousand six hundred and forty-nine...wait, everything was coming under control now. He turned and smiled at the girls. "Hey! Where're you girls headed?" He wiped the sweat off his brow with the hem of his basketball jersey.

"Nowhere special. We thought, like maybe we'd walk to Haagen Daz or something. You know?"

The sun glinted on Paige's braces and on some soft, blonde hairs on Jamie's chest. Man, she was the shit!

"Buddy."

"Yes, Ma."

"Come here, please."

"'Scuse me, girls. I'll be back in a minute. Wanna wait for me?"

There was much giggling and shuffling. Jamie wouldn't meet his eyes.

"Buddy!"

"Coming, Ma." He flew to the kitchen door to the sweet sound of,

"We'll wait."

Buddy dashed into the kitchen and was greeted by Rose's,"Buddy, just what do you think you're doing out there?"

"Ma I-"

"Don't those girls have anything better to do on a Saturday morning? Don't they have underwear to wash, bedrooms to clean?"

"Ma-"

"Get rid of them, you hear me." She raised her voice.

"Ma, please. You're embarrassing me!"

"Please, nothing! I'm sick of you! You and white girls! How do you think I feel? Boy, what the hell is wrong with you? You don't think I'm pretty? Why is it that only white girls interest you? Are you sick? Don't you like yourself? Don't you like your family? Your race?" She peppered him with the familiar questions.

Buddy became alarmed as he watched her work herself up into what his Dad called her 'bad black thang'. "When their ancestors were painting themselves green and running around Europe naked, buggering people's sheep, yours were in established medical schools in Timbuktu, or ruling and living in civilized African kingdoms. Boy, stop bringing us down."

Shit! The girls might hear her, and he'd be branded a racist at school. There would go his cool jock image, not to mention his girls. God! Couldn't she take a chill pill?

"Ma, you're gorgeous," he shouted desperately. He tried to put his arm around her but she shrugged it off. "Ma, black girls don't like me."

"Stop that foolishness, boy. Just because they have more pride than the white trash you hang out with, and they won't chase down your black butt doesn't mean they don't like you-you fool!"

Oh God, he was in for it, he thought. She was definitely on her favorite topic now and she was flying. This could go on all day. He anxiously glanced through the window and she caught him.

"Boy, I put you in both Jack and Jill and that new Martin and Harriet Organization. You're in the Buds of Promise singing your little black heart out every Sunday in the Baptist church and you still can't find a black girl who interests you? What've we done wrong?"

Buddy wisely refrained from reminding her that she also got nasty when she thought black girls were interested in him. She'd said awful things about Tiffany Price when she claimed that she caught her looking at him too long, at a Jack and Jill meeting. She looked up to the ceiling where her copper pots hung gleaming in the morning sunlight. Maybe she thought her God was hiding inside them for she seemed to be addressing the pots. "Lord, why me?"

She walked toward him and he retreated. She was unpredictable when she got into the power like this. She stopped at the breakfast nook, and exchanged her Architectural Digest for Ebony magazine.

Out of the corner of his eye he saw his little sister Sydney standing in the dining room enjoying the whole scene. Rose saw her too.

"Look at your sister," she screamed. "Isn't she beautiful?"

Sydney smiled triumphantly.

"But no; some black jerk like you would bypass her for a little white tart who just wants a piece of black action. I should have stayed down South and raised you in my hometown; there would've been none of this foolishness. The Bible says the only thing you can do with a fool is to bury it. But I never understood what this really meant 'til I had you. The damn fool will get itself killed!"

Sydney, obviously enjoying the drama, made a throat-slitting gesture.

"The father of one of these little, white tarts is going to kill your black ass, and your father and I will have to bury it!" Rose shrieked.

Suddenly she rolled her Ebony magazine into an offensive cylinder, rushed at him, and smacked him sharply across the side of the head with it.

"You self-hating Oreo! Get out of my sight!"

She tried for another blow but connected with air because he was celeritously obliging her. He was already halfway out the kitchen door.

"I'm outta here," he flung over his shoulder as he leaped down the kitchen steps back to sunshine and hot white girls all waiting outside for him. Oh yeah!

"I've got five sticks sitting in the garage and each one's got your name on it!" he heard in his flight.

Right! Let his Mom talk. This was it! These girls would put out for him. Look at them in those swimsuit tops with their nice, smooth legs all hanging out of their shorts. Phat! They must've come from Paige's pool. He'd swum there with kids a few times, and Paige'd let him slide his fingers under her swimsuit. She was all right, Paige. These girls could go on dates with him. They let a guy cop a sly feel now and then. This was no problem with them. There might even be the biggie soon. Maybe he could set that up.

Let his Mom keep her black girls. He couldn't get past those black mothers to ask their daughters out even if he wanted to. They'd hit him upside the head and tell his Mom that he'd insulted their precious daughters by daring to invite one of them out on a date at the tender age of fourteen. When his Mom thought one of them was looking too hard at him in church, she talked about her the same way she talked about the white ones – worse sometimes, because she felt their mothers should've taught them better.

Not to worry, he'd get them later. But these white girls were now. They were hot. That hair! That smell! That skin! The way they talked... The things they'd do! Sheeit! White girls were banging!

"Hi, girls." He flashed them the million-kilowatt movie star grin.

10

Men!

Maxi soaked her paintbrushes in turpentine. She looked critically at the remembered seascape she was painting. It was the rocky beach in front of her grandmother's house with the sea spume capturing the dying light just the way she wanted it to. She admired her handiwork and decided she could reward herself with a lunch break. Then the 'phone rang.

"Hello," she said happily, smiling at her painting on the easel. She heard a muffled sob on the other end."Hello, hello? Felicity? Honey is that you? What's wrong? Are you alright?" Maxi gripped the 'phone with both hands. "Stop crying."

"I'm not crying," gasped her sister."Baby, you are. Tell me what's wrong. Remember you're my baby sister and I love you. Tell me what's the matter?" said Maxi urgently.

"It's George, I caught him with another woman," sobbed Felicity.

"What?! Are you sure?"

"I saw him!" Felicity sniffed.

"How dare he!" said Maxi.

"He dared. He's just like all the rest of them. The men on this island are like dogs in heat; their brains are in their balls. They're depraved!" she wailed.

"Oh, Honey, I'm so sorry," said her sister. "Shall I come?"

"Yes, I'm so confused, and embarrassed."

"Don't be, you didn't do anything wrong, he did."

"Well actually, I kind of did a few things..."

"What, Honey?"

"It's a long story."

"I've got the time."

Felicity blew her nose. "I thought he loved me!" She sobbed anew.

"Hush, Baby, I'm sure he does. Tell me about it. I'm not defending him, but you know his father, his uncles and his brothers all cheat on their wives. You told me that yourself before you moved down there; remember? It's not surprising if he does the same thing. It's a learned behavior, and from what you've said it's the way Bahamian men have learned to behave."

"I know," Felicity sniffed, "and I do love it here. It's almost perfect. My law practice is doing so well. George is going into politics like his father and uncles and we're so important..." her voice broke.

"Of course you are, Baby," said her sister soothingly.

"People kiss up to us because of who his family is. And I still love him! You never think something like this'll happen to you."

"Do the boys know?"

"Of course not, they're too young to be exposed to this. I'm going to raise them to not ever do anything like this to their wives-even if they are Bahamian males." She blew her nose.

"Good luck with that," said Maxi grimly. "Felicity, what exactly happened?"

Felicity sniffed and started her recital. "You know I've been trying to land Sir Clifford Manning as a client."

"Yes, you've mentioned it six hundred times, I believe," said Maxi. "You wanted to beat out George and all the other lawyers on the island."

"Well I had an in and I had it set up. He represents millions. He plans to build a resort with gambling and a golf course on the island."

"Wow! That's serious."

"I pumped my friend Gretchen; she's friends with his sixth wife. I learned that he has a passion for seafood, short skirts and navy blue is his favorite color."

"I can guess the rest-"

"Of course, it's a no-brainer! I boned up on his company then finagled a business luncheon with him through a mutual acquaintance at this fabulous new seafood restaurant on Cable Beach. Of course I wore the navy blue silk suit that I bought in Paris last spring. I had the skirt shortened. All signs pointed to go."

"Sounds good to me, if he was looking for a liaison, but didn't you say he needed a local lawyer?"

Felicity snapped, "Didn't you hear me! Of course I covered the legal aspects. I'm on a lot of hotel boards, have a host of local contacts and our firm represents over a dozen local businesses. Obviously I know my way around the local legal quagmire plus I'm very easy on the eyes."

"Okay, okay, just checking; so what about George and the contract?"

"Oooooh," Felicity cried again. "I was sitting with Sir Clifford, and I was schmoozing with the best of them when I happened to glance across the room. George was sitting by the window having lunch with a common-looking thing!"

"A thing?"

"Yes, a jail-bait thing! A little wharf rat thing."

"How old was this thing'?"

"About sixteen," she sniffed back tears.

"Really, Felicity, I hardly think George went after a child."

"How do you know? Anyway, I saw this thing reach across the table and hold my husband's hand. They laughed! Then he kissed her-right there in broad daylight!"

"Oh, Sis!"

"I excused myself, I think I mumbled something and next thing you know I found myself at their table. It was weird because I don't remember walking there."

"Uh oh!"

"So I said, 'Hello George', and he knocked over his water glass and mumbled some nonsense about the slut being a client he was giving business advice to about opening a boutique – like I was born yesterday."

"Well he had to say something," said Maxi reasonably

"I suppose. So I'm standing there feeling so disconnected, and the bitch smiles at me. So I swear, I just kinda slipped into this fugue state or something weird where I hear someone shrieking, 'Give me this pocketbook you bitch, my husband's money paid for it, like he paid for you'. Next thing you know I'm holding her goddamn pocketbook and she's screaming curses at me!"

"Sis!"

"Then I get that disembodied feeling again-"

"Dear God-" groaned Maxi.

"And I hear that same voice bark this time, 'give me that blouse, Bitch- my husband's money paid for it', and next thing you know, I'm ripping off her goddamn blouse and screaming curses at her!"

"No! You didn't!" said her sister.

"Yes I did-tore it right off her bony, black back."

"Felicity, Honey! I'll be there just as soon as I can get a flight. Take it easy, please?"

"Do you know the bitch wasn't wearing a bra? And she jumped in my face and slapped me! So I hauled off and punched her in the face. She clawed me. I bit her and-"

"Felicity stop!" Maxi tried to suppress her laughter. "You didn't! What did George do?"

"He just sat there. I think he was in shock. As for Sir Clifford, I think I blew the contract. I sneaked a glance at him and his jaw had kind of dropped down to his chest and his eyes were popping. I've been too embarrassed to contact him since. But then, this happened yesterday-"

"Go on; what happened next? Did George break up the fight?"

"Sort of. The Maitre d' came and yelled. He didn't want to get involved I guess because of the bare breasts, they were bouncing all over the place and they hung real low for someone her age. They were so annoying looking-jumpity, jumpity like shit slung around in a sack. I smacked her across them."

"You didn't. How could you bring yourself to touch another woman's breasts?"

"Get mad enough you'll touch anything. Anyway after the maitre d' got enough of an eyeful he yelled at George to separate us. So George kinda got into the middle and grabbed me and took me out of there. I saw him slip the Maitre d' some money."

"Oh, Sis, what a dreadful experience; I'm so sorry that happened to you, you deserve better! I wonder what happened to the girl. I guess they must've used the money to buy her a new blouse."

"The bitch! If I ever see her again I'll definitely rip off her blouse since this time I'll know beyond a doubt that my money paid for it."

"Honey, she probably has more than one blouse."

"I guess," Felicity admitted reluctantly. "Anyway, you know what pissed me off?"

"No; what, Baby?"

"On the way home, George kinda looked at me out of the corner of his eye and all big and bold he sighed and scratched his crotch!"

11

The Trip

"Working on a Saturday afternoon, Madam Tycoon?" said Maxi, coming on to Charlie's patio where her friend sat typing at her laptop.

Charlie looked up in pleased surprise. "Maxi! When did you get back? I thought you were still settling Tatty into her new camp." The women hugged.

"I got back yesterday. The camp's great. Tatty's the only black kid, but the white girls seemed friendly enough. Lennie let me in on his way out. I wanted to surprise you. I see you and Evadne have packed up practically everything."

"Yeah, a lot of stuff's already at the Angloville house. I can be out of here any time I want to now. The new people are scheduled to move in at the end of the school year, that's in about two weeks. Sit."

Maxi sank onto a chaise next to Charlie. "That's right; you were waiting for Gee to finish out the school year in Mamaroneck before you moved. Your school gets out so much later than Tatty's school. She's been out for over a week already."

"Uh huh, but it's like Mama used to say, 'man proposes, God disposes'; who'd have imagined what happened to Germaine."

"Oh, Charlie, that was so horrible. When are you going to court?" Maxi looked at her friend with concern.

"We're still talking with the district superintendent. Walker, my lawyer's handling it-we've filed criminal charges. Emotionally I can't deal with it right now, it's too much."

"I know," Maxi reached out and touched Charlie's hand sympathetically.

"I get so filled with rage when I think about it. I have to distance myself from it for awhile. Lennie's fit to be tied-you know that whole macho thing. Someone wanted to besmirch his daughter so he has to kill them. But he can't so he blames me for it. He went kind of crazy"

"What can you expect? It's his daughter. He's protective."

"I know. I can't let him meet with the young thug and his parents, because I don't know what he'll do. He's not a man who denies himself anything."

"It's a mess. How's Gee doing now?"

"I spoke to her last night. She's good. It's lucky for us that Mumtaz hadn't gone back to Trinidad for the summer before all this happened. She came over and was so sweet and supportive. She was like a big sister to Germaine."

"I remember you said she stayed over for a few days. I'm sure Gee appreciated it."

"She did. Mumtaz flew with her to Trinidad and she's staying at Lennie's Mom with her 'til Gee's ready to let her go. So Marita's in heaven, she gets two grandchildren at once. Usually Mumtaz hardly ever visits her."

"Trinidad's the absolute best place for Gee right now. It's so much easier to be black in the Caribbean. I would have hated having to grow up in this country."

"Yes, you guys had it easy down there," said Charlie.

"That's what Gee needs right now. She's got oodles of people there who care about her and proof that people can be black, rich and happy and even freely marry outside their racial group, like Lennie's parents."

"And get so racially mixed up that they no longer know what they are – like Lennie's mother," Charlie added.

"Don't knock that. She's still part of a group and accepted, no matter how mongrelized."

"You're right, Germaine does need the Caribbean," said Charlie tiredly. "I'm little use to her right now. She's at that oedipal stage where Daddy's king and his family by extension reigns supreme. She doesn't want to hear a word from me. I spoke to Phoebe about it. She says I should just wait out this stage."

"It's good that you talked to Phoebe she's an excellent psychologist. Girls can be so quirky at this age."

"I see that daily. I don't know what I would've done without Mumtaz."

"I'm still amazed by Mumtaz being so nice. She always seemed vain and shallow."

"I know, I guess that's the curse of great beauty. People prejudge you and Mumtaz never did anything to make us suspect that she was nice."

"Right, Germaine's fixing up to be quite a little looker herself. I love that short haircut on her. She's so gamine with it, like a little Halle Berry."

"Isn't she? She's got her father's looks."

"She resembles you too, Charlie. You know you're stunning."

"Thanks for the vote of confidence but you know I don't pride myself on my looks. Give me brainpower and I can buy looks. Any competent plastic surgeon and cosmetic counter will fill the need."

"You got that right," said Maxi with a laugh. "So onto the next thing, Mrs. I-can-buy-whatever-I want. Are things any better between you and Lennie now that Germaine's gone?"

"Not really, should they be?"

"Yes, now you two have time to talk to each other. I know it's not a honeymoon but it can be a good time if you use it well. You might even rekindle the old spark.

"No way!"

"Think about it."

"Let's have tea?" said Charlie exiting her program and closing the computer.

"Good idea," said Maxi.

They entered the house through the kitchen door and Maxi said, "I'm going to Nassau tomorrow to visit my sister, Felicity. Her husband, George; you remember him, tall, handsome, muscular and very opinionated-well she caught him fooling around. She's devastated."

"Poor Felicity," said Charlie, "Hold on a minute. Evadne." she called out.

"Yes'm" said Evadne, coming into the kitchen.

"Please fix a tea tray for Mrs. Paine and me; we'll be in the living-room."

"Yes'm."

"You just got home and you're leaving again. Jordan must be climbing the walls," said Charlie as the women headed for the living room.

"Poor baby, he is. But he's sweet; he understands that Felicity needs me. She was practically hysterical today. We don't have a Mom so we've got to be there for each other and I'm the big sister so it's a no-brainer. You need to get away, so if you came with me when the two lovebirds get back together I won't be the proverbial fifth wheel."

"You've got to be kidding," said Charlie sitting on a packing crate and motioning Maxi to do the same. "I'm in the middle of moving and considering expanding my business and you want me to sidetrack to the Bahamas – tomorrow no less!"

"Why not? Germaine's fine and she's in good hands. Take a mental health vacation. Look at you! You're completely wired."

"I can't leave; I've got too much to do."

"Charlie, you're too bright not to know that you're functioning at your worse right now. You're dealing with marital problems, the awful thing that happened to Germaine and of course your business. Stop looking at your watch! Are you going somewhere?"

"No," said Charlie with a shamefaced smile.

"You're not expecting anyone?"

"No, come on Maxi. It's just a habit," said Charlie.

"I know, but it shows how programmed you are. Jump off the treadmill, and come to the Bahamas. 'It's better in the Bahamas!'"

"My God," said Charlie, "When did the Bahamas Tourist Board give you a job?"

"When I saw that my friend needed a break. Seriously Charlie don't you know when to say Uncle? That stuff isn't going anywhere, it'll be right here when you get back still waiting for you to deal. But you'll deal better for having been away for a while.

"Thanks Evadne, put the tray on that box," Charlie said to Evadne who entered the room with a tea tray.

"Evadne, are you looking forward to working at the new house?" said Maxi taking a cookie.

"I'm not going with Miss Charlie, Mum. I have to stay in Mamaroneck so that I can pick up little Ronesha when she gets out of school at three. From next week I start to work for Miss Rose."

"Yes," said Charlie sipping her tea. "Rose needs someone, her latest housekeeper left last week."

"Not again!" said Maxi laughing. "Good luck, Evadne, power up those supersonic, dust-busting skills if you plan to work for Mrs. Architectural Digest."

Evadne smiled and left.

"Charlie, think about what I said," Maxi told her friend later as they parted. "Call me if you change your mind."

"At one o'clock in the morning Maxi's 'phone rang, "Hello," she said groggily. "Is that you, Felicity?"

"No, it's me, Charlie. I'm coming."

12

Better in the Bahamas

An unforgiving tropical sun pounded Charlie and Maxi as they crossed the tarmac to the customs area at Nassau International airport. Most of their fellow passengers-mainly young, white tourists, wore little. A vivacious, dirty-blonde woman in the tiny shorts known as booty-cutters that revealed a pimple on her left butt cheek, was already a hit with the young Bahamian officials at the airport.

Felicity met them. She hugged Charlie, and then fell into her sister's arms with tears and exclamations. Finally she whisked them away in her blessedly air-conditioned, chauffeur-driven Bentley. Brilliant sunlight washed everything. They passed Spanish-style villas, coconut trees, casuarinas and gardens riotous with brilliant unfamiliar tropical flora. A line of banana trees preceded their passage through a village where they stopped for a group of goats to finish their progress across the road. Little wooden chattel houses dotted these narrow streets. Children horsing around with a water hose appeared to be playing with liquid rainbows. Then they were running parallel to the ocean again.

Charlie and Maxi sank luxuriously into the upholstery and duly admired everything. It was a picture postcard ride with Felicity as tour guide.

"It's beautiful, I can see why you live here," Charlie said to Felicity.

"Thank you. It has its advantages," she replied as they pulled into a circular driveway, in front of a sprawling, white, modern, house with lots of glinting glass.

"Sobers, after you park the car, bring the bags up to the guest-room, please," said Felicity to her chauffeur as he opened the car door.

"Yes, Ma'am," Sobers replied.

A neatly uniformed Haitian maid opened the front door. The cool interior was all pale pastels, white marble, glass and blonde wood. Colorful pictures by local artists hung on the walls. Picture windows and sliding glass doors framed a beach view beyond the garden wall.

"My God, talk about the good life, when can I move in?" said Charlie.

"Listen to her," said Maxi, sinking into a love seat. She turned to her sister, who joined her on the seat. "Her new home is magnificent. It has to be seen to be believed."

"I wouldn't go that far," said Charlie, looking around the room. "But it's nice, thanks to Maxi, here. She helped me whip it into shape. Felicity, what clever use you've made of color. I feel as if I'm undersea."

"Yes, Sis, take a bow, you've done a great job. Entering this room is like sipping some long, frosty, tropical concoction that provides instant surcease for whatever ails the drinker," Maxi said and sprawled back against the cushions.

Felicity rose with a laugh. "You artistic types, was that a hint? Would you like cool drinks? Charlie, try some mauby. It's a great tropical drink, made from tree bark."

"I'm ahead of you, island girl. I too am of 'Caribbean extraction'. I spent many a summer at my grandparents' home in Barbados quaffing mauby, and yes, I'd love some."

"I should've known you were originally from the Caribbean. That's why you have such good taste." Felicity teased. "Actually they don't drink mauby here. A friend brought this for me when she went on vacation to Barbados." She spoke to her kitchen by intercom then said, "Come, I'll show you to your room; Sobers must've taken your bags up by now. Bette will bring our drinks upstairs."

The bags, as predicted, were in the guestroom; a large airy room dominated by a king size bed made up with pale Porthault linens. More local-looking art adorned the walls and lace curtains billowed at the windows above the air conditioning vents.

"I have got to paint this view, it's so tranquil," Maxi exclaimed looking out the window.

Her sister snorted, "A visual oxymoron. There's no tranquility here. And all this," she waved her arm to encompass the room and the view, "is why these men are so crazy. It's too much! They can't handle it. I could smack that little bitch again."

"Felicity, honey, its going to be alright," Maxi said embracing her sister.

Felicity snuggled into her big sister's arms and whimpered, "Too much heat, too much money, too few rules. They just can't behave themselves." Then she sobbed noisily.

Charlie felt uncomfortable and welcomed the interruption of the maid, Bette, with the drinks. She politely drank hers with the sisters then slipped into her thong bikini; grabbed her beach paraphernalia and headed out.

It felt wonderful to walk practically naked in the tropical heat. She breathed in the flower-laden air around her and silently thanked Maxi for persuading her to come, she needed this. Today she was Charlie, tourist, with nothing but relaxation on her mind.

Charlie closed her eyes, and turned her face up to the sun. Its blinding light made kaleidoscopic patterns behind her closed eyelids, and she basked in its heat. She visualized it burning away all her New York problems and cares. She was free...

"If it be true that any beautiful thing raises the pure and just desire of man from Earth to God, the eternal fount of all" declared a sonorous, male voice, "then woman, I have found salvation!"

Charlie jumped. She had thought herself alone, yet this Bahamian man (for so his accent told her) was here, disturbing her reverie.

"Who the devil are you?" She whirled on him and instantly regretted her big-city-woman hostile reaction. He was gorgeous; with a rippling dark muscular body with red skin tones, he wore drawstring cotton pants loosely tied on his hip bones, exposing a flat, hairy belly. He looked at her with the face of an ebony angel and conveyed such frank admiration coupled with amusement that she had to be flattered.

"Beg your pardon, fair lady, don't be alarmed. We haven't met yet." He doffed an imaginary hat with a flourish and bowed from the waist. "Roderick Baine, George's cousin at your service."

"So you're not a prowler, good!" Charlie said smiling involuntarily.

"It gets better. I also know who you are. You're one of the American ladies expected today?"

"Yes, I'm Charlie," she said with a smile. "Sorry if I seemed hostile. But you startled me. Do you live around here?"

"No, I've recently returned from the UK and I'm staying with George, over there in the guest cottage, 'til I get settled." He pointed past the hedges in the direction of the beach. "You should drop by some time."

"Sure." She looked at her watch. "Nice talking to you. But if you'll excuse me, I'm headed for a shady spot on the beach with these." She held up her magazines. "Ciao."

He plucked a nearby flower offered it to her. "Here, welcome to Nassau."

"Thank you." She held her back a bit straighter and sucked in her already flat stomach before she took the flower.

"The pleasure's all mine," he said, looking at her quizzically.

Turkey! she thought, but unexpectedly felt herself blush. She walked away quickly, feeling off balance. Odd that he had one green and one brown eye.

Afternoon tea was served at four o'clock on a shady patio amidst a riot of flowers. A cool breeze off the nearby ocean made it a pleasant spot."I met your other house-guest earlier, on the way to the beach. He seems nice," said Charlie.

"Oh, Roderick, yes, he's George's cousin," said Felicity, looking a bit puffy eyed. "He's probably no good, just like the rest of these damn, Bahamian men. He was married to an English woman. She was okay; we hung out with them sometimes when we were in England. They have two sons. He's independent and usually won't even join us for meals 'though heaven knows he's welcome. The amount of food we cook and waste in this house is incredible. The kids love him.

"He seems to be quite a character," said Charlie.

"Is that how you were occupying yourself this afternoon," said Maxi teasingly.

Surprisingly, Charlie again felt hot blood rush to her face even as she forced a laugh and said, "'Scuse me, I'm married!"

"So is my husband," said Felicity dryly.

"Felicity, what is that flower? It's incredible," Maxi said, pointing to a large exotic bloom on a nearby bush.

"Gosh! I can't remember. It's a hybrid. We're working on it at the Garden Club. We came up with a name for it at the last meeting-something Latinate, but it's completely skipped my mind," said Felicity.

"Well, it's lovely. I hope its name does it justice," said her sister.

"Are you girls up to a party tonight with the local big-wigs?" Felicity asked. "A minister-government, not theological, is having a get-together. You might enjoy it."

Maxi looked anxiously at Felicity. "Sis, are you sure you're up to this sort of thing already?" She protectively covered her younger sister's hand on the table with her own.

"Sure," responded Felicity, in a brittle voice. "I'm not an anomaly here. I've just had my personal baptism by fire like every other foreign and even Bahamian, wife."

"That may be," agreed her sister, "but can you deal with George in public yet? You know people will be watching you, trying to figure out how you're taking it."

"I know," replied Felicity. She stuck her chin out defiantly. "Well I have him. I am the wife, and damn it! I will go to that stupid party with my husband, louse that he is. I'll show these vicious people that I'm not going anywhere; except maybe to the prime-minister's residence one of these days, with the louse-as first lady of this island."

Charlie said, "That's the spirit!"

Maxi looked at her sister appraisingly.

Felicity met the gaze and said, "Max, I'm going to be okay, really. Like I said, these men are all a pack of village rams. So I won't be singled out as the one who couldn't hold onto her man. Look at what Mama did."

"What's a village ram?" queried Charlie.

"It's a West Indian term for a man who sleeps around," explained Maxi."

"Graphic," said Charlie. "I can see him butting away at all the unfortunate village girls leaving havoc in his wake."

"I guess," said Maxi glancing at her sister with concern in her eyes.

Felicity said, "Calypsos here celebrate this type of thing. They praise the village ram's great sexual prowess and disgusting womanizing. He's sometimes described as a 'donkey conqueror', you know; hung like a donkey and completely unconscionable."

"Men are such shits!" said Charlie. "Rap in the US does the same thing, except that our songsters are misogynists. They advocate demeaning and getting violent with women. Let's go to the party. We can't ever let them make us hide."

"Here, here!" agreed the sisters lifting their teacups in a toast.

13

The Package Deal

Japanese lanterns shone softly in the trees behind the honorable Mr. Fitzgerald's large, white, Moroccan style house perched on a cliff at Lyford Cay.

"Great night for a party!" said Charlie, entering the noisy courtyard with Felicity and her family. "What's with the guard at the gate back there? You've got Rockefellers living in this place?"

"Something like that," said George. This is the only gated community on the island. It was created for wealthy expats who value their privacy and possessions. Locals started meeting the wealth criteria, so now Bahamians live here too."

"It's getting a bit cool," Maxi said, as a freshening breeze off the ocean raised goose bumps on her bare arms and set balloons to dancing on the umbrella-topped tables around them.

"That's why they've got spirits at that bar. Let's head there pronto and we'll all be warm," George said chivvying them along.

George and Felicity hailed friends as they made a tortuous path to the bar.

"Look!" said Charlie sharply, pointing to a dark shape on the grass ahead of them. It turned out to be a forlorn, forgotten, black doll with long hair and staring eyes.

"Sorry," said Charlie. "For a moment there I thought it was a baby."

George shook his head. "She hasn't even had a drink yet."

"Ignore him, Charlie," Felicity said. "The Fitzgeralds have children. As you can see, some little girl's going to make a crackerjack mother."

The guests were a well-dressed, attractive, motley crew. Blacks predominated, interspersed with a judicious smattering of Whites, Conkey

Joes (Creole Whites) and enough East Indians and Chinese to qualify for rainbow coalition status.

Poolside, a steel band softly played Schubert's Ave Maria and liquor flowed from the bar. Uniformed waiters circulated, serving the ubiquitous Bahamian conch, in all its party forms-conch fritters, soused conch, scorched conch, cracked conch-prepared, it was said, for the virility of their men.

Men wore leisure suits, bush jacket suits, kente cloth shirts or dashikis. Their ladies mostly sported the latest from Europe and America's fashion houses. A few stalwart souls, who insisted on buying local, wore dresses from Burdines and other popular bastions of cheap fashion in Miami, Florida-the place for quick shopping trips and clandestine love fixes.

"Who or what on earth is that?" Maxi asked her brother-in-law.

They all looked to the tall, fierce-looking man she indicated. Clad in a green, mid-calf length tunic and black Turkish trousers, he wore his long hair in dreadlocks topped by a red fez. His mid-chest length beard was elaborately braided and decorated with gold balls. A diminutive, perfectly proportioned, Asian woman in a tight cheongsam hung onto his arm.

"That's our Minister of Culture, Alpha Omega, " George said.

"Say what?" said Charlie.

"Alpha Omega," reiterated George, obviously enjoying her amazement. "He chose that name after he shed his 'plantation patronym' and reinvented himself linguistically as a new black man. He always wears the black liberation colors; red for blood, green for the Earth and black for the people. You women must meet him. A word of warning-he gets offended if you don't address him by both of his names. He considers them "'hermeneutically significant.'"

"'Scuse me," said Maxi. "Repeat that in English please."

"Hermeneutics, you know, the science of interpretation and seeing something in its larger context. If I got this correctly, his name flies in the face of compromised black history. The buck stops with him, the Alpha and the Omega-the beginning and the end. He is a New World, new man. He has reclaimed himself from a debatable past and now owes nothing to the White man. He takes full responsibility for himself. He is his own past and future or something like that. He's seen you and obviously wants to meet you. Let's get those drinks and go over and talk to him."

Alpha Omega had been eyeing the women as had most of the men at the party. They smelt new blood, and like sharks with fresh blood on the water, they were closing in for the promised feast. The 'nigger network' had already announced the arrival of unencumbered, attractive, American women to the Knowles household. These men cared nothing about husbands at home. They lived by the motto from the local calypso

Indiscretions will be concealed,

No charge

It's part of the package deal."

They were the deal and the night was young. If hot, loose American women called, it was in-your-face time for attendant wives and sweethearts. Antibiotics could always be taken later.

"Alpha Omega," George hailed him, drink in hand. "Meet my sister-in-law Maxine Paine and a friend, Charlene Gopilal. They're visiting from Stateside-Westchester, right?"

Alpha Omega turned to the women. "Charmed, dear ladies. I'd like you to meet my lady, Petal." He held onto Maxi's hand just a beat too long, and gazed intensely into Charlie's eyes. He was a hair's breadth away from salivating.

Felicity was not amused. She could be felt radiating heat. This further example of the general randiness of the Bahamian male appeared to gall her. George of course was totally oblivious as he surveyed the lady Petal with a foolish grin on his face.

Petal offered a limp hand to be shaken. Her long, red nails somehow managed to rake Charlie's hand.

Surprised, Charlie regarded the young Asian flower with interest and observed, "Terrific party!" as she accepted a conch fritter from a passing tray. She tasted it. "This is good." She turned to Alpha Omega. "It's such a treat to get away from the touristy sections and meet the real people who live in a place." She gazed sincerely into Alpha Omega's eyes. Take that Petal! After all, she was on vacation and could bullshit with the best of them if necessary.

Alpha Omega rose to the occasion. "I'd be happy to give you a tour of our beautiful island Charlene. I can show you places where your countrymen have never set foot. Tomorrow I'll pick you-"

"Alpha Omega, catch you later," interrupted George catching an unmistakable look from Felicity. "They've got to meet their host. The honorable won't stand for beautiful ladies ignoring him." He hustled them off.

"This is refreshingly different from our American parties," said Maxi later, sipping a rum-punch.

"How so?" asked Felicity.

"Men and women are actually talking with each other instead of men over here and women over there," replied her sister.

"What is it with these black Bahamian men and the heavy Oxford, English accents?" Charlie asked. "If I close my eyes I swear I can almost imagine I'm somewhere in the British Isles."

George explained. "The upper classes here used to ape the British; many of them studied in England or Scotland. They practiced the accent and brought it home with them to remind the rest of us of their superiority. The more plebeian of us affect American or just plain, old, Bahamian accents-no matter where we studied. I've also heard of Bahamians going to the airport on a Sunday afternoon outing and returning home with American accents."

"You've had too much to drink," said his sister-in-law with a laugh.

They meandered through the courtyard and Charlie and Maxi were introduced to what seemed like the entire large party. They joined in some conversations and eavesdropped on others.

"I tell you, his wife never suspected he was a damn 'batty man' until she caught him."

Charlie whispered to Felicity, "What's a batty man?"

"Here batty is slang for butt, so it's pretty much self explanatory," Felicity replied

"Oh no! I wouldn't want to be that wife; she can't compete at all," said Charlie.

"Felicity, dear, I'm so glad you came." A short, plain, woman in horn-rimmed glasses, and a Liberty-Print shirtwaist dress enthusiastically exchanged hugs with Felicity.

"Ruth, good to see you-meet my sister, Maxine Paine, she lives in the U.S., and her friend, Charlene Gopilal. Ruth's a partner in our law office," said Felicity.

They shook hands all around and Ruth asked,

"Felicity, will you and George be joining us in Madrid this summer? We're taking the kids to the time-share. I'm dying to practice my Spanish and broaden the boys' horizons. Your boys would love it."

"George and I haven't decided yet. It's tempting. Right now they're in Florida in summer camp."

"Good for you! I told you they were ready to sleep away from home. Get back to me on the Madrid thing. I see John from Immigration over there. I've got to check something with him-that case we discussed last week." She hurried off.

"What do you think about the P.M. appointing Crawford to that cabinet post?" asked a pretty woman in a pink silk sheath.

"Sheer nepotism, my dear," responded a bearded type in a bush jacket. "But if you don't help your friends when you're in power, when will you help them?"

Another group was in hot debate.

"Obviously the Bible is not literal. How can you, a supposedly rational, intelligent person, believe otherwise? It's all allegory."

"No. Faith is a necessary component in Christian doctrine. 'Unless ye become as little children,' etc."

"Children believe anything. Didn't your mother make you go to church about three times on Sundays? Well I did and I know my Bible, from Genesis to Revelations."

Charlie found the party exhilarating and exotic. In the background a calypso about a gay man asked:

Who put the pepper In the Vaseline?

Oh Lord, I can' stan' this t'ing!

She felt dizzied by it all-the liquor, unfamiliar faces, accents, concerns. The throbbing beat of calypsos and goombay music pulsed in her blood. Men flirted outrageously with her. She felt sexy and desirable.

"Having fun yet?" asked a familiar voice behind her.

Charlie turned and confronted laughing eyes, one brown, and one green. "Oh, it's you-George's cousin," she smiled up at him. "You're funny. Actually I am. I feel as if I've suddenly gone to the other side of a fun house mirror. Everything is unfamiliar and it's all so much fun!" She laughed and flung her arms out slopping champagne down the front of Roderick's dashiki.

"Oops. Sorry! Damn! I always seem to be apologizing to you," she said as she dabbed at his chest with a greasy paper napkin that had held a fried conch fritter.

He caught her hand and held it. "Relax," he said softly. "Come, let's take a walk. Fresh air will do you good." He took her champagne flute and set it on a passing tray.

Maxi and Felicity exchanged looks as Charlie and Roderick walked away. Roderick shepherded Charlie, through the crush of dancing bodies and intriguing conversations.

"The poor, silly, man! That Knighthood's completely driven out what little sense he ever had. He had a genealogist research his roots. Now he has a replica of his coat of arms and Scottish tartan hanging in the hallway of that silly castle he brought over from Scotland and had reconstructed down the street. Claims he discovered he's the rightful laird."

They passed a conga line snaking along the perimeter of the dance floor. The line vibrated with sexual energy as the calypso declaimed,

If you can't get a woman

Get a man...'

Someone grabbed at Charlie's hand to pull her in. Roderick firmly disentangled her from the clutching hand and led her to a narrow walkway that descended to the beach.

The susurration of the night wind in the coconut trees beckoned them forward. Charlie, to her surprise, felt relieved to leave the party laughter and music behind. They descended the rocky path to the beach, with the occasional lizard darting in front of their feet. Roderick held her hand to steady her as she tottered at times in her wildly impractical, high-heeled sandals. Once, she slipped and he caught her and held her in his arms for a few seconds. She thanked him and held her breath as they looked at each other then wordlessly resumed their descent.

Charlie felt confused. She was taking a chance. Date rape did happen. But he was behaving differently from the men at the party. Did he still find her attractive? Also was she the kind of woman who went tit for tat with her husband? Anyway she was too old for this sort of thing, if it was 'this sort of thing'.

When they reached the beach she kicked off her shoes and waded into the sun warmed, now moonlit ocean, hiking up her skirt and squealing. She would not think about what she might want from this disturbing, attractive man, or he from her; or why she had left the safety of the party to be alone with him. She was on vacation, and so was her mind. Charlie stayed in the water for as long as possible and waded. Roderick sat on the beach and watched and waited.

14

The Morning After

"Well, what did you think of the party?" asked Felicity next morning, plunking down on the chaise in the sunny guestroom.

"Great!" said Maxi; "All those preying men do wonders for a girl's ego. Sorry, I forgot, Hell! The come on *is* nice! It must be terrible, as Daddy used to put it, 'to live and die and never have anyone even ask what you're selling'".

"And our Daddy certainly asked," Felicity observed. "And, just like Daddy, all these men ever want is new pussy. I told George that I could be new pussy too-to some other man."

Charlie said, "Not bad. Anyway, I'd take this any day over our dull, predictable parties with the same boring, homogenous Westchester and Connecticut professionals."

"Yes," agreed Maxi. The men discuss sports, or sometimes actually watch it on TV. Their wives power-broker positions in Jack and Jill, The Links, The Girlfriends, or some other inane black organization which gives them the chance to dress up in designer clothes, dump their kids, and trip out of the house to discuss other friends not in the same organization."

Charlie added, "They also discuss shopping and houses-they're mad about houses. If you buy a new house they'll find ingenious ways to get a tour of it. Their little darlings' progress is another hot topic. A darling is always performing somewhere or winning something. BAPs and their brothers-"

"What're BAPs?" asked the amused Felicity.

"Black American princesses of course-the children of Buppies, who are the black version of Yuppies," explained her sister.

"They're like the JAPs," Charlie continued. "They're indulged, successful, little, cut-throat kids. Watch out America!" They laughed in recognition of their own children.

So what's bad about that?" asked Felicity.

"Nothing, but it's not party conversation! It's boring, no spice." said Maxi.

"Now, I broke the mold with my last party," said Charlie. "I threw together one heterogeneous group of niggers in the true sense of the word-both black and white, and the fireworks were incredible."

"You don't appreciate your assets," Felicity said in amazement. "It must be wonderful to have men who don't have to jump around and brandish their penises, so to speak, to prove that they are men. I've met your men. I think they're sweet. They respect their wives, and most of them can converse with a woman without making her feel sexually threatened."

Maxi said, "So I'll party with your hot, sexy men with the brandished penises," she laughed and ducked the pillow that her sister flung at her head. "Then I'll go home to my sweet Westchester, black, American man who wouldn't dare misbehave, because this West Indian girl has become a bad, liberated, black American woman. I'd tie him up in his sleep and bobbit-with a rusty knife too-and he knows it!"

"Well, Miss Smarty, don't you turn up your nose at your Caribbean sisters. Just last week a local man was fooling around and his wife found out. Guess what? When he fell asleep she stuck his penis to his belly with crazy glue. So take that, Miss America!"

They rolled on the bed and laughed till tears streamed down their faces. When they had recovered somewhat Charlie said, "I still say there's something about your men." She remembered Roderick's flat, hairy belly and Puckish teasing charm. "They're so sexy! There ought to be a law against it."

"Yes," admitted Felicity. "Sexy children; they misbehave in front of Mommy to show how cute they are. I want a man, not a bad-behaved little boy. Didn't your mother ever tell you that there are some men you have fun with and some you marry?"

"Amen to that." said her sister.

"Amen!" echoed Charlie, and they went downstairs to breakfast.

The meal was served on the patio now awash with morning sunlight. The riotous tropical flowers and plants fronted an ocean of the most intense blue Charlie had ever seen. "Why do I live in Westchester?" she asked looking around her. "Let's switch."

Felicity poured Darjeeling tea from the big silver teapot and said, "You'd be begging for your old life back before the end of the first day,"

"Ma'am, Lady Vera's on the phone." The maid said, bringing a cordless 'phone.

Charlie and Maxi raised eyebrows at each other over their teacups.

"Thanks, Bette." Felicity took the call. "That was my friend, Vee. Her husband's a local politician. He was recently knighted in the Queen's birthday honors. We're going to Miami today, to shop for our kids. They have a European class trip coming up. My boys will be leaving again the day after they return from visiting their Grammy on Abaco Island. Want to come with us? We'll be back late afternoon."

"I'll see," replied Maxi. "When do you plan to return to work?"

"I'm not ready yet." Felicity said irritably.

Charlie looked at her sympathetically and quickly changed the subject. "What's the story on that pale, little Oriental woman at the party with Alpha Omega last night?"

"That's Petal, she's in the man business."

"What's that? Prostitution redefined?" asked Maxi.

"I guess you foreigners wouldn't know." Felicity laughed at their perplexity. "Women like her have children for important men in the community – the sort who don't want it said that their child is seeing life real hard and the Daddy, who of course is rich, and powerful locally, won't give a cent to the child's mother. These people are family conscious that way."

"That's like having a permanent hostage! How can they fall for that?" said Maxi.

"You know men are generally stupid about that sort of thing. Here, if you're young, cute, light-skinned or dark, with a good grade of hair, and immoral-you can get away with anything. Also, knowing every sexual trick in the book is probably an asset. These people are not normal," Felicity said bitterly.

The women fell silent and Maxi patted her sister's hand.

"It's okay, Sis," said Felicity. "I'm not some fragile hot-house flower who'll wilt in this scorching, tropical sun. I'm going to hang in there."

"Right on, Paine women have the right stuff. Look at how Momma tamed our wild Daddy. You stay right here and whip that George back into shape."

Charlie rose. "I'll leave you sisters alone to kick things around. I've got to see a man about a horse." She looked at her watch, grabbed her tote bag and headed down the steps.

15

Ms Tourist

Charlie looked at her watch then took a deep breath and rapped firmly on the guest cottage door. It was a bit after 10:00.a.m.

"Hold on," she heard Roderick call from inside.

She smiled as she thought of how she had escaped explanations to Maxi and Felicity. She'd have to call them later; this was bordering on rudeness. But what could she say? It felt slightly wrong to be here. She was just a tourist being shown around by a native of the place, she reassured herself. Suddenly the native stood in the open doorway.

"Boo!" he said, and laughed.

She joined in nervously. "You startled me, again."

"Good Morning, you sure are one nervous woman. Come on in."

"Am I too early?"

"No, right on time, I just finished breakfast. I should've taken you out for a Bahamian breakfast." He moved magazines off a love seat and motioned her to sit there.

She sat and placed her bag on the cluttered coffee table. "That's okay, I had to spend time with Felicity and Maxi-girl talk, you know. But thanks for the sightseeing invitation. I'm sure Felicity wants to be alone with her sister, she's taking this George thing really hard."

"Bad business that." He looked at her soberly and shook his head. "So, enough about them, what shall we do today? Would you like to drive around the island? Is there some particular spot you're hankering to see?"

"None, I place myself entirely in your expert hands."

"I see you're a wise woman. Okay, we'll play it by ear. We'll drive around; stop anyplace that tickles your fancy, and later lunch al fresco from a roadside stand, you're going native today. I'll have you back by tea-time."

"Sounds wonderful; by the way, this roadside stand business-you guarantee no Montezuma's revenge?"

"Charlie, have I ever led you astray?"

"Never, in the less than twenty-four hours I've known you."

"Good, keep believing in me-that's the ticket. We'll mix business with pleasure and drop by some sites I promised a developer friend I'd take a look at. We plan to build a community out East near the water. You can tell me what you think.

"Sounds good."

"Hey! You're not one of those green people, are you-the sort who doesn't believe in destroying the natural habitat to provide habitats for humans?"

"Well, now that you mention it, I could be a moral watch-dog. Is that what you need, a conscience?"

"No, I've got plenty. I plan to build tiny burrows for all God's creatures that'll be displaced, I'll even burn candles for them," he said with a wink. "But seriously, we plan to use Feng Shui principles in our community. We have a Master coming in from the US to advise us on this." He started tidying the room.

"Very nice, I'm impressed," said Charlie. She smiled at him. "Let me help you, so that we can get out of here while the day's still young?" She stood.

"No, sit. You're my guest, let me do the work." He gently pressed her back down onto the seat. Then he clicked a remote control, and filled the room with new-age sounding piano music.

Charlie sat back on the rattan love seat and watched him and wondered why she was there. He'd been a perfect gentleman the night before. He'd talked about growing up in Nassau and appeared interested in her life. They'd been comfortable together. He didn't seem to want anything from her. She caught him looking at her and they smiled at each other. "I love that music? Who's playing?" she asked.

"George Winston, the CD's called Winter. Great isn't it? It always makes me think of England; cold, remote and beautiful at times."

"Is that why you returned home, because you didn't feel a part of that society?"

"No, I always planned to return home. Events made it sooner rather than later."

Charlie called Felicity and informed her of the sightseeing jaunt with Roderick; then they took off in his yellow, mini Moke, the consummate, tourist car; a jeep with no top or sides. There was no room for conversation because the wind blew their words away, so Charlie relaxed and enjoyed the sights. But she was ever conscious of the man by her side. He was disconcertingly attractive. She was married.

Last night, they'd talked on the quiet beach and much to her surprise she had fantasized about taking off his clothes and saying, "don't talk, just make love to me." Maybe she shouldn't have come out with him today. She sighed aloud.

"Penny for your thoughts," Roderick shouted against the wind.

"What?"

"What were you thinking? You seemed so far away." He stopped the car, and helped her down from the high-sided Moke. They were in a deserted beach area. Sea grapes grew in the scrub near the water. The ocean beyond the pale gold sand sparkled.

"Believe me; you don't want to hear my thoughts. They're boring to anyone but me. I was thinking about my business and how long I dare stay away."

"Charlie," He said sternly. "No thinking about work today. Now about this location, what do you think about it as a development for me?" He grinned impishly.

"I see. No business, just monkey business-yours! We'll both think about my restaurants then maybe I can afford one of your over-priced homes. Let's discuss possible new items I can introduce at my Fordham Road location-that's the busiest one."

"Touché; but seriously, what do you think about this spot? It's up for grabs now and I might invest with a developer – we'll put down some roads, power lines, top-notch security systems. Right now it's all kind of behind God's back. But it could fly."

"It might," she agreed, her thoughts disturbingly on him, not his development. "Hey! Race you to the water's edge. Last one there's a ... a ..."

"Buys dinner tonight for the winner," said Roderick shedding his shoes and taking off for the shoreline."

Roderick won. When she reached the water he caught her in his arms and spun her around laughing. When he let her go, their eyes met and her nipples hardened. She felt flustered. This was not the platonic reaction of a proper married woman.

They swam, dived and bumped into each other. Charlie had not been this relaxed in years. Later they visited another of his potential sites, this time they floated in a peaceful bay, with water as still as glass.

"This place is unreal," said Charlie, looking around at the rock enclosed natural pool in which they swam, framed by a perfect beach.

"Because it's beautiful?"

"Yes, and remote, like your George Winston music," She dived under and he dived after her. They competed to see who could stay under longer.

"Ready for lunch yet" asked Roderick later as they climbed back into the Moke.

"Please, I'm famished."

"Me too; lunch here we come."

Roadside food vendors provided an exotic feast of hot, greasy conch fritters, pineapple slices, guineps and coconut water. "Is this how the natives eat?" asked Charlie.

"Actually this is how the tourists eat; the natives now eat with the Colonel and McDonald's."

"I should have guessed. I should open a franchise here."

"You should. Here, have some coconut water." He passed her a coconut, with the top cut off and a space cut out for her lips. "Use it like you would a cup. Good, tilt your head back. That's it." They ate in companionable silence and Roderick introduced her to guineps, small, fleshy, pink fruit in a firm, green skin.

"Great lunch," said Charlie. She dabbed her lips and wiped her hands with wet naps looking around in contentment. "What on earth!"

Roderick followed her gaze to a young, white couple – tourists most likely, engaging in oral sex in full view of everyone on the public beach. "Sorry, our government unofficially permits that kind of thing. They don't want to offend these tourists who have no respect for our country. So we put up with displays like that rather than act and possibly stanch the flow of the tourist dollar. Let's go." He looked furious as he pulled Charlie up off the rock and they headed for the car. "We'll go to the underwater park."

"Good idea," Charlie said as they left this more recent version of The Ugly American behind them.

In the park's submarine room they admired the fishes swimming by on the ocean floor and sometimes looking in at them. They visited Fort Montague then zoomed by the Adastra Gardens to see the flamingos. They passed Government house, and Charlie was properly impressed. Roderick pointed out countless hotels along their route. By teatime Charlie pleaded exhaustion and they headed back to Felicity's.

"Charlie, about that dinner tonight, can I take a rain check on it?" Roderick asked.

She looked perplexed.

"You've forgotten already! Remember the race that I won this morning, on the beach? You lost, and you're to buy me dinner. But I'll have to take a rain check. I just remembered I already have a dinner commitment for tonight."

She nodded, too hot and exhausted to talk.

"Old friends invited me. Hey, why don't you come with me? Please? You'll like Steve and Bert. Bert's an old flame of mine." He laughed when she visibly started. "No, I didn't swing that way, Bert's actually Bertha, but no one ever calls her that."

"It's a brutal name. Didn't her mother like her?"

"Very much I think. That's why she named her specially. Ever heard of A Boy Named Sue? "

"You know that crazy song too?"

"One of my favorites; please say you'll come. I'll call Bert. It's a small dinner party; you'll enjoy it. Pick you up at 7:30?" He smiled, and gave her knee a friendly squeeze.

Charlie's uterus contracted. She whirled through the air on a carnival ride and her stomach dropped back into place after the rest of her body. Holy shit! she thought; this can't be happening. I'm too old for this type of thing. I've got a teen-age daughter!

She beat down her body and said demurely, "Anything you say." Then she lay back against the upholstery, and tilted her visor down. This was almost forgotten territory.

Back at Felicity's house a red Lamborghini was parked in the driveway.

"Who's driving that beauty?" asked Charlie admiringly.

"Our famous lady Vee," replied Roderick. "She and her ancient husband are the new plunderers of the Western world; rather, her husband, Sir Trevor McEwen is. They're a Bahamian couple.

"What on earth did he do?" asked Charlie.

"He bought a Scottish castle, transported it here and re-erected it stone by stone then did his own rape of Europe. He acquired tapestries, rare artifacts and priceless antique furniture from all over, put it all in his benighted castle by the sea and left it."

"You wanted him to stay there and admire it?" Charlie asked.

"No," he replied, pulling up and helping her from the car. "As he and baby wife tripped around the globe, the heat and sea air attacked and destroyed the priceless treasures. He didn't have the wit to air-condition the sorry place."

"That's a shame," Charlie said as Roderick walked her to the front door. She stole a glance at him and admired his expressive mouth. She fantasized those indignant lips on her own.

Charlie rang the doorbell and Roderick said, "See you at eight?"

"Why not? I'll call you if there's a problem."

"Okay, you go on in and meet the robber baroness. She's delightful."

"I'd be delightful too, if I had that kind of money," said Charlie. "Later," she caroled as the maid answered the door and let her into the house.

16

Sophie

"I never did thank you properly for getting Rorie into The Boulé," said Sophie to her lover as she languorously trailed her fingers from his navel up to his neck then back down again.

"You just did," Grantley replied, kissing the top of her head as she lay in his arms. This bi-weekly tryst was such a release. Sometimes things got so hot that he feared for his heart, but what a way to go. He smiled and stroked her firm belly. "I can't believe you now have a teen-age daughter."

"I'm a good Catholic girl, I am; and when we get hot, we get married-so we marry young!" she pouted, as she climbed onto him and deliciously ground her hips into his pelvis. Then she laughed into his face, as his mounting interest became increasingly evident. "Here's more thanks!" she said.

"Oh Lord, woman, what am I going to do with you!" He chuckled and tried to roll her off him.

"Just love me?" she said in a little girl voice.

"Baby I do, I do," he grunted huskily, hungrily cupping a breast and easing her upwards so that he could tongue it.

"Grantley," she said as she arched her back for this caress, "What's Rose wearing to the Fitzwilliams' anniversary party?"

"Christ! I don't know," he said annoyed. "Why don't you ask her? She's your friend." He took the nipple into his mouth.

"She's your wife, and I don't want to ask her. I'm asking you."

"Damn it, Sophie!" he said, hanging onto the nipple and speaking in a muffled voice. "I don't get involved with women's fashions." He chomped away. "If it means that much to you, call her and discuss your clothes. That's what you want to do, isn't it, but who the hell knows or cares what a woman's wearing to a party that's more than a month away?"

Obviously, I do." She gripped him tightly by the hair on his head.

"Ouch!" he said. She decreased the pressure and he returned his full attention to the task at hand and sucked greedily. "Anyway, you know you look good in anything you put on." He mumbled this between mouthfuls before diving back to his full time job of burrowing his face between the magnificent breasts and rolling them around his cheeks. Then he reverted to suckling the large right breast with its hard, brown nipple.

"I care. I've never been to a Boulé event before, and this will be a Boulé event because he's the president. But somebody, ahem, ahem; never got my husband into the organization until now so what do I know about how the wives dress? But I'm going to a Boulé event," she trilled.

Sophie rolled off Grantley, making the nipple pop out of his mouth. She sat tailor fashion on the bed facing him, arms raised above her head in exultation. Her heavy breasts bounced in excitement. Grantley groaned and reached for them again.

"Sophie, we've only got about twenty-five minutes left. I have a two o'clock patient; let's not waste time talking nonsense. Come to Poppa," he said tenderly.

"Big schmuck!" she laughed, pushing him away. "Talk before we do anything else naughty," she said archly. "Anyway we can leave this place together; no one we know comes to Yonkers."

He lay back, put his hands behind his head, and looked at her.

Sophie jumped off the bed and started doing a lascivious dance. She ground her hips in a circle while her hands gracefully held her long, heavy hair on top of her head. A patch of sunlight illuminated the gold of her body, and she knew she looked good standing there, with her golden brown pubic bush on fire from the sun.

"What do you want to know?" he said, getting erect again as he watched in fascination. The way she stuck out her butt and touched herself, in ways he wished he could be touching her now; this was making him crazy.

"What do you Boulé boys talk about? I know wives can never attend the meetings. Do you get in there and play with each other? And I mean play."

"Did anyone ever tell you that you're crazy? Why did you want your husband to join an organization that you don't trust and that you claim to know so little about?"

"Because," she said softly, stroking her breasts and sliding her hands up and down her torso, slowly and oh so gently. "Because;" she studied a breast, then stopped for a second to pluck out a hair from the surrounding areola before continuing her dance and her speech. "Because I am relatively young," she stroked her pubis;" smart... and somewhat beautiful. I want to attend the best parties... Be seen with the best people... and, my darling," she swooped down on him suddenly, tweaked his now erect penis, then ran back to her patch of sunlight that was filtering in through the partially drawn drapes at the Yonkers Holiday Inn.

"Come back," he said hoarsely.

But Sophie continued. "I want contracts for my architectural firm. Black contracts, white contracts, Set Asides – I want it all. That's an influential group of black men in your li'l ol' fraternal organization. They can throw a lot of business the way of a blood brother's-"

"Isn't there an N word for stuff like that? Like nepotism?" he said, laughing and enjoying the show.

"Now, now!" she responded, moving her body in wave-like motions and running her hands over her hips and belly, accentuating their flare. "You guys are the ones always preaching economic determinism for the black community. Well, I want your boulé to be my ticket to economic success. I'm black!"

"Is that why you're here with me?"

"No, honey pie," she drawled. She put one hand on her hip and came slowly toward him, pelvis first. She grabbed hold of his now fully erect member. "This is why I'm here with you. It's why I've been with you right from the start." She slid her hand up and down the shaft a few times then hopped on. "I want you for you," she whispered, as she bent forward and kissed him on the lips.

He held onto her tightly as they moved quickly to his second climax of the afternoon. It was now seventeen minutes past two; there were two o'clock patients to be seen. But God, she was something!

17

Meeting The Natives

Charlie sprayed on perfume and admired her image in the mirror, dark skin glowing against the white summer dress. There was a tap on the door and Maxi entered.

"Going out with that man again tonight!" Maxi said.

"Why not? I'm a tourist and I'm enjoying myself. Wasn't this your prescription Dr. Paine." She wagged her finger at Maxi and said; "Don't give me that look."

"What look?"

"The, 'married lady, you're playing with fire look'."

"You said it, I didn't." They smiled at each other then Maxi turned her attention to her magazine and Charlie headed for the door.

Roderick gave a long, low, wolf whistle when Charlie descended the stairs.

"Charlie, you have set a new standard for pulchritude in the Bahamas.

O thou art fairer than the evening air

Clad in the beauty of a thousand stars."

"Thank you, kind Sir," she replied.

Steve and Bert's large contemporary house bordered a golf course. Several cars were already parked in the circular driveway when they pulled up. A butler led them to the party in the backyard where their host, Steve, a short burly man, kissed Charlie soundly on the lips before she could object.

"I heard about Felicity's gorgeous house guests," he said, "but I wasn't prepared for this. Wow! Welcome American cousin, kissing cousin." He bussed her again.

"Bert, you still haven't taught this old vagabond company manners?" said Roderick. He hugged and kissed his slim, dark, beautiful hostess. She seemed to float in a flowing, white, Indian cotton outfit.

Some men just can't be house-broken," said Bert. Her voice was low and husky. She smiled at her husband and put her hand on his shoulder. Little bells on her charm bracelet tinkled. "But I love him this way. He's my wild man."

"Grrrrr," said Steve, obligingly, then he hugged his wife with a laugh.

The guests sat around the pool deck with the setting sun as a backdrop. The men wore bush jacket suits in pale colors. The women were varied in their dress.

"Roderick, absolutely topping to see you again, old chap. Jolly good show returning to your native land and all that," a large, black, Bahamian with a heavy, Oxonion, English accent boomed, rising and clapping Roderick on the back. He shook Charlie's hand. "Gregory Montgomery, at your service; meet my wife Maude."

Charlie suppressed a smile as she wondered if this one had been to the airport or England to pick up his accent.

"Hello, ducks," said a pale, freckled blonde with a cockney accent. "Nice t'meet y'." She gave a wet fish handshake. "Try this drink, it's good."

"Thank you, I will," Charlie said.

"Charlie, Gregory's our family doctor; I was in school with the old reprobate. Come meet the other guests," Bert said leading her away. "This is Malthus, our priest; and his wife Camille."

"Priest?" said Charlie.

"The Church of England," Bert smiled at her. "Anglican priests can marry."

A tall, handsome Bahamian in a clerical collar rose and pumped Charlie's hand. "Charmed," he said.

"His wife, Camille," said Bert.

"Pleased to meet you," a mousy- looking woman with short, badly processed hair shook Charlie's hand.

"This is Angelica Sands, a professor of sociology at our local College, and her husband, Tyrone, a banker," Bert continued.

"Charlie, we met last night at Hugh Fitzgerald's party. I know, you don't remember me." Angelica chuckled. "It seems as if the whole world was there and you met everyone."

"Just about, nice to meet you – again," Charlie said with a smile.

"Let's sit." Roderick put his arm around Charlie's shoulder and steered her to a pair of empty chairs next to the Priest and his wife.

"Charlie, do try our Bahama Mamas," said Bert as the butler approached with a tray of red drinks.

"Don't mind if I do," she said and took one. She sipped it and declared it delicious.

A maid bearing a tray of conch delicacies followed the butler.

"Try the scorched conch," said Roderick.

"Is this a set-up Roderick?" said Tyrone. "Plying the lady with liquor and conch, and then taking her home alone-naughty, naughty!" He wagged a finger.

There was general laughter and cries of "Roderick," in mock stern voices.

Charlie felt embarrassed and for a moment wished that she was unencumbered and that it could be that sort of date.

Malthus turned to her, "Charlie, the strangest thing happened to me last Sunday. I was christening a beautiful baby boy; scion of an old Bahamian family."

"Malthus, I wish you would do more funerals," broke in Camille. She turned to Charlie; "They pay more."

"I will, dear," Malthus said. "The baby wore an elaborate christening gown that's been in their family for generations. Suddenly I felt this warmth on my hand. For a second I thought it was the Holy Ghost, then I noticed that the water in the fount was yellow-:"

"Yes," said Camille. "The young mother forgot to diaper her baby. Can you believe it?" She burst into gales of laughter and Malthus sat back and looked pleased with himself.

"Can I have another of these?" said Maude holding out her glass, unsteadily.

Bert signaled the butler who came from the bar with a refill. Gregory frowned at his wife as she thirstily downed the Bahama Mama.

"Angelica," said Charlie. "I met Alpha Omega last night, he's fascinating. Do many Bahamians share his views?"

Tyrone exclaimed, "That nut! He should be certified and kept away-"

Angelica interrupted. "Tyrone, will you please stop it! Your mouth is going like a sick nigger's backside, and there is no sense in what you're saying." Then she explained the phenomenon of Alpha Omega-her way.

"My dear, I hope I'm not being presumptuous" said Malthus to Maude, "but do you miss England a great deal, living here?"

"Oh, no," she said. "Gregory's England to me; he sounds just like the BBC. Why he's more British than I am. Occasionally I want grits and stew fish for breakfast. But Gregory always prefers kippers, and scones and marmalade." She giggled.

"How charming," said Malthus.

"That's why I love him so much." Maude took a sip, and then hiccupped. "The other nurses on the service dared me to go out with him, because he was colored and all; but I didn't care."

"You went out with your future husband on a bet?" said Camille.

"It was courageous of her," said Malthus, patting his wife on the knee.

Maude continued, "He was always oh so proper. But I knew right from the start that he fancied me. I was younger, and thin and pretty." She looked wistful and her china doll, blue eyes filled with unshed tears.

"You're still pretty," said Malthus gallantly and untruthfully.

"I'll have another of-hic- these," said Maude as the butler emerged from the house with more drinks.

"Maude, you've had enough," said Gregory,

"No, luv, this is smashing." She waved the glass in his general direction, tossed her blonde curls and sloshed the drink onto the short, tight, sausage skin of a dress that encased her soft, plump, little body. "Oh!" she whimpered.

Napkins and club soda were hastily supplied for damage control then Bert rose and said, "Let's go in to dinner. We've used place cards so you won't have the bother of deciding where to sit."

Chopin etudes played in the background as the omnipresent butler smoothly served the exquisite meal, complete with palate clearing sorbets.

"What a wonderful wine," said Roderick. "Did you pick it up locally?"

"Course we did. You can get everything you need on this little rock of ours." responded Steve. "Here, let me have Thaddeus give you a refill."

Bert tinkled her little crystal bell and summoned Thaddeus and added, "That's true. We offer everything here." She turned to Charlie; "Children here even have the option of using either the British or the American Educational system."

Angelica said, "The American offering attracts mainly children of Americans stationed on the island. Most locals know that an in-depth British education is far superior to the generalized American offering that creates academic Jacks of all trades and masters of none."

Charlie bristled. "Why be so narrow? There's so much to know. You Anglophiles run the risk of producing ignorant, narrow, culturally illiterate kids."

"You Americans with your buzz words," scoffed Angelica. "There are too many people in your country knowing too little about too many things-and claiming expertise on everything, no less! It's frightening! Remember Pope's Dunciad.

A little learning is a dangerous thing
Drink deep or touch not the Pierian spring.
There shallow draughts intoxicate the brain
And drinking largely sobers it again.

America should read this every night!"

"She's right," said Gregory. "You have a culture of instant experts. Look at that ass Shockley for instance. He won a Nobel Prize in what was it-physics? Suddenly he's an expert on genetics and psychology and proclaims black people to be intellectually inferior to the White race-and he got a following!"

"It's akin to Chaucer's little joke about autcorite,'" said Roderick. "In The Prologue he comments that once someone is considered expert in one field their opinion is automatically given validity in other areas of which they are totally ignorant. Autcorite has become a big American problem."

"America the land of the pundits!" roared Angelica, raising her glass in a toast.

"Let's go into the drawing room where we can be more comfy," said Bert. She tinkled her bell. "Thaddeus bring the post-prandial stuff to the drawing room, please. Who's for coffee, tea, espresso, cappuccino? Let's sit in the conversation pit; it's nice and cozy there."

"Lovely meal," said Malthus.

There was a general buzzing of compliments as they followed their hostess into the room where the sweet sound of Marsalis playing Stardust welcomed them. Bert led the way down to a sunken circular, white Italian leather sofa.

"Isn't it inconvenient that every time you want to have a conversation in this house-hic- you have to come down into this conversation pit?" asked Maude clutching the remains of her Chablis as she carefully descended into said pit.

Her husband winced. "Dear, have some soda water or fruit juice it's so good for your complexion. We want to keep the roses in those cheeks," he said as he pinched her cheek and drew tears to her eyes. .

Malthus rescued her. "I agree with you, my dear. The concept of a specific conversation area can certainly be restrictive. It is not new, however. The ancient Romans for example had very activity-segmented houses. In modern times Bill Gates is a worthy descendant in this tradition. Here, let me carry that for you." He gently disentangled her fingers from the glass.

The all-important exchange of ideas resumed with coffee, liqueurs and chocolate.

"Steve," said Tyrone. "What do you make of this lesbian business with you-know-who's wife? I see your newspaper didn't touch it.

"What happened?" Charlie asked Roderick, who now sat next to her.

"A local politico arrived home unexpectedly and found his wife in bed with his sister. At least they kept it in the family," Roderick chuckled. "He made such a ruckus that the maids rushed upstairs and had to stop him from killing both lovers."

No!" gasped Charlie.

"It's too embarrassing for the family. I won't let my newspaper touch that story; I was in school with the man. The whole thing's bloody unnatural," said Steve.

"No, "said Gregory. "I can see two women being attracted to each other, they're soft and cuddly; but two big hairy men going at each other sure beats the shit out of me."

"Sexism!" shouted Bert. "I can't see women being attracted to other women. As they say, a good man is hard to find, and a hard man is good to find. There's nothing a woman can do for me sexually but show me which direction a good man just went in!"

"Come now," said Malthus. "Surely there's more to this business than hardness and softness. It's a fusion of both body and spirit. Every night at bedtime I read my wife a passage from the Bible and then one from the Kama Sutra or a similar book. The sacred and the profane are both necessary for a joy-filled Christian marriage." He clasped his wife's hand and she clung to it and lowered her eyes. "I see God in my wife's face at the moment of climax and together we soar above the terrestrial plane." His voice reverberated passionately in the room.

Roderick said, "Too often we see sex as a purely physiological stimulus/ response situation. There's a whole underlying spiritual richness and ritualistic aspect that we miss completely. During the act we're so busy thrashing around that we often don't take the time to be still and truly experience union with the other person."

"You are so right," said Angelica. "In many so-called 'primitive cultures,' a woman will spend an entire day preparing for that night's sexual encounter. The other women help her depilate her body, bathe and scent herself. She then prepares an elaborate meal for her returning warrior. All day she is focused on the coming night and its promised delights. Those women do not have our sexual problems."

"Yeah, they also don't have our incomes," muttered Charlie.

"East Indians, have well known, ritualistic sexual practices that elevate the act to the level of religion." added Roderick.

"Big deal, Hindu screw," said Gregory. This earned him a quelling look from his hostess and a comment, sotto voce that sounded suspiciously like "ignorant brute."

They further intellectualized sex, and Charlie let her mind drift. Roderick's hand on the sofa touched hers for a moment, and was still. She held her breath and contracted her pubococcygal muscle. He removed his hand and she diligently did a series of regular rhythmic Kegel's contractions- in readiness for her own warrior later that night? She sipped her Drambuie and looked around. Maude, with a mesmerized expression on her face, was staring at Roderick as he expounded on the elements present in good sex. Charlie became furious. She suddenly felt proprietary toward Roderick. She looked daggers at the woman. Maude flushed in consternation at the steady, unprovoked flow of hatred emanating from Charlie to her.

The party soon broke up. The guests thanked their host and hostess for a splendid evening. Charlie looked at her watch. She'd hire a butler and duplicate this party in New York. She'd guide all discourse into intelligent, meaningful channels and squelch any attempts to introduce the worn out topics that kept her friends from soaring conversationally.

"Did you enjoy yourself?" Roderick asked. He covered her hand with his for a moment.

She felt awkward at the familiarity of the gesture. "Definitely, I like your friends."

"Good. There you go again with that mysterious smile. It makes me wonder what's going on inside that beautiful head of yours.

And she half smiles to Earth, unknown
Smiles that with motion of their own
Do spread and think and rise."

Charlie wondered if the night would end with her in his bed. She looked at him and her lips slowly curved into a smile.

18

His Anandalahari

"Walk on the beach?" Roderick asked Charlie as he helped her down from the Moke. "Please say yes; it's too beautiful to go in yet."

Charlie hesitated. Her heart thumped and she felt danger and excitement. This could be a turning point. "Sure, why not? I should try to walk off some of that delicious food."

"Let's leave our shoes here," said Roderick as they strolled onto the beach beyond the garden wall.

Charlie slipped off her shoes and again felt a faint thrill of forbidden things. Was this all she would be taking off before she reached the safety of her room again?

They walked not touching each other and Roderick said, "One of the things I missed the most about home was seeing the stars at night above the ocean." He stopped and looked out to sea. Whitecaps scudded across the surface of the water. "Look at that moon. How could I have left this?"

Charlie leaned against a coconut tree and looked at the sky. But she thought about Roderick. She was seriously turned on. All that talk about sex was unsettling if you had no sexual outlet.

"Want to play Ducks and Drakes? Do you know how to?"

"Of course," she replied, picking up pebbles. "Watch me." She tossed the pebbles out to sea. One skipped five times.

"Hmm, not bad," he said. He threw and his skipped eight times. "I have the advantage of being the home team. You're the visiting team."

"Okay, watch this."

They tossed a few more rounds of pebbles then continued their walk.

"I love the stars," said Roderick looking up. "In the Metropolis you can never see them, but here...Look! There's the Big Dipper, Orion." He pointed them out to her.

She felt close to him, and small and vulnerable standing on the empty beach contemplating the heavens. They really were insignificant, in the grand scheme of things. How long would they be here on this earth? Could it matter if in the short time allotted to us you did something to make you happy that didn't hurt anyone else? The way she felt right now, she was no better than Lennie because she dressed her adulterous impulses up with starlight. She wanted to touch Roderick. She wanted him to touch her. She wanted him.

Roderick looked at the sky and quoted,

I saw Eternity the other night

Like a great ring of pure and endless light

All calm as it was bright.

Charlie wanted to kick him, could he stop it with the damn poetry! She was on fire and here he was looking at the sky and spouting nonsense. She smiled grimly and said, "That's beautiful."

"You're starting to like my poetry," he said.

"Uhuh. Tell me; how did you acquire all that knowledge about sex. It's impressive. I had no idea that people put that much effort into such a basic function."

"I studied texts from various cultures on the subject. Human sexuality has always fascinated me. There are and have been taboos, obfuscation, downright misinformation, and religious strictures around this basic urge. Look at Tantric sex or sex as advocated by the Gita or the Taoists. That is, of course, if you're interested. I get carried away and have to be reminded that not everyone shares my passion."

Charlie shared this one at the moment. Her nipples were uncomfortably erect; and he hadn't even touched her yet. If he kept on babbling this way she might yet go home untouched. "Oh, I do, I do!" she exclaimed. "You've introduced me to ideas I've never even dreamed of. Your friends are so...so... intellectual. You don't take things at face value. I like your world."

Would you like to come and see my Anandalahari?"

"I'd love to," she replied with alacrity.

They headed slowly for the guest cottage. Charlie had butterflies in her tummy and was positively dizzy with desire.

The illustrations in the Tantric texts, Anandalahari, were beautiful. They aroused not lust, but awe. She wondered how human beings could contort themselves in such fashion. She vowed that she would not let him throw out her back-no matter how much she wanted him. The man, not the pictures, aroused her lust. She was on fire.

Roderick spoke in a scholarly manner of the wealth of sexual lore in the Pillow Books of the Taoist Chinese. He droned on about the philosophy of Tantric Sex. "Introducing a sacred dimension to sexual loving reveals the divinity in both partners to each other... Tantra views sexual union not only as sacred but also as an art. Mental sexual intercourse is the most powerful feeling you can ever experience..." He showed her erotic texts and pointed out their fine points on which he then expounded at length. Her blood raced as she imagined them as the protagonists in the erotic pictures he displayed; those expressive hands roaming her body, that mobile mouth roaming her body, that man-in her body.

Suddenly he stood. "Charlie, I've over-tired you. Come I'll take you back to the house. It's way past your bedtime, Love. This is the second night in a row that I've kept you up jawing my head off about all kinds of things that you probably don't even care about. I'm sorry."

He pulled her up from the rattan love seat. She wouldn't meet his eyes. She wouldn't let him see the rage in hers. He was just a common garden cunt-teaser.

He deposited her at the main house then walked off jauntily, whistling Chopin's Tristesse. Charlie did not know that when he went home, like Onan; he too, spilt his seed in the wrong place.

Charlie flew into the house and up the stairs. "Maxi, wake up," she said shaking her friend violently.

"Wha', Whassamatter?" Maxi rubbed the sleep from her bleary eyes and regarded her friend. "What!"

"He didn't sleep with me."

"Congratulations! He's not supposed to, you're married." Maxi said flatly and pulled the cover over her head and turned over onto her stomach."

"Maxi, I want him to."

"Say what!" Maxi turned her head and peeped out from under the cover.

"I can't stand this. The man is a goddamn cunt-teaser." Charlie stamped her foot.

Maxi propped herself on her elbow and squinted at Charlie. She said, "You wake me up and tell me this. What do you want me to do? Call the guy and say 'please fuck my friend, Charlie, so that I can get a good night's sleep?'" She pulled the cover back over her head and nestled into the bed.

Charlie pulled the cover down. "You know damn well what I want you to do. I want you to listen to me."

Maxi resignedly sat up against the headboard squinting and yawning and said, "You sound like an adolescent boy with a bad case of blue balls. What time is it?"

"Two eighteen."

"No wonder I feel like a wreck. Sorry Charlie, I know it must hurt, but it's after midnight and you're going on like a frustrated mink." Maxi stifled another yawn.

"You have no idea what I'm going through."

"Tell me about it. Tell me about sex with a stranger in the age of AIDS."

"Oh, Maxi, go to hell. I'll tell you about sex with a latex condom and spermicide.

"Charlie, what's gotten into you? Or rather; not gotten into you."

"Sure, joke about it. Your husband takes his sex regularly like vitamins. Mine is catch as catch can. I generally don't want him, so we indulge sporadically just to see if maybe we're missing something-you know? Maybe sex got better while it was dormant. Who the hell knows what?" Charlie paced the room. "I want that smooth talking, poetry spouting, cunt-teasing, erudite son of a bitch."

"Whoa, what got you so worked up?"

"He did, with all his fine talk about the religion of sex. He got my motor roaring all the way to nowhere." Charlie stamped again in disgust and burst into furious tears. "I hate him. I hate him," she sobbed and flung herself across the bed, pounding it rhythmically with her fists.

Maxi sat on the edge of Charlie's bed and sighed. She rhythmically rubbed her friend's back and crooned, "It will be all right, trust me. He'll come to you. He'll come to you."

Charlie fell into a fitful sleep. Maxi donned her peignoir and slipped out of the room. She roamed Felicity's deserted, dew-soaked garden in search of supplies. She disturbed sleepy lizards and insects, as with flower basket and garden shears; she preyed on plants and flowers. The things one did in the name of friendship; she sighed and snipped. Soon she had all that she needed and she bore her botanical supplies off to Felicity's large, white, high-tech kitchen.

The night kitchen was colder than the garden had been. Maxi felt a chill from the white ceramic tile floor mounting up through her flimsy marabou mules. She turned on the bright recessed lights and methodically searched appliance garages, kitchen island, and every storage area until she had assembled everything. Soon the food processor whirred and the microwave-convection oven nuked and Maxi perched on a transparent, Italian, lucite stool by the kitchen island. She sipped Perrier and hummed a popular calypso, tapping out the catchy rhythm on a rung of the high stool.

"Just 'cause she fat, tap, tap tap.

She win' like dat. tap, tap, tap."

she sang and bopped along with the song. Soon the oven beeped and she stood and placed her hand on the door. In Patois she murmured old words regularly interspersed with the invocation "Ouvri bayi pou moi" (open the gate for me). She felt a cold presence, but undaunted she murmured the name of her loa-the special saint that would protect her, while involved in these activities. She also invoked the protection of the god Damballah, as she shivered with the sudden chill, and pulled the charmeuse peignoir more tightly around her thin, silky nightgown.

Maxi removed the sweet-scented Botanical potion. She strained the liquids into a Tupperware bowl and placed the floral-herbal solids in a ziploc sandwich bag. She carefully squeezed out the air, sealed the bag, and chanted ancient words, while holding these objects and a package of birthday candles in her hand. She swayed rhythmically with the words that invoked the help and strength of Ossange, the herbalist god. She gathered the rest of her ersatz armamentarium up off the counter; placed everything on a tray, and bore her offerings upstairs to her friend.

"Charlie, wake up." She shook her. "I'm going to help you. Listen carefully."

Charlie, now in nightclothes, sat up reluctantly. "This had better be good. I finally got to sleep after-" She shut up when she saw Maxi's face. "Okay, okay I'm sorry. What is it?"

"Do you still want that bozo, Roderick?"

"Shit!" said Charlie disgustedly. "Does a nympho want to get laid, does Rose want to have unnatural relations with her house-Of course I want him!"

"Charlie!" said Maxi barely stifling a laugh, "Well, you can have him."

"What are you going to do, lasso him and bring him to me?"

"No, better than that; he will come to you of his own accord. Here, put this under your pillow."

"What's this, Island hoodoo?"

"No; payback for getting me through Stats 101 at Howard

She laughed as she helped her friend slip the gris-gris bag-for such had ziploc been transmuted to-between the pale Porthoult bed linens. "Listen to me, Charlie. It's easy to get a man who's interested. Keeping him is another matter-for that you might need Dr. Ruth or Dr. Joyce Brothers."

"What've I got to lose," Charlie said. "What do I do?"

"First you pick a color." She held out the birthday candles.

Charlie chose the blue one.

"Now we place the candles here." Maxi produced juice glasses filled with salt water, sand, garden dirt, celery seed and pennies. She placed the candles in them, arranging the yellow and red candles in a pattern with white votives at the cardinal points. Finally she put the blue in the middle in a crystal ashtray. Then she spoke quietly.

Charlie looked away. She did not want to be too involved with things she did not understand. She thought of Roderick. She was slowly undressing him...

"They're grounded now." Maxi's voice brought Charlie back from her reverie.

"Concentrate on them while I light them." Maxi flicked on the long, red butane lighter that Felicity used for barbecues. She lit the candles. "Leave these burning as you go to sleep. Look at them occasionally and think their colors. Visualize Roderick where you want him to be, doing what you want him to do-"

"Woman, are you mad? Is there a fire extinguisher around that you can use on this bed if I do that?"

"Fool!" Maxi said with a laugh. "Tomorrow morning take a shower, and then soak in a tub of tepid water to which you have added this." She held up the Tupperware bowl.

"What's in there? Frog shit?"

"Soak in the solution for seven minutes and read the sixty-eighth psalm aloud. Here, you can use my Bible." Maxi placed the bible on the night table with the bowl. "Does your watch have a stopwatch attachment with an alarm? It does? Good. Pat yourself dry with a white towel. I'll have one in the bathroom for you tomorrow. Then dress in white."

"Easy so, huh?"

"Yup. That's what it takes. Now go to sleep. See him where you want him to be, doing what you want him to do. He'll be there."

"I warned you, the bed can't take the heat. X-rated dreams, here I come!" Charlie said with a chuckle.

Charlie fell asleep staring at the flickering candles on the bureau. They stood phallic-like on a makeshift base of slowly hardening candle wax. The facets in the heavy, crystal Waterford ashtray on which they sat, danced in the lambent light. Charlie soon drifted off, peaceful as a baby, while visions of brown penises danced in her head.

19

Meanwhile in Manhattan, NY, At the Marshall Chess Club

Alexei approached the chess table where the girl sat. He slipped his hands inside his pants and thoughtfully rearranged his genitals into a more comfortable configuration.

"Wash your hands before you touch my chess set," said the child coldly.

The Russian swore under his breath and complied, then returned to the game.

Twelve year old, Sydney gave Alexei the chess stare-a baleful, hostile look that showed nothing but utter contempt for its recipient. The man reddened and kept his eyes on the board. He drummed his fingertips furiously on the tabletop. The knot of men around the table observing the game was silent. Alexei reached out; his hand hovered over his Queen then withdrew. He looked at his clock – he had two seconds left.

Sydney sang under her breath, to the tune of It's beginning to look a lot like Christmas,

It's beginning to look a lot

Like Checkmate...

Alexei's clock beeped. He had lost. He swore. He furiously toppled his King on the chessboard then glared at the small, skinny, black girl with the unblinking, basilisk stare as he rose abruptly and upset the board. Laughing, Sydney leapt up and avoided the flying pieces as Alexei stalked off.

Igor, Sydney's coach, took her notation sheet off the table. He examined it and smiled and nodded. "Dubro, Dubro," he muttered in approval. Then he helped her pick up the scattered game pieces and replace them on the board. "Good girl, you played well. Had he not lost on time you would still have crushed him in the next five moves and you have fifty minutes left on your clock. We go over it now? Da? Sit," he said.

"Sure," said Sydney. She looked around. "Where's Mom, I'm hungry."

Igor laughed. "You are always hungry. Your mother is not here; she probably went to the Ladies Room. I told her your game would soon be over and we both knew your first words would be 'food'."

"You did? Good!" Sydney beamed at him and set up the opening she had played with Alexei.

"Wait," said an observer with a heavy Russian accent. "What if he had done this?" He rearranged the pieces into an alternative move to the one Alexei had made.

"Then I would've done that." Sydney made a move that still kept her ahead.

The man laughed and patted her on the head. "One of these days you will bring even the great Kasparov to his knees, yes?"

Sydney grinned and he went away chuckling.

"Shall we play a friendly game while you wait for your mother?" asked Igor.

"No, let's continue going over the game. There was a part in the middle game where I wanted to play an alternate combination that I wasn't too sure about-here." She jabbed at the notation pad and set up the position in question. "And see, I did that King's Indian thing I've been studying and it sorta didn't work so I had to improvise." She and her coach pored over the board and the crowd around the table began to disperse.

"Darling, did you win?" said Rose breezing into the room later. She placed a large paper bag on the table. "Your lunch was just delivered. I was downstairs waiting for it."

"Yeah, I won, thanks for the food, Mom." Sydney started downing sushi before Rose could finish setting out her meal on the table. "This is really good, I love eel. Did you get food for Igor? I have forty minutes before the next round, so I'm going over the game with him."

"Good girl, my own little Pachunga Princess," Rose kissed the top of her daughter's head, and smiled at Igor. "I gave one of the guys money to pick up McDonalds' for you. He was going there for his own lunch. He should be back soon."

"You're too kind," said Igor.

"Nothing's too good for the coach of a winner," trilled Rose with a smile. "See you guys later, I'll be over there reading if you need me."

"'Bye, Rose," said Igor.

"Uuumf," said Sydney, as eyes on the chessboard and mouth full of sushi; she waved goodbye to her mother.

In the adjoining room, white men and boys sat at chess tables playing quietly. Rose found an empty seat and snuggled down in the comfort of the deep leather, ox-blood, wing chair. There, beneath great, dark, Italianate oil paintings of chess grandmasters, living and dead, she once more thanked her lucky stars that she was not a soccer Mom standing in the rain cheering on her child's team; but a chess Mom, sitting indoors in comfort with no obligation to watch anyone do anything. She was of the elite.

Rose yawned and pulled that month's Architectural Digest from her tote bag. She smiled as she munched on a carrot stick. Bathrooms and bedrooms were amazing; you could do so much with them. She was soon lost to the world.

"Excuse me."

Rose looked up at a smartly dressed, young, white woman.

"Are you Sydney Inniss' mother?"

"Yes, I am," said Rose.

"Good," the woman smiled at her. "I'm a reporter, my name is Jeannie Searles." The woman stuck out her hand and Rose shook it. "We're starting a sports magazine for young women," she continued. "We want your daughter to be on the cover of our first issue. Chess, as I'm sure you know, is a sport that's becoming increasingly popular in this country."

"Yes, the sport of kings," said Rose with alacrity. "What a great idea. Sydney can be an inspiration to other girls. We need more females in chess."

"Absolutely!" agreed the reporter. "And your daughter's a superstar in the chess world. She became the youngest female chess master in America, I'm told. Can I come to your home and interview her in her own environment? I'll also bring a photographer, of course."

"Of course you may," said Rose warmly. Already she could see her chintz sofa profiling in the magazine. Her new color scheme was wonderful. She'd buy a large picture to hang on the wall behind the sofa; maybe she'd match it to the rug. A new lamp..."

"Mrs. Inniss," said the reporter.

"Oh, I'm sorry, you said something?" Rose came back abruptly from her thoughts of decorating splendor.

"Yes, would next week Friday be good for you?"

"Sorry, we'll be out of town. We're nearing the end of the scholastic chess year, so there are a lot of important tournaments coming up. Let me see..." Rose pulled her Palm Pilot out of her handbag and consulted it.

"My goodness, you are organized," said the woman admiringly.

"You have to be to do something like this, how does three Fridays from now sound?" said Rose as she calculated how much longer the current reupholstery job would take. She'd have to add custom made throw cushions; they'd be ready in time. The family had to look erudite so she'd buy some of those impressive looking, leather bound books by the yard. They could be left casually on tables and of course on the new extra bookcase she'd purchase..."

"Wonderful, I'll see you then." The reporter snapped shut her notebook and shook Rose's hand. "Here, please take my card. I'll call you to confirm."

Rose scanned the card into her Palm Pilot and returned it to Jeannie saying, "My husband will be there too."

"There's a husband?" Jeannie marveled. "This is incredible-she's a black girl doing all this and she comes from a two-parent family... "

Rose held her peace. She imagined her house and daughter featured in a national magazine to the envy of all her friends. She ostentatiously dropped her PDA back into her oversized Prada tote.

"Hi, Mom, what's up?" Sydney bounced into the room and came and perched on the arm of her mother's chair.

"Sweetie, why aren't you in the tournament room? You couldn't have finished your game already."

"I wish," the child said with a laugh. "No, I wanted to walk around a bit; this guy spends a long time thinking. Mom! I'm up on time and he seems scared of me." She hugged herself in delight. "And he's no Pez dispenser either, he's a real International Master-and I'm winning Mom! Can you imagine *me* beating an IM?"

"It'll be wonderful if you win, Darling. We'll have to go out and celebrate. But remember, he's the level above you so don't be surprised if you lose. Sydney meet Miss Searles."

"Please, call me Jeannie," said the reporter, shaking Sydney's hand.

"Sorry, I can't. My parents consider it inappropriate for me to call adults by their first names."

"What a charming child," said Jeannie to Rose over Sydney's head.

"Thank you," said Rose looking longingly at her magazine. The article on renovating master bathrooms, accompanied by glorious pictures, was calling her name. When would these two leave her alone?

"Sydney, congrats on your chess success. You're one of the youngest chess Masters in the country, the only black, female at this level, and you're representing America for the fourth time in this year's international competition in France. Way to go!" Jeannie Searles tried to high five the girl, but Sydney did not respond. She merely said thank you.

"You used an interesting term just now – 'Pez dispenser', what do you mean by that?" asked Jeannie.

"Kids call some of the old guys Pez dispensers. They once were good and had high ratings points. Now they've lost all their marbles but they keep playing chess. We beat them easily and gain lots of points off them – it's like they're dispensing candy."

"Wow! But don't they eventually lose all their points along with their minds," asked Jeannie with a laugh.

"Nope," said the child. "There's a floor-two hundred points below your highest point and you can never drop below that."

"Interesting; how'd you like to be on the cover of a magazine?"

"I don't know; ask my Mom. Mom, I saw this perfect fork, if he'd just move his king to E3, then kaboom!" She punched her palm and laughed excitedly.

Jeannie smiled at her and said to Rose, "You have a lovely daughter, she is so pretty. I'll see you in three weeks. Good luck, dear," and she was blessedly gone.

Sydney's watch beeped. She leapt off the arm of her mother's chair. "Break's over, wish me luck," she said and rushed back to the tournament room.

Rose returned to her magazine. She nestled into the chair contentedly and resumed her reading. Soon she drifted off into a pleasant sleep.

"No! No! Noooooo!"

Sydney's screams mixed with background shouts jolted Rose awake. Heart in mouth she sprinted to the tournament room where pandemonium reigned.

Sydney sat pounding the table and screaming while her opponent watched her. On the floor nearby, two men rolled, grunted and rained blows on each other, curses in a guttural foreign tongue interspersed their fight. There was a sudden yelp as one bludgeoned the other with a metal, chess clock.

"Igor! Do something, get my child!" yelled Rose to Igor who had positioned himself out of harm's way, against the wall on the opposite side of the room.

"I am so sorry. It is dangerous there," said Igor eyeing the rapid exchange of punches.

Rose flew through the melee to her daughter, exclaiming, "My little Pachunga, don't be scared, Mommy's here, they can't hurt you." As she threw her arms around her daughter there was a crash and a chair flew through the air. They both ducked.

"Stop them! They will kill each other!" Igor screamed from his sanctuary, across the room, pressed up against the wall. Men waded in and with difficulty separated the warriors.

Sydney's screams and table pounding intensified, and she yelled, "No! No! No!" and sobbed wildly.

Rose became alarmed. She slapped Sydney lightly across the face. "Stop it!" she commanded.

"No! No! No!" the child screamed hysterically.

"Sydney! Stop this now!" Rose commanded a new sharp tone in her voice.

Her daughter shut up. "It's not fair! He's a stinking cheat," she sniffled.

"What happened, Baby? Tell me," crooned Rose, stroking Sydney's hair.

"I reached out to checkmate him with my pawn and I got distracted 'cause Alexei screamed really hard, 'cause Vlad bit him." She gulped.

"Why would people bite each other in a chess tournament?" asked Rose.

"Alexei tried to advance Vlad's clock when he thought he wasn't looking, but Vlad caught him and bit his hand. Alexei's scream startled me and I accidentally touched my king instead of my pawn!" She bawled and her thin shoulders shook.

"And you lost," said her opponent. "The rule is, touch move, little lady. You know that."

"Urrghh!" Sydney screamed and crashed her fist onto the table, scattering pieces.

"Sydney, you're out of control," said Rose sharply. "You have ten seconds to compose yourself." She paused. "Now apologize. If you ever behave like this again you will no longer be permitted to play chess. *We* don't allow this."

"Sorry," said Sydney. She extended her hand and her opponent shook it.

"You played well, little girl. One of these days you'll be a force to reckon with."

Sydney bit her lip and drew blood. She rose quietly. She looked at her opponent. "I'm taking this up with the tournament director, and if necessary, with the U.S. Chess association. You won't get away with it. I did beat you and I *will* get my points. I don't care if you're an International Master."

Rose followed her and Igor fell in behind them.

The august bust of Frank J. Marshall, former USA champion and long dead founder of this gentlemen's chess club; sat on a credenza at the front of the room, observing the blood sport of chess in America at the end of the twentieth century.

20

Had we but World enough and Time

"Okay, everybody up! Its hoodoo time," Charlie announced loudly as she headed for the bathroom.

"Go 'way, I'm not your personal Mambo," Maxi mumbled sleepily, from her bed. She pulled the bedclothes up over her head.

Charlie stopped in front of the mirror on the bathroom door to appraise her cleavage in the low-cut nightgown. She liked what she saw. "What the hell's a mambo?"

"Voodoo priestess," Maxi mumbled snuggling deeper into the bed. "God, I'm tired! Do as I said last night. If Damballah appears-"

Charlie stopped, with her hand on the doorknob. "Say what?"

"If Damballah appears-he takes the form of a large snake, a boa-constrictor I think; well, if he appears, remain very still and say, 'go in peace.'"

"Island girl, you've lost it? I won't have freaky snakes in the bathroom with me."

"Fine," said Maxi, yawning again. She rolled over onto her stomach and peeped at Charlie with one eye. "Don't have Roderick. Stay horny."

Her friend remained in front of the bathroom door, apparently irresolute.

"Go ahead, I was kidding about the snake," Maxi said. "Good luck."

Charlie entered the bathroom, stripped and scrutinized her naked body in the full-length mirror-definitely not bad. A few gray pubic hairs marred the picture; she plucked them carefully then performed her ablution ritual.

Soon, outfitted in a white halter sundress and no underwear, she carefully applied make-up and piled her hair on top of her head. It was sexy, yet innocent, with tendrils falling around her face and neck when she pulled out the pins at the right moment it would tumble down, just like in the movies. She'd had a relaxer last week so her hair could tumble. She popped a birth control pill, and sprayed on some Volupte perfume. She was ready. Not bad for a forty year old, in fact, damn good!

"Good luck," Maxi called sleepily as Charlie left the room.

"Thanks," Charlie flung over her shoulder as she headed downstairs to see what the day would bring. Her mind was made up. She would go for it. She deserved sexual pleasure. She would no longer ignore the strong physical attraction. If the voodoo kicked in-he was hers. She walked onto the terrace preoccupied with the minutiae of planning an affair. Who would provide the condoms? Should she? Would he?

"Roderick!" she cried in surprise; for there he stood, tantalizing in white jeans, a pale colored Rugby shirt and topsiders; delectable.

"Good morning," he saluted her. "I came to kidnap you from Felicity and these Anglophiles in the great house. They no doubt plan to fill you up with bacon and eggs or kippers, but a Bahamian breakfast awaits us. Come sample my wares."

Charlie looked at him and slowly smiled, then immediately blushed. She looked at her watch, to avoid meeting his eyes. Voodoo? She did some Kegels in anticipation. Just then, Felicity, in a swimsuit, with a matching cover-up strolled onto the terrace.

"Morning," she said, "Roderick, what a surprise. You're here early. Join us for breakfast. How was the party last night?" She stretched out on a chaise in a sunny spot.

"Great, did you enjoy yourself, Charlie?" He touched her shoulder.

Charlie nodded and tensed as she held her breath at the intimacy of the gesture.

Roderick apparently oblivious to her reaction continued, "I'm here to tempt Charlie to join me for an island breakfast. You don't have any plans for her, do you?"

Felicity looked up from slathering sun block onto her thighs. "No, I don't. Charlie, where's Maxi?" she asked.

"She'll be down later. She wanted to catch a few more zzs," Charlie replied feeling vaguely disloyal at abandoning Felicity.

"Okay, go enjoy." Felicity waved her away and turned over onto her stomach.

The day was magnificent. Birds sang and a briny smell blew off the nearby ocean. The colors around them were as intense as Charlie's emotions. She walked beside Roderick with her thoughts in tumult. They hadn't made plans to have breakfast. This supernatural thing, if that's what it was, was scary. She felt uneasy. Roderick was a wild card. She didn't know what to expect from him. He could still be teasing.

Roderick interrupted her ruminations; "Life's a precious gift on a day like today. It can awe you," he said then quoted:

God's in his heaven

All's right with the world.

Suddenly he hugged her, throwing her even more off balance.

The fragrance of fresh perked coffee welcomed them. Today the room was immaculate, the furniture gleamed and vases of freshly cut flowers sat on the coffee table and the dining table. "I was working while you slept. Here's your repast. I went 'over the hill' for it. That's where 'true, true Bahamians' live and serious native food is cooked.

"I recognize Felicity's 'under the sea' look in decorating," Charlie looked around in wonder. "What're those flowering plants at the window? I didn't notice them yesterday."

"I picked them up this morning. I don't know what they're called, but I liked them." Roderick said as he walked past her to the laden table.

"Breakfast is served, Madame," he announced, pulling out a chair with a bow.

"Thank you, kind sir," Charlie replied and sat at the table, covered with a glistening, white, damask tablecloth.

"Roderick, yellow rose petals in finger bowls!? You don't do things by half measures do you?" Charlie laughed and dipped her fingers into a bowl.

"Glad you didn't drink it. One of our local politicians attended a state dinner in London and drained his finger bowl, pronounced it tasty too."

"You're so ridiculous," she said. "Sit and let's eat, I'm starved." She looked at him and smiled as she imagined him as the *piece de resistance* of the proffered feast.

"Here for milady's delectation we have grits." He raised a pewter dish cover. "Johnny cakes, boiled fish," he uncovered the others. "This morning you eat like a true-true Bahamian."

"You're extremely organized," Charlie said.

Roderick clicked a remote control, and the sound of castanets followed by a sweet, plaintive melody filled the room.

"What's that? "Charlie asked with pleasure.

"An old favorite, Miles Davis' version of Rodrigo's Concerto de Aranjuez.

The lush, romantic emotionalism of the piece was heady in the small area. Charlie heard sexual desire, yearning and love finally requited and consummated in the haunting dirge. Suddenly Roderick stood behind her, with his hands on her shoulders.

"Hungry?" he murmured into her hair.

Her heart stopped.

His hands slipped down and forward 'til they cupped her breasts. There was no mistaking his intentions. She stiffened, surprised. He whispered in her ear,

Had we but world enough and time,

This coyness, lady were no crime."

Fire spread through her loins as he gently placed his hands on her shoulders and turned her around to face him. He gazed into her eyes. She felt as if she were in a movie observing herself-this was a ridiculous seduction scene. It just didn't happen this way. She stifled the impulse to laugh. He declaimed:

We would sit down, and think which way

To walk, and pass our long love's day."

He gently kissed her forehead, and tilting her face upwards he traced a line from her eyebrow to her chin. She watched him, mesmerized. What the hell was he doing?

An hundred years should go to praise

Thine eyes, and on thy forehead gaze

Two hundred to adore each breast;

He moved a hand down and gently squeezed her right breast and stroked the nipple through the thin cotton, all the while gazing into her eyes.

But thirty thousand to the rest:

An age, at least, to every part,

And the last age should show your heart.

For, lady, you deserve this state;

Nor would I love at lower rate."

Charlie was out of her depth. Was that his problem not wanting to be too fast? This sure was different. But it was exciting. She was turned on. If this was how he played she'd have to learn his game. She put her arms around him to hurry things along. But he disentangled himself and holding her two hands in his, dropped to his knees in front of her and declaimed:

But, at my back, I always hear
Time's winged chariot hurrying near."

He placed his hands on the sides of her hips and slid slowly past the hem of her dress to her bare knees.

The grave's a fine and private place,
But none I think do there embrace."

Charlie was hot putty. His eyes held her captive as he lifted her dress hem centimeter by agonizing centimeter. She was faint with desire and some embarrassment because she wore no underwear. When the dress could rise no further, she tugged it off and let it fall to the floor then pulled the pins from her hair, and let that fall too, carelessly around her shoulders.

...while thy willing soul transpires
At every pore with instant fires,"

Roderick's finger traced the outline of her mons while his other hand rested on her buttocks and held her fast.

Let us roll our strength, and all
Our sweetness, up into one ball;

he said before softly kissing her pubis. He parted the lips of her vulva and flicked in his tongue to touch her clitoris. She shuddered and dropped to her knees in front of him. He stroked her trembling back as they knelt, his erect penis pressing pleasurably against her inflamed vulva. Never before had Charlie been this sexually aroused. It almost scared her. She clung to him as he urgently whispered:

And tear our pleasures, with rough strife,
Through the iron gates of life.
Thus, though we cannot make our sun
Stand still, yet we will make him run.

Yes, yes, she cheered in her mind as Roderick rose and pulled her to her feet. She came up to him like a puppet. His will was her will. She kept her eyes on his and followed his cues. They were going to tear those pleasures. She was ready. She did her Kegels madly.

"I want to adore you."

She nodded dumbly. This was a new one to her, but it sounded good. He led her into the cool darkened bedroom. He pulled back the blue bedspread and settled her onto the neatly made-up bed. She noticed sunlight stealing in through the slats in the closed shutters. A white lizard on the wall, disturbed by the humans scurried behind the dresser mirror. Then Glory be! she saw a pack of latex condoms on the bedside table.

Charlie lay on the cool, blue sheets and waited. Roderick undressed quickly and unselfconsciously. His body was magnificent. She quivered in anticipation when he knelt on the floor beside the bed. Her clitoris throbbed as though it had a heart of it own.

"I'm going to worship you," he said.

He touched her foot and she caught afire. She melted as he gently rubbed her big toe, then placed it in his mouth and sucked it sensuously. He slowly moved his hands over the bottom of her foot pressing various points. New exquisite sensations of pleasure flooded her. Her body assumed a life of its own; twitching and arcing like a burning, mindless thing.

He inched upwards, touching and kissing every part of her. His questing fingers even explored her scalp. Only her engorged genitals and breasts were excluded. Just before she could beg him to worship these areas too, he turned to them. His hands reverently violated her, and then his tongue followed. She experienced pure bliss as he venerated her mons veneris.

He picked up a liqueur glass of Grand Marnier from the night table and carefully trickled its contents onto her navel, then her nipples, clitoris and the inner lips of her vulva. Slowly, and with exquisite artistry, he licked it off, savoring it like nectar. She feared she would lose her mind with pleasure. She became jelly and felt utter molten madness. He kissed her deep, dark and sweetly then climbed onto the bed. Rampant, he straddled her as he slipped on his condom. His strange unmatched eyes glowed as he lay by her side and gently parted the lips of her vulva. Then he entered her.

There was a nightmarish quality to this union. It was beyond lust. She was in deep and she knew it. She could not just get up and walk away from what was happening there today. He had cut to her core. They heaved as one body moving on itself. Their movements were perfection. Their dance held life itself at bay. They whirled off into the stratosphere. She was the blazing sun; he was God's own finger. This was ecstasy.

Charlie struggled upwards, and straddled Roderick without breaking their rhythm. Mounted on his rod of redemption she rode him, screaming, like the last horse out of hell. She felt empowered. She was wild warrior woman; she could crush coconuts with her vagina. She held him in a cock-lock and silently blessed her Arab friend Fatima, who years ago had taught her the trick she would now use. She crunched her powerful well-exercised vaginal muscles and in a series of strong wave-like motions milked his penis.

Roderick instantly forsook Shakespeare, Marvel and Yahweh. He plummeted down, down, down to his ancestral gods. There in a jazz riff, he bawled for murder, called for his mother, sobbed, and made unintelligible sounds. When Charlie heard him speaking in tongues she knew that she'd done it right. Fatima had used this reaction as a criterion for success.

Charlie now gave herself up totally to the experience. She let go, and became part of the white light glowing inside her head. In a cataclysm, they exploded within seconds of each other. Shaken, they could not meet each other's eyes.

"Was it good for you?" Charlie finally asked Roderick.

He looked stricken, until he saw the mischief in her eyes. They laughed, then held each other tightly and drifted off into exhausted sleep.

21

The Georgia O'Keefe Problem

"I take it you made the beast with two backs since you're not climbing the walls this time," Maxi said as Charlie strolled onto the patio looking smug and happy.

"Maybe I did," said Charlie in a singsong voice, "Where's Felicity?"

"She and George have gone to the marriage counselor, I prevailed on her. They started today. Also she got the contract with Sir Clifford. He admires the spunky way she defended her territory. But getting back to you, from the look on your face I'd say you did it." Maxi sat up in the recliner and pushed her sunglasses back into her hair.

"Yes! Yes! Yes!" Charlie said beaming. "It was wonderful! Incredible! Fantastic!" She flung herself onto a nearby chair, and chortled with delight.

"Idiot," said Maxi affectionately. "And thank you Damballah, Roderick and all others, living or dead, natural or supernatural who made it possible. Now I can sleep at night again."

"No, you can't. Now I have to talk about him. He is so wonderful! I really felt something between us, it's weird."

"You felt nothing! You just had a piece-apparently a good piece, but a piece nevertheless."

"A piece! Are you crazy? This man just showed me things I never knew before-tenderness, passion, playfulness and hokiness too, and you call what we did 'a piece!' I can still feel him. I can smell him.

"Puhlease, what do you know about this; you've been on starvation rations for so long? Tell you what, I'll try him and tell you if he's up to snuff."

Charlie sat up abruptly and mock-aggressively said, "I'll kill you."

"Maybe so, anyway, you've been longing for this. It was good. But don't overrate it. It was just that-a good piece. So you formed what I'll call for want of a better descriptor, a cunt connection."

"You've definitely lost it," Charlie assured her.

Maxi stood, and paced the terrace. "Hear me out, Charlie. I know how you feel. I'm not putting it down. You've formed what I describe as a cunt connection, or young love."

"Yes, Dr. Paine, you and I are real young."

"Oh, Charlie! Remember the days when you could lubricate just thinking about a special man or boy? You reacted like a Georgia O'Keefe flaming cunt if he just held your hand; God help us, if he touched your breast. Remember? That one area of your body responded, connected to him. It was purely a cunt connection. It's all right there."

"This isn't. It's more widespread-like if he's seeped into me."

"Trust me, he hasn't. You were due for this. You're a late bloomer. You were too busy overachieving in college, and afterward, to get connected by the cunt like the rest of us dizzy girls. We were busy falling in love, having one night stands, and generally getting it out of our systems."

"That's not true. I fell in love; I went out on dates too."

"Yeah, but you were preoccupied with your work. Nothing ever really hit you, not even Lennie-you weren't mad for him. You were the nerd's nerd. So at forty, wham! You get socked in the pelvis by a smooth, sexy guy and form a cunt connection."

"He's not smooth. He's, he's... I don't know. He's certainly different and I do feel something for him that's beyond lust."

"You don't. You love Lennie, you love your family; you won't hurt them. Come on! You letch for this man; he's your lost youth. Put a condom on him and screw the devil out of him if you must. But get it out of your system then go home to your family. For God's sake don't upset your child. And by the way, you don't know where he's been, or where the people he's been with, have been."

"I thought you'd understand. Roderick's not just what you call a 'cunt connection.' Sure, I want him that way. But he's much more. We're friends. I'm connected to his mind. I admire him-"

"So, go take a self improvement course. It'll be much less emotionally expensive.

"He's knowledgeable but not a show-off. He's funny, sweet and sensitive, full of poetry, a fantastic lover-"

"If he's so wonderful, how come his marriage didn't work?"

"Did Felicity tell you anything about that?"

"No, but we both worry about what's happening to you. You're not a man, Charlie. They screw around as naturally as breathing then go back to their families as if nothing had happened, often carrying diseases. But women-we get emotionally hung up. We want to be with the guy. We want to leave our families, and for what? A cunt connection! A rush of hormones to the groin that will subside if left alone. Don't do anything rash that will eventually hurt your family. Go screw him-several times if you must."

"Thanks for the permission," Charlie said dryly.

Maxi sat at the foot of Charlie's chaise. She placed her hand on her friend's knee. "But don't you dare talk about feeling something special for him. You letch for him, you love your husband. He's your family. You have history with him. Sure, he's a shit, but aren't most men? It's what they've been raised to be. But since it's no fun for most women to love each other that way, we love them."

"Maxi, that's a terrible thing to say. Aren't you perfectly happy with Jordan? You're sure horny enough."

"Come off it, Charlie, no one's 'perfectly happy'. Sure I love my husband. I'm cunt connected to him at times and realize I'm lucky to still have that feeling after sixteen years of marriage. But he's no angel. Neither am I, for that matter. Jordan has to imagine himself in charge at all times; thinks he makes the big decisions – sees himself as the big honcho."

"So? Who can blame him? Power's nice. Everyone should want it."

"I guess. But I don't need the show of it. I massage Jordan's ego and let him maintain his power fantasy. It's no skin off my nose. Besides, it's hard being a black man in America. He's near the top of the heap, but his position's not secure. He's dealing with them-you know, White, corporate America-and every day, they try to cut his balls off."

Charlie sighed, "You're right, I know. But Lennie brought this on himself. He's an ass-hole, a lazy one too. Look at that Guyanese doctor affair. Can you imagine the humiliation I felt?"

Maxi rose and hugged her friend. "Charlie, I know it's hard. Sorry if I seem to be playing the part of your conscience."

"You're right it is hard. Lennie behaves like a spoilt child. He's got such a sense of entitlement. He fools around and expects Mom to forgive him when he looks at me all doe-eyed. Naturally he expects Mom to put money into his accounts when he overspends and can't cover his ass so his creditors are dunning him. Once he forgot himself and actually called me Mother!"

"Oh Charlie," Maxi looked at her friend sympathetically. "You work hard and you deserve a break. Enjoy your affair then come home with me to your family. They love you and you love them. Lennie's the father of your child. Come on, grow up, girl." She squeezed her friend's hand.

Charlie smiled weakly.

22

Whirlwind

Charlie spent the week of a lifetime with Roderick. They swam, talked, and made love then talked some more. She felt as if she'd known him all her life. He was playful, easy to talk to and he made her feel carefree. Suddenly she was open to happiness and possibilities. Sometimes she even forgot that she was married and had a child.

Felicity and Maxi left the couple to their own devices, after assuring Charlie that she and Roderick were welcome to join them any time they wanted to. On a hot Sunday evening Roderick dined with the family. They sat casually on the terrace as cricket and night bird sounds serenaded them from the trees. George joined them for the first time since the women's arrival. Tonight he played chef, in a large tuxedo emblazoned, plastic apron. The perfect host, he manned the gas grill and barbecued a large grouper.

Felicity appeared less hostile toward George. Charlie and Maxi silently blessed the marriage counselor and wished the couple many more successful sessions.

George asked heartily, "What's been happening? What've you ladies been doing? Roderick, you been taking them sightseeing?"

"I'm doing my part to keep them happy," he said with a look at Charlie.

She flushed and quickly looked down.

"Help yourselves to salad please," urged Felicity. "Roderick try the rice pilaf and pass it around; here." She gave him the bowl.

Dinner was pleasant. Charlie blushed a lot, ate a little, and kept up delicious, hidden body contact with Roderick throughout the meal. Yes, Maxi was right, she was connected by the cunt; and she loved it. She did some Kegels exercises, contracting and relaxing her vaginal muscles to make sure sex stayed as great as it was.

Soon everyone decided to call it a night. Maxi retired to read a book. Felicity and George left to play squash at their club, and Roderick invited Charlie to go boating.

"At this hour? You've got to be kidding. How will you navigate?"

"The same way I do in my car at night-by headlights and the available light. It's a straight ride to Cornelia Island. Bring your suit, we can swim when we get there."

"In the cold ocean?"

"The water's at its warmest now. It's absorbed and retained all the heat from the sun. It's hot right now. So try it, you'll like it." He winked at her.

"Well, okay, just for a while. I really should turn in early tonight and read a good book. Maybe the Anandalahari you lent me?" She looked at him innocently.

"Come and we'll bone up on different interpretations of the philosophy. Then you'll read it later with a fresh take. I'll get you back to your book in time," he promised gravely.

Charlie ran upstairs for her suit and towel. She found Maxi reclining on the chaise, writing postcards. "Hi!" she greeted her friend before rifling through a drawer. "I'm going for a swim; ah, here's my swimsuit."

"Enjoy your swim." Maxi responded with a wink.

"Will do," said Charlie as she headed out the door stuffing things into a tote bag,

That was heap powerful juju you worked the other night, Island Girl; if we bottle that stuff we could become billionaires. Want to go into business?"

"Oh, go away," said Maxi with a laugh. "Please note; I can't raise the dead, so use moderation in your sexual demands on that poor man."

23

Kissing the Joy

Who was Cornelia?" shouted Charlie above the engine's roar. She sat in the prow of the speeding boat, wind and water whipping her face.

"You didn't meet her?"

"Should I have?"

"Definitely; she's absolutely gorgeous."

Charlie felt a bit jealous at this praise for the unknown Cornelia. She also felt his eyes on her. She turned and met his laughter.

"Cornelia's the boys' lizard. They found her on the cay we're going to. They named it after her. She's rather beautiful with shining eyes and a long yellow-green tail. I'll introduce you."

Charlie shuddered visibly. "Please, you don't have to. Just say hello for me. She'll understand I'm sure."

They smiled at each other and lapsed into companionable silence. The boat's wake made silver sparkled spume in the navy blue water. Charlie watched it happily.

Soon they reached the cay. Bright moonlight bathed the scrubby beach with its sparse trees. Roderick jumped out and pulled the boat as close ashore as he could. Then he dropped anchor and he and Charlie waded in and unloaded their supplies.

A crescent moon and stars provided the only light, and tonight the stars put on a show for them. They could see the entire cay. It was mostly beach with some shade trees, unidentifiable vegetation and the ubiquitous coconut trees growing further inland.

"This is perfect!" Charlie exclaimed. "I feel as if we're the last people on Earth."

"We are, tonight."

Roderick spread a gaily colored, summer weight blanket on the white sand. He set up their picnic, lit a citronella candle; and then surveyed his handiwork with a smile.

Charlie looked at the prepared area and felt an irrational rage. Suddenly she blurted out, "Am I on tonight's menu? Is it entertain the tourist time again?" The surprising words slipped out before she could stop them.

He looked as if she had slapped him. "Charlie," was all he said.

She felt terrible and exposed. "Sorry, sorry, I shouldn't have said that. I could kick myself. It's just that-I'm so confused! I've got a husband and child waiting for me in New York. What am I, a supposedly respectable married woman, doing alone on a cay in the Bahamas at night with you? There's a word for women like me."

"Yes, beautiful," he said and gently touched her face. She slapped his hand away and he said quietly,"Okay, what are you doing?"

"I don't know," she said in despair. "Why am I letting you into my life in this way? Why am I here?"

"I thought it was obvious," he replied.

"What do you mean?

Roderick quoted,

He who bends to himself a joy
Does the winged life destroy;
But he who kisses the joy as it flies
Lives in eternity's sunrise.

"I can't say it any better than that."

"Great," said Charlie. "I majored in business not literature, but did I just hear you say that we should treat this as an extended one night stand, a passing 'joy'?" Her voice was tight and her fists clenched. "Are you a hit and run driver? What's the bottom line Roderick? Hell! What's the use of all this? I'm married; I shouldn't be here in the first place. I have no right to ask you anything." She looked ready to cry.

Roderick wrapped her rigid body in his arms and gentled her. Then he tenderly opened the clenched fists and kissed the open palms. "That's not what I meant. Let's not analyze everything to death, Okay? Can't we just enjoy this now and ask questions later?"

"No, we can't. I don't sleep around Roderick. This is a first. But I don't know what I want-or have the right to want."

"Sit down," he said and pulled her gently down to the blanket. "This is coming out all wrong." He momentarily cradled his head in his hands in a gesture of frustration. "Look, that's not what I meant –"

"I'm married, unhappily, but never the less, married. And I have a child. But I feel something for you. I don't like this situation and I'm all mixed up I don't want to get involved any further. I'm too old for this."

"I know," he said. "So am I." He put his arms around her and nuzzled her neck. "Let's talk about it, and about why your hair smells like strawberries."

"Can't you ever be serious," she exclaimed.

"Yes, I can. What brought this on?" He lay back on the blanket and gently pulled her down to lie on his shoulder with his arm around her.

Charlie became conscious of the dropping temperature and the heat from his body. A sand crab scurried across their blanket then down its hole. The crashing of the waves on the nearby rocks provided background music for her confusion. "I don't know what's gotten into me. I guess it's partly because I spoke to my daughter this morning. She's fine and happy she says, and so am I and I feel guilty about it. I shouldn't be here."

"Charlie, I'm not insensitive. I know you want me to say that I love you."

She bristled.

He said, "Hold on, that's a reasonable expectation. I too, don't see sex as a sport to be played with any willing partner. What's happening between us means something to me. I was attracted to you from the moment I met you. That swimsuit probably had a lot to do with it."

She swatted at him. "Will you be serious."

"I am," he said and kissed her hair. "It showed your beauty," he whispered while his eyes danced.

"Stop it," she said. "Talk to me."

"Fine, Charlie, I wanted you from that first night on the beach. But obviously that's crazy. I'm walking away from a painful, failed marriage. There're children involved... Then I met you. This isn't easy for me either."

"Yes," she whispered not caring. "Do you love me?"

"I care what happens to you. I want to be with you, to touch you, to taste you, to hear you laugh ... to please you. I want you to be in tune with me. No, I want us to be in tune with each other, and I want you like hell."

"You love me!" she crowed in triumph, and rolled on top of him throwing her arms around him.

He laughed then kissed her with increasing passion. Soon he gently disentangled himself. "Wait a minute," he said. He went to the bag and from a dark case took out a long shining silver object that glinted in the natural light. It was a flute. He sat in front of her and began to play it. He played something unfamiliar, high-pitched and haunting.

When he finished he carefully placed the flute on the blanket and took her in his arms. "I'll serenade you again later." he promised.

Soon they were both naked in the moonlight and she worriedly asked, "What happens if someone comes."

"Then we'll come too, and play to an audience."

They slowly excited each other then they fused sexually. He sat upright, bent knees firmly planted on the blanket, straddling her. The starlight lit up his face and he looked saturnine with his odd mismatched eyes. He picked up his flute, and to her wonder, began to play.

The lament of Consuela's Theme rose to the heavens. Waves of peace washed over her as she listened. The music was inside her and around her. The stars were in her vagina. She reeled off into eternity, a part of everything around her. The closeness she experienced was frightening. It almost hurt physically to be that spiritually entwined with another human being.

At last, after indefinable time, he carefully placed the flute by her side and slowly moved his hips in the familiar archetypal rhythm. This brought the usual pleasure and release. They completed the act of love in finite space and time.

"What happened?" she asked him later as she recovered, blinking at her surroundings.

"We loved," he replied, and she felt herself absorbed in the warmth of his smile

They remained unashamedly naked while he showed her the rest of the cay. Further inland they found wild flowers. They picked them and twined them into each other's pubic hair.

"Shades of D.H. Lawrence!" he exclaimed. "People really do this!" He admired the purple passion flower he'd twisted into her springy pubic hair. "We're the new Adam and Eve."

"Right on target," she said. "You know that Eve, or Lucy as they now want to call her, was black and originated in Africa." She sprang up. "Catch me Adam or the species won't go on." She screamed with laughter and ran for the beach. He caught her, and there on the sand they again did their bit for the human chain.

Afterward they snacked on macadamia nuts and tart exotic fruit, while they drank chilled Campari and club soda from carefully transported crystal, balloon glasses.

Charlie smiled at the thought of the ludicrous picture they made. She picked a crushed flower from Roderick's pubes and offered it to him. He took it and kissed her hand. After this, how could she return to Westchester and Lennie? God help her, she didn't even miss her child.

24

Lola

The Land Rover purred over the George Washington Bridge as Lola hummed along with the jazz station. An instrumental version of Where Or When was playing. Leroy turned and smiled at her and reached over and squeezed her hand.

"I missed the kids, but it was great having you to myself. What do you say we leave them with the folks a bit longer?" He kneaded her thigh affectionately.

Lola slapped him playfully on the arm, "You're bad, drive on and get my kids please; I miss them. We're all moved in now and we need them to fill that big, old house. It spooks me when I'm alone there." She stretched over and kissed her husband on the cheek. "I love you." She looked around her happily at the Sunday traffic of families heading into New Jersey.

Everything was perfect. They'd found the perfect house. She had the perfect husband. She hoped to make friends with Charlie, who was now her neighbor; Rebbie had got her into Jack and Jill. She was on her way to the perfect life ... "I ran into Lennie, yesterday at the cleaners. He said Charlie's out of town, but he wants to invite us over just as soon as she gets back. Wasn't that nice of him?" she said.

"Yeah, real nice," said Leroy.

"What's the matter, Baby, don't you like Lennie?"

"Sure, but I can't get excited about a dinner invitation or whatever it is they want to do I'd rather be home with my family. I get tired at work. I like to relax when I come home, not go sit in someone's house making small talk."

"Oh, Leroy," she said softly and briefly touched his hand. They listened to the Jazz station and sang along sometimes as they continued on their way to the Poconos. As they neared the farm, Lola said, "It's real nice of your Mom to do that ham for Rebbie. I felt bad asking her."

"She loves you, Honeychil'-like I do. You're the daughter she never had. Ask her anything."

"You guys are all so nice. Sometimes I feel I don't deserve you."

"Never feel that way, Baby. We all love you." He squeezed her leg again and winked at her.

"Baby, can we try to find this antique store?" She held up a paper with directions written on it. "The decorator said it's around here, somewhere."

"Sure, why not."

"She said I should go to antique stores and experiment with different pieces that I like and feel might work."

"Sounds good to me."

"Make a left here." She furrowed her brow and studied the directions again. "Sorry, it's more of a follow the road kind of thing. Turn around and go back."

Leroy retraced his steps good-naturedly while Lola navigated. "Leroy pull over, its there!" she said excitedly five minutes later.

He skidded into a dirt parking lot next to the little Pocono Antiques store and walked around to the side of the car to help her down. "Maybe you can pick up a few pieces here for the ski house, you know, give it a more homey kind of feel. Right now it's so Swiss Chalet spare, you almost expect little rosy-cheeked Swiss Misses to come dancing out."

"Oh Leroy, you know I'm not good at that sort of thing. The ski house is so beautifully furnished already I wouldn't know what to add. Help me?"

"Sure I will. Let's see what this place has." They entered a dim little store, cluttered with years' worth of bric-a-brac and dust.

A bell rang and a wizened, old white woman came hobbling on a cane from the back of the shop. "How're you folks doing today? Can I help you with anything special," she said in a raspy voice and followed the greeting with a phlegmy cough.

"No, thanks, we're just browsing," replied Lola.

The woman sank into a dusty, stained, old, overstuffed armchair. She lit a cigarette and puffed away on it as she watched them with watery blue eyes. "Call me if you need anything." She leaned back and half-closed her eyes.

"Baby, I don't know what to look for?" Lola whispered helplessly.

"Yes, you do. What do you like? Imagine this furniture is all shined up and winking at you from Bloomingdale's sales floor. What do you think about this little escritoire?" Leroy pointed to a dusty old writing desk.

"I guess." She approached the old thing dubiously.

"Let's look at it," Leroy continued. He rubbed off some of the dust and a dull brownish wood emerged. "You could keep it in your study and store household bills in it. Interested?"

"I guess."

He slid up the slatted opening. "Plenty storage for pens and stuff, maybe even a laptop. What's this?" He opened a clever little drawer that was partially hidden. "Secret storage, nice touch; like it?"

"Sure..." Lola wandered off and examined a silver filigree necklace with a heavy marcasite pendant. "Baby, look at this," she said excitedly and held it up.

"You want it; you got it," he said. He took the necklace from her and fastened it around her neck. "See, that wasn't so bad. You bought two great things. You're a whiz at antique shopping, Baby; don't let anybody tell you otherwise." He turned her around and kissed her on the nose.

Leroy lugged the desk to the front and indicated the necklace Lola wore, "How much do we have for you?" he said to the old woman.

The woman reluctantly roused herself and completed the sale. Leroy and Lola left with their finds, Lola wearing the necklace, which Leroy had the old woman shine up for her.

"Now let's get our kids," Lola said happily.

25

The Call of Home

Roderick drove the women into town. They visited the straw market for souvenirs then joined Felicity in Solomon's Mines for duty free perfume, crystal and silver.

"That heat was oppressive," said Maxi when they got back to the house.

"God, yes!" agreed Charlie. "I thought New York in the summer was bad, but it can't touch this. Absolute hell! But such beautiful people," she said, looking fondly at Roderick.

"Don't try to clean it up, you're criticizing my native land!" he joked.

"Mrs. Paine," the maid said, coming into the foyer.

"Yes," said Maxi. She paused on her way upstairs with her packages.

"There was a long distance call for you this morning. Your husband said to be sure to call him as soon as you got in."

"Thank you, Bette," said Maxi. "I'll try him now." She went into the drawing room to use the phone.

Felicity looked up from sifting through the day's mail on the little Sheraton table. She said, "Bette, don't go yet, anyone for a cool drink? It's about an hour to tea-time."

"Great idea," said Roderick. "Coconut water if you have any. I can't seem to get enough of it since I've returned home."

"We noticed," teased Felicity. "The coconut vendors downtown all cried when you left."

"I'll have the same, its addictive," said Charlie.

"Bette, bring the drinks to the terrace please," said Felicity. She headed there briskly, high heels clicking, guests in tow, and newly arrived catalogues under her arm.

Roderick did a shuffle step and sang:

Coconut is a' i'on

Coconut

Mek you strong like a lion

Coconut

Charlie said, "Roderick, you've got a poem or a song for everything"

"No!" they heard Maxi cry out as they passed the drawing room door. She dropped the 'phone and face in hands sank back against the sofa.

"What is it?" said Charlie as they all hurried into the room.

Ashen-faced, Maxi cried in great wrenching gasps that shook her entire body.

"Sis, what's wrong!" said Felicity, as everyone crowded around in concern and Maxi cried even harder.

"Jordan?" Felicity took the receiver. "What's going on? Maxi's just sitting here bawling and I can't get a word out of her... Oh no! Oh, the poor little thing. Are they sure? ... Oh Jordan, I'm so sorry. I'll put her back on the phone."

Maxi motioned her sister to hang up the phone.

"What is it?" said Charlie, impatiently, kneading her friend's shoulders.

"They think Tatiana may have bacterial meningitis, but further tests are needed. She's getting a spinal tap now," said Felicity.

"Oh no!" gasped Charlie.

"Poor kid," said Roderick.

Felicity dropped to her knees and hugged her sister, who, head in hands, sat on the sofa. "Maxi," she said, "are you sure you don't want to talk to Jordan any longer."

"No; tell him I'll call him back, no; give me the phone." She swallowed hard. "Jordan-" she said and then she burst into tears again and ran upstairs with Charlie in hot pursuit.

Once more, Felicity picked up the phone. "Jordan, this is horrible. If we can do anything let us know. She'll be on the first 'plane out of here. I'll call with the flight number... Give Tatty our love. We're praying for her." She hung up.

"Let's get organized," said Roderick. "Felicity, get their tickets. I have a friend at Bahamas Air who'll bump people, if necessary, and get them on the first New York flight."

"Thanks, Roddy," said Felicity. She touched his shoulder, and then went upstairs.

In the guestroom, Charlie and Maxi were tossing things into suitcases as Maxi moaned, "I should be there. She needs me. How can she have a spinal tap without me being there?"

"Shh," said her sister. "You'll be with her tomorrow. She's fine with Jordan for now. Remember; he loves her too. Give me your tickets so Roddy can make return reservations." She took them and headed for the door.

"If it's meningitis, tomorrow may be too late!" Maxi's voice broke and she sank to the floor in fresh tears.

"Roddy, please come for the tickets," Felicity said into the intercom then hurried to her sister who sat on the floor, sobbing and clinging to Charlie, who also had tears in her eyes. "Maxi, you'll be with Tatiana before you know it. Jordan has already left to meet her. She's being airlifted from the camp to Columbia Presbyterian Hospital. They'll have the results by tonight. Shall I come back to New York with you?"

"No," Maxi whispered. "Your boys will be home soon. Your family needs you and you have that new contract with Sir Clifford to worry about. I'll be fine with Charlie," she said, then started whimpering like an animal.

As the women watched her solemnly, Roderick fetched the tickets and left quickly.

"I've always been there when she needed me! Now she's having a spinal tap without me? My baby!" Maxi wailed suddenly.

"You're a good mother, she'll pull through," crooned her sister. "Kids are something. Much of the time you can't stand them, but as soon as something happens to them you can't stand yourself with the anxiety and sheer hell that you go through."

"Isn't it the truth," said Charlie. "This time tomorrow we'll be back in New York." "Charlie, I hate doing this to you, I know you don't want to leave yet. But I'll be so glad for your company on the plane." Maxi blew her nose and cried some more.

"Sis, stop it. You'll make yourself ill too," Felicity commanded as she dabbed away Maxi's tears. "Here, blow your nose." She gave her a fresh tissue. "Tatiana needs you to be strong right now, so start practicing."

Maxi turned streaming eyes to her sister. "Sorry for losing control," she said softly.

"Everything's going to be all right. I guarantee it," Felicity said confidently and a look passed between the sisters.

"I'm not worried anymore," Maxi said softly. "I know it will."

26

Offshore Education

At dinner that evening Maxi was calm and pale. Tatiana's spinal tap had ruled out meningitis. Further tests were being done, and she was in intensive care in a coma. George tried to inject a note of heartiness into the subdued atmosphere.

"Felicity, this is wonderful," he said taking seconds of the rice and crab and the accompanying fresh native tomato salad.

"Pass it when you've finished please, George," said Charlie. "I swear if I lived in this country I'd become as fat as a hog."

"Somehow I doubt that, Charlie," said Felicity with a smile. "I've heard of how hard you work. Running between your different restaurants must keep you thin. Now I have to watch it; my work's more sedentary than yours. I need to take more time off to exercise."

"What's this?" said her husband. "You women trying to upstage us; boasting about who can work harder? Pass the rice'n crab please. Oh God it's hard work doing justice to this food!" He mopped sweat from his brow and renewed his attack on the food.

"How can you can eat this heavy delicious food year round? If I lived here I'd max out on salads to beat this heat, and of course to control my gluttony. Pass the rice'n crab when you've finished, please," said Charlie.

"Charlie, my stomach stays at ninety eight point six year round; so there's no need for anyone to throw a salad at me and try to call it a meal. I want real food every day of the year – hot food," said George. He handed her the dish. "Careful, it's hot."

"Thanks," said Charlie.

Felicity laughed. "See what I have to deal with? We can't ever declare a salad season."

"Your cook you mean. No one has more household help than you island people," said her sister.

"But we work just as hard as you!" retorted Felicity. "We work outside the home, then come in and deal with crazy children and super spoilt men with multifarious needs."

"That's got to be rough," said Charlie, "especially since you guys routinely use nannies and chauffeurs and as we already established; cooks." She smiled, "Just teasing!"

Maxi said, "In America we have to deal with teachers who have lowered expectations of children once they see a black skin. And you don't know who is a closet disciple of Jenson and those Bell Curve Guys. What're their names? I keep on blocking them."

"Richard Herrnstein and Charles Murray," supplied Roderick.

"Yeah, that's the crew," Maxi said. "So you have to push your black child academically and with the extra-curricular activities until you swear you'll drop from the effort. If you're black you have to be better for them to even notice you – cliché but true."

"Come on, Maxi, its not that bad," interjected Charlie, happy that her friend had been tempted into the conversation. "All our kids are doing well academically. I don't know of a dumb, black, upper-middle class kid."

"That's because we push them so hard, Charlie. You would have to be real dumb, to be dumb, if you were one of our kids," Maxi retorted.

"How can you live like that? It must be horrible for the children. That kind of pressure would break me. I know my boys couldn't take it," said Felicity.

"It comes with the territory," said Maxi. "All their friends, both black and white, don't even mention Asian because the word stress was invented to describe their schooling-are in the same boat. But blacks have to push harder, because we have a credibility problem in white American society. The Leviathan of racism is always breathing down our necks; it makes us keep our children on the move"

"You know," said George, "I'm going to say something that's not going to make me popular at this table, but it has to be said. Black Americans are always bitching about their credibility problem in their society and 'the man' keeping them down." He belched softly and continued, "You people-"

"George, I wouldn't go there if I were you," said Felicity.

He ignored her. "I've met black people in America with life styles comparable to mine and they're still crying about 'the man' and their oppression. What oppression!"

"The fact that often, unlike in your situation, they can't rise any higher than they were when you met them," said Charlie. She regarded George over the rim of her wine glass.

"For God's sake, Black Americans should just get up off their duffs and take their share of the pie! Work either within or without the system to change it. But do something don't sit around and cry about it," George retorted.

"Easier said than done, I worked my butt off day and night to get my business started-with no help from anyone. Granny always said 'the only way hard work could hurt you was if it fell on top of you'. No one tried to stop me-because I was a black female. There are lots of men out there working as hard as I did, but they won't get my results."

"You're one of the exceptions Charlie," said George. "You're smart, have Caribbean values and I guess were in the right place at the right time. Many of your American countrymen just expect a handout. America has created a welfare mentality that often stands in the way of Black success."

"Will you stop that!" said Charlie, incensed. "That's the absolutely worst kind of patronizing racism. Translate-the rest of your group ain't worth shit, you're the only good nigger there is. There are a lot of non-West Indian blacks working hard and doing well in America, Brazil and where ever else the Diaspora threw us up."

"Charlie, I hate to see you under fire," said Roderick, "but I understand what George is getting at. We didn't always have it easy in this country. A generation ago the country was run by a white oligarchy. But our fathers collectively said 'enough of that.' They shut down the country-blocked off the airport, among other things, and got their candidate into office. Like your critic Stanley Crouch points out, in the same way that 'you sing the blues to get over the blues' you use government to rid yourself of the blues of government.'"

"Yes," continued George. "And do you know what the first thing was on our new black government's agenda? Education. It was a moral imperative. Like the Jews, we said, 'never again'. Now we have a whole first generation of black professionals who would have been running around here strung out on drugs, or screwing tourist women for a buck, had it not been for our fathers taking their destiny into their own hands and moving with it. The country now has the pick of this new, savvy, educated black litter, in elections."

"No fair," said Maxi. "It's a different situation. For one thing, look at the numbers. Blacks here are the majority. In America we're a minority; what is it? Approximately thirteen percent of the population?"

"Something like that," corroborated Charlie.

"Yes, and our white folks are slick," said Maxi. They'll take you into the system if you've got the credentials. Then they'll slam you in the head with the glass ceiling. You don't advance past this point, niggah! So there's generally this obvious disparity between black and white. "

"So what about the O'Neals and Parsons of this world." said Roderick.

"Smoke screens," Maxi retorted. "The few of us that make it through the divide get the big rah rah with the white media leaping up and down, congratulating themselves on wonderful America which can spawn black Horatio Algers. The face of the escapee from blackness is everywhere and the message is, 'See what brains and hard work can do.' Bullshit! That was the exception that proved the rule. There's more than a handful of talented blacks in America."

"Excellence will always be rewarded," intoned George.

"In a colorblind society, sure," said Maxi. "But our society isn't colorblind and the ceiling separating us from the top isn't glass-it's lucite. Glass you can break, but this thing won't even crack. Still, some little no-count white will zoom right through it and make twice as much money as the black man or woman who trained him in the first place."

Charlie said, "You learn to live with it. They don't want you to make it in their America, so I made it my America! I too can manipulate it. When I went for my business loan I didn't appear too bright. They figured I'd be mediocre or fail, but they'd have done their duty by giving little black double minority me a loan. They'd get their business Brownie points – not their fault that the dumb nigger failed."

"Ingenious," said Roderick looking admiringly at Charlie. "A covert economic determinist; you should go teach the rest 'to sing the blues.'"

She smiled at him and continued; "I've had former black classmates brighter than myself turned down for the same loans because they didn't know how to play the game."

"So how do you feel now, knowing that they didn't want you where you are?" asked Felicity with interest.

"It's no problem, now," said Charlie. "They accept me. I've proven myself. I've become part of the 'talented tenth' of the Negro population that Dubois said would be on top. It's like being an honorary white person in South Africa under the apartheid system."

"I swear, I couldn't live that way," said Felicity. She shook her head. "As I said before, I'll come shop, go to the theatre and then get the hell out."

"You adjust," said Charlie. "I live well. You just have to let Whites know you're as good as-pardon me, better than, they are, because you had to work harder for everything you have. Then you have no problem. They can't get at me because I have money; but to be poor and black in America, now that would be pathetic and dangerous."

"Charlie, I wish it were that easy," said Maxi with a sigh. "Sophie's daughter went to an expensive camp in Vermont last summer. There were few blacks there-she was the only black girl in her cabin. You know they never put all the blacks together. They spread our children around so everything looks integrated. Sophie never got the full story of what happened, but Penelope's still in therapy recovering from the experience."

"Hmm," said George. "Do we know that the kid wasn't obnoxious and just got her comeuppance?"

"George, she's a nice kid and she was outnumbered racially; so I'd side with her and not with them," said Maxi testily.

"Oh, George, let's just blame the victim why don't we, especially if she happens to be a black female," Felicity added.

"In spite of all this craziness our children are doing fine academically and otherwise," Charlie said.

"They have no choice," said Maxi. "If they fail they hit the bottom. If their white girlfriend fails, chances are she won't. She'll get the benefit of the doubt, they won't."

"Enough of this depressing topic; I hate to be uncouth, but what's for dessert? I've just loved all the Bahamian food I've had so far," said Charlie.

"Then you'll love what you're getting tonight," said Felicity. "Guava duff, with a rum hard sauce."

"Terrific. My hips will hate me tomorrow," said Maxi.

They finished dinner and sat around and talked for a while. Finally Roderick said:"Charlie, coming for a nightcap?"

"Sure, I'll run upstairs and get my cardigan."

"You don't need it. I'll keep you warm.

"Mmmm" she said, "Okay."

George looked incredulously at the couple. "Well I'll be damned!" he said as they bade everyone goodnight and walked out into the tropical darkness, arms around each other.

27

That Sheep May Safely Graze

Charlie and Roderick strolled through the moonlit garden to the music of hidden cicadas.

"Poor Maxi, I 'd completely fall apart in her shoes," Charlie said.

"No you wouldn't. From what I know of you, you'd assemble a medical dream team, and offer a bounty to the one that got her out of the woods," Roderick rejoined.

"What's not to like in that scenario?"

"Hey, if it works..." He shrugged his shoulders.

"Enough of this!" She looked around at the beach-bordered garden. "Don't you ever have bad nights here? You know your low down, dirty nights. Nights when the moonlight does not gleam on the water, when you don't hear the crickets and their friends, and it's not the perfect temperature. You know that kind of night?"

Roderick chuckled and threw his arm around her shoulder, pulling her even closer to him. "No Charlie," he said. "I put in a special order for you, that all your nights would be special. But if you want, I can cancel it."

"That's okay, I can live with perfection. Thanks." She tiptoed and kissed him on the cheek; and they smiled at each other and entered the guest cottage.

"I'm going to miss you Charlie." He held both her hands and looked into her eyes.

"Yeah?" she said, meeting his gaze.

"Yeah," he mimicked.

"You sound so strange saying 'yeah.' I'm going to miss you too," she said.

"This is not necessarily goodbye. How do you feel about a commuting romance?"

"It can be done."

"Good, then that's settled," Roderick said briskly. "I have something for you."

She sat on the love seat and admired his retreating buns. He soon returned and put on a CD of wind instruments playing stately cadences.

"Roderick, what is this? It sounds like the song the old cow died on."

"What!"

"You heard me, island boy. The song the old cow died on. Don't tell me you never heard that expression before."

He laughed. "Actually, I haven't. But you did kind of hit the nail on the head. This is from Greatest Hits of 1721 and this selection is That Sheep May Safely Graze. So you see, it's ovine rather than bovine; the old cow's cousins, but you're in the ballpark."

"Don't you have Quincy Jones, or Cleo Laine, or something! Christ, anything but this! No good ever came of black men listening to music with titles like That Sheep May Safely Graze. This is downright depressing."

"Why does it depress you?"

"It's so White! and sad too. It reminds me of childhood summers spent in Barbados with Mom's parents. They were old and strict. Sundays were ridiculous-church twice that day, Rediffusion, the local radio, playing church services or music like this all day. By night time you wanted to smash the damn Rediffusion box up against the nearest wall."

"You should be glad your Grammy was religious. When women reach that age they turn to either rum or religion."

"Roderick, stop it," Charlie laughed and slapped him playfully. "Rude boy!"

"My Dear, we'll have to do something about this distaste for good music won't we? All this passion needs to be redirected into the right channels. I can't have you going through life not loving Bach's 1721 hit song. I guarantee you, before this night is over whenever you hear this song or any of the others on this C.D. you're going to love them."

"What's this, Pavlov's dogs revisited?" asked Charlie

"Maybe," he smiled. "You'll have to be the judge of that."

He handed her a package from the sofa table. It was small, square and extravagantly wrapped in pale pink, mylar paper, with exuberant curlicues of silver and lavender ribbon.

"Ooh!" exclaimed Charlie sitting and holding the gift. "I almost don't want to open it, it's so pretty." She looked up at Roderick and her eyes misted over.

"Go ahead, open it," he urged.

Inside sat three, little, golden balls in ascending size order; the smallest slightly bigger than a standard sized marble.

"Oh!" she exclaimed in surprise. "What on earth is this?"

"A present," Roderick smiled, enjoying her look of perplexity.

"I can see that. What do I do with it?"

"And well you might ask. They're Ben-wa balls. What? No light of recognition in your eyes? When you return to cold New York, and go about your quotidian days sitting by the fireplace on a cold winter's night-you with your knitting, your husband with his latest medical journal-"

"Is this sun-stroke or liquor talking?"

"Reading glasses perched on the tips of your noses," he continued. "Insert two of these little presents into your vagina-you start with two then build your way up to three-then rock in your chair and think of me."

Charlie gaped at him. "You're sick!"

Roderick roared with laughter. "If you could see yourself, Love. Try it now, please. Shall I put them in for you?"

"No, thank you," she responded stiffly. "And what makes you feel that I go around sticking foreign objects up my vagina."

"They're not foreign objects," he explained patiently. "They're yours and will not harm you. They've been in use for centuries-ladies in the Orient swear by them I hear."

"Why would I do this, again?"

"Because you want to live a little and experience something new and wonderful that is non-fattening, contains no chemicals or electricity and can only increase your pleasure quotient and enhance your life."

"Well if you're sure-"

"I have it on the best authority. My offer to help you insert them still stands."

"Get out of here, I can do it myself." She rose and headed for the bathroom. Soon Ben-wa balls in place, Charlie returned and sat in the rocking chair.

"Now, listen to your body," said Roderick. "We'll experience this together." He smiled and rocked the chair vigorously; his attention firmly focused on her face. At first Charlie returned his fixed gaze and then her mind drifted. This man rocking her, playing soothing music for her was her home. He was taking care of her in a way no one ever had before. Waves of tenderness for him washed over her accompanied by a pleasant lassitude.

"Anything happening yet?" he inquired.

"Like what?" she said drowsily. "I'm enjoying your rocking and, incidentally, your music. It is relaxing."

Roderick rocked the chair a bit more quickly. The music swelled and became demanding. He rocked harder. Charlie's feelings of lassitude fled. Deep in her womb something was happening. A gentle feathery tickling was becoming persistent and pronounced. It was now a tiny flame. She focused in on it, unsure of what it meant.

She remembered when Germaine, her newborn had first been placed at her breast. That tightening of the uterus was here again. But this time instead of pain, there was a deep feeling of urgency and love for the man whose head she was now gripping in her mounting excitement.

Suddenly Charlie's womb caught afire. She panted. The room whirled. Roderick's strange eyes blazed. He rocked with one hand and reached for her breasts with the other. Gently he turned a nipple as if turning up the volume on audio equipment. High mewling sounds ripped from her and blended with the bright music that painted pictures of pastoral summer days, fluffy clouds, and fat grazing sheep gamboling in the meadows. Charlie was an electric storm building up power above the peaceful scene. Her toes curled.

Roderick's hand moved slowly down her body leaving a tingling trail of heat in its path down her belly. His eyes pinned her to the chair even as her emotions caused her to expand beyond it. Her uterus contracted furiously. This was crazy!

She howled. She gripped his hair more firmly as from the waist down she felt hot, pleasurable, liquefaction. He softly stroked her clitoris. The molten liquid roared into a conflagration. She shrieked and together, she and the music rose to a crescendo. If she died now it would have been a life well spent. Incredibly, the intensity increased. She threw back her head, arched her back, and flexed her toes in a screaming orgiastic frenzy.

Roderick knelt in front of her and rocked even faster. He whispered urgently, "That's it. Let go. Let go!" while his strange mismatched eyes glowed like a devil's.

Charlie bawled from her depths as her entire body contracted and flamed anew. He stopped rocking the chair and covered her face, neck and breasts with kisses. Then he buried his face in the heat between her legs and kissed the throbbing contracting slit, even as his hand squeezed her breast.

"Why, Charlie you're blushing down here," he said. He pulled apart her vaginal lips and gazed in awe at the deep wine berry color of the swollen, blood engorged flesh.

This exposure perversely escalated her excitement. She was now beyond shame. Her hands dropped to his neck. She wrapped her legs around his shoulders and came again in a final shuddering collapse.

"Come to me," he said. He disentangled himself then half lifted her from the chair. She could scarcely stand without support.

"What did you do to me?" she asked weakly.

"Wasn't that what is popularly called 'good loving'? Don't say you've never had it before. Oh my! Good thing we're not in the main house. They would've sworn I was killing you. Your erotalalia would have brought them running."

"Speak English."

"Fine; love cries," he translated.

"What was in those damn balls?"

"Oh, a substance that moves and warms up as you move. It does things for you sexually that even I with all my love, knowledge and sexual prowess? Ahem, ahem, can't do. Did you enjoy Bach and develop an affinity for sheep?"

"Pervert!" she said, laughing weakly. She stroked his face. "Did anyone ever tell you that you're completely nuts"?

"Yes, I'm nuts over you," he said, and kissed her. "Come let's take out the balls. They're taking up my space and it's my turn now."

"You know, one of these days you're going to go too far," she said in wonder.

They retired to the bedroom for a night of slow, quiet, bittersweet lovemaking, with Bach in the background setting the pace. All too soon it was time to awaken and return to the sleeping house.

"Know something," Charlie said, "that intensive immersion technique does seem to have worked. I kind of like Bach now."

"Another session and you'll become his greatest devotee, I promise you. I plan to work on Ravel's Pavanne for a Dead Princess next, and really pull out all the stops." He lightly squeezed her buttocks, and left an exciting tingle.

"No, next time you'll give me my boy Marsalis, or Spirogyra."

They smiled at each other. The rising sun lit their way through the dew soaked garden with its awakening morning sounds. Charlie started to miss Roderick already.

28

Welcome Home

New York, and home-a scared looking Jordan met them at the airport. Tatiana had viral encephalitis and was slipping in and out of a coma. Maxi in tears clung to her husband and chided him for leaving Tatiana with strangers while he came to pick her up. Charlie felt unutterable sadness as she turned down their offer of a ride. As she climbed into a cab that reluctantly took her to Harlem and her 135 Street restaurant; she thanked God her own daughter was fine.

The Internet, faxes and the telephone had made things run smoothly in her absence. Lennie had tried to play restaurateur but employees in daily contact with their boss rebuffed him at every turn. As Charlie went through her books she considered flying to Trinidad to bring back Germaine. The child had never flown alone and this was not the time to start.

"Mrs. Gopilal,"

Her manager pulled her back from her thoughts, "Yes, Laron, what is it?"

"That order of whiting that was supposed to come in today seems to have gotten mixed up with something else. Come and see. We don't know what to do with this thing."

Charlie followed him to the kitchen.

"Chil' I in had this in ages; it not popular in these parts."

"Wha' you sayin'; y'all don' eat conch up here?"

Charlie's ears pricked up, at the word conch. Was this a sign?

"Griselda," she said, "did we get conch by mistake?"

"Yes Ma'am. I from the Virgin Islands an' we eat this all the time, but these Yankees actin' like if it goin' bite them." The woman gave a rich belly laugh.

Was this God or serendipity? Charlie said, "Laron, return this for now, but we will carry this product in the future. I plan to add conch fritters to our repertoire."

"But Mrs. Gopilal no one here knows anything about cooking conch."

"They'll learn. I'll get a recipe developed. We'll test market it here in Harlem. There are enough Caribbean people to start getting it off the ground. If it's good it'll fly on its own by word of mouth; and it will be good. Bahamians can't get enough of it."

"Yes Ma'am."

Charlie phoned Roderick. "Roddy, I'm so excited; guess what I'm going to do?"

"Come back to the Bahamas and make passionate love to me?"

"That too," she chuckled, "but I also plan to add conch to my menu and open a branch of **Charlie's Chicken** in Nassau! Can you try some of that island nepotism for me and see who I have to talk to and what palms I have to grease?"

"Of course; anything for my ladylove. You don't waste any time do you, my lady. This is the best news I've heard since I returned home. Of course the delectable owner of **Charlie's Chicken** will make frequent visits to her Nassau franchise."

"Of course."

"Bring on the conch!" roared Roderick.

"Nut," said Charlie affectionately. "Talk to you later." She hung up the 'phone. She smiled and blushed as she remembered the night before. This thing with Roddy was madness. She had no idea where it was going but she knew she didn't want it to stop. In fact she was fairly sure that she couldn't live without it at this point. God, good sex was addictive! And the packaging was fantastic. She sighed and called Lennie.

Lennie picked up Charlie on his way home. They pecked each other on the cheek as if nothing had happened and he said, "You're looking good. Enjoyed your vacation?"

"Thank you, I did enjoy myself. How did you spend your time?" She pictured Lennie as a sexually over-stimulated, experimental rat running amok stopping at cage after cage for relief with little pink-nosed, red-eyed female rats. It made her smile.

"Well, girl, I managed to keep your business afloat. It needed a man's touch. Those people that you have working for you are rude. And they don't know the first thing about business. It was hard work." He squeezed her hand.

"Thank you, Lennie. You really didn't have to."

"Course I did. How was the trip? I missed my two girls."

At her questioning look, he appeared uncomfortable and said; "You and Germaine are the queens of my heart."

"Of course we are. I can hardly wait to see Germaine. I might fly to Trinidad and get her this week."

"Good idea," said Lennie. "After that the next trip will be all of us. Let's go to Hilton Head. You and Gee both like it there."

"I can't. I plan to expand down South and into the Bahamas, so there's a lot of work to be done; you know-meetings, site searches, feasibility studies."

"Woman, you're something else," he said approvingly. "By the way, Rose called. They're back from Hawaii. Sydney won first place in the chess tournament there and before she left she beat an International Master. Rose says that's the level above Master, which is the girl's level."

"She did?" Charlie said excitedly. "Wow! That little girl is unstoppable. She's showing them who's king. Rose swears that some day she'll be the first black, female, Grandmaster. I'll call her; I know she's bursting with pride. Is there anything else happening?"

"The usual; the cops still beating the shit out of black people. They just shot another black boy in the back last week. A cop beat up another one for truancy. I tell you, if we had a son he would have to grow up in Trinidad. This place scares me."

"Oh, calm down, for God's sake. How could you put a son of mine in the same category as the boys getting shot? Our son, if we had one, would be growing up rich and smart in an exclusive Westchester community. The money in his pockets and the expensive clothes on his back would buy him all the respect he needed. He'd also have the good sense not to put himself in harm's way. Bullets would not be for him."

"Well, I hope you're right. But I almost don't feel comfortable here now. I've been listening to that Reverend Buxley-you know the little loud mouth black man who dyes his hair blonde."

"That clown?" Charlie laughed.

"Go ahead and laugh. There's a lot going on in this country that you don't know about because you read the New York Times and the Wall Street Journal. I've been listening to this Reverend guy on the radio and he's saying some frightening stuff."

"Who cares what that fat clown says? He's always running around with busloads of unemployed black people following him and screaming 'right on brother.' Gimme a break!" She chupsed, "Listen, Lennie, I grew up in this country-In Harlem, so you can't tell me anything about this place that I don't already know. What you're talking about does not apply to us. Money protects us." She glared at him.

Germaine came running out shrieking, when the car pulled up to the front door of the new house. Charlie gasped. She jumped out of the car, caught her daughter in her arms and showered her with kisses.

"When did you get back, Sweetheart?"

"This morning; Daddy wanted to surprise you. Granny had a friend who was coming to New York on a shopping trip, so I traveled with her. She was really nice. We ate roti and channa and pawpaw on the 'plane. You should've seen how the other passengers looked at us; they wanted our food!"

Thank you "Lennie. This is the nicest thing you've ever done for me." Charlie choked with tears and clutched her daughter to her. She stroked the short, glossy, stylish hair. She was so different from the sad, sullen child who had left a few weeks ago.

"Mummy, I missed you. I love the new house. Everything's finally been moved in. Wasn't it terrific of Daddy to move us in while we were gone?"

Charlie was momentarily taken aback, and then she laughed and said, "It was wonderful of him." She silently blessed the decorator, the new staff and Evadne who before she left to work for Rose had made it possible for Lennie to lie yet again. She walked into the house with her arm around her daughter's shoulder. "You've grown taller since you went to Trinidad, I don't have a baby anymore." She squeezed her daughter. "Isn't the house magnificent?" Charlie's heart glowed as she looked at the highly polished dark wooden floors, crystal chandeliers and burgundy window treatments that colored the setting sunlight filtering through them.

"I love my room," said Germaine. "It's huge. I can roller-blade in there."

"Don't you dare. Do you notice how tranquil it all feels? I had a Feng Shui decorator work with us."

"What's Feng Shui?" asked Germaine.

"It's an Asian manner of creating harmony – like in this room. Things are placed in a configuration that encourages a positive flow of energy which will result in good outcomes for –"

"Oh, Mom!" said the child.

"All right, all right! See what I got you!" Charlie reached into the large basket she had purchased in the straw market and pulled out a shiny silver box. "Ta da!"

"Mommy!" Germaine ripped off the box lid, "It's beautiful!" she shrieked. "They're just like the earrings Dushanti wore at school last year-but prettier. And you got me the matching bracelet too, thank you, thank you. I love you!" She hugged her mother enthusiastically, and then ran to a nearby mirror to try on her new spoils.

At dinner that evening Charlie told her family about Tatiana's encephalitis; later she called Maxi at the hospital for an update.

"The poor thing," said Maxi, "she can hardly talk. She slips in and out of consciousness. She's on a drip now and anti-seizure medication. Earlier she had such an intense headache that she was screaming. Charlie I don't know if I can take this. Seeing her so...so..."

"Shhh, she's at one of the top hospitals in the country. It's going to be all right. I'm praying for you. I'll be in as soon as visitors are allowed."

"Thanks," Maxi whispered. "And thanks for that cute teddy bear holding the balloon bouquet. They're keeping it for us at the nurses' station. You can't have stuff like that here in the ICU, but I like to go out and look at it. It lifts my spirits and reminds me that there's still cheer in the world. You're so thoughtful." Maxi's voice broke.

"Now stop that, you know I'm here for you! Be strong."

"Charlie, I'm trying," sniffed Maxi. "But it's hard. She looks so... so..."

"She'll get better, I've put in an order with God and I won't accept anything else," Charlie said firmly. "Look after her and I'll be over soon."

"Charlie, you're a nut, but thank you," Maxi whispered with tears in her voice as she hung up the 'phone.

Charlie felt sad and alone as she opened Germaine's door a crack and looked at her own sleeping daughter. Her arm was loosely thrown around a large stuffed animal and she sighed in her sleep; she was healthy and safe. Charlie closed the door softly. She walked past unpacked boxes in the wide hallway and went upstairs to her office. She'd make enough money to always keep her safe, and if anything ever happened to her she'd have enough money to make it better.

29

The Maids

Rose's eighteen-month-old son was howling. Midian's little face was red with rage and he shook his fists, but Evadne his baby-sitter was busy. The conversation was sweet and Evadne had no time to be constantly bending down and picking up toys in what the foolish-bitch-mistress called the child's weaning games. Let the blasted Tele-Tubby stay on the ground. She was nobody's slave, that woman was insane. She had come to the park to enjoy herself and chat with the other maids, not run behind some hardheaded little black boy. This job was not working out the way she had planned.

Evadne considered her charge ugly like sin, and red! Shit! But why she couldn't work with white people and get some pretty, little, white-skinned child with soft hair to look after? Or even a half East Indian child like Miss Charlie's daughter. She had a good grade of hair, don' mind it still needed a bit of a straightener. But no; every day she had to explode this little, red, vagabond's nigger knots wid a' almost useless comb. Once the boy's hard hair had even broken the little comb. She looked enviously at Sondra's charge, all soft golden curls and pink-cheeks in the crisp, spring air.

"Yes, she buy dese fancy Moan somet'ing plates and t'ings for the occasion," said Evadne, ignoring the howling child.

"Is a white plate wid pink and purple t'ings on it?" asked Gracelyn.

"Das de one; you know it?" asked Evadne.

"De mistress was admiring 'dem in a cattylog an' she show me," said Gracelyn.

"Get on wid de story nuh?" said Sondra, tenderly wiping dribble from the white baby's chin. "You too sweet!" she said tenderly pinching her little fat cheeks.

"She sho is dat," agreed Evadne finally giving in and picking up the tele tubby. She handed it to Midian who promptly flung it away again with a loud bellow.

"But looka he doah nuh!" exclaimed Evadne.

"He too passionate," said Gracelyn. "He like he want a slap."

Evadne chupsed, shook the stroller threateningly then went on with the story.

"Yes, like I tell you. Dis Miz Inniss real great an' foolish. She in dis PTA t'ing and always talkin' bout de white ladies on it like if she and dem is frien's."

"My mistress is de president," said Sondra proudly. "Dey always comin' by de house for discussions and t'ings."

"For truth?" said Evadne. "Miz Inniss never say she went to your lady's house."

"Well, I never see she at any o' de meetins dere now dat yuh mention it. It does only be de white ladies," Sondra said.

"Well, like I tell you. She go to dis Bloomindale's an' buy dese t'ings special- de plates I did tell you 'bout. "

"De Moan plates." put in Gracelyn.

"Yes, dem. She say dey expensive. She skin she teet' like a roas' dog when she show dem to me. An' she buy dis patty t'ing, an' she buy cheese and so much fruit! She rent some big fancy silver t'ing to do de coffee in, an' she have dis ruggy Jewish t'ing to serve too. I like it bad, you know. It taste good."

"You mean ruggelach," said Sondra. Miz Ben-David buy it all de time."

"Yes, an' she have de bagels and cream cheese too. She get she nails done an' all mornin' she wuk me like a dog. She shoutin' polish dis, move dat. She behave like a cent kite wid a swishy tail. You know de kind dat cheap and always flyin' all over de place makin' a lot o' foolish noise?"

"Yes! I in hear dat expression fuh a long time!" and Gracelyn clapped her knees and laughed uproariously.

"Well," continued the raconteur. "All de time she sweatin' like a pot cover. De time passed when de white people did suppose to come. She say she on some committee and dese are her members. Some coolie woman show up-Miz Baboo or somet'ing so. Well, dey waited. Not one o' de white women came. Miz Inniss was too shame."

"Oh shit!" said Sondra. "But dey treat she bad. Nobody call and say nuttin'?"

"Not a one," said Evadne triumphantly. "But dah fuh lick she! She feel she better dan me an' you. She one o' dese black women dat always feel she shit could make patty. I glad dey whip she. God doan like ugly!" She gave a wise nod.

"But you right." supplied Gracelyn. "I never wuk fuh black people!" and she ran her fat, black fingers through little Chaim's blonde curls. "No sirree. I want de real ting. I stay home fus. It would be like changin' black dog for monkey to go out an' wuk wid dem. Dese black people aroun' here too poor-great. Dey feel dey is somebody. My mudda did always say 'when dish rag turn table-cloth, table does get upset'."

"Girl, I need de money. Neddy havin' li'l problems now, you know how it go. My last mistress arrange dis job fuh me 'cause she had to move. So although I tek another black job, like you I would really prefer white. Dese nigger people does don' know how to behave. Dis Miz Inniss too high fallutin' wid she self. If you could hear how she does answer de phone. 'This is she'," Evadne mimicked in a mincing voice. "And compared t' de white folks she in even got a cup o' warm spit t' she name."

"But how you could stan' dat?" queried Sondra she smiled fondly and shifted the stroller so that the morning sunlight would not shine directly into little Megan's blue eyes.

"I wid you on dat!" exclaimed Gracelyn. "When I did firs' startin' out at dis ting, I wukked fuh a black woman. Like your Miz Inniss she was poor-great. An' she was as lazy as butter is greasy! She in help me do nuttin'. But she always complainin' dat I does don' finish she wuk."

"Is de truf, dey always behave so. Dey want to kill yuh wid de work," said Sondra.

"Well, one day even dough dis bitch see me strugglin' wid all de hard wu'k she put some o' she husban' pants wid de laundry for me to wash and iron. Well chil' you know me. I had to call she up on dis, 'cause you know dese black people, dey will stone you wid shit den hang you for stinkin'," said Gracelyn.

"Is de truth," Sondra said.

Gracelyn continued. "She get nasty, an' I tell she I never t'ought I would see the day when one Caribbean woman would treat another one so. An' she fire me on de spot fuh pointing out dat me and she was one! So bosie, I in know how you could stan' dem."

"Chil,' is a job." Evadne explained, "An' I can' do any better right now. But when I get my green card I goin' go to Maryland an buy a driver's license then go wu'k for white people up in Connettycut. I hear dat is real money up dere and de people too nice; dey does even let you drive dey car," said Evadne.

"I did always hear dat," said Gracelyn. "I hear too dat de white mens does like to sleep wid women like we. You might even get a little light-skin, straight hair baby."

"You go 'long," said Sondra with a laugh. "Wha' white man goin' look at she wid she big, ugly, black self.

"You don' worry 'bout dat. My day comin'," said Evadne. "When I swishin' 'roun' lookin' sexy, an' bendin' over lettin' him get a' eyeful o' de bubbies it gon' be like dey say; 'yuh can't carry de butter an' put in puss mout' an' think dat he won't lick it!'" She gave Midian his toy. He clutched it, and his bellows of rage subsided into whimpers.

"Look, I have to go now," said Sondra. "Miz Ben-David like to call 'roun' nap time to check on Megan. So I'll see you ladies tomorrow, early o'clock."

"I have to go too. Is this boy's nap time now and Miz Inniss does get mad and carry on if he not in de bed by eleven o'clock," said Evadne.

Suddenly a white toddler rushed up to them. They smiled indulgently at him.

Splat, splat, splat "brrrrr." He spat swiftly on all three maids and stood out of arm's reach watching them with interest as he bubbled more spit.

"Shit! He got me!"

"Wha' de-"

"He's a ass-hole or what?"

The three maids were thrown into general consternation. Before they could act, a young white woman ran up and grabbed the boy.

"I'm so sorry," she apologized breathlessly with some type of European accent. "I'm his au-pair." She turned to the child and shook him. "Johnny, apologize at once. Don't I always tell you not to spit at anyone?"

"But Anastasia," he pointed out with the irrefutable logic of childhood. "These aren't real people, they're black people." He blessed them all with a beatific smile.

30

Pool Party

It was pool party weather. A large group of Germaine's friends from her old school and children of family friends descended on Angloville to attend her end of school-year bash. Charlie was gratified to see so many children come to celebrate with her daughter.

Mrs. Padowski accompanied her son to the pool area to find Charlie. "Now you behave yourself," she said to her son. "Don't give Mrs. Gopilal any trouble. Dad's taking me for a driving lesson; we'll get you afterwards." She tried to kiss the boy goodbye, but he ducked and ran off in a breathless hurry. She laughed indulgently and said to Charlie, "Mrs. Gopilal, what time shall we pick up Lech?"

"At six," Charlie said. She looked at her watch

"Thanks for inviting him, we'll see you then, bye," said the woman looking around to include her son. "Lech, No!" she screamed.

Charlie spun around as Lech, holding his nose, leapt feet first into the deep end of the pool.

"Noo! That's my baby, and he can't swim!" The distraught mother rushed to the side of the pool. "And I can't swim either!" she added as she leapt into the water behind her son. She went down like Enron stock. Charlie stared in disbelief. Yes, there they were thrashing around at the bottom of her pool.

The children gathered excitedly and pointed and commented on the duo.

"She's still holding onto her pocketbook."

"Yeah, old Lech's gonna mug her down there."

Charlie herded the excited children away from the pool's edge. Her thoughts raced. She could leap in and ruin her hairstyle. Would her contact lenses pop out in the water and render her purblind? Her two hundred-dollar swimsuit wasn't supposed to get wet. Where was the damn lifeguard? Delayed by melanin no doubt.

"Heeelp!" Charlie shouted.

The adults on the pool deck kept up their conversations.

"Damn!" She rushed to the kitchen off the patio. Maids were preparing trays of food and Lennie for once seemed to be doing something useful.

"Lennie, come quickly. Two people are drowning in the pool."

"Don't bother me, I'm getting ice," he snapped.

"What?" Charlie felt as if she were in the twilight zone. She rushed back outside feeling the beginnings of a major headache. She would have to jump in and try to get them herself. They were still struggling in the water. "Heeelp!" she screamed again as she mentally prepared to take the plunge.

A fully clothed figure hurtled past Charlie and dove into the pool, the lifeguard at last. Strong, young, brown arms brought up first the boy, then the mother. He handed them spitting and gasping to the now assembled knot of adults, on the deck.

"Oooh, nasty," said a child. "Look at the boogers coming out of their noses."

"He almost ruined my party!" shrieked Germaine. "He said at school that he was going to jump in the deep end although he can't swim."

"What happened?" asked Lennie, approaching with the ice bucket.

Charlie glared at him.

The lifeguard performed artificial respiration on the boy, and a doctor in the group did the same for the mother.

"Omigod! The father's outside waiting. They were just dropping the boy off!" Charlie said. "Lennie, go tell him what happened."

"What?" said Lennie uncomprehendingly.

"Charlie, I'll do it." Rose briefly touched her friend's arm; then she was gone to return quickly with a distraught man muttering rapidly in an unfamiliar language. Mrs. Padowski was given dry clothes and the couple accepted the invitation to stay with their son, who, once revived, refused to go anywhere but back into the water.

The lifeguard/party director organized dance competitions, competitive diving, water races, and Charlie's friends crowded onto the deck to root for their kids.

"Move it, Barry!"

"Yay, Monifa! Monifa! Monifaaa!" screamed Heather. She leaped up and down, red-faced as her little darling was cleaving her way to second place behind Anita's daughter, Tulani.

"Oops!" Heather exclaimed as she fortuitously kicked a ball into the water in front of the winning Tulani.

Charlie saw Anita clench her fists and purse her lips.

"Anita what's wrong?" said Heather as she trained her camcorder on Monifa, climbing beaming and victorious out of the pool.

"What you did wasn't nice," said Anita choking back tears.

"What're you talking about? You couldn't have seriously expected Tulani to beat Monifa. Monifa's taken swimming lessons since she was four. You didn't let Tulani learn to swim 'til she was eight."

Tears sprang to Anita's eyes as she bit back a reply.

God, those people were strange thought Charlie. Anita showed the truth of the new adage 'the meek shall inherit the earth; they'll get ground into it.' Charlie shook her head mentally and looked at her watch. The water-ballet troupe should soon be here. After they performed and tried to teach the kids a few of the routines the party would end-blessed relief!

Finally the last stragglers departed, replete with food and loaded party bags. Charlie thought longingly of snuggling up with Roderick. She'd tell him about the near drowning and Heather's cheating for her daughter. Had she, Charlie, been like this too, nasty and competitive with her own child? So much had happened recently that she hardly remembered who she was supposed to be, what she had wanted. The only thing she was absolutely sure she wanted right now was Roderick, with him she could forget children, the party and the stress of the last few hours. He had showed her that there was more to life than just work and winning. With him she had rediscovered happiness.

The phone rang. It was Maxi. "Charlie, you've got to come. Jordan's out of town on business and Tatty's taken a turn for the worse. She must've picked up something in this damn Intensive Care Unit. I need you. I'm going crazy." Maxi sobbed into the phone.

"Hang on, I'm coming."

"Wait, Charlie."

"Yeah?"

"Bring two candles; one yellow, one orange."

"Yes, Mambo."

Charlie hung up, packed an overnight bag with her laptop, the candles and a few changes of clothes; then went in search of Lennie. She updated him on Tatiana's condition.

"You go ahead, I'll hold the fort," he reassured her.

She thanked him and went to Germaine's room.

Moonlight flooded the bedroom as once more Charlie watched her healthy child sleeping and felt blessed. She tiptoed over to the bed, past the clothes and CDs on the floor. Some kids had brought gifts, and these were spilling out of gift bags and boxes. The careless debris of early adolescence was even on the bed. In the midst of the mess Germaine slept – a beloved pig in her unique sty.

Charlie stood quietly and looked at her daughter. Tears ran down her face and she said a prayer of thanks for her own healthy daughter. Suppose it had been Germaine, instead of Tatiana, in the ICU? Poor Maxi, what if Tatiana died? Charlie bent and kissed Germaine, the child stirred in her sleep; then Charlie tiptoed out of the room and softly closed the door behind her. Her heart ached for her friend.

31

Jack and Jill

"Charlie, Sydney won the Hawaiian Open, Chess championship," Rose whispered. Her face was wreathed in smiles as she slipped into the empty seat next to Charlie at the_Jack and Jill meeting.

Charlie whispered back, "I heard, congratulations. Give her a hug for me."

"How's Tatiana doing?"

"So much better, when I stopped by last night she was almost looking like her old self again. They came out of the hospital this weekend. It was hairy there for a while! Poor Maxi was a basket case. Tatty's temperature kept spiking, she slipped in and out of consciousness-

"Yes, I heard," said Rose.

"Shh," hissed the woman next to her.

"Tatty's recuperating at home now, but it'll take awhile," Charlie finished.

"Will you stop it?" Another woman turned around and said.

Charlie and Rose smiled at each other and started to pay attention to Matefi.

"...Some people still have not paid for their tickets to the Fellowship brunch at Our Savior's Baptist church. Their names will be read out at the next..."

"It's the same old same old," said Rose. "I'm going to the hospitality table. Shall I bring you something?"

"Yeah, some grapes if they have them, and a piece of cheese," Charlie said looking at her watch.

Matefi droned on with club business and Charlie doodled on the back of the minutes of the last meeting. She found the random shape she had made reminiscent of a penis-Roderick's penis. She furtively glanced at her neighbor on her right, to see if she'd noticed. Thank God, she was paying attention to the meeting.

"Anything interesting yet?" asked Rose. She returned munching on a celery stick. She handed Charlie a plate of fruit and cheese."

"Thanks, nothing yet; they're still giving group reports. The junior teen group went to Playland Amusement Park and enjoyed it. They recommend that-"

"Shh!" hissed the woman in front again. She turned and glared at them. "Go outside if you must talk."

"Sorry," Charlie and Rose said in unison.

"...and if you don't bring in all your ticket money by December fifteenth I'll have to read your name out from the floor as being unfinancial."

"Doesn't this make you sick?" Charlie said to Rose. "Every year it's the same stupidness. These people have no class."

"Uh huh, and no money," agreed her friend. "But it's going to be good tonight. I came to this meeting for the entertainment. They're warming up, listen to them."

A hostile babble of voices was erupting from the floor.

"Is she crazy?"

"Read out my damn name. See if I care. My family goin' have Christmas. Where the hell she thinks people goin' get six hundred dollars from for tickets in December?"

"You know, people should not get into organizations they cannot afford."

"I don't believe she said that," gasped Charlie in delight. The remark had been made coolly, but got a hot reception.

"Who is the fool that said that? I just know I didn't hear right," a large, dark complected, woman thundered, leaping up and belligerently regarding her fellow club members through round, wire framed eyeglasses.

"Ladies, please! We'll be here all night," begged their president. "LaToya-Marie, please sit. If anyone has anything to say, kindly raise your hand; when I recognize you briefly address your remarks to the floor, and then sit. But let's not spend a whole lot of time on this topic because we have too many other things to discuss tonight."

A horrible clamor arose as women practically leaped out of their seats, waving their hands in the air in their fervor to be recognized.

"I think we must take the economic climate into consideration. That is just too high a price to ask for tickets that are mandatory for members to sell."

"... this was supposed to be an elitist organization. We have to keep a certain tone so that ticket price is reasonable. My husband and I just attended a banquet where we paid a thousand dollars a couple for tickets."

"Madge never learns does she?" Rose whispered to Charlie in delight. The two women grinned at each other and settled in for the fireworks.

LaToya-Marie was on her feet again in an instant. She stabbed the air with her fat, dark finger and testified as she snaked her ample neck about like a swollen boa constrictor preparing to strike. "Now you listen to me-"

"This is hot!" exclaimed Charlie. "Get down, child!"

Women murmured their approval of the theatrics and a general air of expectancy spread throughout the room.

"Ladies, ladies!" implored Matefi in despair.

"The days are gone," continued LaToya-Marie moving her neck with the agility of a Balinese dancer, "when yellow people with house nigger mentality like you, can dominate a black organization."

"But who's she calling 'a house nigger'? Rough dark skin sure makes many of us envious. Umm uummm uummmh!" said a voice from the floor.

LaToya-Marie didn't respond. Big and bumptious, she plunged on and mimicked Madge. 'We paid a thousand dollars for tickets.' Well, bully to you and your thousand dollars. But some of us just can't afford to pay for *four* hundred and fifty dollar tickets at the same time-and don't have friends we can sell hundred and fifty dollar tickets to just before Christmas either!" LaToya-Marie breathed rapidly, opening and closing her mouth in an alarming fashion reminiscent of a guppy. She accompanied this by whirling her finger in a circular motion and ended pointing directly at Madge.

"LaToya-Marie!" roared Matefi. "You're completely out of line. Sit! I'll expect a letter of apology for this-to both Madge and myself!"

But Madge needed no defenders. She rose red-faced and firmly retorted to LaToya-Marie, "Well, you shouldn't be in the organization then. We are white phenotypes. We are paradigms of the best that black society has to offer-financially and intellectually; plenipotentiaries of-"

A roar drowned out the rest of her words.

"Save me! The girl has brass balls, " said Charlie, now seduced from all doodling and lubricious thoughts of Roderick.

"But she's suicidal," chuckled Rose. "Hey, that's Lola over there. So she's in now. She's nice. I hear Rebbie's made the poor woman into her personal Step'n Fetchit."

"Typical Rebbie, why does Lola let her? She's moved to Angloville, Lennie saw her recently. I haven't had the chance to invite them over yet. Since I returned from the Bahamas, things have been crazy-what with poor Maxi's problems and my expansion plans-Hey! What's with LaToya-Marie? Looks like she's trying to pass a kidney stone."

LaToya-Marie's friends were trying to subdue her. They vainly endeavored to push her bulk back down to the chair. Heather stood on tiptoes and dabbed perspiration from LaToya-Marie's fat face. She barked at Anita to massage her friend's heaving shoulders as LaToya-Marie grunted, sweated and signified. She roughly slapped away Anita's bony hand and testified.

"You feel you're all that because your skin is lighter than a paper bag and your blasted hair can blow in the wind without you using a straightener. Well this isn't Washington and a Paperbag and Blow club for people like you; this is Jack and Jill in Westchester, New York, in the twenty-first century! And let me tell you something else, bitch-" The accusing finger wagged at its enemy.

"None of that language!" screamed Matefi. "Apologize!"

" Dealing with black people's money's a serious thing," someone observed.

"... people like you ain't worth shit!" continued LaToya-Marie, "walking 'bout the place so seditty like Miss Priss-"

"LaToya-Marie, that's enough!" thundered Matefi. "I mean it this time. One more word from you and you're out. I'll personally see to it. If I have to crawl to National Headquarters on my knees over cut glass, I'll have you out! I've never seen this type of behavior in this organization before; never!"

LaToya-Marie subsided into her chair like a huge punctured Thanksgiving Parade blimp. She panted and glowered at Madge.

The room audibly registered disappointment at this speedy defusing of that night's highlight. Things moved along quickly until Matefi broached a new proposal.

"... Our executive committee met with their executive committee and the new organization, Ladies of Character was formed. This group is a blend of women from The Links, Jack and Jill and the Junior League. The focus of this group will be to foster racial harmony between us all, and to help us interact amiably so that understanding and friendships across racial lines can be possible for our children-and us too.

A hostile buzz, like the approach of killer bees arose in the room.

"You won't catch me befriending no white bitch."

"Their little heifers just want to get their hands on our black boys. I'll bet they're all putting their mothers up to join. I'll rot in hell before I turn some hot STD infested white girl loose on my black prince."

"Oh God! Don't say that!"

"Girl, when I marched in the sixties a white piece o' shit as old as dirt looked me in the eye and got ready to spit on me."

"So what, some people got killed! I'd spit on you too," declared a West Indian accented voice.

"Damn it!" An American arose and looked around with flaring nostrils.

"Well, child," continued the original narrator. "I told him m' name wasn't Gandhi and m' name wasn't Martin, it was Becky-Sue Haynes. And if he spat on me he'd better be prepared to die for it. And I pulled m' switchblade from m' little pocket-cause I wasn't stupid like those other peace marchers-and I said, 'Come boy, lemme slice you from ass-hole to appetite, then plunge this thing into yuh ol' leprous heart'. And you expect me to be friends with his daughters? Shoot!"

"God! You Americans carry so much racial baggage."

"What's that? What's that?" said Vera, a small pale woman.

"I said you Americans carry too much racial hatred. Why can't you relax and enjoy people as people? Where I come from in St. Vincent we're all friends with each other."

"Then why the hell don't you go back there?" shouted someone.

"Look at me, I'm a hybrid," the Vincentian continued. "I can't deny the yellow in my skin from my white ancestors anymore than I can ignore the kink in my hair from my black ones-and neither can you!"

"Oh shit! Whiteness done made the girl mad," roared Heather. She catapulted her yellow bulk out of the protesting chair to get a better view of the ill speaker.

"Listen, honey chil', here in these United States of America, a nigger is a nigger. That MD degree you hefting around don't make your shit sweeter than mine to the white man. You're still a black, nigger here. So haul your narrow ass."

"I'm not really black," caroled a mocking singsong voice. "My grandfather is part French, and my great uncle is white, and m' grandmother's sister's cousin is part Chinese!"

"Fiona, you're too much!" laughed the speaker's friend.

A deep American voice rumbled, "I told my little Betty-you know my baby in the six to eight, age group-'Honey there are three types of people you can't marry. One: a convict, two: a drug addict, and three: a white man. Marry one of them and I'll beat you into bad health."

"Jesus, these West Indians make me sick!" said someone else. "Why the hell they didn't stay in the islands and continue spawning with the white people, I don't know."

Charlie thanked her lucky stars that Maxi had not made it to this meeting. This was not a night for bi-racials to be out. Why do we hate each other so much, she mused? And why the hell am I here? I don't like these women. They're vicious! I could be home with my child, I could be in my office working, or ... she smiled and let her mind drift to remembered scenes with Roderick. She concentrated on flexing her vaginal muscles in a Kegels contraction. A girl could never exercise too much; one-two-three, hold-two-three. Where was Roderick now? What was he doing ... She'd stay in shape.

Rose excitedly jabbed her in the side with her elbow. "Charlie, pay attention; it's heating up again!

"To hell with all-you!" sang out a West Indian accented voice. "You Americans are always claiming that you're mixed with American Indian and you have old white ancestry from the South. That bullshit doesn't impress West Indians. We had a real educated, black, middle class before you jokers. Not a whole set of Pullman porters bowing and scraping to white people, but doctors, lawyers-"

"God damn it! You come to people's country and talk to them so!" Heather sprang up again, light glinting off the gold threads in her beige cashmere sweater set.

Anita, by her side, blubbered, "Why can't we all love each other? We're all black!" Honk, honk! She blew her nose stentoriously and dabbed at her streaming eyes with the mucous laden tissues.

"Isn't this a bitch? She's enjoying this as much as anyone else," said Rose.

Charlie whispered, "Her Dad's a preacher, so she has to put up a good front."

"Hypocrite!" hissed Rose.

"... and yes I'm a West Indian with an attitude! What cha gon' do 'bout it!" The speaker stood arms akimbo, eyes flashing, and feet firmly planted on the ground. She looked defiantly at the room and seemed capable of flaring off-springing up in the air and flinging up her skirts, if the altercation got hot enough.

"Oh, sit! The meeting will come to order," said Matefi, but her voice lacked conviction. "The meeting is adjourned." She gathered up her pocketbook, whispered to her vice-president and walked out the door.

"Ladies, let's be nice," said Mona the vice president. "Matefi has to take care of some business, but we can all stay a while longer and socialize. Refreshments are available at the back of the room. The ladies on the hospitality committee have gone to a great deal of trouble for us, so let's enjoy."

A full moon shone through the open window onto the elegant, waiting repast, as once more, Charlie wondered why she was there. She gathered up her pocketbook and left behind Matefi.

32

Hotel Hijinks

"Fine, I'll transfer you to my secretary and we'll set up a meeting for next week." Charlie looked at her watch and punched line two. "Yes, the conch must be here before six tomorrow morning," she barked. There was never enough time. As she punched another button her secretary's voice announced over the intercom,"Nassau, Bahamas on line four."

"Thanks, Kathy, I'll take it. Hold all other calls." Charlie swung her chair around from the computer screen and spreadsheets and smiled. She tilted back her chair, put her feet up on the desk and said softly, "Hi, Sweetheart what's up?"

"You know what's up when I think of you," said Roderick's voice. "There's been a change of plan. I'm coming today. How does this afternoon, 3 p.m. at JFK sound? I'm arriving on Bahamas Air."

"It's possible," she said with a smile.

"If there's a problem I can take a cab and see you-"

"You idiot! Of course I'll be there." She burst into a laugh. "Roddy, this is so wonderful! How come?"

"The Swiss businessmen I was to meet with next week will be in New York this week talking with their people who handle this hemisphere. They want me in on the meeting. This thing could get really big because they're anxious to get into the Bahamas. They want to finance me. I guess I'll be their Bahamian front man. I'm willing to talk."

"Roddy, be careful. I'd hate you to become a black puppet for some white money men who'll use you to rip off your country."

"As I said, we have to talk."

"Fine, fine, just be careful. Where will you be staying?"

"Midtown, at the Hilton; is that close enough for you?"

"Perfect. See you later."

"Hey, don't run away. I've got more news. The guy handling your restaurant application in the ministry's an old school mate of mine, so it's a shoo-in; anything for my woman."

"Your woman, hmmm, I like the sound of that. Are you my man?"

"I'll show you later."

If ever any beauty I did see,

Which I desired, and got, 'twas but a dream of thee

So pick me up later, I want to be with the original. Love ya."

"Love ya."

Charlie concentrated with difficulty after this. There was more work than ever. Potential expansion plans were under way. She was providing emotional support for Maxi and helping Germaine make a successful transition to her new neighborhood where she stood out like a blackbird among a flock of white pigeons. But all this was no longer enough; she'd seen the other side of the mountain. What she needed was an adult to share her life with. She needed Roderick. He was fun and sweet and playful; she deserved him. She wondered what had caused his divorce.

"God, woman; I don't remember you being this beautiful!" Roderick exclaimed later, as he enfolded her in a huge bear hug.

"Will you stop it? Flattery will get you everywhere." She laughed and enthusiastically returned the hug.

"Great!" He hugged her again and this time he patted her bottom.

She laughed and pushed him away. "Get off me. This is New York. Here, I'm a proper married lady." They regarded each other with ill-concealed lust and laughed.

Charlie expertly maneuvered her way through Manhattan's slow, rush hour traffic. An hour and a half later despite homicidal cab drivers, killer buses and suicidal pedestrians they arrived at the midtown Hilton.

"Charlie, I don't know how you did that, but I need a drink. That traffic was unreal." They surrendered the car to valet parking and Roderick's luggage to a bellhop. Roderick checked in quickly and Charlie used the 'phone then they followed the bellhop to the elevator. "Want to go to the bar for a drink before we go upstairs?"

"You're kidding, right?" Charlie looked at him with undisguised lust in her eyes.

He laughed and threw his arm around her shoulder. "Right," he pulled her close. "Any chance of your husband having spies planted here?" he whispered into her hair.

Charlie considered the very real possibility of meeting Lennie himself, there on his own tryst. "No," she said, and her face momentarily clouded over. They rode the elevator to Roderick's room in silence.

The bellhop opened the door to a room from which issued haunting, unfamiliar music. "We must have the wrong room," Roderick said, entering nevertheless. "What's going on?" he asked at the sight of a beautiful, East Indian woman sitting on a little carved stool playing a sitar. She looked at him, smiled and continued playing.

Charlie whispered in his ear, "Just setting the mood; I've boned up on the Kama Sutra as well as your Anandalahari."

He pinched her bottom covertly, and started a preparatory fire inside of her as he pulled a bill from his pocket and gave it to the waiting bellhop. There was a knock on the door. "Charlie, does anyone know you're here? Will I meet a man in a gorilla suit singing welcome, or maybe an irate husband or two?"

Charlie showed her dimples. "Just answer the door, my rajah."

"Did I win a game show?" Roderick asked as a room service waiter wheeled in an elegant meal. "This looks like King for a Day, or some such thing."

"You're my Rajah. Let's eat."

The waiter served the lovers unobtrusively then left. They constantly touched hands, gazed into each other's eyes; and played with their food. Finally the food was cleared away, the sitar player departed with her instrument and a generous tip from Roderick and they leapt on each other like beasts.

Charlie finally broke away and panted, "Let's take a bath together."

"Whatever you say, ma'am; is there a eunuch in the bathroom drawing the water?"

"Dang! It was on my to-do list but I forgot to hire one. We'll have to do without this time, come." She stood on tiptoe, pecked him on the nose then led him into the mirrored bathroom where they splashed in warm scented water, talked and drank champagne. Charlie wondered if this type of idyllic relationship ever survived marriage. "Dry you?" she offered when they were finished. He readily accepted.

"We're on my territory now, so into the bedroom and let's do things my way."

"Yes ma'am. But I must first stipulate that I don't hang from chandeliers, perform acts involving household pets or livestock and although I heartily endorse both the Anandalahari and the Kama Sutra I lack the suppleness to perform at that level."

"You'll do what I say!" She laughed and swatted his naked bottom with the damp bath towel. "What a beautiful ass! I can't wait to get at it."

"Not as nice as yours," he said, catching her in his arms and grinding his body into hers as he kneaded her muscular butt. They pressed their bare bodies together, for a kiss, which rapidly grew in passion.

"Stop," Charlie said huskily, breaking away. "Go into the bedroom and lie on the bed before it's too late and you ruin my plans."

He looked at her quizzically. "This is getting curiouser and curiouser. What am I letting myself in for?"

"Please," she coaxed. He humored her and Charlie soon stood in the doorway, drinking in the glorious sight of the man she yearned for, waiting-stretched out on a bed, with a stupendous erection-just for her.

"Now close your eyes, lie on your stomach and don't talk." Charlie turned on a jazz station and gently massaged subtly scented oil into Roderick's toes. He groaned appreciatively. She straddled him and slowly moved upward spreading the oil all over his body. She repeated the process when he rolled over. Finally she blew on the oil on his thighs. It grew pleasantly warm and tingly, then hot. She kept up the blowing all the way to his genitals, spreading heat in her path.

Roderick groaned appreciatively. "What is that?" he asked.

"Yankee ingenuity. You like?" she said mischievously. "I have science helping nature along since I don't have words and time to read the Oriental erotica like you. Fooled you with that Kama Sutra stuff didn't I."

"Any way you want it," he said huskily.

She dropped her head down to his toes and slowly licked, and nipped her way upwards. She took his testicles into her mouth and hummed in a deep tone, creating sonic vibrations that soon had him shouting and jolting on the bed. Then she applied a vibrator to his testicles. "Technology to the rescue!" she exclaimed. He howled, and then was off speaking in tongues again. Before he could come she jumped on him and rode him to a roaring climax.

Afterward she nuzzled up against him. She lazily scratched concentric circles around his navel with her freshly manicured, red nails and enjoyed the rough texture of his pubic hair. "Roderick, you've got to leave some of that jungle stuff back in the islands. We don't carry on that way in this part of the world.

He caught her hand and held it. "Please. We should have met fifteen years ago. Now the spirit is willing but the flesh is weak. I must rest," he begged.

"You don't love me," she said in a hurt voice that belied the amusement in her eyes.

"You witch! That will be it for the rest of my short life if you won't let me rest."

They kissed with sleepy affection, and he held her close 'til both sank into exhausted sleep.

33

One Summer's Afternoon

"I don't know what I would've done without you, Charlie," Maxi said, looking gratefully at her friend as they sat on Maxi's sunny patio on a glorious October, Indian summer afternoon.

"I don't know what I would've done without you over the years. It's my turn to be useful now."

"Oh, Charlie, "Maxi squeezed her friend's hand on the table.

"What would poor Germaine have done if she didn't have Auntie Maxi to fill the gaps while Mommy was out there busting her butt to keep caviar on the table, and Daddy was 'otherwise engaged', shall we say?"

"Charlie, you're one in a million." Maxi said with a laugh. "Thanks, anyway. It's a good thing we're out of that hospital room. You single handedly filled it with fruit, stuffed animals, balloons... What were you thinking of? I was living in a horn of plenty."

"Oh, Maxi, come off it. Are we exaggerating just a wee bit? Anyway, Tatty deserves the best-she needed distracting."

"She certainly got it. We never knew what to expect. Where did you find that accordion player? She and all the other kids on the ward absolutely loved his music. You're incredible."

"It's the least I can do. Remember, she's my god-child. I don't get the chance to spend much time with her, so thank God I can give her stuff she enjoys."

"Speaking of enjoyment, what's happening with Sydney lately? That's one kid who never gets any down time. Is she chess champion of the world yet?"

"Not yet, but I hear the kid loves what she does and really does want to spend most of her free time competing in chess tournaments," said Charlie.

"Good for her," said Maxi. "Have you seen Rose lately?"

"Yes, last week at the Jack and Jill meeting, we sat together. Has she been up to visit since you got out of the hospital?"

Maxi laughed, "You've got to be kidding. She's not going to visit. When she discovered the state of Tatiana's health she went into hiding so that if I was looking around for a friend I couldn't mistake her for one and maybe ask for help."

Charlie looked sympathetically at her friend then they both looked across the patio at their daughters playing Scrabble, Tatiana in her wheelchair. "Tatty's going to regain her health one hundred percent," continued Charlie. "I know she will: she's a fighter."

"That she is," agreed her mother. "By the way, has Rose had sex with her house yet? I hear she's doing something to it again."

"Not yet," said Charlie, with a laugh. "Last I heard she was starting to get intimate with new living room furniture."

"Figures," said Maxi. "Poor Grantley's a saint to put up with her obsession."

"I know; he's such a nice man. Sometimes I feel sorry for him. I wonder why he puts up with her mad passion for their house, it's never finished. She's always doing something else to it."

"He must love her or he would've walked long ago. Speaking of which, Charlie; how's your love-life these days, or should I not ask?"

Charlie took a sip of her lemonade then said softly, "Great, since Roderick's here."

Maxi studied her friend. "Charlie, hold that thought. I must prop up that sunflower. It's going to fall and smash its face any minute now.

"Go ahead. I'll watch."

Maxi fetched garden supplies from the nearby tool shed and set to work.

Charlie talked as Maxi propped the flower. "I feel this need to make a stand, but I don't know how. Sneaking around in hotel rooms cheapens what we feel for each other. I don't want to be like Lennie."

"Then don't be." Maxi squinted critically at her handiwork. "This relationship is how old and your marriage is how old?"

"Ahh, Professor Paine, but love is not quantifiable by time lapses with higher numbers equaling greater happiness and are we forgetting your famous cunt-connection theory or hypothesis? Well, I'm still connected and I'll have him, whatever way I can get him. But that doesn't stop me from disliking the present way.

"Ah, that good old cunt connection," sighed her friend slipping off her gardening gloves and setting aside her tools. "Is he upset with the present arrangement too? Remember what I told you in the Bahamas, Charlie? Enjoy him, but don't hurt that innocent child. Look at her. Can you really deprive her of her father? And how will you tell her about your lover?" She looked at her friend, then pointedly again at their daughters.

Charlie too looked across the patio at their twelve and thirteen year-olds. The girls, dressed in camp shirts and shorts, sat at a black wrought iron table, playing Scrabble. Germaine's brow was furrowed in concentration. She looked just like Lennie.

"That's not a word! Gimme that dictionary!" Tatiana demanded. This was followed by giggling and a playful scramble for the dictionary.

"She's so vulnerable," continued Maxi.

"Tatty's improving," Charlie commented. "She's got energy and her speech is better."

"Yes, thank God they got to her in time. Her short-term memory's still pretty shaky, but all in all she's doing so much better. Scrabble's good for her."

"Will she return to school later in the year?"

"We're playing it by ear, but I'm hoping she can. She gets hopelessly bored sitting around here all day. The homebound teachers only come a few hours a week. She misses interaction with the other kids. "

"Poor Tatty, she'll get better. She's come a long way from where she was in the hospital. By the way, thanks for telling me about the Emotion Lotion. The results were beyond my wildest dreams."

"You liked it? I bought mine at a Sweet Sensations party, sort of like a Tupperware party; they unofficially call it Fuckerware. A bunch of women sit around examining sex merchandise samples then order what they want. Our hostess had a smorgasbord of delights. The lotion was the sanest thing."

"I'm glad you got it. Order some for me next time."

"I will. It was a gas to feel this thing actually turn hot as we blew on it. We were rubbing it on our hands and blowing on it like kids-hysterical!"

"I want to attend one of those parties."

"Sure, maybe I'll host one. Madge did the last party; she said she invited you. If you're in a hurry we can go to a sex shop and browse."

"At our age, I don't think so! You have a party and invite me."

"Fine, Charlie." Maxi smiled at her friend. "You're like a child with a new toy. Good thing you didn't discover sex while you were in college, you'd have flunked out."

Charlie laughed, "Roddy's professor friend was right. Sex is so much fun when you plan it; the anticipation, a set agenda-"

"Hold on, Madam Tycoon, you're not planning a hostile take-over. You can't cover every eventuality. Heaven help us if the poor devil is tired, or thoughts of your beloved husband stop him from getting it up. What then?"

"We'll cross that bridge when we come to it. We've got the rest of our lives." Charlie leaned back in the chair, stretched out her legs and smiled contentedly.

"Right, try some of this stuff on Lennie; you might like what you get."

Charlie's smile vanished and she bolted upright in the chair. "Maxi, don't you understand that I don't want to sleep with Lennie. I'm not a whore! I have strong feelings for Roderick. I'm talking relationship with sexual exclusivity. This is not an interlude."

"Neither is your marriage."

"It was for Lennie. Anyway I'm tired of always toeing the line and doing what people expect of me, and for what? Who are people anyway? That pack of losers I had at my party? The carrion crows in Jack and Jill who won't even wait for a corpse to start their feeding frenzy?"

"Charlie, what you're saying may all be valid, but you owe it to your child to try to make your marriage work."

"Well, she'll have to take an IOU on that one. Lennie doesn't know how to relate. He doesn't talk to me unless he wants something; but get him in a social or work situation, and you can't shut him up. He doesn't know how to make love. It was all a big macho thing with him of frequency-you know, fast, often, and to hell with how I felt. He didn't care how I felt. I never knew what good sex was 'til Roderick. I never knew about love, or what it was to relate, really relate, to a man. We're friends as well as lovers-great lovers. You want me to give this up? You've got to be crazy."

"Charlie, maybe a good therapist can still turn it around for you. Look at what it did for Felicity and George."

"Apples and oranges, I don't respect Lennie anymore. He doesn't have the ambition or the balls to study for his boards, pass them and get a decent job and his own private practice. He's embarrassing! So he fucks around to prove his manhood. I've had it, putting up with his shit just to provide a father for Germaine. I have needs too. I want a man I can respect and love-and not have to protect myself from every time we have sex because I worry about where he's been and whether he's bringing AIDS back with him this time."

"Charlie, I'm so sorry." Maxi touched her friend and glanced anxiously in the girls' direction.

"Okay, no more Lennie talk. Now help me plan this dinner party for Roderick. It's got to be the last word in elegance. We need a dynamite menu, wonderful décor, you know-the works. You're better than any party planning service."

"Boy! Between you and Jack and Jill I sure do get a creativity workout. Of course I'll do it for you. I missed planning Germaine's end-of-the-school-year party."

"I'll invite Lola and Leroy. They just moved to Angloville. They bought a terrific place down the street, a former embassy. One of those little European principalities that's always fighting ran out of money; so they shut up shop, didn't care who they sold to, and Leroy snapped it up. Another black family got into Angloville."

"Good for him! I guess that *you don't have to live next door to me/ just give me my equality* stuff doesn't hold water anymore. They've got to live next door to you now. You're right up in their faces in that former bastion of whiteness."

"Yup, we can live where we want to. It's no different here in Chappaqua."

"True, but at least we're not the very first to colonize the neighborhood. Marguerite's been here for ever."

"How are she and Homer doing? I hear she's drinking more. Rose says she was soused at a recent fundraiser and had to be taken home."

"Poor Maggie, she's not cut out to be a politician's wife. The spotlight's killing her," replied Maxi.

"Poor thing, I guess she overdosed on politics. Her father was a politician too."

"Ah well... By the way, how was last week's Jack and Jill meeting?"

"As usual; everyone hating everyone else and fighting to the death. What do you expect? Bunch of turkeys! but they sure were entertaining."

"Sounds familiar."

"Maxi, did you hear a car?"

"Yes, I'm not expecting company. Delores will get the door."

A few moments later a mother and daughter duo sailed onto the patio wearing matching Laura Ashley summer frocks and flower bedecked sun hats.

"Monica, what a pleasant surprise-and Caitlin too!" said Maxi hugging them,

"We were so worried when we heard about poor Tatiana. We had to stop by and see how she's doing." said Monica.

"I'm glad you came. You're both so pretty and summery looking. Caitlin, how you've grown!"

Monica tossed her dark hair behind her back, and Caitlin her blonde one as they gave the same smile and stood in flattering poses.

"Yes, hasn't she," said Charlie. "You're all legs Caitlin. Monica what have you been feeding this child? I want some for my little shrimp."

Monica beamed and brushed cheeks with Charlie then turned to Maxi. "We brought Tatty something. Dear, we have something for you," she called out to Tatiana.

"Hi, Tatty, hi, Germaine." said Caitlin approaching the girls with her mother.

"Hi, Caitlin, hi Mrs. Bruce," responded the girls in unison.

Caitlin handed Tatiana a large, prettily bowed, gold box of Godiva chocolates and Monica air-kissed both girls.

"Ooh, Tatty," said Caitlin, "you've got split ends."

"Yeah, sure," Germaine hissed at the girl. "What's split is your stupid eyes seeing things that aren't there. Tatty, don't mind her, your hair's fine."

"Well, she does," Caitlin said stubbornly. "Tatty, I'll call you when I get home and give you the name of a great product I use on my own hair. It's specifically for black hair and it works. You try it and maybe your hair can get like mine, see how long and strong it is?" She shook her head and agitated her heavy, well-trimmed, naturally blonde hair, relaxed to mainstream American perfection.

"That's disgusting, flying your dandruff all over the place," said Germaine.

"Ladies," interrupted Monica. "Be nice. Germaine, don't be so hostile; dear, people won't like you. Caitlin, honey; why don't you take on the winner of the Scrabble game? She has a tremendous vocabulary," Monica assured Maxi and Charlie returning to their end of the patio.

"I'm sure," murmured Maxi, looking sharply at Charlie, who surprisingly was holding her peace. "It's sweet of you to come by and visit."

"We've been house hunting in the area. Today we drove around to get a feel for the neighborhood then decided to kill two birds with one stone and stop by to see how Tatiana's doing. She looks good. How long will she be in the wheelchair?"

"We don't know. It 's lovely of you to stop by, it's been such a painful, stressful, lonely time for her," said Maxi; "We don't get many visitors."

"That's a shame, it happens when you live off the beaten track. You guys are in real country up here," responded Monica.

Maxi laughed. "To a Riverdalian I guess we're 'real country,'" she said.

"Ma'am, are these ladies joining you for tea?" asked the maid coming onto the patio.

"Of course, see if the children want fruit juice or decaffeinated iced tea."

"Yes, Ma'am."

"You're house hunting?" queried Charlie as she looked at her watch. "What's wrong with your place? I heard you just finished redecorating."

"There's nothing wrong, of course. It's lovely, as you know. But Caitlin has become horse crazy so we decided to get a bigger place so she can have her own horse and stable it at home. For that amount of land you need to be upstate."

"True," responded Charlie; "someplace like Pound Ridge or Bedford with the literati and glitterati, I guess."

"Naturally, but there will be trade offs. We'll miss the multi-ethnicity of Riverdale and its proximity to the city. Caitlin, however, is willing to forgo that. Right now she's so in love with horses that she'll gladly switch."

"For a horse she doesn't even have yet!" Charlie shook her head.

"Yes, for a horse," said Monica firmly. "Haven't you heard that girls who love horses have later sexual maturation? Apparently it's a sort of immunization against sexual precocity."

"I'll bet," said Charlie with a grin. "All that rubbing up of the clitoris against a saddle and bouncing it on the leather must keep those girls in a constant state of sexual excitation. They're too drained to even think about dealing with boys."

"Mommy, will you please tell these girls that 'polyglot' is really a word?" came a shrill command from the girls' corner.

"Of course it is, darling. I'm coming," sang Monica gracefully rising.

"Your Mom isn't a dictionary," Germaine glowered at Caitlin and said. "If it's not in this talking dictionary, we're not accepting it."

"Oh!" said Monica in surprise. "Are all three of you playing? I thought the winner was going to challenge Caitlin."

The girls remained silent as Germaine checked the dictionary.

"Mommy," said Caitlin, "They didn't know words like 'xu' or 'qanat', and just because they're not in this stupid, useless dictionary they won't let me have them." She thumped the offending dictionary. "Of course they don't even have the Official Scrabble Players Dictionary. The third edition is the most recent," she said to the girls with a sniff.

"Well, darling, you have to realize that not everyone is as erudite as you, nor do they have your advantages. You must be patient, honey. Tatiana, love, don't you have a better dictionary than that?"

Tatiana looked obstinate and did not answer. Maxi quickly came over. She rested her hand lightly on Tatiana's shoulder and patted the child. "Really, Monica;" she said, "We're placing way too much emphasis on a children's game of Scrabble." She firmly grasped Monica by the arm and walked her toward the table where tea was now set out. "I do have an Oxford English Dictionary, somewhere. It's very thorough, and if they need it I'll fetch it. Let's have tea."

"You must understand that Caitlin plays tournament Scrabble and she uses the official Scrabble dictionary. She's had so much more exposure than your girls because she's at the UN school."

"Really?" said Charlie.

"Yes, apart from grueling academics, one of the many wonderful things about her school is its ethnic diversity. As a black family at a high-income level, we did not want to place her in a setting where she would be the only black child. At her school she's in an international community and living in Riverdale continues this experience for her."

"Go ahead, Miss Caitlin," said Charlie. "You people always were cutting edge."

Maxi looked at Charlie suspiciously but got only an innocent expression.

"Well, anyway," continued Monica, "Caitlin's friends are the children of diplomats and UN reps. Also we travel a lot with her, so she has become mature and sophisticated beyond her years. Apart from this, she's a natural brain with an incredible grasp of world affairs and human nature."

"I couldn't stand to live with a child who was smarter than I am," said Charlie.

"I don't think that's what she's saying," said Maxi containing her amusement. "She's just showing us how and why Caitlin is different from ordinary run of the mill kids."

"Exactly," agreed Monica. "She's mature enough that she can now be moved to a community like this and not be harmed by its lack of diversity. Maxi, this seed cake is superb.

"Thanks. Girls," called Maxi, "please come, serve yourselves."

Tatiana rolled over in her wheelchair followed by the two girls.

"Caity, darling, let's show the girls that picture of you with the horse you're going to get when we buy our house." Monica passed a picture to her daughter who showed it to the two girls.

"Which one is the horse?" asked Germaine with interest.

Suspicious snorting sounds issued from Charlie and Maxi who both quickly looked downwards-Maxi to examine her hands, Charlie to admire her own well-shod foot. Tatiana howled with laughter.

"Did you girls enter that national writing competition that Caitlin just won?" asked Monica sweetly.

"After I won that national writing competition, Daddy got me a new laptop with the works. Of course I have cable access to the Internet, digital camera, my own FAX line-I already have my own regular phone line. Do you guys use the Internet much up here?" said Caitlin, only too aware of the possibility of a hideous digital divide between herself and the assembled bumpkins.

Tatiana and Germaine rolled their eyes at each other and remained silent.

"I guess you're not too computer literate here in the boonies. When I move here, Tatty, we'll see each other more often and I'll show you my computer stuff. You know we're getting a huge place so that I can get that really cute Arabian horse and have him live with me in his own stable."

"Now, Caitlin, that's only if you promise to be a responsible owner and look after your horse by yourself," said her mother with fussy severity.

"Oh, Mommy, I will, I will!" she promised. She jumped up and down and her hair bounced gracefully on her slim shoulders."

"No, not again!" shouted Germaine.

"What?" asked Charlie.

"Her dandruff's in our food now!"

34

The Dinner Party

"This sherried grapefruit appetizer is quite wonderful, Charlie, " said Rose.

"Thank you," Charlie replied. She looked approvingly down the length of her table that seated both husband and lover. Flowers and Rigaud candles scented the air and Marsalis jazz standards played in the background. "Did anyone see the article on the educating of black children in the Sunday Times?"

"I think I did... Oh now I remember," said Grantley. "It was provocative. Rorie, your magazine should tackle this issue more."

"We will. What did the Times say?" asked Rorie. "I haven't read it yet."

"They touched on the creating of special schools for black boys, and the various teaching methods being tried in these schools," said Charlie.

"Bad situation," said Rorie, he shook his head gravely as he worked his grapefruit spoon into the fruit. "If you isolate them academically from the main system you're practicing segregation. Meanwhile they're dropping like flies out of a system which practices educational racism and disproportionately detains or suspends them."

Charlie felt smug. Roderick wasn't the only one with serious well-informed friends. Then her eyes fell on Grantley. He looked preoccupied. He wasn't involved in any of the conversations at the table, damn him. This party was no place for a wet blanket. She'd have to draw him out.

"Can't you provide support within the system that will enable them to reach the academic and societal behavioral norm," asked Roderick.

"They won't do the necessary extra work. They're not Asians!" said Maxi.

"Oh dear, this all sounds so complicated," said Lola in a worried voice.

"It won't affect you, Lola," said Charlie. "Your little boy will grow up in an affluent, white neighborhood with one of the best public school systems in America." She turned to Jordan; "If I had a son I wouldn't put him in a school exclusively for black males. They already have one in New York-it's called Rikers Island."

"Charlie!" said Maxi laughing.

"What's funny about the Rikers Island School," queried Roderick.

"It's not a school," giggled Maxi, "it's a jail."

"Come now, Charlie, that's not quite fair," said Jordan.

"But she's right," said Rorie. "Black men represent about six percent of the general population, nine point nine percent of the college graduate population, and forty seven percent of the prison population. So, to continue Charlie's point, they stay on that track into adulthood."

"Big deal, your figures just reflect the economic situation. You stay out of jail if you can afford good lawyers," stated Sophie; "where'd OJ be today without Johnny?"

"But it doesn't have to be this way," persisted Rorie. "It costs thirty thousand dollars a year to keep someone in jail. That money could be better spent, say ten thousand dollars per year, per child, for a mentoring program or additional school programs to help lessen the educational and digital divide and get them off the jail track and onto the academic track."

Roderick looked interested and Charlie patted herself on the back. She noticed Grantley off in his own world again. What was his problem she wondered with annoyance. He should join in the conversation at her end of the table-he had a son. She turned toward him and knocked her knife rack onto the floor. Damn! She ducked to pick it up. "What!"

"Charlie, are you all right?" asked Roderick.

"I almost lost my balance but I'm okay now." Beneath the tablecloth Sophie's long, pale gold leg had reached over to Grantley's lap. Her unshod foot was between his legs with toes firmly gripping and rhythmically squeezing his semi-erect penis. Charlie's snowy white serviette covered the head of the moving, black organ, fluttering gaily in a dance of concupiscence. Furiously Charlie retrieved the knife rack.

"I take it your magazine's doing an article on this topic," said Jordan.

"We are, that's why I'm up to snuff on the figures," said Rorie.

Maxi declared, "I'm sure you've also come across the fact that White teachers tend to label active black boys as hyperactive and aggressive, in other words pre-criminal-"

"So you just get in there and make sure your child gets a fair shake." interjected Rose. "And you keep them busy. That midnight basketball deal was an excellent idea. My son spends a great deal of time playing basketball. I know it keeps him out of trouble."

Rorie advised, "Keep it that way. They won't cut him any slack if he's ever accused of anything even slightly illegal. Black youths are six times more likely to be incarcerated than their white peers when neither has a prior record."

"Oh God! With the stats again!" said Sophie, his wife in disgust. "No one cares, lighten up; we're not your readers."

"Getting back to those figures, it's incredible that you put up with this," said Roderick.

"What can we do, immigrate?" asked Rorie. "Also, my brother, with all due respect to my dear wife, I have more numbers that'll wake you up. Black youth comprise fifteen percent of the population under fifteen, but make up one-third of youth referred to, formally processed by and convicted in juvenile court. How do you like them apples?"

"It must make you want to send your son to Africa or the Caribbean for safe-keeping," observed Roderick.

Charlie looked at Grantley. This was a good time for input from him. Her heart stopped he was breathing more rapidly and grinning. Dear God, he couldn't plan to come in her napkin!

"Our boys have a problem," said Maxi. "The failure rate of upper-middle-class black boys in the public schools is ridiculous. Take Jesse's son-he now wears a do-rag on his head, hangs out with the black boys from the Projects and his grades mirror theirs. He's all thugged out. The family's desperate, and the kid refuses to see a therapist."

"Typical story, when women had a problem they started their 'take our daughters to work day.' But we can't do that for our sons because white men rule this country and as Holmes-Norton pointed out 'Take our Sons to Work Day,' for Whites would be as necessary as a White History Month. So once more black boys get shafted," said Rorie.

'Grantley, how do you keep your son motivated?" asked Charlie.

Grantley ignored her and brow furrowed in concentration remained in his own libidinous world. Oh dear God this can't be happening, thought Charlie in consternation.

"Grantley!" said Rose sharply looking at her husband in amazement.

All eyes turned to Grantley who with an obviously supreme effort said, "What?"

The question was repeated and conversation resumed with Grantley back on task.

Maxi said, "My friend, Gail moved her family to Greenwich to give their son the benefit of a superlative school system. They live in the smallest house in the neighborhood, the kid has the poorest parents-never mind they're both professionals-and probably has the lowest IQ; he's not a particularly bright boy. He's now messed up on drugs, obviously has low self esteem and is failing out of school. "

"You've now scared me too. We didn't have problems like this when I was growing up; kids wanted to get ahead," said Leroy. He looked at Lola's worried face. "Don't you worry, Baby, we'll make it."

"Of course you will," said Grantley warmly; "I am."

Lola smiled at him weakly.

Charlie daintily dipped her fingertips into her crystal finger bowl with the floating rose petals. "Everyone finished?" She scanned the table then tinkled a little golden bell. Two butlers quickly replaced their first course with soup. She caught Roderick's eye and they smiled at each other. Roderick here at her table felt so right. He should be host to her hostess she thought wistfully. She checked on Grantley. He was sipping his soup with a smile and an expression of extreme concentration that boded ill for her serviette. "Grantley," she said.

"Huh!" He started and spilt his soup. Sophie sitting opposite him gave a little cry.

"What a set of nervous Nellies!" exclaimed Maxi, with a laugh. She looked at the foot of the table where Charlie sat, flanked by Grantley and Sophie. Sophie colored and Grantley busied himself with the napkin in his lap.

"I'll get you a fresh napkin." Charlie rang her bell.

"No, really it's all right," protested Grantley.

"Nonsense, I won't have you sit through dinner with a soggy lap," Charlie insisted. This was too good an opportunity to make him zip up. The serviette was duly replaced. "Grantley you have a son-" Charlie continued.

"Huh?" he said, again appearing distracted. Oh God, had he unzipped again Charlie wondered. She noticed Rose looking exasperatedly at him. Charlie persisted, "Buddy's been in the local public schools for at least eight years. How's it for him?"

"Good so far," he replied.

"That's because I stay on top of things. Sometimes I go to school with him and sit in the classroom," said Rose.

"You're joking!" said Leroy.

"No, I'm not. This is how I keep him on track. He pulls himself together real fast when I do this because you know he doesn't want me there." She laughed. "And I'm not the only mother who does this and it's not just black mothers."

"I'd say you're all overreacting," said Jordan.

Rose chatted on, oblivious to the little tableau being played out downwind from her. "Do you have a better suggestion? Smart black girls are a dime a dozen, but boys..."

"Seems as if you ladies think a smart black boy is an oxymoron," said Rorie.

"I definitely get that impression," said Roderick. "I hear the gene for intelligence is passed from mother to son and you upper-class, Black-American women here are all highly intelligent. I take it you're not anomalies, so what gives?"

"The system," said Maxi. "It seems to be rigged against black boys."

"It is. So I told Buddy that if his grades drop below a B+ it's off to military school for him. Meanwhile Sydney gets upset with anything below an A+. What's the matter Grantley?" Rose asked, concern in her voice.

Grantley was breathing as if having some kind of attack. All eyes turned to him.

"You okay, old man?" queried Lennie rising from the head of the table.

If he comes in my dinner napkin, Charlie vowed, I will burn down his house-and tell his wife. She thought she heard the sound of a foot hitting the floor and caught a smug, satisfied expression on Sophie's face. Charlie smiled despite herself; she had always admired nerve. She also had to get the table's focus off Grantley's plight. "Lennie, he's probably reacting to some pepper, aren't you Grantley?"

Grantley nodded gratefully and Lennie returned to discussing insider trading and the recent vicissitudes of the stock market with Jordan and Leroy. Charlie exhaled. Poor Jordan had recently lost a bundle in the market and needed a wailing wall. Lennie should go back to being it. "Drink some water," she urged Grantley, "You'll be all right," even as she thought, damn fool, playing with fire at her dinner table. The man probably had a vicious case of blue balls right now. Oh well, Rose would reap the benefits of this one... She gave Sophie a pointed look and Sophie coolly returned her gaze.

"Lola, I hope we're not scaring you, you're quiet tonight," said Charlie. "That's a lovely necklace you're wearing."

"Thank you," said Lola blushing as all eyes turned to her and focused on her décolletage where the necklace nestled.

Leroy said proudly, "She picked it up at a little antique shop in the Poconos recently. My wife has an eye for treasures."

"She does," said Lennie, looking approvingly at Lola's creamy, voluptuous chest.

"To get back to educating our kids, you're limited in the school system because you can never be part of the good ol' white girls' network," Maxi said.

"True," agreed Charlie. "But you can get involved through the PTA, I've done it. Of course there's a limit to how far you can go with that. They have voting blocs and hog most of the power in their secret meetings in each other's homes. Rose, last week I was in Loehmanns, and that skinny Goldberg woman – you know the one with the crazy child who was selling his psychotropic drugs to the other kids?"

"Oh, yeah, I know who you mean; that weird kid Zack," replied Rose.

"Yeah, well, she called out 'hi Rose' to me. Her friend, Rifka, corrected her and said I was Charlie. Do you know what the bitch said to that? 'I call all of them Rose.'"

"That's heavy," said Rorie.

"Charlie, have you joined the Angloville Junior league yet? I hear they're considered the best chapter," said Sophie.

"Why should I?" said Charlie. "I'll just make regular cash contributions."

"Hey, Charlie, you're paying protection money so that your daughter can go to their daughters' birthday parties," said Rorie with a chuckle.

"Whatever," said Charlie. "Lola, have you joined any local organizations yet?"

"I don't have that kind of nerve," said Lola.

"Hey, Charlie, maybe she can join the local DAR chapter – you know, The Daughters of the American Revolution," said Rorie.

"Not quite," laughed Charlie, "though I'm sure they have one. Lola, I can see that you're going to need someone to show you the ropes. Do you jog?"

"Yes," said Lola mystified.

"Well, so do I. I'll pick you up at six tomorrow morning and we'll jog on the high-school track. A lot of people are out there at that time so it's perfectly safe," said Charlie.

"Oh, Charlie, would you? I'll be ready," said Lola excitedly.

"Great, it's a date then," said Charlie.

"Charlie, are you on a committee for Jack and Jill's Fund Raiser? Maxi and I are working on decorations. Want to join us? You too Lola," invited Rose, "and guess what, Sophie's grandfathering in, she's coming in this month." She smiled at Sophie.

"This month!" exclaimed Maxi. "But we don't take in new people until spring. And Sophie," she turned to her, "you grew up in the Caribbean like I did, so you weren't in Jack and Jill as a child, how can you grandfather in?"

"Rorie was in Jack and Jill and I proved special need for Penelope. So we're in," retorted Sophie.

"Great! You can be on our committee," said Rose.

"I suppose," said Sophie unenthusiastically. "As I said, it's for Penelope. She has no black friends at her school. The black kids are all from the projects and are in the bottom academic groups; so of course she has no interaction with them. Rorie feels this is a problem. Whatever." She shrugged and took a sip of wine.

"I saw her at Bloomies recently," said Maxi. "She looks so grown-up these days."

"Thanks," said Sophie. "I'm not looking forward to coming into Jack and Jill and mixing with people I wouldn't be caught dead with if I had my druthers. We're doing enough social work in my family right now. Rorie has become a Big Brother to a fatherless, twelve year old kid from the Projects. Like I say, bring our daughter's potential rapist right on into the home, why don't you." She looked distinctly put out.

Charlie broke the uncomfortable silence which followed. "Roderick, we must refill your wine glass." She tinkled her bell and summoned the butlers to refill all the wine and water glasses then Rose spoke.

"Sophie, you've got a point about Jack and Jill. When the kids were young and we went to Lincoln Center to see The Nutcracker; the kids in velvet and Mommy in cashmere and mink-I wanted Junior League women around me, not some low class hurry-come-ups from J and J with no idea about appropriate behavior or dress. J and J has gone down over the years."

"That sounds horrible but unfortunately it's so true," agreed Maxi.

"You women are something else!" declared Rorie with a shake of his head.

"Let's take in a Broadway matinee, and then plan our decorating scheme over tea at the Palace, shall we? Last Sunday Grantley and I had tea there. They have a harpist who will make you swoon. She played some of Joabim's Brazilian love songs and I swear we fell in love all over again, didn't we, Honey?" said Rose. She reached for her husband's hand. He squeezed it and obligingly gazed into her eyes. Sophie smirked.

35

Joy to the World

"Race you to the end of the block!" Buddy yelled as he whizzed past Abie. "Wheeee! He laughed as the cold wind whipped his face and stung his eyes to tears.

"Hey, wait up," yelled Abie. "I dropped my yarmulke."

Buddy slowed. Abie circled back, swooped down on the yarmulke, and then flew past Buddy. "Eat dust, Butt-munch!" he yelled as he disappeared around a corner. Buddy dashed after him, and they wove alarmingly in and out of the traffic. Soon they were in unfamiliar territory where small, close together houses mixed in with two-family homes.

"Hey Buddy! That girl you've been sweating."

"Who?" said Buddy, grinning.

"You know, that girl. Wha's her face? Yeah, Jamie. She lives in this neighborhood. My Mom and I picked up my cousin Dorrie from her house last week."

"Where's her house? Boy! There must be a gazillion lights in this place."

Several houses were outlined in lights. The Virgin Mary and the Christ child vied for precedence over Santa and his reindeer. Snow White and the seven dwarves waved Merry Christmas from an animated display. Up and down the block illuminated winter wonderlands competed with each other.

"If my Dad had to pay this kind of light bill he'd blow his stack. Mom already does the laundry at night so she can get the lower, non-prime time rates." Abie commented.

"Really? I'm gonna start playing my video games late at night so we can get those good rates too," said Buddy.

"I can just see your Mom letting you."

This mention of Rose had a sobering effect on the boys who remained quiet for a while.

"Hey, Abie, you know the way back home?"

"Sure I do. Here's Jamie's house."

They approached a small, white, frame house enclosed by a picket fence. On the front lawn the words PEACE ON EARTH GOOD WILL TOWARD MEN blazed in front of an illuminated crèche. The boys threw down their bikes, vaulted over the low gate and bounded up the narrow walkway to the house. A Christmas wreath hung on the door, and all the front windows in the cramped looking, little house, gleamed. Abie and Buddy jostled each other to see who would get to ring the bell. Buddy got his elbow in Abie's throat pushed his chin up in the air, and as Abie clawed at the restraint, Buddy slammed the bell hard, twice.

"Yes!" The door ripped open. The missing link stood before them. He was huge. He wore large jeans and a wife-beater, revealing a gold cross nestling amidst dark curling hair on a startlingly hirsute, barrel chest, at the boys' eye level. Abundant underarm foliage flourished beneath powerful biceps and his bull neck balanced a large head with close-cropped salt and pepper hair. The creature could crush rocks.

"Yes," he snarled again as the boys gaped at him. His bulk blocked the partially open door and he regarded them balefully for the length of a heartbeat. Finally, the lumpen creature hiked up his jeans and said, in a voice that seemed to come from the depths of his toes, "Whadda y' want?" Hard brown eyes with little light regarded the boys with disfavor.

"Uh...uh... We've come to see J-J-Jamie?" Abie said.

The man looked scornfully at the boys, his eyes rested longer on Buddy. "Youse people come to see my daughter?"

"Youse? Huh?" articulated Buddy appearing not to understand.

The brute's eyes flared into life and reactivated Buddy's brain.

"Uh! Yes, Sir! We's people have come to see J-J-J Jamie." He desperately tried to speak the lingo of the natives.

The man turned to Abie. "Why you bring this smart ass here?" He closed the door abruptly and vanished into the house.

"I so don't belong here," muttered Abie. He looked at Buddy, who shrugged his shoulders then whispered urgently to Abie,

"Man, he's mad-ugly! You think Jamie's adopted?"

Abie whispered back, "Hush, he might-"

"No Daddy! Nooo!" Screams interrupted them. "I didn't..."

Whop! Whap! Pow! The violent sounds of blows being administered followed.

"No, Mario... Don't! She's only a child." They heard a woman's sobs.

"Noooo!" This was followed by a blood-curdling scream.

"A nigger! A stinking nigger!" Pow! Pow!

"Let's split-Now!" said Abie urgently tugging at Buddy's sleeve. But his friend appeared to be in a trance.

"Nigger!" they heard again.

Buddy looked puzzled. He shook his head, like a dog trying to get water out of its ears. Then the door flew open and a younger, harder version of the missing link stood there.

"Youse kids-" the newcomer snarled.

"Daddy, please-" they heard loudly through the now open door. "I'm sooooorry," followed by more shrieks.

Buddy's hair stood on end, and he broke out in a sweat.

"Mario, no!" the woman screamed bloodcurdlingly this time. "They're only children."

There was the thud of something heavy falling and the creature at the door spoke. "I said youse kids, git! 'Specially you, niggah! Should know better than comin' roun' decent people' homes askin' for their sisters. I oughta-"

They never discovered what he oughta. They were out of there. They leapt the fence and plunged into the street. Buddy tore his leather jacket, Abie lost his yarmulke; but they didn't stop. They pedaled away furiously.

"Shit!" muttered Buddy. "What a dick-wad!"

"Yeah, that was one shit-load o' trouble!" agreed Abie. "Now what am I gonna tell my Mom about my yarmulke. Uncle Ira brought it back from Israel for me."

"Just tell her it's gone," Buddy said off-handedly.

"Yeah, like how you're gonna tell your Mom that you just happened to split that new leather jacket."

"What! Where? Oh shit! Now she'll be on my case in a big way. Damn that girl!"

"Who, Jamie?"

"Yes, you retard, Jamie! If it hadn't been for her I wouldn't have torn my damn jacket." Buddy set his face grimly, and pedaled his fine black self away from the scene of his ignominy.

"I guess." Abie seemed lost in thought as they rode. They remained silent until they reached the Post Road and headed toward the Sound.

"We'll be passing Paige's house soon. Let's stop and say hi," said Buddy.

There was a sudden crash as Abie and his bike went down.

"What happened Abie, you all right?" asked Buddy stopping to help his friend.

Abie stared at Buddy in disbelief as he picked himself up off the ground and dusted off his pants. Suddenly he kicked furiously at a nearby tree stump. There were tears in his eyes. But all he said was, "I ran into that son of a bitching stump. Fuck it!"

"Maybe I will," said Buddy slowly. "Maybe I just will." He gave a slow ruminative grin.

36

Waving the White Flag

"Roderick, what's the investment climate in the Bahamas with your new government?" asked Rorie. "My magazine's planning a special on black paradises. You guys have the perfect set-up: no income tax, a moneyed black professional class, a black government..."

"It's not perfect," said Roderick, "but it's as good as it gets and it's home. I really appreciate it after having lived abroad for the last fifteen years." A lively discussion on the pros and cons of overseas investments followed.

"I like to keep the business in the family and invest black," said Rorie.

"Suit yourself," said Charlie. "My color's green. I have no allegiance to any other color when it comes to business."

"I don't blame you," said Rose. "It's a racial characteristic of ours. We don't have any sense of allegiance to each other even among our own in Jack and Jill. If those women discover anything that can be beneficial-a tutor, a program-they don't share it."

"Oh, Rose, come off it, everyone needs a competitive edge," Charlie observed. "If I share with Jack and Jill, when my child succeeds at the same level as their children she doesn't look dazzling because they're all shining. I don't see you pushing chess as an activity for J and J kids to embrace?"

"Surely you want success for as many members of your race as possible. It can only help to dispel the negative beliefs this society holds about you," said Roderick.

"But then she would not be singled out as special?" Charlie retorted. She glanced at Grantley to see if her dinner napkin was in danger. He wore a foolish look that made her suck in her breath sharply. Didn't his mother teach him not to come at people's dinner tables? If they got through this night without mishap she swore she'd never invite those two anywhere again.

"That's an interesting conundrum," said Jordan. "At what point should self interest give way to the common weal and-"

"Excuse me," said Charlie. "Sorry Jordan. Everyone finished?" She tinkled her bell and sorbet succeeded the soup course. She hoped this interruption would distract the sex fiends from ruining her party.

Is Jack and Jill planning anything special for Christmas this year?" asked Sophie.

"I haven't heard," replied Rose. "Why?"

"I like to be prepared," said Sophie.

Rose replied, "I'm sure we're doing something. But they're still trying to decide if to celebrate Kwanzaa or Christmas. The usual are we Black or are we American dichotomy-as if the two things are mutually exclusive, but Kwanzaa-"

Rorie interrupted. "Don't you realize that just being black is a political statement in this country? You mean Jack and Jill doesn't automatically celebrate things like 'the fourth of you lie'. We still tell his-story like in your Junior league? I see the feminists have herstory, when will we learn ourstory and celebrate it."

"That's not fair," put in Jordan. "We're still trying to integrate the various parts of our past into a palatable and usable whole. It's going to take awhile. Indulging in Americana doesn't mean we've forgotten Goree. We've got to integrate into the mainstream if we want to succeed."

"Yes," said Rorie, "but as Dr. King said we're 'integrating into a burning house, we need to become firemen.' If we mainstream our kids into a culture of drugs, alcohol abuse, cut-throat academic competition, teen suicide, a glut of money, early, casual sexual experience –"

"So what's the option, stay poor and noble in the ghetto? At least the moneyed sexual experience is accompanied by birth control and all the other bugaboos you mentioned can be helped by money," said Sophie. "I'll never let anyone make me feel disloyal to a cause because I can buy beaded, Fabrice gowns from Nieman Marcus. Fabrice is black and I support him." She looked around defiantly, but no one disagreed.

Charlie wondered if Sophie could titillate with her toes and offer up serious opinions simultaneously. There was a limit to what her napkin should have to go through.

"Is loyalty to 'the cause' and having money considered mutually exclusive in this society?" queried Roderick.

"Excuse me, please, Roderick," interrupted Charlie glancing around the table before tinkling her little bell. The entrees arrived. "You were saying Roderick?" encouraged Charlie as the butlers departed.

"It sounds as if blackness is supposed to impose a substandard lifestyle despite the opulence that surrounds us here and in the houses of so many blacks in this country. In the Bahamas I guess because we're the majority, it's taken for granted that black people with money will live where they want to and as comfortably as they can afford to."

"Here too, to a certain extent," reflected Rose. "But other blacks will envy you. So it's that old crabs in a barrel syndrome. You know one crab tries to climb out of the barrel and the others pull it down so that they all stay trapped."

"That's human nature," said Charlie. "Everyone wants to be the HNIC"

"What's that?" asked Roderick.

"The head nigger in charge," replied Charlie. "Or we like to be the first, or the only. Hell, why deny? It's great to be uniquely successful."

"You'd get further if you banded together," observed Rorie.

"You've got to be joking," declared Charlie. "Band with envious people who want to see you drop to their level? You don't understand the hatred the black underclass has for people like us," she said grimly as she suppressed visions of Germaine's tearful face and beautiful hair scattered on the floor. She wished she could check on the situation under the table again. Those two were being awfully quiet. Could that fool produce enough ejaculate to drip onto her floor? Was it acidic? Could it stain her Persian rug?

"They are the ones who need the example in unity," Roderick asserted. "In London things have become so bad for people of color that the East Indians are now banding with Blacks against the Brits. Otherwise we all lose."

"Humph!" sniffed Charlie.

"I think our history in the New World made it difficult for us to bond, Charlie," said Rorie. "Remember we were sold into slavery by our own people. Then we were repatriated, totally deracinated, and now folks turn around and tell us we should love the motherland that's been messing with us for over two hundred plus years. Patria? Not mine! I'm sorry, I spit on the American flag!"

"Easy guy!" said Jordan.

"There's nowhere I can comfortably educate my kids!" said Rorie.

"What about private schools?" asked Leroy.

Maxi sniffed derisively. "Private schools are just a different set of problems. Black mothers there judge each other by the clothes they wear, the car they drive. They still don't bond-crabs in the barrel all the way. We as a class are still so insecure and superficial."

"Yes, and I hear white kids generally consider all the black kids to be the deserving poor on scholarship-ABC kids," supplied Rose.

"Acronym for 'a better chance;' a scholarship program that puts bright inner-city kids into good private schools," Charlie explained to Roderick.

Maxi said, "When our kids befriend these kids who look like them, they discover the divide. These kids can't ski or play tennis and are often more sexually precocious."

"That's true," interjected Rose, "They tend to have the same morals as the white kids-you know anything goes for *them*! Plus we don't feel comfortable having our kids hang out with these kids in the South Bronx. You can catch a stray bullet there or get raped on an elevator."

"Thank God my children are too young for me to have to deal with this yet. I don't know what I'll do!" cried Lola, looking in consternation at her husband.

Roderick said, "This pretty much mirrors what's been happening on your college campuses. The white students take it for granted that most black students are there as part of a quota, not because of academic ability and the ability to pay."

"Shades of Shelby Steele," said Rorie grimacing and taking a drink. "Yeah, that's your equal opportunity working."

"Depressing," sighed Maxi. "The only thing worse than white racism is white paternalism, when they –"

"Aaaaah A A Ohhhh! Achoo!" Grantley sputtered explosively and appeared taken over by a mighty sneeze.

God damn it! thought Charlie, that was no sneeze. The bastard ejaculated into my table napkin and is doing a cover up! Her nostrils flared. She breathed slowly and deeply, begging God for control enough to make it through this dinner party. She wondered maliciously if the ejaculate would overflow onto his pants. He was fumbling about in his lap with the handkerchief that he'd pretended to sneeze into, and with her napkin too, of course.

"Bless you," said Rose.

Charlie smiled. If Rose knew what was happening, 'bless' would not be the word preceding 'you.' Sophie was looking intently at her husband as if absorbed in the conversation. Charlie thought she detected a trace of a smile; bitch!

"So achievement notwithstanding you're seen as undeserving affirmative action babies depriving this world's Bakkes of their rightful place in the sun," observed Rorie.

"It's a bitch?" said Charlie. "What do you think about learning styles? Some educators have concluded that black kids can't sit still long enough to learn like white kids. We suffer from genetic ants in the pants syndrome. Ergo, black kids should be allowed to hop around more, like the jungle bunnies the educators say we are, and possibly reason inferentially in mid flight. It has also been 'discovered,' of course, that blacks generally cannot do the more formal, inductive and deductive reasoning."

"If I ever hear about my son leaping through a class-room unchecked, while he reasons inferentially that teacher and I will make the news," Grantley asserted warmly.

"Roderick are you enjoying these bits of Americana that are not necessarily in the news?" asked Jordan wryly.

"This type of growing up experience must either produce very strong or very messed up people. Judging from my dinner companions, I'd say it has had the former effect, so no doubt your children will be okay too," Roderick countered.

"Spoken like a true diplomat," said Jordan heartily and they laughed and finished off their Javanese Jambalaya.

The anise fruit salad and gelato elicited groans from everyone, but they polished that off too. Charlie observed Grantley surreptitiously stuffing her dinner napkin into his pocket. Well, he could certainly have that one, she thought with disgust.

Lennie shepherded their guests into the living room. "Shall we sit here or in the conservatory?" he asked. "It's turned a bit cool, we could light a fire here." He went to the fireplace and pulled from the brass fire box what looked like a thick roll of dollar bills."

"Lennie, what on earth is that?" asked Maxi.

"Burning bucks, I have enough money to burn some of it to keep us warm," he said with a wink.

"I like that!" declared Grantley, roaring with laughter. "Pass it here and let's have a look at it. Now where did you find something like this?"

"In the bank of course," retorted Lennie as he carefully lit a fire, using the 'money'.

The sated guests opted to sit in the conservatory for coffee and liqueurs. They sank blissfully into large, padded wicker chairs, surrounded by indoor plants, with the illuminated fall landscape visible through the glass walls. As they listened to Miles play Round about Midnight; flames in the adjoining living room crackled and consumed what looked like dollar bills. Charlie fantasized herself and Roderick hosting this gathering then sitting together by the fire and discussing their party after the last guests had departed. She would lie in his arms and absorb his warmth and love.

"This is the life," sighed Lennie comfortably. "Anyone want anything else?"

"No space, old man, but thanks," said Jordan.

Roderick set down his liqueur glass and rose. "I must be going now; I have to catch an early flight tomorrow. Nice meeting everyone." He shook hands all around.

He said to Charlie, "I look forward to doing business with you. I guess you'll be in the Bahamas again when all the paperwork is complete?"

"You bet!" she said. "I love you," she mouthed soundlessly, and he smiled formally as he shook her hand at the door.

The other guests soon left. Charlie watched the last lights vanish down the driveway then slowly walked across her entrance hall. She no longer saw its beauty. Standing under the five-foot chandelier hanging from the cathedral ceiling she felt only emptiness. Roderick should not be departing with her guests. She sighed. She climbed the stairs to her bedroom and turned off the downstairs lights. In the darkness a mood indigo washed over her as she opened the door to the master bedroom and Lennie.

37

A Quotidian Saturday

Rose muttered and slammed through her sleek, sunny kitchen. It was Saturday morning. Evadne, that lazy, rude, ass of a maid should be here when she really needed her-weekends! when husband and children were underfoot making a mess of the house. She couldn't stand it; her house would soon have that lived in look. "Damn!" she exclaimed as she spilt coffee onto the pristine countertop. Swiftly she wiped it up and harbored even more horrible thoughts about Evadne who should have been there to do her menial duty.

The chess interview was in four days and the cushions still had not come. How could her living room be featured in a national magazine without them? She might have to buy ready-made cushions in a store. She shuddered at the thought of imperfect matches. Also her black hairdresser at Bloomies had just married and left town, the jerk! Now she'd have to travel into the city to get her hair done because none of the top notch (make that white and luxurious) local salons had hairdressers who could fix black hair. She could go to a ghetto hairdresser in a black community like Mt. Vernon; but she'd be trapped there for hours with loud people who didn't speak Standard English or give a damn about time. She could end up with that stiff ghetto fabulous look. Blast!

Rose heated up the griddle to make pancakes and her dark thoughts continued. Here in Westchester blackness could consign you to a ghetto setting for ethnic things like hair and religion. The Sundays when there were no chess tournaments; she and her family had to desert their upscale lifestyle and sit in a black church in a not-so–nice neighborhood where they could worship with other black people and her husband could charm potential patients. Sometimes being black in America could be hell. She scowled and dropped an egg on the floor in her annoyance. "Damn!" She hitched up her silk caftan and bent to clean it.

"Morning, Sunshine," bellowed Grantley, her smiling husband, as freshly showered and dressed in navy blue sweats he entered the kitchen.

Rose jumped, and narrowly escaped bumping her head on the kitchen island. She gave him a sour look.

"And the top of the morning to you too buttercup," he said sitting at the counter.

"Go to hell," she replied, scowling at the glop on her shining, ceramic, tile floor.

"What's the matter?" Grantley asked, pouring himself a cup of coffee.

"I need weekend help. This is wrong. I shouldn't be cleaning a kitchen on a Saturday morning.

"Wrong? Slavery and murder are wrong. You have the Long Island Sound in your backyard, a new, state of the art Bulthaup kitchen - for which you said you'd sell your mother on the street. And you say this is wrong?

Rose rolled her eyes. "Yes," she snapped. "I need weekend household help. Am I supposed to make myself a slave to my possessions; spend the weekend cleaning them? I'm married to a dentist and I will have the accompanying lifestyle. I promised myself that on my wedding day."

Grantley's eyes flew open, but all he said was, "Tough, this dentist is only having his family around him on weekends." He picked up a copy of Emerge magazine from on the table and sipped his coffee. "Hey, this is an old frat brother!" he said in surprise.

"Who?" asked Rose, looking up.

"This guy, Peter Phipps." He showed her. "We were at Moorehouse together; he transferred to Princeton, poor devil. Then he went on to Harvard law. He's heading up some international commission to Rwanda." He perused the article and Rose finished cleaning the floor and started making pancakes.

"Mom," Sydney bounced into the kitchen in her pajamas, "I can't find my notation pad with the games from the Pan Am tournament. Igor needs them. He wants to choose the best to submit to Chess Life for publication.

"You'll have to wait until Evadne comes to work on Monday. I have no idea where she put them. Of course you can always look for them yourself."

"Right," said the girl, dismissing the ridiculous suggestion. "Are we leaving soon? I can't be late for a tournament."

"We'll get there on time, okay! Damn it sometimes this chess can be a nuisance. There's always a tournament," her mother grumbled.

"I'm taking a bye on round two, you can be grateful for that. I should play all the rounds. It's a Grand Prix tournament. First prize is a guaranteed six thousand dollars!"

"You don't need six thousand dollars. Your father makes plenty. You need chess fame and I need to Christmas –"

"What the hell are you telling that girl? I don't 'make plenty,' as you put it. You just spend plenty. Let her go out and win six thousand dollars if she can. Have you lost your mind woman?" said Grantley.

Rose rolled her eyes. "Sydney go get ready, we'll be leaving soon. Call down to the basement and tell Igor when you're ready to have breakfast. You two can eat together and plan strategies."

"Bye all," said Sydney and ran up the back stairs laughing.

"Where's Buddy?" Grantley asked as he flicked on the TV.

"Turn that off," Rose screamed. "It's too early for that. I can't even hear myself think. Buddy's spending the weekend at Columbia with Jason, remember?"

"Vaguely, aren't you a little ray of sunshine this morning." He lowered the volume slightly. "What's the problem Rose, PMS?"

"Go to hell." She slapped a plate of pancakes in front of him. "Here. Is Midian still sleeping?"

"Last time I checked he was. Where are the sausages?"

"Coming!" She speared two sausages from the toaster oven and dumped them onto her husband's plate. "Don't awaken that child 'til I leave. I don't need him wailing and screaming to come with me. I can tolerate children exactly one at a time."

"Rose, don't say things like that. I know that you don't mean them, but one of the children might overhear you.

"Tough."

"Suit yourself." He shrugged and turned to the article and his breakfast.

"Grantley."

"Yes dear," he answered, eyes firmly fixed on his magazine.

"Grantley, I need you to take Midian to his Jack and Jill activity this morning."

He looked at her in dismay.

"It's at the Nature Center," she continued. She whirred fatback and spices in the mini processor and spoke above the sound of the motor. "A naturalist will tell them about woodland creatures and allow them to pet some of them."

"I don't believe this," he said. "Just what a two year old boy needs on a Saturday morning-a naturalist to tell him about-"

"Leave here at ten," Rose yelled above the machine, "so you'll reach by ten thirty. She turned off the processor, and continued in a normal voice as she sautéed the mixture on the gleaming silver stove. "You must be on time because you're dealing with white people. It's not a black see-you-when-you-get-there activity."

"Your Jack and Jill people won't be on time, trust me."

"Just see that my child is there on time. His clothes are at the foot of his bed. He's wearing that little Tyrolean peasant outfit I picked up at Saks last week."

Grantley grimaced but said, "Something sure smells good. What's it?"

"Marinade for this leg of pork. It's a recipe Maxi gave me long ago." She lifted a grid-bottomed container holding a leg of pork from the deep sink. "Those West Indians love their spicy food. This has so much stuff in it!" She frowned and added more spices and wine to the fragrant, simmering mixture on the stove.

"I can't wait." Grantley exaggeratedly licked his lips. "Mmm."

Rose snapped, "If I'd known it was going to be this much trouble I'd never have considered fixing the damn thing." She made vicious slashes in the hunk of meat and forced a dry spice mixture into them. Then she tied the whole thing tightly with kitchen twine and poured marinade over it.

Grantley watched with interest. "What will you serve with it?"

"Green beans, corn and white rice; this has to be rolled in herbed flour before cooking, to give it a crisp crust. I'll shove it into the convection oven and put it on automatic before we go shopping later. Let the oven figure out how long it'll take."

"Mmm," breathed Grantley again, rubbing his hands this time.

Rose, Sydney and Igor got to the tournament on time. Sydney won her game in ninety-four minutes. Igor stayed at the club for pick-up games and Rose, with time and Sydney on her hands, had a manicure, went to the supermarket and got home to discover that Grantley had also done his part.

"He loved it," Grantley assured her from where he sat on the floor in the messy family room, back against the sofa, eyes glued to the giant screen of the television set eating ice-cream from a tea-cup. "The naturalist waited twenty minutes, and then left because Midian and I were still the only ones there."

"You're joking!"

Grantley chuckled. "Your friends started arriving about fifteen minutes later. So we toured the place and saw the creatures on our own. But of course we couldn't get the hands-on stuff. That fat, yellow, woman; what's her name? Heather? She wanted to beat the little white woman in charge because you folks didn't get the promised show. Last I heard she was planning to sue."

"Give me a break! This is what I dislike about Jack and Jill. Money shouldn't be the only qualifier. That's why Monica and I plan to start Fauntleroy and Amelia."

Grantley didn't touch that one. "We almost brought you a present. Midian wanted to bring the snake home but your friends convinced him you wouldn't appreciate it."

"Mommy, when are we going?" asked Sydney running into the family room.

"Going somewhere?" Grantley asked in surprise.

"Don't you remember? We're taking them into Manhattan to see the Department store Christmas windows, Sydney's bringing Germaine. We're going to Bloomies. Then we're visiting F.A.O. Schwartz for Midian.

Sydney ran up the stairs shouting, "Midian! Where are you?"

"Oh, that's okay; you're taking Midian with you." Grantley looked back at the TV and tossed a handful of pretzels into his mouth.

"I said *we*." Rose narrowed her eyes.

"We nothing," retorted her husband. "Jordan and I booked a squash court for this afternoon. I'm not going to call him at the last minute to cancel. When you plan this kind of thing you have to give me advance notice."

"You and your bloody squash! We planned this a month ago. This is the only day we have free before Christmas." She yelled and glared at him.

"See you later." Grantley got up off the floor and stretched, precariously balancing a cup in his hand.

"What's in that tea cup you're holding, and where is its saucer?"

"Midian and I picked up some Butter Crunch ice-cream, want some? There's plenty in the freezer." He took a last spoonful then tipped the teacup to his lips and drained it. "Ahhhh," he said with pleasure.

Rose shuddered. "No, thank you. I suppose you didn't want to use an ice-cream dish. We keep them for this purpose."

Grantley ignored her. He picked his jacket up off the sofa and shrugged into it. "Bye," he said and left the room, stumbling momentarily over the train set in his path.

Rose's heart contracted as she looked at her family room. Several cushions were on the floor where he had been sitting. A bowl of pretzels was spilt on the carpet, and two, empty, single service juice boxes were capsized on the coffee table. Waves of despair washed over her. She sat, close to tears, on the sofa; the mess, the mess!

"I have to do a couple of things before I play squash," Grantley called, and then the front door slammed.

"Midian! Sydney!" Rose wearily pulled herself up off the sofa and yelled. "Come right now if you plan to go out with me.

"Coming, Mom," Sydney yelled back. "I'm on the phone. I told Germaine we're leaving now.

"Then hang up and let's go."

The children came clattering down the stairs. Sydney grabbed their coats from the closet, thrust her brother into his down jacket, and the two of them ran out behind their mother into the cold December afternoon.

38

A Morning Run

Charlie breathed heavily and looked at her stopwatch. "We improved our time this morning," she panted as she and Lola jogged off the Angloville high-school track and sat on the nearby bottom bleacher.

"Did we?" Lola wiped her sweaty face with a small towel then stuffed it back into her fanny pack. "This is the best way to start the day; it makes me feel so good." She did some neck rolls. "I can hardly believe it's winter, the weather's been so mild. Thank you Charlie, I'd never have done this without you."

"Thank you too. You're a godsend, Lola. I love being outdoors early in the morning and it's great to have a friend to exercise with. Want to run for another fifteen minutes then do a cool down? I'm getting chilled sitting around. Hi," she smiled and waved at a passing white woman, one of the many morning regulars.

"Sure," puffed Lola doing a stretch, "but not as fast as before. I'm a bit tired today, okay."

"Yes, I noticed that you're not your usual perky self, anything wrong?"

"No, I was up really late last night; you know." She blushed and looked away.

"Ho, ho!" said Charlie with a laugh. "It's okay, we can stop now I have a long day ahead of me, anyway so I'll burn the calories later. You apparently burnt yours last night."

"Oh, no, Charlie; really!" Lola blushed. "We can run; come." She took off down the track with Charlie behind her. They ran in silence until Charlie's stopwatch beeped.

"Phew! I felt that," Charlie stopped running and jogged in place. She looked at her watch. "I must be getting old. Let's call it a day; it's almost six-thirty?"

"Sure," said Lola, stopping too. She flopped forward panting, and stretched out her back muscles. "Charlie, how can you say you're getting old," she twisted in her friend's direction. "You're in better physical shape than I am!"

"I wish," said Charlie, giving her a smile. "You don't know how these old bones ache at night when I crawl into bed and rub down with both Bengay and Tiger Balm."

Lola laughed. "Stop it. But seriously, how can you do so much? You're gorgeous, successful, smart, and nice too; you've got such a great life – fabulous home, beautiful family. Gosh! It must be wonderful to be you. I saw that article on you in Ebony magazine, and I wanted to call them and say, 'Hey! That's my friend and you don't know the half of it. She's a terrific person too, the absolute best friend anyone could ever have!'"

Charlie smiled at her new friend. "That's sweet of you, Lola, thank you, but I don't walk on water-not yet, anyway."

Lola returned the smile. "Bet you could; ever tried it? Want to stop for coffee and bagels? I'm treating this time?"

"Sure," Charlie looked at her watch and smiled at the younger woman.

"Charlie, do you feel odd living here?" Lola asked as they pulled into a parking space at their local Cosi.

"What do you mean?" Charlie slid out of the high SUV.

"You know, everyone's white, we're black. Do you feel they don't want us here?"

"Not really, maybe a few people wish we weren't here, but the majority probably don't care one way or the other."

"You really think so?"

"Of course," Charlie opened the door and they entered the warm coffee shop.

"Morning, ladies, nice day," the proprietor greeted them. "Having the usual?"

Soon at a table by the window they warmed their hands on steaming mugs of latte to a background of mellow jazz. Then they attacked their bagels with gusto.

"Rebbie's been saying that maybe it's not good to live here. She says that I'll become white in my thinking. But we take the kids into Harlem every Sunday to attend the Abyssinian Baptist Church and Leroy tithes. What more can I do?" Lola looked helpless.

"That's preposterous. Don't let Rebbie upset you; she's just jealous. And don't try to live your life to please anyone but yourself and maybe your husband if he deserves it."

"Oh, he does," said Lola.

"I know," Charlie smiled at the younger woman and patted her hand. "By the way, I love those oatmeal-raisin cookies you let Germaine help bake yesterday, thanks."

"It was my pleasure. I love Germaine; she's a sweet kid. My little ones look forward to her coming over after school when she has the time. She's becoming quite a little baker. Did you taste those great chocolate cupcakes she made last week?"

"I did and Lola, you're a godsend. You don't know how good it is to have a friend nearby. I hate not being able to spend more time with Germaine. I had to schedule a weekly mother-daughter date so that we can spend quality time together. Maxi's hands are full with poor Tatiana. If it weren't for you..."

"Oh, Charlie, you know I'm here for you. Germaine's like a little niece to me. Tomorrow she's baking a Sock-It-To-Me cake with me and the kids. They're excited that she's coming over."

The two new friends smiled at each other over their steaming lattes.

39

Peace on Earth

Front, front," screamed Midian, pointing to the front passenger seat.

"No!" shouted Sydney. "You're too young to sit there. The seat belt will be restraining your stupid face."

"Front," he repeated stubbornly.

"Put the damn car seat in the front and let him sit here," Rose ordered.

"But Mom-"

"Mom, nothing, you have a friend going with you. Most of the time you have me to yourself-I sit for hours at chess tournaments with you. He gets his mother today. He sits here! And what's more we'll listen to his Raffi tapes, so shut up!"

"Mom!"

Rose smiled in malicious triumph and sang along loudly with Raffi,

Willaby, wallaby wusan

An elephant sat on Susan."

Midian crowed in delight, the Jaguar roared into life and they were off to pick up Germaine.

"Gosh, Mrs. Inniss, this is the most traffic I've ever seen in my life," Germaine declared as they crept through Manhattan traffic to the strains of Wee Sing's Spanish Carol.

"That's Christmas for you. We should have taken the train," replied Rose.

"I hate the train," said Sydney. "You always have that long walk afterwards; you can never get a cab."

"Sydney, the long walk's nice. You get the chance to buy stuff from the street peddlers, like every few steps," declared Germaine.

"Oh yeah," said Sydney.

Rose rolled her eyes. They parked on Third Avenue in the seventies and the children groaned.

"Mom, you could've gone into a garage off Fifth Avenue within walking distance of F.A.O. Schwarz," wailed Sydney. "You know I hate walking."

"No garage boy is touching my big silver baby. She stays here or we can go home. Get the stroller from the trunk and start walking."

Eventually they reached F.A.O. Schwarz. Rose hunkered down inside her mink feeling disgruntled. She wasn't a little old Jewish lady to be running around in a mink. Grantley really should buy her a fisher. She'd be damned if she bought it for herself!

"Mommy! You must buy me this!" Sydney exclaimed, pointing out a huge stuffed dog, taller than herself. She hugged the toy to her.

Rose looked at the price tag. It read seven hundred-dollars. She blinked. "Do you have a job, little girl?" she questioned. "Get off that animal. Where's Midian?"

Germaine said, "Caitlin has that dog, Mrs. Inniss. You know they have this apartment in Riverdale with little rooms. Well the dog takes up half her bedroom and she uses it as a chair. It's so funny." The two girls giggled.

"She would," Rose replied. Suddenly she noticed the empty stroller. She grabbed Sydney by the shoulders and demanded, "Where's my son?"

"I don't know," muttered Sydney. "He wanted to get out of the stroller and look around. So I let him. Here's the stroller."

Rose's heart rate quickened and she became conscious of the loud thumping of her heart. Remembering her friend who'd recently had a stroke she concentrated on taking deep abdominal breaths. Suddenly she erupted, "God have mercy! And you're supposed to be bright. Midian!" she screamed. She ran wild-eyed through the store pushing people willy-nilly to the side as she searched for her lost son with the eyes of most of the shoppers on her.

Sydney looked at Germaine and shrugged her shoulders. The two girls wandered away and were soon making music as they walked on the giant piano keys on the floor.

Suddenly there was a loud crash followed by a triumphant voice shouting, "Look, Mom!" Midian emerged from beneath a former towering display of boxes of Beanie Babies. "I want this one," he said, waving an ugly bat in the air. Rose ran to her son, took him by the hand and pulled him away quickly as employees rushed to the scene. "Now I want to see Santa," chortled Midian. "There he is!"

Rose gathered the children and herded them out of the store. Near the entrance a white security guard approached them. He gripped Germaine by the arm.

"Come with me please, Miss."

"I beg your pardon," said Rose, taking hold of Germaine's other arm.

"What?" said the startled child.

"Ma'am let her come with me quietly. She's been shoplifting."

"What!" They all shouted in unison.

"How dare you!" said Rose tight-lipped and pale. But she followed the store detective because you never knew with other people's children. Much later, they marched out of the store. A store manager assured them that mistakes often happened. There was no reason to bring race into it.

Rose was not looking forward to running this by Charlie later. She pressed her gloved fingers to her furrowed brow and forged ahead. She'd taken note of all the people involved. She got the embarrassment; Charlie would get the money. Some people had all the luck. That Charlie didn't need any more money, but now here she was with the chance to win at least a million dollars in a can't-lose lawsuit! Damn! It just wasn't fair! Why couldn't they have thought that her daughter was a thief, she thought bitterly.

"Look!" said Germaine, pointing to some black street performers, break-dancing and body popping to rap music. They joined the gathering crowd. The girls got into the music, moving to the beat. "Phat!" Germaine exclaimed, getting her groove on.

Midian crowed with delight at the spectacle. A little boy with a missing front tooth passed a hat around and Rose willingly gave fifty cents. She got a warm feeling from helping her own. They moved on to admire Saks's Victorian Christmas window, then the children all clamored for food.

"There's falafel. I'll have that." Germaine walked over to the cart.

"You do that, I'm getting a good, old fashioned, American hot dog," said Rose.

"Mom, you shouldn't have a hot dog, they're carcinogenic," shrilled Sydney.

"Everything in moderation," said her mother looking around for a hot dog stand.

"Do you think we'll find a sushi cart?" asked Sydney. "I want California rolls."

Rose said, "You don't eat sushi off the street. The upholstery of my car won't be able to stand it; have something else."

"Oh, fine," said Sydney following her friend to the falafel cart.

"This has been fun," said Germaine when her friend joined her. "Thanks."

Midian tore into a pretzel, slobbering and ripping like a young wild animal."Yuk!" exclaimed his appalled sister as Germaine giggled and averted her eyes.

"Mind your own business. You don't have to look at him." Rose defended her son.

They visited the windows at Lord and Taylor and Bloomie's. They shopped exhaustively at the latter. The crowded store left Rose drained and ready to go home.

"Please, Mrs. Inniss, may we go into the Village and see Barney's window. Everyone says it's wonderful this year," said Germaine.

Rose studied the child for a moment. "No, not even if they were giving away thousand dollar Versace tote bags. No way will I go anywhere but home right now. Have you any idea how long it would take to fight this traffic to get into the village?"

"Mommy, please!" Sydney begged.

"Mommy, hell! Everybody walk. To the car!" Rose purposefully strode ahead.

"Please, Mommy," said Sydney as they headed north; "Can Germy sleep over? Then you or Daddy could take us to New Roc tonight; we could see a movie, go on that ride, and eat at Applebee's. It'd be so cool, even Midian could come."

"I'm not going anywhere tonight. My feet are killing me. I've got decorating magazines to consult. That reporter's coming over next week with a photographer and I'm definitely not ready. The powder room towels should be a teensy bit lighter. There's too much terra cotta in that pink and-Oh my God!" She stopped abruptly.

Rose gaped at her car. A window was smashed. There was glass all over the seat and her radio and C.D. player were gone. They must have disabled her alarm. She stamped her foot and immediately cried out in pain.

"Dammit! I think I broke my god-damn toe!" She burst into noisy tears and dropped her packages to hug her foot.

Sydney attempted to soothe her mother. She patted her back. She murmured that it was okay; but Rose was inconsolable, so Sydney entertained Midian instead.

Rose eventually calmed down. She cleaned the glass off the car seats; rejecting offers of help, then took everyone in a cab to the local precinct to report the accident. She got the forms necessary for her insurance company and many tedious hours later bundled the children into the car and headed back to Westchester.

They had a cold time of it, driving window-less in twenty-degree weather. The girls whined and complained all the way, Midian cried and Rose yelled. She dropped off Germaine and after what seemed like an eternity reached her home. It was finally over.

Wearily, Rose came into her house through the garage entrance. The children dropped their coats on the floor in the mudroom and scampered off. She let them; she was beyond anger. Like a robot she walked into her foyer and hung her fur in the hall closet. She sighed and picked up that day's mail from off the floor in front of the mail slot. She put it on the foyer table. A tired, irritable looking woman with a pale, pinched face stared back at her from the mirror above.

Rose went upstairs. She slipped into a heavy, warm, caftan and came back downstairs to see about dinner. "Sydney, call Sal's and order a pizza."

"Yes Mom," said Sydney.

"Pizza! Pizza!" Midian bounced up and down with glee.

"And order me a bowl of minestrone," she commanded.

"Yes, Mom, should we get extra cheese and pepperoni for Dad?"

"Of course not; that's far too much cholesterol."

"Zooooommmmm, zzzoooom," Midian streaked in front of Rose pretending to be some kind of vehicle. He careened through the room steering himself with an imaginary wheel and bumping into everything in his path.

"Oh God, child, stop that or go to bed!" Rose snapped. "Go into the family room and play quietly. Your train's still set up in there. Your father almost broke his neck when he tripped over it this morning." Her marabou mules clicked on the wooden floor as she swept past him, headed for the kitchen.

"Vroooooom," went the vehicle as it headed for the family room.

Rose turned on the kitchen lights and adjusted them to dim. She opened the fridge, placed the marinating meat on the counter and fished out sparkling water from behind it. Tonight she would be good to herself. She poured the water into a crystal goblet and floated a lemon slice in it. Then she sat at the kitchen island, took a Tylenol and washed it down with the water. She would pretend today had never ever happened.

"Where's your mother?" she heard in the distance.

"In the kitchen, Dad"

"Hiya!" Grantley breezed into the kitchen and pecked her on the lips. "What's cooking? Hey, I don't smell anything. What's going on? What happened to the pork roast?" His eye fell on the container of marinating meat. He opened it. "What the hell is this? I've been thinking about this pork all day. I played two hours of squash, saw an emergency patient, jogged for half an hour. I'm wiped out. The only thing that kept me going was thoughts of this pork." He was almost crying. "Woman, where the hell's my dinner?"

"On the way over from Sal's," she said coldly.

"You didn't roast the pork leg and you're giving me pizza! I'm a hungry man and I want real food!" He glared at her. "Woman, cook the goddamn pork now!"

Rose did the only thing any self-respecting black woman of her acquaintance would do. "Get the hell out of women's business, you ass!" she yelled. She snatched up the leg of pork, and smacked him across the face with it. The marinade ran like blood down his shirt. That was the last thing she remembered before passing out after seeing myriad stars.

40

Bedtime Stories

Charlie closed Harpers magazine and smiled at Germaine. "That's it for the night, Pumpkin. What an interesting article," she said rising, "We'll have to finish discussing it tomorrow. It's amazing how companies get away with placing cell 'phone towers and other potential environmental toxins in poor neighborhoods. I want you to always remember; the best thing you can do for the poor is to never become one of them. Study hard, work hard and make sure you can help them but never ever join them."Germaine sighed in exasperation. "I know that, Mommy." She yawned sleepily. "What are we reading tomorrow night?"

"An article on the rise of gated communities in wealthy neighborhoods. Then you'll read Octavia Butler's The Parable of the Sower for yourself, it's about life in a gated community in the future and the need for them. We'll discuss gated communities after this. We have to keep that gray matter stimulated. Wrinkle, wrinkle little brain," she said, and bent and kissed her daughter on the forehead.

"Night, Mommy, I love you."

"Love you too, Sugarplum," Charlie said. She turned on the CD player and the sonorous strains of Mozart's Symphony Number 35 in D Major filled the room.

"Oh, Mommy, not tonight," said Germaine with a frown.

"Every night and several times a day, if you can painlessly boost your IQ by listening to Mozart or complex jazz, why wouldn't you? Tomorrow night you can listen to Miles, okay?"

"Anything is better than this. 'Night, Mommy." She frowned and turned her back.

Lennie was lying in bed watching television in their bedroom. He looked up when Charlie entered.

"Charlie," he said, "did I see you this afternoon on Angloville Avenue with Germaine and some girls?"

"Yes, I took the afternoon off. Germaine wanted to go for ice cream after school with a group of her new friends. We went to Haagen Daaz. "

"Good, she's settling in."

"Seems to be," said Charlie, heading for her bathroom. "She's invited to a birthday party on Saturday."

"It's good that you're spending time with her; girls need their mothers." Lennie observed before turning back to the TV.

Charlie was thoughtful as she changed into a nightgown and robe. Was Lennie accusing her of neglecting Germaine? When she came out he was still watching TV.

"Coming to bed?" he asked.

"No, I've got work to catch up on. I'm going up to my office." Charlie was disturbed as she mounted the spiral staircase to her office in the crow's nest above the bedroom. Did Lennie suspect something? A cold, crescent moon shone through the open skylight. She closed it and sat in the dark, at her black steel and glass computer center. She rocked back in the chair, put her feet up on the desk and clasped her hands behind her head in thought. She was spending far too many late nights here in this aerie hiding from Lennie. Phone sex with Roderick's seductive voice telling her wild things was a turn on. Cyber sex on the computer with him was fun too, he was creative as hell; but it wasn't enough.

She thought about the past few weeks. This was no way to live, not when you reached her age and worked as hard as she did. The situation was becoming increasingly intolerable. She wanted Roderick. Damn it, she deserved Roderick! She needed to toss some ideas around. She called Maxi.

"Isn't it a bitch? When I wanted Lennie he was nowhere around, now I can't escape him. I almost think he knows about Roderick. He's being so nice. He surprised us with tickets to Aida last week. We did the family thing-dinner at Mars 2112, then the theater. Germaine was in heaven."

"So you guys had dinner with Martians in purple spandex?"

"We did, and it was no weirder than Lennie playing pater familias. We rode the spaceship down to the restaurant. Lennie had a Martian eat with us –"

"Stop it!"

"He was probably erect the whole time because the Martian was sexually ambiguous. We know he rises to the occasion."

Maxi laughed. "Give it a rest Charlie, at least he's trying."

"Sure. But he's not doing it out of family love. You know nothing makes you as attractive to a man as his knowing that you're no longer interested in him. He's always watching me now. I can almost feel the heat from him."

"Charlie, I know you don't want to hear this, but you two can still reconcile."

"You're right-I don't want to hear it. I must be getting like Roderick because I've got these words from a song stuck in my head. Remember,

I can bring home the bacon

Fry it up in a pan

Well I did that, but while I was out there busting my butt to bring home the bacon and do all that good stuff, he was out there following his heat-seeking scud and making me feel sexually inadequate."

"Charlie, that was the past; he's trying now."

"Give him a Brownie point but I still resent it. I can't love him anymore. In fact, I hate him, because now it's too late. I always wanted to have a real family with my child's father. You know, like The Cosby show, the perfect black family, or that hokey 50s Father Knows Best."

"Yeah, I can just see you playing second fiddle to 'Father'."

"I can 'yes, Dear' a man as well as the next hypocritical woman who knows its going to pay off like a son-of-a-bitch later; in bed or in the jewelry store. But it has to be *my* man exclusively."

"Charlie, you're a card. But seriously, it's not too late to reconcile with Lennie. You can still have all that. If you want it to work I can help you."

"I don't; but out of curiosity, how?"

"Get a blue candle-"

"Oh, Lord, do you have shares in a candle factory! No, I take that back. Every time you've burned your candles so far things have worked out, Mambo. But this time I don't want them to work out so I'm not burning, and don't you."

"I can't. You have to want it too."

"Good, how's Tatty doing?"

"Much better, her tutor still comes every day. But sometimes her brain's not on, then she can't retain a thing and gets so irritable and frustrated."

"The poor thing, this has got to be so hard on both of you. Can I do anything?"

"Charlie, you know you're doing everything and more. I'm going to ban the UPS truck from my block. You're spoiling my daughter."

"And what's wrong with that?"

"Oh, Charlie, you're hopeless," said Maxi with a little laugh. I'm hoping she can go back to school next semester."

"Germaine and I will be up next weekend if I can get through enough of this damn paperwork. This Bahamian expansion is giving me a headache-the licenses, palms to be greased, general bullshit! Everyone craves a piece of me. I've never felt so *wanted.*"

Maxi chuckled, "I'm sure it'll prove well worth the aggravation to you, right?

"Right," Charlie laughed; thoughts of her naked body entwined with Roderick's in the sunny Bahamas made her laugh richer, and made her do some Kegels on the spot, in preparation.

Suddenly they heard Lennie. "Charlie, Charlie. Girl, you're working too hard.

"Maxi, I'll talk to you later. I've got to look busy."

"Go and be nice," hissed her friend.

Charlie quickly turned on the computer, hung up the phone, and put on her reading glasses. She was poring over a spread sheet when Lennie's head appeared at floor level. She suppressed the urge to stamp down on the ascending head.

"You're really working hard on this Bahamian expansion," he said sympathetically. "When are you coming to bed?" There was a pause. "I'm lonely."

Charlie met his eyes and felt mixed emotions. Rage at what was, vied with sadness for what could have been had he only tried to establish a relationship with her sooner. She too paused, and then said, "I'll be right down. This expansion will affect my company's stock, so I've got to be on top of everything when I meet with the money guys next week."

"Okay, I'll leave you to do your thing. But remember, I'm waiting." He gave her a look she did not want to interpret, and then he retreated.

Damn! She was in trouble. There was no way she would ever sleep with Lennie again. Even the thought of it made her skin crawl. This was just too little too late.

When Charlie came downstairs an hour later, Lennie was lying in bed, erect; watching a couple have sex on the Playboy channel. He smiled at her, and her heart sank.

"Be there in a minute," she said. She fled to the bathroom and found her salvation.

"Lennie, what the hell do you think you're doing?" Charlie yelled. "I'm tired telling you not to throw your wet towel on the toilet bowl lid. It's stupid, nasty and lazy."

"Move the damn thing if it bothers you," he said testily, "and come out here."

"For what?" she asked. "The ten second special on the good ship Gopilal?"

She heard the bed creak as he sat up. "What do you mean by that?" he said.

She came out of the bathroom and confronted him. "I mean what I said. I'm tired of you and bad sex."

"You're crazy! You've been working too hard. You were up there drinking?"

"Go to hell. I'm not you. You need a keeper-I don't. You can't even hang up your own damn towel, for God's sake. Obviously it has to be moved before someone uses the toilet, so why put it there in the first place?"

"You back on the towel shit again? You're really crazy. Look, get out of the way." He gestured for her to move from blocking his view of the TV screen. "And while you're at it, if it bothers you so much go move the damn towel yourself."

"Turn that bloody thing to hell off and listen to me when I speak to you," she screeched, remaining in front of the TV.

"Move," he shouted, rising up from the bed.

"No. I'm tired of taking shit from you, you big, lazy, ass-hole turd. Move your butt and pick up your god-damned towel now."

"You fucking crazy! Who the hell you think you' speaking to like that. Move to rass from in front of the fucking TV, before I knock the shit out of you!"

"Come, and I'll call the cops and put your black ass out on the street."

His eyes blazed at her; hers blazed back at him.

"You're sick. I'm getting out of here. I'll sleep in the guestroom. What's with you? You forgot to take your Prozac today?" He stormed out of the room.

Not a bad night's work, thought Charlie. She hummed as she went into the bathroom and did her nightly rituals. Then, all clean and moisturized, she lay against her backrest, arranged the comforter cozily around her and channel surfed 'til she found the Tonight show. She was soon laughing with Jay Leno as she freshened her nail polish.

That night she had sweet dreams-she and Roderick positively wallowed in connubial bliss as they raised their perfect child, Germaine.

41

A Manhattan Afternoon

This is definitely the way to go," said Rose, getting into the chauffeur-driven limousine Charlie was providing. "I've always wanted to see Cabaret, thanks, Charlie."

"I owe it all to you," said Charlie. "My lawyer got to the store brass and they didn't even try to put up a fight. We settled out of court. Even if I go broke tomorrow, Germaine will have no problem, paying for college, graduate school and whatever else she wants later, thank you."

"Amazing that they didn't try to go to court," said Maxi.

"They know they were wrong. Do they want to send a message to people like us to stay away from their store? Most people don't want themselves or their children to be publicly humiliated, and political correctness is in!" said Charlie.

"I don't know what I would have done if that had happened to my family or me," said Lola; "poor Germaine."

"Poor, rich, Germaine," muttered Rose.

"Some people have all the luck," said Sophie.

"Maxi, how's your little girl doing now?" Lola asked.

"She's much improved, thanks for asking. Her disposition's great; she's out of the wheelchair and will probably be back in school by spring."

"Way to go! That Tatiana's a fighter. I remember her as a toddler standing up to me because she wanted to sit in the front seat and I wouldn't let her. Maxi, remember when I called you to find out if she had pit-bull family?"

"Oh, Charlie!" said Maxi with a laugh. "Her recovery is entirely due to Chun Do Sun Bup, a six-thousand year old Korean healing system. We've been going to their Manhattan center daily. She was a different person after the first treatment. She came home and walked! Scout's honor! Now she's in and out of the wheelchair. I swear they can cure anything; all those diseases that western medicine can't handle-piece of cake to the Chun Do Masters!"

"That's wonderful!" said Lola. "No wonder you look so terrific. You've got a glow about you."

"Thanks. It's because the whole awfulness of an incurable illness has been lifted from me and I'm doing the Chun Do training myself. It's a wonderful thing to do," said Maxi. "I've regained my focus, I'm centered-It's better than therapy. I now chant daily."

"Tell me more about Chun Do. Leroy's Dad has prostate cancer and he's not doing too well. This might be something for him to try," said Lola.

"You won't regret it," Maxi assured her. "They teach you to harness energy, which they call ki or chi, and use it to heal yourself. At first Tatty couldn't do it so they did it for her with Chun Su treatments. Now she's improved tremendously and does the energy training for herself. Every day I look at her getting better in front of my eyes and I thank God for Chun Do Sun Bup. They gave her back her life. I love the Masters, they're god sends. "

"Wow!" said Lola softly.

Maxi talked more about Chun Do healing, and they chatted and enjoyed the ride to the theater and their post-theater Jack and Jill committee meeting.

"Look, look!" Sophie cried suddenly.

"What?" said her friends.

"That building!" Sophie pointed. "I designed it with my firm. It was my last big project. I've been able to take it slow and easy this year thanks to the proceeds from that big, beautiful baby. Isn't it wonderful? Aren't Set-Asides fantastic? I'm in love again." She blew the building a kiss.

"Go on, girl, flaunt it," laughed Charlie.

"We'll toast this later," Maxi said.

"Rose, I love your sunglasses, they're real cute; where'd you get them? They're Italian aren't they?" Sophie said reaching to take the sunglasses; but Rose recoiled.

"No, don't. I have a bit of photosensitivity right now." Rose waved Sophie off and tried to push the glasses more firmly into place; but they fell off revealing slightly darkened skin around her right eye, unsuccessfully disguised by make-up.

"Oh Boy! What have we here? Did Grantley finally catch her fornicating with the house?" Maxi murmured to Charlie.

"Maxi, behave yourself," Charlie hissed, trying to keep a straight face.

"What's with your face?" said Sophie.

"I walked into a door," Rose said shortly.

"I know," clucked Maxi sympathetically. "Its name was Grantley."

Rose glared at her. "It's not what you think." She reluctantly related the saga of her husband and the side of pork.

"No! You're kidding!" howled Maxi, holding her sides. "I'm going to wet myself. I'm sorry, Rose." She went off into peals of laughter again.

Rose ignored her, "So, Lola, how's Angloville treating you?"

"It's a terrific place," Lola said shyly. "We're enjoying it."

"She's going to give the neighbors something to talk about. You should see her renovation plans. Her place is going to be fabulous. Lola, tell them what you plan to do," Charlie urged. "You'll blow them away. You've got such great taste and good ideas."

The women smiled encouragingly at the younger woman and she shyly talked decorating with them. For the rest of the journey they quietly discussed color schemes and themes for the upcoming Jack and Jill ball. When they reached the theater their little committee had made the decision. It would be a Black and White Ball-the height of elegance, causing friends and enemies alike to talk about them.

"Great! I look sensational in black", exclaimed Maxi.

"Here we go again. You two horny animals will stay home screwing up a storm to celebrate you in black," observed Charlie dryly.

Maxi blushed, and her friends laughed.

"That was terrific," Rose said later as they walked out of the theater. "That old woman was a tough old bird the way she ditched the old guy when she realized that loving him would present problems later; hats off to the playwright. Usually women are shown doing dumb romantic things that hurt them in the end."

"That's true," said Maxi. "She sure refused to take on his baggage."

"I take it you guys don't believe in love and doing the honorable thing, like trying to escape together, or trying to hide the old codger. Some people did stuff like that and it worked out," said Charlie.

"Rescue fantasies," opined Maxi. "They rarely work in the real, hard-assed world."

"Uh-oh! Hang on to your furs, ladies. Here comes a suspicious looking group of white people," said Rose

"This will be the day that I die," said Sophie nuzzling down into her fur against the brisk winter day. "No one tells me what I can wear; definitely not a group of white terrorists walking around preaching animal rights."

"They probably won't bother us. I'm a black woman, so they don't know how I got this fur, or what I'd do to keep it. And I will die for it," stated Rose glaring at the approaching white people.

"Oh, come on, Rose," said Charlie with a laugh. "It's a piece of dead animal. Surely you're worth more."

"I am. But this mink set me back too much for me to have some freaky white person rip it off my back, spray paint it red, stomp on it and then hand it back to me. They can't tell us what to do anymore. And I don't take that shit!" said Rose.

"Oh dear!" said Lola, increasingly nervous as the approaching Whites inexorably bore down on them.

"Nothing's going to happen, Lola; the car will be here in a minute," said Charlie. "Are you guys skiing over the coming Thanksgiving break? Germaine says your little Sandra told her you have a ski house in the Poconos."

"We do, Leroy loves the place. He built it himself and did his own decorating. He's so proud of it. But we can't leave town; we're trying to get the Angloville house ready by Christmas, so we're letting Rebbie use the place."

"Good Lord, cut Rebbie loose, Lola. She'll suck you dry," Charlie said in an exasperated tone.

"She's been kind to me and has shown me the ropes, sort of. I don't know what I would've done without her. But of course you're much more helpful and knowledgeable than Rebbie," Lola quickly added.

"Am I hearing right, Rebbie kind?" said Rose with a laugh. "You believe that and I've got a bridge I can sell you."

"Oh no, they're almost upon us. I don't like this," said Lola almost wringing her hands with worry.

The other women looked distinctly uncomfortable and Charlie marveled that grown black women got worked up over the approach of a seemingly harmless group of Whites. Then she remembered tales of white women clutching their pocketbooks and bounding across the street to be out of the orbit of men like her husband and her friends' husbands-decent, conservative looking, college educated black men in three piece suits with six figure incomes and carrying heavy mortgages. She gave a mental shrug and got into their limo as it pulled up.

"It's a shame that you can't wear your furs comfortably in the city anymore," Rose said, once they were settled in and headed across town to the Palace.

"Isn't it?" said Sophie. "I suppose I could buy an expensive woolen coat to wear in the city. You don't know what those nuts back there were about. I hate this." She pouted.

"I'm getting like my sister in Nassau. I come into the city briefly, do whatever I came for then get the hell out before something bad happens," said Maxi.

"Enough of this, Let's go to tea and have a lovely time," said Sophie. "Tea's on me to celebrate my building."

Tea at the Palace was a gracious affair. Charlie let go of Roderick, Lennie and all the complications of her life, as the soothing ambiance enveloped her. The muted beige and gold made it a pleasure to sit sipping fragrant tea and nibbling on dainty cucumber sandwiches, while the harp music washed over her.

"This is what I miss most about not living in the Caribbean; tea-time," said Maxi.

"Me too," said Sophie, "It is the most pleasant meal. We must do this more often."

"Let's," agreed Rose. "Isn't that Colette sitting over there with Phoebe's husband?"

"Where?" asked Marguerite. "Oh, I see them. Oh, no! Poor Phoebe."

"Rose, did you go to the Epsilon fashion show?" asked Sophie. "I missed it.

"I left early-those clothes were tired looking! Tell me which of us black Westchester socialites is going to run around wrapped up in Kente cloth?" Rose challenged.

"That big-Momma-wrap-up-y'-head-and-come stuff was all they showed?" asked Maxi.

"It was," said Rose. "So most of us ignored the fashions and chatted."

"I love Africa as much as the next deracinated, black woman," said Sophie. "But I exercise for hours so I can look this way. I'll be damned if I hide this body in yards of fabric. You don't have to have a big butt and belly to be African."

"Oh, you bad Eurocentric fool," said Charlie with a laugh. "Don't you want to be some black man's fertility symbol?"

Sophie said, "Show me some slinky ethnic stuff and I'll find my roots fast-thin and proud." She raised her china teacup in a salute and sipped her tea daintily, pinkie sticking out at the correct angle.

"To money, and a tiny hiney," said Charlie, raising her teacup too.

"Hear, hear," said the others, joining in.

"What's a hiney?" asked Sophie.

"A behind," said Rose, daintily dabbing her lips, with the gold napkin.

"Hey, do you think they're, you know-having an affair?" whispered Charlie; glancing over at Colette and Phoebe's husband.

"I'll bet they are" declared Rose. "See how he's looking at her? Oww, she's dessert."

"Umm hmm" said Maxi, "Just look at them."

"It must be nice, sighed Charlie."Do you think they've reserved a room here for afterward?"

"They'd better, if not they're going to do it on the table," said Rose. " Look at them."

Maxi added, "I wonder if he's found her Graffenberg?"

"That G. spot nonsense," snorted Sophie, "wherever did it go? A few years ago everyone was hunting for it and the women who claimed they'd found theirs were on TV acting as if they'd found religion."

"Yeah, I remember," Maxi said, "Maureen trotted out patients who testified that they'd found theirs and reached Nirvana."

"What is this G. Spot?" asked Lola.

"A waste of time," snorted Sophie.

"Speak for yourself," declared Rose. "Grantley and I found mine, and whenever I have the time or the energy we do our Graffenberg bit and it's nothing short of sensational."

"How d'you do this Graffenberg stuff?" asked Lola shyly, blushing furiously.

"It's real easy once you get the hang of it," Rose asserted. "But I can't tell you here." She waved expansively at the room and knocked over her water glass. "Oops! I have an article I'll fax to you. Give me your FAX number."

"Thanks, here, I'll write it for you." She passed the number over.

The women companiably nibbled at scones, preserves and clotted cream, then turned their attention to the dessert cart, groaning with its sinful bad-for-your-hips pastries.

"I'm going back on Weight Watchers tomorrow," declared Maxi.

"You and me both," agreed Rose, delicately nibbling on an éclair. "My husband, to whom I am not speaking; says the only things he wants big, are his house and his car."

"The only things?" queried Sophie, to a general chuckle.

Well, that other's a given, isn't it?" said Rose with a laugh.

Charlie looked thoughtful as she flirted with a chocolate covered strawberry. Finally she said, "If we could all start over again, which would you go for; the great career, or try for the great home life. Mind you, the home life is not guaranteed, husbands could stray anyway, no matter what you do. But you could provide a place that's psychologically nice to come home to and where you could raise happy kids."

"Spare me!" said Sophie. "That exists solely in Hollywood."

A heated discussion followed and Charlie felt an unbearable longing for Roderick. She did her Kegels exercises. She had to call him that night. Even phone sex was acceptable at this point. This wasn't just an affair was it? What was it Roderick had said?

He who kisses the joy as it flies

Lives in Eternities sunrise

She wouldn't analyze so much. Germaine could still get her happy home. She *could* let 'the joy' fly from her-but later much later, she needed Roderick now. It was a bitch to want someone this much and not have him. If she did not see him soon she would not be responsible for her actions. She'd climb the walls and masturbate vigorously in public. She grinned at the thought.

"Charlie, why are you laughing at poor women who have no choices," said Rose accusingly.

Charlie wisely kept her own counsel. "It's Kafkaesque irony!" she declared. Before anyone could challenge her to explain this, she looked at her watch and exclaimed, "Look at the time? I promised Germaine I'd be home in time to meet her bus this afternoon."

They all examined their own watches, and muttered about busy schedules as they gathered up furs and bags and left discreetly, without glancing in Colette's direction.

42

These Endearing Young Charms

Lennie walked into the house and the haunting, old melody of "But What If All These Endearing Young Charms" drew him to the music room. He slipped into the room and watched his daughter with pride. Germaine's thin hands plucked the harp strings, rising and falling like leaves swirling in a dance, she teased out the melody from the golden, concert harp.

"Bravo! Bravo!" he said applauding loudly at the end of the piece."

She looked up, startled. "Daddy, when did you come in? I didn't hear you."

"I know; that was beautiful, Kitten. Play something else for your Old Man."

"Okay, but just one more; that piece had a lot of loud passages and glissandos and arpeggios – they're murder on your fingers. I still haven't developed enough calluses to play that kind of music comfortably for long periods."

Lennie flinched and came over to his daughter. Wordlessly he took her hands and examined the fingers. "Let's jam, Baby," he said softly. "We'll do Satin Doll together. You give me the first few chords then you can rest your little hard hands." He sat at the piano and Germaine played an elaborate chord introduction to Satin Doll. Lennie came in with piano and voice for most of the song and Germaine blended her voice and harp with him at intervals. They finished with a flourish and much laughter.

"That was great, Daddy. Why are you home so early?"

"Can't I come home to spend time with my number one daughter?"

"Sure," she smiled at him and played a glissando, and then she put up the harp pedals and came and sat on the piano bench next to her father. "Let's do Heart and Soul".

"Heart and Soul comin' at ya! We jammin' in the name of the Lord!" He played an elaborate chord sequence then they launched into the simple duet. "We're a couple of cool cats," he said when it was over. "Want to walk to the village for ice-cream?"

"Too cold for that, but I'd take a car-ride to the Pizzeria."

"Why not," he said, tousling her hair. "Let's go."

They made the five-minute drive to Ye Olde Pizza Shoppe in the village shopping area. "Let's sit here," said Germaine choosing a table at the glass-fronted entrance of the deserted Pizzeria. Lennie ordered then slid into the booth opposite her.

"Are those girls in your class?" asked Lennie, pointing out some teenagers looking into a store window across the street.

"Yeah, they are."

"You should invite them over some time. Do you want to ask them to join us?"

"No, I didn't say they were my friends. I said they were in my class," she said dully.

You're right, sorry; stupid me." He slapped himself on the forehead in a clownish gesture then looked at her and said in a serious voice, "Tell me, Germaine, what's going on with you? Lately you've been down at the mouth."

"I don't know what you mean?" she said, not meeting his eyes.

"Yes, you do, Miss Gee, look at me please." He gently put his finger under her chin and turned her face toward him. "There! Who's got the most beautiful face in the entire world?"

"You do, Daddy," she said and laughed.

"No! No! No! You forgot I passed it on to you. The King has had his run; now it's the princess's turn! Here's our food." They sat in silence as the waiter served them, and left the check on the table; then pizza in hand, Lennie continued softly. "Germaine, tell me, what's bothering you."

Her eyes clouded and she blurted out, "I don't have any friends."

"You could've fooled me. You're on the soccer team and have a whole slew of teammates. Remember, you haven't been in this town very long, give it time. Hey! Didn't you and Mom go for ice-cream last week with a car-load of girls?"

"Yes, but I don't like them." She ate silently and looked through the window at the girls who had crossed the street and were approaching the pizzeria.

Lennie continued, "Why not? They seem nice enough. Are they mean to you?" He looked worriedly at his daughter over the last of his slice.

"No, they're nice," she said slurping up her milkshake.

"So what's the problem?"

"Oh, Daddy, they're just different, okay?"

"How, Kitten?" They finished their food and rose. Lennie left money on the table, and waved to the owner. "Want to walk?"

"Sure, Daddy."

He opened the door for her and they stepped out into a cold, winter afternoon. The street was gay with the red and green of Christmas interspersed with some blue and silver Hanukkah displays. Yards of synthetic ivy wrapped the lampposts and a Salvation Army Santa stood outside the supermarket ringing a bell and collecting donations in a huge black cauldron. Lennie and Germaine dropped money into the cauldron then stopped to admire the merchandise in an impressively decorated Gap display window on the tree-lined street,

"Germaine, tell me, why you don't like the girls here," Lennie asked quietly.

She looked up at him. "You wouldn't like them either, and you wouldn't like it if I liked them. Apart from being snobs, and nasty and competitive about everything-"

"Since when has that bothered you, Miss straight A student?" Lennie teased.

"Since they take the books out of the library before a paper is due, and always ask me my grades and try to look at them when papers are being passed back."

"Not good," said Lennie thoughtfully.

"French is awful. Most of them are fluent and have perfect accents because they have French au-pairs or have been vacationing in France for the past few years. Four of them are French."

"So, we'll get a French au-pair. What else?"

"Oh, Daddy, they're different! They're into boys in a major way. Around here they date at twelve! Mom would kill me if I even asked to go out on a date, and I'm thirteen already!"

"You poor old lady, and she wouldn't; I'd do it for her," said Lennie smiling down at his daughter.

"They wear make-up already, Daddy. Some of them smoke cigarettes and marijuana. They're allowed to stay home alone and they have make-out parties where they drink and do drugs. They take Ecstacy and think it's cool to destroy property and harass people in stores. They say I'm weird because I won't do that kind of stuff and I don't think it's funny!"

He squeezed her hand helplessly and they walked in silence.

"I wish we'd never moved here," she said in a small voice. "And by the way it wouldn't have been cool to ask those girls to join us in the Pizza Parlor."

"Why not, Baby?"

"'Cause you're a parent. You're not supposed to be seen in public with parents. They like to act as if they just landed here from Mars," she said bitterly. "I really caught it when Mom came with us for ice-cream. At first they thought she was my maid. When they found out she was my Mom..."

Lennie looked down at his daughter helplessly. The pain on her young face made his heart ache. "I'm sorry, Baby," he whispered.

"These people are very different from us." She said dully. "Daddy?"

"Yes, Honey."

"Do you really think I'm pretty?"

"You're beautiful, Angel. How can you ask me that?"

"Well how come no one else thinks so? No one my age in school anyway," she added bitterly

Lennie went silent. Then he looked at her and said gently, "That's because you're Black and they're White, and this is America, Baby. Are there any black boys in your class?"

"Daddy, I'm the only black kid in the entire school, probably in the entire village except for Lola's little kids."

Lennie's heart was heavy. As they came to Le Bijou, the local jewelry store, he said, "Gee, let's stop in here." Lennie browsed until he found a silver necklace with a little, heart-shaped, silver locket. The locket opened to reveal space for two miniature photographs. He purchased it. "Here, Baby," he said giving it to her. "You wear this every day. We're going to go right now and get our pictures taken-the two most beautiful people in the world. You wear this with our pictures in it and always remember you're beautiful and who loves you." Just then his beeper went off. He checked and saw that it was a call from Colette. He turned off the beeper and said to his daughter, "Come, Baby, let's go get our pictures taken."

They stepped back out onto the Angloville street. A light snow had started to fall. In the distance they heard laughter and the clanging of the Salvation Army Santa's bell. Old-fashioned street lamps and twinkling, white lights in the sidewalk trees held the impending twilight at bay. But darkness was in Germaine's eyes as her father held her hand and they headed for the photographer's Studio. Lennie's expression was troubled. He squeezed her hand gently as they walked into the cold whiteness with snowflakes gusting around their feet.

43

House Call

I wanna
Li' Li' Li' Lick you
From yo' head to yo' toes
An' I wanna,

Music blasted from the speakers. The party rocked. Revelers caroused throughout the ski house. Ecstasy and opium peddlers did brisk business. Shrooms had their fanciers and cokeheads were not slouches. A happy conga line wended its way from the living room with its strong, sickly sweet scent of marijuana from a supersize bong, it snaked up the stairs through the loft and bedrooms, interrupting couples on the beds; then meandered back down to the kitchen for refills on libations. Young, white, Ivy-League America was partying.

"Yo! Where's the fuckin' beer!" yelled the leader getting no response from the keg's spigot.

"Where's the fuckin' beer."

"Where's the fuckin' beer." The line took up the chant.

"Man, this is hot!" said Buddy, as eyes shining he entered the ski house and breathed air thick with marijuana, nicotine, clove cigarettes and exciting, illicit odors he could not define. "Wow! Thanks, Jay, I had no idea a party could be like this." He stared at a laughing group where men poured liquor into a funnel inserted in the mouth of a bare-breasted girl with a silver nipple ring and hair a shade of red not seen in nature; his nature rose as his breathing quickened.

"Stick around me, kid. I'll show you the ropes. The girls said it'd rock. These girls that I was in Jack and Jill with got hold of the key to their parents' ski house-So here we are." Jason flung his hands in the air and did a little dance. "Oh yeah!"

"Hey, Mr. Bojangles; you made it-who's the young cutie?" said a fat, black girl, bearing down on them with a hard lemonade in her hand.

"Hey Mikki, or is it Makki? I still can't tell you two apart. What's with the bitch drink? I hope you've got more serious stuff than that. This is my young cousin, Buddy. Youngblood's spending the weekend with me and I'm giving him a taste of college life. You know, let him see what it's like to hang with a college crowd. It'll encourage him to study hard so he can be like us some day. Right m'man?"

"Sure," said Buddy with a grin.

"Well, enjoy. Go on into the kitchen, there's beer there for you he-men; some of the guys brought their own forties. If you want more serious stuff they're organizing round-the-world upstairs. That'll put some hair on your chest. There's a Mexican area with Tequila, Russian with vodka, America's got apple pie shots-the kid will love them. You get a shot of rum, then cider, than someone sprays whipped cream into your mouth; it's the best! I'm headed there now. I'm gonna get shit-faced tonight. Woo eee, parteee!" the girl made a circle with her large hips then laughed and moved off sucking on her bottled bitch drink.

In the kitchen was an identical, fat, black girl. "Jason," she screamed, and rushed and enveloped him in a hug. "You got my e-mail, I am so glad to see you!"

"Yeah, it's been a while. I brought my cousin, Buddy."

"Great." She said softly, "It's always good to see another black face, you know what I mean. I e-mailed a few other kids from the old Jack and Jill lists, but they're scattered all over the place now. So it's this U-Penn crowd here except for you two. You're at Columbia, right?"

"Yeah," said Jason.

"Well, thank God you two came." She whispered, "This party's so *white.*" Then she stuck her head out the doorway and yelled, "Someone bring in another keg from the deck, please! Here, kid, help me, move this empty one," she said to Buddy.

As Buddy obliged, Jason tossed some trail mix into his mouth and left to join the party. Soon a new keg appeared and guests swarmed the kitchen for refills. Buddy stood to the side feeling lost as he watched the party and waited for Jason's return.

"Lemme at that keg. I can drink as much as any man here!" declared a petite blonde, elbowing her way to the keg then knocking back a plastic cup of suds, following it with a rapid refill.

"Move shrimp," a huge, dark-haired, woolly mammoth of a woman broke from the pack, shoved the blonde to the side good-naturedly and had her time at the trough.

"She-man!" snarled the smaller woman.

Crash!

"Oh, shit! What was that?" yelled the black twin who was still in the kitchen.

"The statue that was on the pedestal in the living room," replied her sister nonchalantly as she danced in carrying a plastic cup of vodka and an almost empty bowl of pretzels .Her lower face was smeared with whipped cream, she giggled. "The kids were throwing stuff at it to see who could hit it first. Some other kids are playing Beer Pong and they keep missing the cups and knocking over stuff. They've had to take so many penalty drinks for missing that they're all like completely smashed! The women are drinking as much as the men. There's a Goth chick that's got a wooden leg! Man, this party's on fire!" She threw the last of the pretzels into her mouth and barked with laughter.

"Say what?" said Makki.

Buddy watched wide-eyed as Mikki chugged the last of her drink, grabbed a wine cooler from an ice chest, and then pawed through the sticky, overflowing kitchen counter until she found a half-empty snack bag. She emptied most of into her mouth and some into the bowl. "Someone's got to make a snack run," she observed as she chewed. "We're out. We need more of these spicy pork rinds they're-"

Makki interrupted. "Damn, Mikki! Look around you! They're trashing the place-"

"Come play, Flip the Cup; you can be on my team. It's fun!" She popped the top of her brilliant magenta drink and slurped thirstily. "You half fill this cup and chug it, then you have to-"

"Fuck it, Mikki! Look around you!" shrieked her twin.

"Yeah, the party's slammin'!" Mikki exclaimed. "You know what? You need to get a buzz on. You're too uptight." She put her drink on the counter, clapped her hands and shook her big booty as she sang,

The men them at the party, party, party

All a dem is sexy, sexy, sexy.

Oh Lord, have his mercy.

A flushed, red-nosed, drunken youth staggered into the kitchen. He squatted behind Mikki, wrapped his pale hands around her big body cupping her breasts and freaked her. She laughed and took a thirsty slurp of wine cooler, then put her hands over his, and did a slow, deep, satisfying grind into him as she sang,

Me feelin' irie, irie, irie

Lord, have his mercy"

"Mikki, stop this now! Lose that dong with the luminous nose; they're trashing the place! Some virgin bitch popped her cherry on the white comforter upstairs; there's goddamn cum and bloodstains all over it. Mom's gonna kill us. There's beer, urine and wine stains on the carpets! The bathrooms are disgusting. A jerk threw bottles down the powder room toilet bowl. There's shit on the floor! And on top of the bottles! The toilet's clogged up and overflowing. It smells like fuckin' ass down there and it's just as bad upstairs. Mikki, Help! We've got to get these ass-holes out of here!"

"Peashe, shishter." The drunken youth admonished then nuzzled Mikki's neck and mumbled, "Wanna go upshtairsh?"

"So help me, you fucked up cocksucker; you leave this room with my sister and I'll fuck you over!" Makki yelled at the drunk.

"Sister, chill!" laughed Mikki guzzling more wine cooler.

"Yesh, shish, chill!" The youth squeezed Mikki's large breasts and she sighed.

"Irie, irie," she whispered and lolled her head back on his shoulder.

"Stop that!" snapped her sister.

"Panteeee! Panteee! Panteeee!" came a wild yell from upstairs.

Buddy followed the shout and saw a robust, young, white man rush downstairs, naked, except for the black lace, thong panty on his head. "Panteee!" he yelled again, pulling it off and waving it in the air. "Catch!" He flung it to a nearby boy, who caught it, sniffed it, said "Aaaaah!" and leered before tossing it to the next young man.

Buddy felt uneasy and looked around for Jason, who was still nowhere in sight. What he did see was a naked, blonde girl with brown pubic hair stumbling downstairs. She ran the gauntlet past young men who groped her in her flight. She lurched to the beige sofa where she sprawled onto her back, limbs asunder, and retched.

Makki, watching in horror from the kitchen doorway, yelled; "Somebody turn her head sideways so she doesn't choke on her vomit."

"Hey, somebody open up her legs some more, I'm not getting a good view!" complained an aggrieved voice."

"Call an ambulance," shrieked a woman's voice, "she could die."

"The bitch won't die, let's have a go at her," said a young man, who with his beard and long hair looked like white society's version of Jesus. The silver peace sign on his necklace danced as he quickly unbuckled, turned the girl's head sideways and set to it.

Why can't I have

Just one fuck

sang the Violent Femmes from the speakers.

"Shit! This thing's getting freaky," said an uneasy female voice next to Buddy who was now feeling queasy. Why didn't Jason come? Why didn't Jason stop them from hurting that girl?

"It's all good", a green-haired lad dreamily assured everyone as he passed the dutchie on the left-hand side.

The group on the floor, playing Beeropoly, popped open some more 40s. Someone belched loudly. The game was getting intense.

A hostess twin with a swain in tow, headed for the stairs. Her sister yelled, "Mikki, don't you dare go upstairs with that skank!"

Mikki, however, bitch drink in hand, mounted the first step. Her twin yanked her sweater. The girl tumbled backward spilling the drink onto herself and her sister as they both tumbled to the floor. The frustrated swain on the second step turned around, looked at the fallen sisters, pulled out his penis and urinated on them. In the background the girl on the sofa softly moaned as the fourth young man mounted her.

"She's sleeping so she won't mind," he said, "I'll take sloppy seconds;" then he took his turn.

"Shit Mikki! Why the hell did you invite all these white freaks?" sobbed Makki rolling out from under her twin and scrambling up. "You know they don't know how to party. All they ever do is talk bullshit, drink, drug and fuck drunk girls! If we'd had black kids, they'd have danced, dry humped on the dance-floor and gone home-They wouldn't trash the damn place." She grasped her urine sodden twin's hand and hauled her up. In what seemed to be an afterthought, she reached out and yanked the drunken young man's penis – hard, screaming, "Take that, ass-hole. Look at us – covered with fucking piss and liquor! I should kick your sorry, white ass!"

"**OW**!" He shrieked in a shrill falsetto as he cupped the sensitive organ and doubled over in pain. "Black bitch, I'm gonna hurt you-oooooooooo!" He started out like Smokey Robinson but gave his finale on the high notes of a dying diva before sinking to the bottom step sobbing out his agony.

"Mikki, Why the fuck did you invite them?!" Makki wailed again.

"Why do y'think? Face it, we're fat and dark; who's gonna take us on? We're sure as hell not gettin' ass from any of the black guys any day soon, they want white chicks, or fine, light-skinned, skinny, black chicks. They don't want us! So what the hell! I told a couple o' white frat guys from my lab section about the house. They said they'd drive over. Maybe we can hook up with a few of 'em later, they're spending the night-"

"No, they're not! Are you mad! Ever hear of AIDS? Or self respect?"

"And look, it's a great party!" Mikki supported herself against the wall and waved at the chaos around them.

"You're fuckin' drunk!" screamed her sister. "Come, let's shower off this shit." She grabbed her twin.

Buddy wished he were anywhere but there. He followed the twins in fascination and fear. They seemed unaware of him. Where was Jason? He dared not look for him in this crowd. The fat sisters would have to do 'til his cousin showed up.

One sister pushed the other into the fetid downstairs bathroom. "Into the shower," she commanded. "What the – she skidded and flailed her arms, fortuitously steadying herself on a towel-rack. "Goddamn vomit!" she said in disgust belatedly sidestepping the mess on the floor. She slid open the door around the tub, put her foot in and screamed.

"What the hell's wrong now?" snapped her twin.

"There's a dead guy in here!" She rushed to the bathroom door, pushed past Buddy and yelled,"Help! Help! Somebody, please help! One of you is dead!"

If I cannot be with you
Maybe I could have a taste
boomed the loud party music.

A woman sporting blonde dreadlocks, a nose ring and a black velvet skirt over blue jeans, came. "What's the problem?" she drawled, swirling ice around in a plastic cup of water.

"Dead guy in the bathtub!" shrieked the twin.

"Lemme see," said the young woman. She hop scotched over the puke, past the feces encrusted toilet bowl and the piss on the floor, to the tub. There she poked in her combat boot shod foot and kicked the man full in the face. He groaned and moved slightly but did not awaken. "He's not dead yet, just drunk off his ass." She looked with distaste at his vomit stained clothes. "Call the medics, he could die. And you smell awful! In fact this place smells like if a goddamn pack of animals crawled in here and died farting! Shit, you people are weird!" She sauntered out of the bathroom shaking her cup of iced water.

Makki hysterically called the police then hung up and yelled, "You shitheads had better get the fuck out of here-the cops are coming."

"Oof!" The last Ivy League kid collapsed, panting on top of the drunken girl. "Gotta go," he mumbled then passed out. His friends dragged him off and one of them jammed a nearby bottle up the young woman's slick vagina. They smashed any breakables they encountered as they high-tailed it out of there; the less wasted dragging the drunk and the stoned. Someone deposited a steaming pile of turds at the open front door, a friend added urine.

Buddy hid in terror. He heard the college kids peel off, tires screeching, cars fishtailing in the snow as they fled helter-skelter, down the narrow mountain road. He trembled and wished for Jason. He had never felt so alone. Finally he came shaking out of his hiding place, behind the far side of the kitchen island and looked around at the mess and the busted furniture. He was numb and scared. He looked longingly at the lighted ski slopes in the distance, so clean and white. He wondered where Jason was. Why hadn't he taken him skiing? Tears welled in his eyes. He wanted his mother. A blast of cold air gusted into the smelly room from the open front door. The fat twin girls sitting together on a love seat, shivered and Buddy's teeth chattered.

"What's going on, where's everybody?" said Jason, breezing into the room with a pretty, green-eyed blonde who clung to his arm and gazed up at him adoringly.

"Where the hell were you?" said Makki. "There's been a gang rape. There's probably a dead guy in the bathtub. Take your cousin and get the hell out-now! The cops are coming."

"Oh shit! Come Buddy; gotta split, m'man," said Jason disentangling himself and running for the door. "Oops sorry, you come too. What's your name?" he said to the blonde girl, holding out his hand to her.

Suddenly they heard the wail of sirens followed by the loud screeching of tires.

"Fuck!" said Jason.

"Quick, this way," Makki jumped up. "The side door-take the kid. Run into the woods. You can come back for your car later." She opened a door and pushed the three of them, jacket-less, out into the frigid night.

Heavy footsteps mounted the wooden, front porch steps and a deep voice exclaimed, "Holy shit! What the hell…" The voice trailed off.

As they stole past a window, Buddy saw Makki close the drunken girl's legs and shudder visibly.

44

At Home with the Gopilals

Charlie said family grace as early morning sunlight flooded the Gopilal dining room and glinted off the glass and silverware on the breakfast table.

"What do you want for Christmas, Poopsie?" Lennie asked Germaine when they opened their eyes.

"Daddy, I'm not Poopsie. Stop calling me crazy West Indian names that have bad American meanings-like Poopsie and Dou-Dou?" she said with exasperation.

"Okay, Boo, is that American enough for you?" Lennie winked at Charlie.

She smiled. Lennie was a good father when he chose to be. They could so easily be the happy family she remembered from her early childhood, except that Lennie was a louse of a husband. Why couldn't they have been like Lola and Tyrone? Those two really loved each other and lived for their kids. It was ironic that Maxi and Lola, her two best friends had good marriages while she; Mrs. Success had-

"Mommy, I said when is Mumtaz coming."

Germaine's voice pulled Charlie out of her reverie. "I don't know, dear, maybe Daddy knows." She felt Lennie's eyes on her. She concentrated on her grapefruit and vowed that he would not get back into her bed. She deserved more than to be a meal ticket and to get badly serviced occasionally. Even for Germaine that price was too high.

"Daddy, do you know when Mumtaz is coming?"

"She'll call. I don't think she's on vacation yet."

"I'll come with you when you go to pick her up. I like the Sarah Lawrence campus. Those kids dress so weird and look so out of it."

"You might look like that one day too, Kitten," he teased. "Of course you'll come. We'll all go-Mommy too." He looked at Charlie.

Charlie smiled, "I can probably come if you give me enough notice." Damn! The time for him to have mended fences was before I got a lover and learned what it was like to make love with a friend she thought grimly. She attacked her grapefruit with renewed vigor.

"Great, we'll go to CPK for pizza afterward," said Germaine"

"So, Gee, you and Mumtaz are very friendly these days," said Charlie.

"Yeah, she's nice. Her big problem is that phony accent."

"I wouldn't say so," said Lennie.

"Sure, you wouldn't say so," retorted his daughter. "She's your cousin. When you were in Trinidad you probably talked just like her. She sounds like a bad imitation of the people on Masterpiece Theater that Mom's started watching."

Charlie took a slice of toast from the rack and smiled broadly. She had to see Lennie's response to this one. But he surprised her.

"Charlie, that's an awfully pretty outfit you're wearing. Is it new?"

Germaine looked at her father in surprise. He and her mother hadn't had this kind of exchange in a while. Charlie did look pretty in a pink suit, but not startlingly so.

"Yes," replied Charlie.

"Excellent taste, you're wearing it well."

"Thank you," she murmured. She busied herself pouring coffee and adding sugar and cream. "By the way Germaine, I'm getting you a French au pair. She arrives later this week. She's been working with a family in Manhattan, but the father-a lawyer-lost his job and they can't afford to keep her. So we lucked out."

"That's great! It's just what Gee needs," said Lennie, again surprising her.

"Why are you getting me an au pair; I thought you didn't like that sort of thing?" Germaine said suspiciously.

"I don't but you got a B+ in French last marking period. Therese can help you. You'll practice French with her and bring that grade up to A+ where it belongs."

"Lennie rose and said heartily," Hey, when you get that French together we'll go to Martinique, Paris if you want. I'll be in early tonight. Why don't we pick up some videos and pizza later?" He stood by his daughter's chair and ruffled her hair.

"Daddy, you forgot. The school's winter concert is tonight. I'm playing harp in the orchestra and I have a solo in the chorale, we're doing the Messiah."

"Of course," Lennie exclaimed, slapping his forehead in mock horror. "How could I have forgotten? I'll see you later at school then; Mommy and I'll be in the audience rooting for you. By the way, that's a pretty necklace you're wearing. Someone has good taste." He winked at Charlie and left.

Damn! thought Charlie again; this is just what Lola thinks my life is-the perfect family. But it's all roses over the septic tank. She smiled at her daughter. "Of course we'll be there, darling. I wouldn't miss it for the world," she said.

"Great," exclaimed Germaine. "I'm so glad that you can both make it."

As soon as Charlie dropped Germaine off at school, she called her lover.

"Charlie," he said, sounding pleased to hear her. "When are you coming?"

"I can't make it until after Christmas."

"Then you'll meet my boys. They're spending their school holiday week with me."

"Is your wife bringing them?"

"No. They're big boys, you'll see. And by the way, it's ex-wife, not wife."

"Oh," she said unenthusiastically.

"Hey, you're not jealous of my ex are you?" asked Roderick.

"No, should I be? Remember, I still have a husband."

"Truuue," he said drawing out the word then he broke into a calypso, *Boy, tell me who do you love?"*

"Okay," said Charlie, laughing. "Sorry. I am jealous. What can I do about it ?"

"Come, make love to me. That'll put everything back into perspective."

"You still think your magic wand has all the answers don't you?"

"Most of them."

"Jerk! Gotta go now. There's another call on the line. I hate doing this call waiting nonsense on a cell phone when I'm driving. Talk to you later. Love ya."

"Love you too. Think of me at twelve fifteen. Better still; let's have a cyber sex date. I'll meet you on-line to guide you to the biggest orgasm of your life."

"Perv!" said Charlie, already throbbing with anticipation. "See ya," she hung up with a big grin on her face and launched into a series of Kegels.

The day flew by and soon it was time for Germaine's program. They had a cold night for the concert. A homogenous group of parents all rich, and white – except for Charlie and Lennie, milled around outside the auditorium.

Charlie glanced at her watch then looked around her. She easily spotted Lennie in this crowd and went to join him. She would put on a show of solidarity for the white folks tonight. She would not support the popular black statistic of single mother or dysfunctional family that didn't know how to behave in public.

"Excuse me, my good man." A tall elegant blonde in a black mink coat advanced on Lennie. "Please adjust the heat. It's far too cold in here."

Lennie looked nonplused. Charlie hid her amusement and sailed to his rescue.

"I recognize you," she said heartily to the woman. "You got busted for running that prostitution ring in Manhattan; I saw you in the newspaper. They said you also turned tricks if business was too brisk for your girls to handle alone. You're famous! And democratic! Lennie, did you ever think we'd meet a celebrity here?"

"What?" asked Lennie, now totally confused. People around them grew quiet and covertly observed the little group where the woman now stood blushing furiously.

"You're quite mista-" the woman started to say.

"I can't wait to tell my friends," gushed Charlie. "Can I have your autograph? Oh dear, I don't have a pen on me. And we thought this was going to be a stodgy neighborhood. But not with you around!" Charlie playfully tapped the woman on the arm and winked broadly at her. She hooked her arm through Lennie's "But it's naughty of you to proposition him, he doesn't indulge. We're both too afraid of AIDS," she stage-whispered. Then nutria cape billowing behind her she swept off with her spouse.

The performance was stellar. Germaine played the harp then sang like an angel. Charlie's mind drifted as she sat in the warm, dark auditorium. She imagined what it would be like to go to a school performance with Roderick. They would sit in the dark and hold hands. It would be so intimate. She sighed, and shifted away from Lennie.

"What's wrong?" inquired Lennie.

"Nothing, I'm a bit cramped, that's all."

She looked at Germaine up there on the stage-the only black child. She didn't look like them, despite her light skin and curly hair, but she qualified financially. Charlie glowed with pride. She would see that she always did.

"Darling, you were wonderful!" Charlie enthusiastically hugged her daughter afterward.

"You think so?" said Germaine, happily munching on a cookie from the refreshments set out for the children and their parents.

"Definitely," asserted Lennie, hugging her too. "This calls for a celebration. Let's go for pizza."

"Oh Daddy, thank you," cried the child, hanging onto his arm. "Can we rent a video afterward?"

"I don't see why not. It's a Friday nigh. Charlie?" he said.

"Sounds good to me," she said.

Lennie was sweet and charming. They ate at California Pizza Kitchen, and then went to Blockbuster Video. "Hey, girls, let's get these." Lennie held up Miracle on Thirty Fourth Street and Frank Capra's It's A Wonderful Life.

"Oh Lennie, that's pure corn," Charlie waved him away.

"Okay. You pick then," he said agreeably. They ended up with his choices anyway.

Armed with microwave popcorn they watched the movies in the den. Lennie sat next to Charlie. She was uncomfortable. She felt his eyes on her much of the time. Finally he nonchalantly draped his arm around the back of the sofa and it somehow ended up touching her shoulder. She shifted slightly and felt the tension as he tried to figure out if she was settling into the arm or rejecting it. They both suspended breathing and movement while Germaine contentedly watched the TV screen, oblivious to the little tableau being played out beside her.

Charlie thought of Germaine. The child loved her father. She remembered her own deprived childhood after her father's death. Then she remembered her deprived adulthood-solitary nights with only Germaine for company and Lennie coming home at four in the morning smelling of liquor and women, his recent flirting at her housewarming party, and at other parties in the past. She thought of Roderick-of talking and laughing with him, his emotional caring for her, of making delicious love. Ever so slightly she eased away from the tentative arm. The arm stayed, lightly drumming the sofa-back.

"Mommy, stop fidgeting," ordered Germaine.

Lennie put his arm back by his side, but Charlie had seen the olive branch and had heard Germaine's unspoken plea for a happy family. Did she owe it to her to try yet again? Lennie was trying, damn him. She slept alone again that night, and after much tossing and turning drifted into a fitful sleep.

45

Brooklyn Jaunt

"You're leaving now?" Charlie said into the 'phone to Maxi. She supported the phone between her ear and shoulder, as she searched for her deodorant. "Fine, I'll be ready. Don't stop for Lola, she can't make it. Her kids have a violin recital this afternoon." Charlie hung up and went in search of Lennie's deodorant.

Lennie was still asleep in the guestroom as Charlie tiptoed past him to the bathroom. She hunted unsuccessfully through the clutter of toiletries on the bathroom counter. She wondered if he would one day be restored to her bed, she hoped not soon. She rummaged through a drawer and found two packages of condoms and receipts for a hotel room used just last week with adult channel and room service charges. There was a receipt dated two days ago, for dinner for two at B. Smith's soul food restaurant. Charlie closed the drawer. She'd use baking soda as deodorant today. She looked at Lennie with loathing on her way out. The leopard truly had not changed its spots. He was willing to make up with her yet keep up his affairs. He rolled over and farted in his sleep, as she left the room.

Charlie dressed and was slipping on her low-heeled pumps when there was a knock on her bedroom door, "Come in," she called.

Evadne entered. "Mrs. Gopilal, Mrs. Alsop is downstairs. She's very upset."

"Thank-you, Evadne, tell her I'll be right down." She glanced in the mirror, grabbed her bag and hurried out of the room filled with curiosity.

The young woman sprang up from her chair, sobbing when Charlie entered the living room. "Oh, Charlie, I shouldn't have bothered you. But I had nowhere else to go,"

"What is it, Dear?" asked Charlie, in alarm, putting her arm around Lola's shoulder and guiding her to the sofa. "Sit, tell me what's wrong. Would you like a cup of tea?"

"No, thanks, I already had breakfast. In fact I was having breakfast when it happened." Lola shuddered and broke into fresh sobs.

"What?" Charlie put her arm around her friend's shoulders.

"That phone call!" Lola's voice broke off and ended in a wail. "I let Rebbie use our ski house," she sobbed. "She let her college kids use it. They had a wild party and wrecked the place. A young woman was drugged and gang-raped; she's in the hospital. A young man drank too much and ended up in a coma. He just died and his parents are filthy rich, show biz folks who're now suing us!" Lola now bawled in earnest.

Charlie was speechless. She squeezed Lola's shoulder comfortingly and silently handed her tissues from a package in her bag.

"Leroy went ape shit!" Lola sniffled. "We're in awful trouble. Some states hold homeowners responsible for under-age drinking on their premises even if they're not there when it happens. Leroy called me terrible names. He yelled at me and told me to get out." Lola sobbed loudly and her eyes and nose streamed.

Charlie fed her more tissues and Lola blew her nose and continued. "Charlie what will I do? I have nowhere to go-that poor girl and the dead boy!" She sobbed afresh.

Charlie felt helpless. She rubbed Lola's back and said soothingly, "Hush, you'll stay here, of course. I've plenty of room. Give Leroy time to calm down, this can be worked out." Charlie felt sickened at what had happened to this innocent. Damn Rebbie!

"Charlie, what will I do? I miss the kids already. We have their Suzuki violin recital this afternoon. They practiced so hard..." She subsided into more tears.

"Lola, I know this is hard for you, but there will be more recitals-many more. The best thing you can do now is lay low and let Leroy handle this. He will. He has to."

Lola blew her nose. "I know; he's so smart, and good. I made this horrible thing happen to him. They destroyed the house; he loved that house so much."

"And he loves you, Lola," Charlie said firmly.

Maxi came into the room. "Charlie, Evadne said you were in here with Lola, are you ready? Sorry, am I interrupting something?" she said at the sight of Lola's pale, tear-stained face and swollen, red eyes.

"Lola has a problem," said Charlie. She put her arm protectively around the young woman's shoulder.

"You can tell her, Charlie, I don't mind," Lola whispered sniffling. "Leroy says it'll probably make the newspapers."

Maxi paled at the story. She hugged Lola, "You poor thing! What a foul thing to happen. I'm so sorry. If there's anything I can do, anything at all..."

"Thank you," said Lola, then she put her head down in her hands and sobbed loudly. Charlie and Maxi fed her tissues.

When she seemed to have cried herself out Charlie said, "Lola, you must stop beating up on yourself. You made a mistake – it was just that, an error of judgment. You're not helping anyone by making yourself sick; so it's back to bed now in my guest room-doctor's orders, come."

Charlie settled Lola in the guestroom. "Please try not to think about it too much. I want you to take a nap and when you wake up do something mindless-watch TV or read; there are tons of books and magazines downstairs. When Germaine wakes up you'll have lunch with her." Charlie and Maxi hugged Lola and left her sniffling on the bed, face turned to the wall.

Outside, Maxi's car was parked in the circular driveway at the front of the house. "Charlie, meet Esther, my new neighbor. She's our navigator today," Maxi indicated an attractive, brown-haired, white woman who sat knitting in the front passenger seat. "Esther, sorry we took so long, something came up."

"That's okay; I just pulled out my knitting and got on with it. I want to finish this for my brother's baby. I'm going to be an Auntie any day now. Isn't it darling?" She held up a delicate little white poncho, and the women exclaimed at its tiny beauty.

"Park your car in the back and we'll use my maid, Evadne's car; you don't want to take a nice car into Brooklyn," Charlie said to Maxi.

"Good thinking," said Maxi as she complied.

"Evadne has a nice car," Maxi said climbing into the back seat of the Corolla a few minutes later. You're right not to drive an expensive car into Brooklyn."

"Yeah, I figured it's cheaper to fix Evadne's if anything happens," said Charlie.

"Charlie, I've looked forward to meeting you, Maxi just sings your praises," said Esther, the navigator, riding shotgun.

"Thank you. But don't believe everything you hear," Charlie said with a laugh as she headed for the Major Deegan and Brooklyn.

46

Ladies Who Lunch

"We can't go wrong getting the children's holiday clothes from Sol's in Brooklyn. He has the absolute best prices," declared Esther.

"Why do Jewish women always know the best places to shop?" said Maxi.

"Because we do our homework," Esther replied smugly.

"I believe you," said Maxi. "I have a Christian friend whose Jewish husband wanted her to convert. She said she would when he started dressing her like the Jewish women in the neighborhood. There's been no more talk of conversion."

"That's a riot," said Esther. "Charlie, get into the right lane. Maxi, I love your-watch out for that truck, Charlie-sense of humor. Here's the Interborough. As I was saying, the clothes are just fabulous. All the best people shop there-politician's wives, diplomats, business people..."

"I can't wait," said Maxi.

"Careful, Charlie, you're straddling two lanes," warned Esther. "Get to the middle of your lane."

Charlie regretted two things: not being in the Bahamas, and not being free to ram her fist down Esther's throat.

"Exit here," said Esther suddenly.

"Shit!" said Charlie swerving viciously into the right lane and almost causing an accident as she successfully exited.

"Sorry," said Esther. "Now keep straight. Oh no! Don't hit that pregnant woman!"

"Esther," Charlie said through gritted teeth, as she slammed on the brakes and the vehicles behind her honked furiously. "I am driving. You say what route to take. But don't tell me how to drive. I'll knock down anyone I damn well please! Okay?"

"Touchy!" said Esther, turning around to wink at Maxi.

"I don't see any street signs," said Maxi. "How do people find their way around Brooklyn, by radar?"

"Naturally, they assume we can't read. So why bother to replace street signs in black neighborhoods?" said Charlie.

On Eastern parkway they drove on a narrow service road behind a large, black Lincoln. The driver stopped suddenly, effectively blocking them.

"Charlie," said Maxi urgently, "for God's sake, don't blow your horn. I want to live to get Tatty's clothes home to her."

Eventually a heavyset black woman emerged from the Lincoln. She reached into the car, took out a package, chatted some more with the driver, and then slowly waddled to a nearby apartment building. After she was inside, the car accelerated loudly and left.

Sol's Kiddies' Fashion Emporium sat on a commercial block dotted with burnt out buildings and overflowing boxes of curbside garbage. People in African robes, Kente crowns, nostril rings, big jeans, short and long dreadlocks all paraded past-Brooklyn was out taking the winter sun. A black teenager danced by in oversized jeans with a Boom Box on his shoulder. His loud rap music urged men to do sadistic things to bitches and hoes. A group gathered around the teenager and executed the latest moves, which all involved clutching at their privates as they rapped along with the music.

"Do we have to get out?" asked Maxi shrinking back into her seat.

Nearby, a loud argument raged. A young woman in a large black and white polka dot, velvet top hat, with the brim turned back and held by a bow as big as her generous backside cussed out a man with abundant locks stuffed into a huge, bright, Rasta tam.

"Blood claat'" he exclaimed and spat on the ground in front of her.

"Now I understand why Sophie said she wasn't up to dealing with Wakim and Abdullah today when I invited her," said Charlie, laughing. "Ladies shall we?" Charlie unlocked the car door and indicated the teeming outdoors.

"Obviously young black men listening to this type of music, led what's her name? that black feminist writer? to pronounce herself more afraid of black men than she was of AIDS," said Maxi climbing out reluctantly. "Listen."

You know you like it like I do
Put your lips around my dick
And suck my ass-hole too.

The boom box blared the golden oldie.

"Their dance is a sort of urban ballet," suggested Esther helpfully as the group of young rappers continued to clutch their crotches and do their dance moves.

"Sociologists probably describe this as the mating call of blackibus urbanus, the black urban ghetto male," said Charlie.

"No doubt," said Maxi. "Whatever happened to sentimental songs like the "Indian Love Call?"This is evil. Let's get into the store." She pulled her black mink protectively around her and wished that she had worn a cloth coat. This did not look like mink country.

"How can Sol have an upscale business on a block like this?" Charlie said. "This neighborhood can scare away his customers."

"Dream on," said Esther as a Cadillac drew up and disgorged several fur bedecked, white women. "Wait till you see Sol's prices. I'd venture into Palestine for these bargains. Why should Sol be in a fancy area? Then he'd charge outrageous prices."

Sol's was everything Esther had claimed. He greeted her enthusiastically. He and several young assistants were everywhere. They pulled things from racks, dived under shelves to bring out overflow to show to customers and popped up out of nowhere to answer questions. Mrs. Sol sat above it all, on a high stool behind an elevated counter. She smiled and monitored a bank of security screens as she rang up goods on the busy cash register.

"Charlie?" hissed Maxi "Look at this price!"

Charlie squeezed her way to Maxi past a group of Japanese women. She blinked when she saw the price tag. "Obviously we've been shopping in the wrong places," For the next two hours they shopped happily at the right place

"Maxi, is that you?" A tall, stunning woman touched Maxi's arm. She was a light-skinned black with gray eyes, wide lips, and a long aquiline nose. Short, kinky, red hair framed her arresting face.

"Omigod! Fanella! It can't be you. I haven't seen you since I left Dominica."

They flew on each other with enthusiastic hugs. Bystanders observed them curiously.

"...we live in Park Slope in the most adorable house with a dock in our backyard."

"...in Chappaqua, I've got a daughter-"

"My husband's a film maker. We met while he was on location at home."

"I'm so happy for you. I've never met a black film maker," said Maxi.

"Lawrence is white! Bet you never expected the little barefoot red girl with hard hair, who ran around your estate picking up the cane breakings, to show up in New York married to a white, film maker, did you?"

Maxi blushed and Fanella gave a great whooping laugh. Just then Charlie and Esther showed up. "Charlie and Esther, meet my sister, Fanella," said Maxi. "Half-sister," she amended at Charlie's look of surprise.

"Charmed," Fanella extended a large, soft, well-manicured hand, glistening with rings, and shook hands with the women.

Maxi and Fanella caught up on each other's lives as they finished their shopping.

"Let's eat some Caribbean food," said Fanella.

"I'd love to," said Esther. "Moishe and I always enjoy Caribbean food.

"Good. Maxi, do you remember Maisie?" asked Fanella.

"Sure. She studied Biochem at NYU, didn't she?"

"Right!" said Fanella. "She has a restaurant around here; the food's delicious."

"Around here?" said Maxi in surprise.

"Yeah, let's go."

Fanella convinced them to walk. They looked dubiously at each other, then at tall Fanella, bedecked in mink, pearls and diamonds-a mugger's dream.

"Well, it's every man for himself and God for us all," said Charlie with a shrug. She looked at her watch. "We won't put this stuff in the trunk, someone will break in if they see us stowing things. You sure it's within walking distance, Fanella?"

"It's right round the corner. Maxi, Maisie will be so happy to see you again." Fanella hugged Maxi and beamed. "Fancy running into my baby sister in Brooklyn."

They walked to a grimy storefront. A sign on the door proclaimed that Married Man Pork, Bull balls and Mannish Water were sold within. Esther looked queasy. Fanella pressed the buzzer and a man with long dread locks peered out, and then buzzed them in.

"All is good," he said solemnly.

"Huh?" said Maxi.

Fanella dug her in the ribs and responded, "All is good. Haroun, how you? Shahrazad here? Maisie changed her name to Shahrazad," Fanella explained to Maxi.

"She in the back cooking up some cow kin soup. You want take some home for you' husban'? You'll have more fun tonight than y' ever had before." He winked broadly.

"You too wicked!" Fanella said clapping him on the shoulder. She turned to Esther and said, "Cow kin soup is made with the bull's testicles." She turned back to Haroun, "What's good today? We want to eat some real Caribbean food."

"Come." He beckoned them into a cramped, dingy room with large boxes lining the walls, a dark, wooden counter stood in front of a Dutch door on the far side.

"Shahrazad!" he bawled. "Shahrazad!"

Shahrazad came to the Dutch door, wiping her hand on a towel. Haroun hit her full across the mouth with the flat of his hand.

"Woman, you take too long to answer me. Learn respect," he said.

The watching women flinched.

"Tell the ladies what is good today." He said, placing the stress in ladies on the second syllable.

She lowered her eyes and said, "Haroun, I sorry I was disobedient and didn't answer you right away. I come as fast as I could."

He looked mollified. "Well see it don' happen again. The Bible say a soft word turneth away wrath. You ladies remember that, an' go treat your own husban's nice." He grinned widely displaying two big gold-capped teeth. "Now go outside again and come in t'rough de next door. That is where we does sell the cook food. Shahrazad goin' meet you there an' take your order, then you come back in here an' eat in the back room behin' dere." He pointed to the dark recesses of the shop. "She goin' bring the food to you."

On the other side of the shop, a group of men stood around a counter debating the day's offerings. Charlie noticed Esther looking dubiously at the insalubrious surroundings and smiled to herself. This was definitely different from Chappaqua.

"They have roti," said Maxi with delight.

"Yes, but look at what I found!" Charlie pointed to the greasy handwritten menu taped to the counter. "Pepper pot! I haven't had that in years. Shahrazad, you used good cassareep to put up this thing?"

Shahrazad glared at her. "It's good enough for the neighborhood people; I don't know about you." She turned to the group of men. "You men were here first. What you eating?"

The women waited patiently while the men gave their order with much discussion and many changes. Finally they left with rotis, cow kin soup and Irish Moss drinks.

A small, thin man with a head full of long, beaded plaits decorated with gold balls, confided on the way out, "Tonight me haffe wreck a pum-pum."

Fanella hooted with laughter, "Get lost, dry foot bwoy."

"Yeah, some sisters goin' have a good time tonight," said Haroun, entering from a back door. "That Irish Moss does make a man irie! Take it with cow kin soup, you know, the cow balls-Lordy, some women in this neighborhood goin' be in trouble tonight. Woooo! Is pure virility time!" He slapped his knee and barked with laughter.

Charlie stole a glance at Esther. She was dead white and appeared dazed. Charlie turned to Haroun. "Haroun, tell me about the pepper pot. What you put in it?"

"Girl, where you from?"

"My mother was from Barbados. What's in the pepper pot?" "

"Oy! Is a Bajan! Well, you an' me understan' each other, cause I is a Guyanese; an' where you think half the people in Guyana come from? Buhbados!" he answered himself. "Well, the pepper pot Miss 'Bados, it have old fowl cock."

"Cock?" said Esther faintly.

"Hey!" laughed Maxi. "He means a male hen. It has to be old and hard for this concoction, because this thing can be cooked for months-sometimes years. You keep adding to it and the cassareep preserves it. It stays on the stove and is reheated daily."

"Sounds a bit like the French 'pot au feu'..." said Esther doubtfully.

"You know 'bout dis too?" Haroun regarded Maxi suspiciously.

"I'm from Dominica and I grew up with your wife," said Maxi. She didn't add, but the bitch won't acknowledge me.

"Oh Lord, oh Lord, but look at my crosses! Is good-looking, Caribbean women fuh so in de place today." He rubbed his hands in glee.

Shahrazad glanced at him out of the corner of her eye as she stood, pad poised, grease shining on her face, waiting for their order.

"I have dis pepper pot goin' tree months now. De cassareep keepin' it good. A frien' bring some special one from home fuh we last summer. His mudder mek it sheself. She have a cook shop in Berbice an' people does fight to taste she pepper pot. It have calf's head in it, all de lean pork you could want. It good! Of course it have in all o'de spices an de other meat too. I was even goin' try it wid a little bit o' de married man pork spice, but Shahrazad feel it would change de taste too much an' the people dem wouldna like it."

They ordered. Esther chose the least exotic dish, curried chicken wrapped in roti.

"What all-you drinkin?" asked Shahrazad.

"You have sorrel?" asked Fanella.

"What's sorrel?" Esther queried.

"Look! Just drink the thing and don' ask foolish questions," said Fanella pushing them out into the street. "Shahrazad bring the food into the back room when it's ready. We goin' see you there. And make that four sorrels," she shouted over her shoulder before ushering her party back into the cook-shop through the other door.

"Come this way," said Haroun. He shepherded them down a short dingy corridor into his 'back room'. There weak sunlight filtered in through pale unwashed curtains of an indiscernible color. A single, low wattage light bulb hung from the ceiling. The four corners of the room each held a table covered with a clean, green tablecloth.

A group of rum drinking, domino players was loud and merry at a table. "Baby want shoes, mudder want panties, I want BVD's." Pow! The speaker slammed his domino onto the table. Loud soka music blared from the jukebox. Esther looked bewildered. Culture shock seemed to be setting in.

"Sit, ladies. You' food soon come," Haroun said then left.

"I've forgotten your name," Fanella said to Esther. "What do you think of Brooklyn?"

"It's Esther," Esther smiled bravely, "and I grew up in Brooklyn, Sheep's Head Bay. But I must confess I have never ventured this far into this neighborhood."

"Yeah?" said Fanella.

"Yes, now that I live in Westchester I just drive in to Sol's, shop and go back home. If I have the time I run over to Sheep's Head Bay to visit my cousins. My folks moved to Florida about ten years ago. But this is all marvelous," she added hurriedly.

"Good," said Fanella. "You must tell me what you think of the curry and sorrel."

"Here's you' food," said Shahrazad, approaching with a tray with steaming plates. She placed them noisily on the table and pulled up a chair. "Maxi, you recognize your schoolmates," she said, acknowledging Maxi for the first time. She waved in the direction of the domino players who were watching them with interest. "There's Big Belly Man, Sugar Foot Daddy, Boysie and Shortgrass."

The men grinned and waved, and Shortgrass, presumably, since he was the shortest there; doffed his greasy newsboy cap to the ladies.

"Hello," said Maxi heartily and too loudly as she waved to the men. It could never be said of her that she did not acknowledge former schoolmates in public.

"So, Shahrazad," said Fanella, digging into her split pea cook-up. "How's business? Do you miss teaching?"

"Child, I can't tell you. I too tired to think. Three o'clock this morning I was right here in that kitchen washing dishes. But Haroun wants to do this, so is all right."

"You're probably better off being in business for yourself," said Charlie. "If you were teaching, you could have been up at three preparing the following day's lesson plans, or correcting papers."

"That's true. And Haroun is happier. He's let his hair grow into dreadlocks and doesn't read the Wall Street Journal anymore."

"Why did he read it before?" asked Esther. "Surely you're not investors." Then she blushed as they all looked at her.

Shahrazad didn't seem to mind. "Haroun used to be an investment banker. He lost his job to downsizing a few years ago and decided to go into business for himself. This is the business he chose. I gave up my job to help him."

"That's sweet," said Esther.

Shahrazad cast her scornful look and she blushed again. "What you all doing down here anyway?" asked Shahrazad.

"Oh, I met them at Sol's," said Fanella. "We were stocking up on holiday clothes for the kiddies. Do you know I hadn't seen my sister in fifteen years? These are her friends." She waved her busy fork in the general direction of the women.

"You ladies have time to shop," said Shahrazad rising. "I have a business to run. I will see you later. Enjoy your food and let me know if you need anything else."

"So that's why his accent keeps slipping," said Charlie. "He wants to be a man of the people. But he can't decide what people, Jamaican Rasta, Guyanese folk or that other weird accent, what do you call it? It's sort of a polyglot basic Brooklyn-black-speak.

"How can someone move from Wall Street to this?" asked Esther bewildered and apparently emboldened by spicy food.

"This is his," Maxi declared. "The same way Maisie a.k.a. Shahrazad, is his, and won't tell him to go take a flying leap. See how he rules his kingdom? His way! God help black men, or at least give strength to the women that choose to live with some of them."

Loud Caribbean selections assaulted them throughout the meal. Haroun came in and raised the volume so that he could hear it better from the front of the shop.

The curry filling from the roti squirted up Esther's nose, as she got too tight a grip on the pastry case and vigorously bit into it. She coughed and looked around with streaming eyes to see who had witnessed this indignity. Her eyes made four with Charlie's, who said sympathetically,

"It's difficult to eat roti."

Fanella heartily pounded Esther on the back and Shortgrass expressed concern from across the room. The rest of the meal was uneventful and enjoyable.

"Maxi, we must stay in touch," Fanella said. "Here's my card."

"You're an importer," said Maxi looking at it. "What do you import?"

"This and that, jewelry, objets d'art, you know the sort of Yuppy-Buppy merchandise. I supply some stores and sell from the house too. Come by one day."

"I will," promised Maxi as they headed for their car. "Fanella, where is your car?" she asked with some concern looking at the descending darkness.

"Oh, it'll be here in a minute. I called from the cook shop when I went to the bathroom."

As if by magic, a large, silver Rolls Royce pulled up in front of them. A white driver jumped out and opened the door.

"Bye," called the women as Fanella stepped into her car.

"Bye, Maxi keep in touch," Fanella called and waved through the open window.

"God, Maxi," said Esther climbing into their car. "Your sister's loaded."

"So it seems," said Maxi, tiredly settling into the back of the little Corolla.

Charlie looked at her watch and started the car. She expertly wove through the traffic with no help from Esther this time. Germaine would love her fabulous new clothes. She hoped Lola was in better spirits, poor woman. She had picked up a few outfits that Lola could give to her children when they were reunited.

There was little conversation on the journey home. Each woman contentedly thought that she had the absolute best buys, and the best child to wear them. So, except for Charlie, they settled in sleepily for the long ride home.

"We should go upstate to Woodbury Commons sometime," said Maxi suddenly, between a series of yawns. "I hear the shopping there is marvelous."

Esther immediately perked up and exclaimed, "Oh, yes! My sister-in-law practically lives in that place. She gets the most divine things."

The shopping conversation gradually petered out as the women nodded off again. Charlie turned on the radio. Anita Baker was singing Sweet Love and Charlie sang along softly,

Sweeeet love

Hear me callin' out your name

I feel no shame, I'm in love.

In two weeks she'd be in the Bahamas with Roderick. Goodbye phone sex, goodbye cyber sex. A real, flesh and blood man was waiting for her; someone she could touch and love and trust, and how she would. The sun set and a light rain began to fall as she headed to Westchester and the house she shared with Lennie.

47
Epiphany

"You've just got to!" Paige sobbed hysterically into the phone.

"Paige, I can't," yelled Buddy hoarsely, near tears himself. "No!" His voice cracked then screeched up an octave. Shit! This new unreliable deep voice was embarrassing at times. "It'll be all right, I swear. My cousin Jason's helping us."

"I've gotta tell my Mom. Suppose I die," she sniffled.

"Paige, you won't die," he shouted. "I'll die if you tell your damn Mom and she tells mine." Tears now ran freely down Buddy's face.

"Buddy?" said Rose entering the room. She stopped and stared. "You're crying! Put down that phone right now and tell me what's going on!"

"Gotta go; talk to you later." He sniffled and hung up. Awkwardly he swiped at his wet face with the back of his hand.

"Buddy, what is going on?"

"Nothing, Mom."

"Do I look like a fool? You're on the 'phone upset and crying about 'nothing?'"

"I'm feeling sort of sick and there's some weird disease going around school and I'm afraid I might have it. It's fatal, Mom."

"And what 'disease' is that?" She eyed him suspiciously

"I don't know, Mom. They haven't even got a name for it yet." Rose started to open her mouth and he hurriedly added. "Well the kid that told me about it wasn't sure at this time and since I'm feeling kind o' sick..."

Rose pushed her son onto the bed and placed the back of her palm against his forehead. "You don't feel warm. We'll have Dr. Charles look at you tomorrow morning."

"Mom! I've got to go to school tomorrow. There's a chem. test I've got to take," he flew up off the pillow and shouted.

"Don't get so excited." She pushed him back down. "Buddy what's going on? You've never been like this over a chemistry test. If you're tested when you're not well your grades won't reflect your ability."

"They will! I've got to go to school tomorrow. It's the end of the marking period, so there'll be no make-ups on missed tests. I'll see the doctor after school. Please, Mom."

"Fine," she said reluctantly. "I'll have Dad take a look at you when he gets in. But I smell a rat and I'm going to get to the bottom of this."

"Mom, Dad's a dentist. Leave me alone, I'll be all right."

Rose studied her son. He looked healthy aside from the strange color caused by the disco light that revolved as he listened to his music. But those tears...

Turn my pitch up

Smack my bitch up...

She heard the music scream. "What on earth are you listening to? Give me that CD right now. If *you* don't respect black women, who will?" Rose angrily thrust out her hand for the offending CD.

"Mom it's not talking about black women. That's Prodigy rapping, it's a white group."

"Give it to me anyway, boy. How dare you join with anyone to disrespect any women? And beware of white boys-they'll lead you astray then come up smelling like roses while you're stinking and going to jail." She snatched the offending CD and stalked out of the room.

Buddy groaned. If his life were a video, he'd put it on rewind and erase that night.

"What the hell's going on in here?" He heard from the hallway. "You're watching TV on a school night! Are you crazy? Turn it off, put on some Mozart then sit to hell down and either do your homework or practice chess on the computer. You have a tournament on Saturday."

"Mom, I just turned on the TV as background 'til I could find The Jupiter Symphony. It has a particular movement that really helps me with problem solving," Sydney yelled back.

"Girl! Stop that right now! You see fool written on my face? And don't you dare yell at me. Look at this face – It's black not white. Don't ever mix me up with your white friends' mothers-you know I'll beat you into bad health if you disrespect me. And take that damn Harvard sweatshirt off your lazy back. This is BCC behavior! That's where you'll wind up with all the other deadbeats who watch TV on week nights."

"What's BCC?"

"The Bronx Community College where the academic underbelly goes-they have to accept everyone. Stay long enough and you get a degree. You could learn to speak Spanglish and even grab a future plumber or truck driver as a husband."

Sydney shouted. "Ma, I don't want a BCC sweatshirt. I'll study, okay? But get off my back!"

"As you wish, child, America has a university for every IQ, so you don't have to worry." Rose sniffed and walked away.

When Rose's bedroom door slammed, Buddy grabbed the phone."Jay, y' gotta help me, man," he hissed desperately.

"Calm down, m'man," advised Jason. "I'm helping you. We're still on for tomorrow, aren't we?"

"I don't know. Now she's scared that she's gonna die-"

"Where'd she pick up that garbage? Women don't die from abortions anymore."

"Well that's not helping me right now."

"Whatever, she's the one having it. She's got to be here before twelve tomorrow; Russ found a way to write her in and waive the fee. So you've got to get her here."

"How'm I gonna do that?" said Buddy in despair.

"Any of the parents know?"

"You kidding? Can you imagine how my Mom would behave if she knew that I'd got a girl pregnant, especially a white girl?"

"It would be interesting," agreed his cousin. "Aunt Rose does have a way with words, and she's not exactly wild about white folks. They must've singed her when she was growing up in Texas." He chuckled. "But Buddy as one guy to another why'd you have to do it? Don't you little guys masturbate and take cold showers anymore?"

"I didn't see you and the kids at that party taking cold showers; anyway it's not what you think, Jay."

"Sorry about that party, m'man, still it's good for you to see what can happen. Recently you've been seeing a lot of what can happen. Want to tell me about this one?"

"There's nothing to tell. Paige was almost naked and she was rubbing her boobs up against me with my thing in her hand. Her friend had her finger up my ass. Goddamn Michael Jackson would've fucked her! In fact, he would've fucked both of them!"

"Her friend? Whoa! Back up brother-man? Were you at an orgy? This is a hell of a thing for a fourteen-year old. Anyway you should have used a condom?"

"I didn't have one, man. A guy I know was selling fancy ones at school. He had discount prices. I ordered neon green with a French tickler; I figured it'd be more likely to score with something like that. But it wasn't coming in 'til that Monday! Jay, she wants me to come to her place tonight and be with her while she tells her parents."

"Whoooaaa!" cautioned his cousin. "Don' do that. This 'a white chick?"

"Yeah," said Buddy.

"Man! Your black stuff would be scattered from Westchester down to Brooklyn after her parents ripped them out. Didja see that Indiana Jones classic where the people just reached in, grabbed out the heart and did what the hell they wanted to do with it?"

"Yes," said Buddy quietly.

"Well, that'd be them and your stuff." There was a long silence on the line. "Man, don't get me wrong. I'm not racist or anything. Here at Columbia I date white chicks-catch hell for it from the black ones-but they're cool. My hottest date was Jeannine, an Australian babe. Love that woman! She was my girlfriend for a weekend-I have this commitment thing. My roomie had to be a sexile for the whole time, you know-couldn't come into our room 'cause the chick an' I were doing a serious hook up. But it was worth it – that girl sexed me up like I was a pasha. But shit man, why'd you get your chick pregnant! You know she could have given you a disease."

"Oh, man!" Buddy eyes filled with tears again. "I don' wanna talk about that right now. Let's get through this thing first, okay?" His voice broke and he blew his nose.

"You okay, cuz?" asked Jason.

"Yeah, Jay, this is so crazy."

Jason laughed. "I know, little Buddy; it bites."

"Don't call me 'little Buddy'."

Jason laughed, "Sorry, you're a big man now; you did a threesome and got a girl pregnant."

Buddy contained his mounting aggravation. "Look it's not that simple, okay? She's a ho'; what else was I supposed to do?"

"That's a bit harsh! You got a slut for a girlfriend?"

"She's not my girlfriend."

"'Scuse me. One would've thought so from the evidence," Jason chuckled.

"Jamie's my girl. Paige is her friend. Remember? The girl I told you about that gives a lot of head?"

"Oh yeah, she plies her trade in the janitor's closet at lunch time sometimes; didn't you tell me that? So your girl was the one with her finger up your ass."

"No!" said Buddy exasperated. "Listen, Paige called me after Christmas. Y' know, things are kinda slow. A lot of kids are out of town. Kids are looking for excitement."

"I remember the feeling," Jason said.

"Whatever. Paige's big sister was home from college and in charge of her because her parents were out of town. But the sister'd gone out with a boyfriend and Paige was sort of lonely and bored. So, she, like, called a few kids to come watch some DVDs. and just hang out"

"I'll bet. Things like The Devil in Miss Jones?"

"Funny. Actually, there was some weird thing called Debbie does Dallas. But it was like sort of gross and nobody really got into it."

"Yeah, right," laughed Jason.

"Well, we kind of loosened up, ordered in some pizza; there were eight of us, four boys, four girls; the girls were mostly mutts 'n sluts. My girlfriend, Jamie, who is Paige's buddy, wasn't there. Because she doesn't, like, live in the neighborhood, it would've been a major deal for her to come. And her father's an animal."

"Is Aunt Rose loosening up in her old age? How come you were allowed to go over to a girl's house when her parents weren't home?"

"I didn't tell her. She thought Abie and I were having pizza on Mamaroneck Avenue, and then maybe we'd hang out at Haagen Daaz or at Abie's house."

"So, that's how you did it. You let her assume," said Jason.

"Well, things kind of got hairy. Paige pulled out some wine coolers and forties. Ben pulled out some Ecstasy."

"You idiot! You took Ecstasy? That shit will eat holes in your brain."

"Well, everybody else did, and so did your ski party people. So we took the Ecstasy, then put on some music and sorta started dancing. Paige drank a lot along with the Ecstasy. Then she started bugging out, as usual. She stripped off her shirt and bra and ran through the house with her big boobs bouncing up and down. This guy Dave caught her and sucked on her tits-"

"Holy shit, you little buggers really did have an orgy!" exclaimed his cousin."

"I don't know man; I'm just trying to tell you what went down! And you keep interrupting!" Buddy yelled, and his voice cracked. "Shit!"

"Sorry dude, this story is so fucked up-down the throat and up the ass."

"Yeah, right; well, like I was saying, David sucked on Paige's tits and I got mad, 'cause she was sort of my date for the evening since my girlfriend couldn't come and all, and she is her best friend."

"I see."

"So I wouldn't talk to her. I called her a slut and played video games for a while. She tried to get back on my good side. Some more kids from the neighborhood came by on a booty call, had sex a few times and left-"

"Drop in sex, nice."

"Then Paige took me up to her parents' room to show me something. We sat on her folks' bed. And man! If you could see the DVD she showed me. It was some kind of *serious* fucking. I sort of sat there in shock imagining Dr. and Mrs. Schraft doing some of that stuff at night – not a pretty picture!"

"You little devil-"

"She kind of sneaked up on me. You know-Paige, next thing I knew my thing was in her hand, then in her mouth and she was rubbing her wet crotch up against me and saying stuff like how she loved me."

"What did you do then?"

"Well, she was like begging me to give it to her. I didn't want to hurt her feelings. So next thing I know, we're on the bed and she has her tits up in my face. Then I hear this laughing and her friend comes into the room. Next thing I know, this chick's naked and rubbing on me with her finger up my ass, and I'm inside Paige, and the whole thing's over. Jason, I swear it was freaky. I still don't know what happened, but I guess I hit it."

"Man, sounds like those chicks raped you." Jason laughed.

"Jay, I'm serious. I didn't like, go over there planning to hook up or anything. She's not even my girlfriend.

"Your girlfriend white too?"

"Yeah, what about it?" said Buddy defensively.

"Nothing, but remember, white folks still don't like to think of the black ram tupping their white ewe. So be careful."

"Yeah, right, but Jason, how come it happened so fast? I was like hardly in before I was out. I always thought it would've you know-lasted longer, been like a major event..."

"That, my lad is what separates the men from the boys. When it's time for you to be a genuine Ebony cocksman I'll tell you how to do it properly. But now is hardly the time for you to risk creating a tribe of little bi-racial babies in Westchester."

"Very funny."

"Seriously, work on that chick tonight and get back to me tomorrow. If necessary, say that you love her. Chicks like that and they'll do anything for love. I'm going to skip classes and meet the two of you at the clinic."

"What time?"

"I told you, well before twelve. Call my cell when you get here. Meanwhile, don't let that white girl get you into her house to tell her parents any shit. 'Cause when those folks finish with your stuff, your dick will definitely be past tense-beyond salvage."

"Yeah, thanks a lot."

"Gotta go now, Jeannine's waiting for some serious stuff from a real cocksman; says she wants to sex me up, no strings." He laughed and hung up.

The phone rang immediately and Buddy grabbed it. It was Paige.

"Buddy, you've got to come over. I'm going crazy," she screeched. "I might die tomorrow. Maybe we shouldn't go through with this. We've got to tell my folks."

Buddy's stomach dropped into his belly and he felt cold. "Wait, Paige!" he shouted desperately. "Don't do that, I'll come. I'll talk to you. But don't tell your folks."

"I'm so confused," she said. "This little baby-"

"That's no baby. It's a parasite! Kill it! Or it'll kill us!" shouted Buddy.

"Buddy!"

"Listen Paige, I love you. Don't tell your folks." The words tumbled out.

"You love me?" breathed Paige. She stopped crying. "I thought you loved Jamie."

"No. I love you. Don't tell your folks. I'll come over. We'll make love, tonight; on your lawn-in the gazebo. Don't tell your folks. I'll sneak out later when my Mom goes to bed."

"Oh, Buddy, you're just saying that," cooed Paige, the sun now shining through in her voice.

"Honest, I'm not, Paige. I've always loved you-Since kindergarten. Don't you remember? I'd always be looking at you and pulling your hair?"

"Yeah, I thought you hated me," she giggled.

"No, baby, that was looove, true love-Like how I feel now."

"You sure? Like about this love thing?"

"Would I lie to you about something like this?"

"No," she said softly.

"You're my girl now," he assured her. "My shorty!"

"Okay, Buddy. I'll see you tomorrow," she whispered. "You don't have to come over tonight. We'll go to school on the bus tomorrow. Then we can, like, sort of slip away from the others and take a cab to the station?"

"Yeah, Baby. That's the ticket."

"Okay, Buddy. And I love you too," she whispered, and made kissing sounds.

Buddy cringed and made kissing sounds back to her. "I love you more than you love me, Sugar Lips," he said.

Buddy hung up quickly and went to his Mom's room. He passed Sydney's open door. She was sitting at her desk studying, a Mozart CD played in the background. He smiled to himself, funny kid; she actually seemed to enjoy that academic stuff. Softly he knocked on Rose's door.

"Come in," she called. She was reclining on her chaise going through fabric swatches and examining them against the light from the brass apothecary lamp. "Darling, are you feeling better?" She looked up at him with concern.

"Yeah, Mom, a whole lot better; hey, Mom?"

"What baby?" she said absently, holding a puce fabric sample up to the lamplight and studying it critically.

"Y' know Mom, I've been thinking about a girl in Jack and Jill., Tiffany Price? That real dark girl with long hair that she wears pulled back in some kind of clip?"

"You mean Madeleine's daughter," said his mother in surprise. "What about her?" I didn't know you'd be interested in her; she wanted to add but bit it back.

"Yeah, well, Mom I kind of wondered if you could, like, invite them over, you know? Like get Mrs. Price to come and bring her daughter. We could play video games in the family room or something...you know," he ended awkwardly, throwing out his hands in a helpless gesture.

"Oh, Buddy, what a lovely idea;" Rose jumped off the chaise and embraced her son. "I knew you'd come to your senses some day. Tiffany's a lovely girl, a bit crude at times, but lovely," she said firmly. "I'll call Madeleine right now and invite her to tea on Saturday. No, I won't make it so obvious because you know how those women are with their precious daughters"

"Yeah, like you with Sydney." Mother and son smiled at each other."I guess," said Rose. "I'll give a real tea-party. I'll also invite Monica and Caitlin-"

"Please, Mom! Not that little bitch-she's a nasty snob."

"Buddy, mind your language with me. You're taller than I am, but I'm still your mother and demand your respect. But you're right; she is a little bitch. I'll invite Nadine and Melissa and Barbara and Bobbi and-Oh Buddy, this will be such fun." She reached up on tiptoe and kissed her son's slightly bumpy cheek. "Buddy, what is this I feel? A hair?"

"Yes, Ma, I'll be shaving soon." He rubbed his cheek and smiled.

"Oh, Buddy, you really are becoming a man; now shoo I can plan this little tea party for you. I'll invite some boys so it won't look suspicious. So, darling, you won't have all the girls to yourself," she said archly, then hugged him again, this time taking care that her breasts not press up against him. She beamed as she watched him walk out the door.

"Night, Ma." He turned around and smiled at her.

"Night, Honey; now let's see... " She opened her escritoire drawer and pulled out that years' Jack and Jill directory. She sat on the chair and thumbed through it. The twelve to fourteen age group... First she'd call

Madeleine, and of course Madge with that cute daughter. She'd definitely use her grandmother's silver.

Rose looked up to the ceiling, closed her eyes, and with fists clenched in triumph she breathed, "Thank you, Jesus," then reached for the phone.

48

It's Christmastime

"Lennie, did you give Marguerite your ponche de crème recipe. She wanted it for her caterer," said Charlie as the family drove upstate to Homer and Marguerite's annual brunch on the Sunday before Christmas.

"I did. Her guests will probably mistake it for eggnog. There'll be a lot of drunk and disorderly people there today once they start imbibing that taste of Trinidad."

"I feel rotten leaving Lola. If only she'd come with us; it might get her out of that depression if just for a little while." said Charlie.

"She's got reason to be depressed. The scandal's in the papers, her husband's not speaking to her; she hasn't seen her kids in weeks-what do you expect? said Lennie.

"I know, but still I feel awful going to a party and leaving her alone. She didn't touch her breakfast. She won't come out of the room; says she feels used-and stupid for having let herself be used," said Charlie.

Mumtaz said, "The papers say that the girl who was gang raped has dropped out of school. I expect she's in some kind of mental institution. The dead boy's Mom was on TV last night talking about culpability and responsibility. She wants blood."

Charlie sighed, "It's all such a mess, so many lives ruined,"

"Why doesn't Lola pack it in and go home. She must have come from somewhere before she got married," said Mumtaz.

"She does, South Carolina. But she hopes that Leroy may still forgive her and she wants to be around if he does. There's not that much love in the world!" snorted Charlie, "but she's young and she'll have to learn.".

"Charlie, will this party be mainly your Jack and Jill folks?" asked Mumtaz.

"Hardly," said Charlie. "Homer's a politician and a former academician, so there'll be those groups. He lives in Pound Ridge with the Broadway types, so they'll be there too and just plain folks like us. Of course J&J people will be there since his family's in the organization and he always invites people's kids; so it'll be one of those standing room only events."

"Doux-doux, any last minute Christmas gift requests?" asked Lennie.

"No, I just hope someone got me a gold crown for my harp, I did mention it a while back. It'll make me look so professional!"

"It will Spooks, you'll look like a harpist from Lincoln center. Remember, you just have to ask and it's yours," said Lennie.

Charlie settled back and thought of Roderick. She smiled in contentment, her man. He made her think; he was teaching her to appreciate so much. She had thoroughly enjoyed the photography exhibition in the city he'd urged her to attend. He was opening up a whole new world to her and she was going to accept it. It was time for *her.*

At the party Homer greeted them in the foyer where they signed the leather guest book. Maids checked their coats and waiters pressed drinks upon them then turned them loose in a room teeming with unfamiliar faces.

"Mommy, look at the robes those people are wearing. It's the same fabric as my African doll's costume. Do you think they're really African?" asked Germaine.

"Maybe, at this level of society when people parade around in their ancestral robes, chances are they really are African," replied her mother.

"Hi, Gopilals," said Maxi, "You just got here? Season's greetings, your gifts are in my car. Germaine, you little vamp," she said kissing her, "your dress is adorable. Tatty's in the rec room, she's graduated from the walker now."

"Cool!" said Germaine and headed there.

"Hi, guys," said Maxi, kissing Charlie, Lennie and Mumtaz.

"What a crush," said Charlie. "I guess Homer's actively campaigning. Poor Marguerite, now it'll be entertain 'til you can't stand the pain. The poor woman has enough of a job just keeping it together for herself."

"Isn't it sad? She's not suited to this type of life or happy with it either. My, this place is beautiful! It's just perfect for entertaining," said Maxi looking around the large living room. An eight-foot tall Christmas tree and gift-packed sleigh dominated the room, which also comfortably housed a grand piano and two sets of country style French furniture. Amidst the heady mix of expensive perfumes and cultured voices a man in black tie with a red cummerbund roamed, playing Christmas carols on a concertina

"...Structuralism deconstruction theory would make you concede that..."

"My, she's got an impressive vocabulary!" Maxi said with a smile, as they heard Mumtaz pontificate in her English accent.

"She doesn't even have to talk for them to listen," said Charlie. "She's young and beautiful with a short, red, silk dress hugging her ass in a vice. Tell me which man here cares what she's saying?" She sighed. "I remember the days when my ass was high and springy like that. You could have bounced a book off it."

"Charlie, behave yourself," giggled Maxi. "We're not over the hill yet. Let's go give old Judge Sanders a thrill. Next to him we all appear to be sweet, young things."

"Good idea," said Charlie. "Wait; let me get a refill on this ponche de crème. It's great." Charlie drained her punch cup.

"The site of the struggle is not here. It's in the inner cities," a speaker declaimed. He flung out an arm, and struck Charlie, knocking her glass to the floor. "I'm sorry. Allow me." The young white man picked up the cup and dabbed at Charlie with a napkin.

"It's okay," she said, pushing him away with annoyance.

He resumed his discourse. "Brand name intellectuals point out the need to de-emphasize the importance of race in..."

Charlie continued the obstacle course through the maze of talk.

"You are your own profit center and should generate your own income. That's what my old man told me and I tell my constituents."

"...this Guggenheim fellow with his ill-conceived plan goes off with the money and years later announces that he has discovered an inverse relationship between brain and penis size, with blacks naturally having smaller brains."

"You've got to be kidding," said someone in the group.

"What ho, Charlie!" Mumtaz greeted her at the punch bowl. A pale, white man of indeterminate age tagged along behind the vibrant, young woman.

"Mumtaz, this punch packs a wallop so go easy on it," said Charlie.

"Fiddlesticks!" scoffed Mumtaz gaily. Her swain laughed too. "As I was saying," she turned back to him, "minority discourse-"

"Sounds like a sexual disease to me," cut in Charlie.

Mumtaz gave Charlie a withering look and walked off to the strains of "...the monological dialogical..."

Charlie joined Maxi and Judge Sanders, pondering whether it was the pursuit of a degree in English that had deprived a normally sensible young woman of the ability to speak popularly understood English, with her own accent.

"Charlie, you're looking charming as usual. Girl, come give me some sugar." The old black Judge gave her an appreciative once over and held out his arms. Charlie pecked his cheek and avoided the octopus arms.

"Merry Christmas, Judge." She winked at Maxi.

"Charlie, meet Candace. Candace, Charlie," he singled out a young white woman from the group around him. "She's a sociologist at New Paltz. She's doing research on the helping patterns of blacks with money. You know... what types of organizations or individuals they make contributions to."

"Interesting, what made you pick this as an area for investigation?" Charlie asked.

"It's generally understood that when blacks make it they move out of the ghetto and forget those they leave behind. It's Blacks who first referred to the N.A.A.C.P. as the National Organization for the Advancement of Certain People. So-"

"Young lady!" thundered the judge. "When did you last visit Hell's Kitchen to persuade your brother to get off crack and give up gang life? Or the South Bronx to lift your drunken father out of his vomit on the street, then take him for rehab. and a job? When you white liberals answer this, then we can answer dumb questions. Why the hell should Blacks with money live in the ghetto? Do Whites?"

"Excuse me, I see someone I need to talk to," said the red-faced sociologist.

"You're still an old bear and I love you for it." Charlie hugged the old man.

"Uh-oh! Lennie had better watch out," kidded Maxi. "There's romance brewing."

"If I were thirty years younger..." rumbled the old man pulling Charlie to his side.

"You old curmudgeon," she disentangled herself. "If you were thirty years younger you wouldn't give me a tumble, you'd be out there looking for 'light, bright and damn near white', like the rest of the eligible black men of your generation."

The judge roared with laughter. "That's why I like you, girlie. No one can bullshit you. I swear, for you I would've made an exception; but I'd have this piece of high yaller on the side for diversion, just to live up to the stereotype." He pinched Maxi's arm and winked at Charlie.

Maxi shook her head. "Now you've insulted us both, happy? Your reputation lives on. Oh, there's Homer, I must say hello. Excuse me." Maxi left.

Lennie appeared. "Hi, judge, how's it going? Charlie, come meet someone."

"Hi, Lennie, m' boy, you're taking this beautiful woman away from me?"

"You'll get more, sir. I need this one."

Charlie and Lennie wended their way through loud, animated groups.

"Why can't a black politician do well while doing good? Whites always do and no one kicks unless they're caught with their hands too outrageously in the cookie jar."

"Tribalism on Ivy League campuses is ruining it for our kids. Black upper-middle class kids have nothing in common with those equal opportunity, low achieving types."

Mumtaz's dulcet tones proclaimed, "...the tenets of cultural absolutism..."

"Jesus! Doesn't she speak English anymore?" Charlie asked Lennie.

"Charlie, don't be hard on the young girl-" but Lennie stopped mid-sentence and his jaw dropped as he heard:

"The gyneolatry of the Southern Caucasian male produced a phallocentric microcosm within the macrocosm crying out for hegemony..."

"Oh, God, girl; you right!" He laughed uproariously and gave a thumbs up sign to his cousin as they passed her, sipping at her ponche de crème and discoursing mightily.

The conversational scraps assaulting Charlie's ears made her feel as if she were in a tower of babble. She swirled the punch around in her cup and followed Lennie.

"So I said to the young whippersnapper, 'my husband is the law'," proclaimed Monica deep in discussion, and not seeing Charlie.

"Right on, sister-'l'état, c'est moi'" came the reply.

". . .tried a leveraged buyout but it was too late..."

"Charlie, this is Pepito Cardoza," said Lennie finally stopping by a bronzed man in a white suit. "He's recently relocated from California, where he has a chain of Mexican restaurants. He's expanding to the East Coast with a flagship restaurant in Westchester. You guys are in the same business." Lennie took a glass of champagne off a passing tray.

"Pleased to meet you, Mr. Cardoza." Charlie extended her hand.

"Enchanted, Mrs. Gopilal." Cardoza bowed and kissed Charlie's outstretched hand. "You are beautiful as well as bright, hardworking and successful. Your husband has been telling me about you. He is a lucky man."

"Oh!" Charlie said, surprised.

"Your aura is blinding. Such a beautiful, spiritual woman!" the Mexican exclaimed.

She speculatively eyed the small, dapper, fiftyish man. Cardoza was handsome and graying at the temples, with what could best be described as a California glow. Gotcha! thought Charlie; New Age, probably vegan, regular colon cleansers, lots of leafy dark green vegetables, grains and mineral water accounted for the smooth, unblemished olive skin and esoteric beliefs. "You can see auras?" she asked.

"Only the really vibrant ones such as yours."

Lennie looked amused.

"Oh," responded Charlie, again too nonplussed by the strange little man to say anything else. She caught a waiter and exchanged her empty punch cup for a bubbling champagne flute. Then she nabbed a dainty crayfish cake from another passing tray.

"Very bad for you," admonished Pepito.

"But very delicious," countered Charlie taking a deep bite. "Mr. Cardoza-"

"Pepito, please."

"Okay, Pepito. What kind of restaurants will you open?"

"Restaurants that serve beautiful, elegant, healthy food; no cuisine minceur, that is insincere. I produce wonderful combinations of the freshest fruits and vegetables with sprinklings of meat and cornucopias of grain in healthy proportions."

"A health food restaurant?"

"No, a haven where I orchestrate the poetry of food; with everything delicious and in moderation. You feel beautiful just eating there-candle light, roses. You must come to dinner, Charlie," he said abruptly. "You are a beautiful woman. It will be a pleasure to feed you."

"Lennie, get me some more of these crayfish cakes, please," said Charlie.

"Sure," he left.

"I love to see a beautiful woman enjoy her food. It is akin to a sexual experience."

"Yeah?" Charlie said, wiping her fingers daintily on the little cocktail napkin.

"Charlie, there you are," exclaimed Rose, pecking her on the cheek. "We just got here. What a mob! We haven't seen Homer or Marguerite yet. Have you?"

"That makes two of us for Maggie," said Charlie. "Rose, meet Pepito Cardoza. Pepito, meet my friend, Rose Inniss."

"Charmed." Pepito gave a formal bow and kissed Rose's finger tips. She raised her eyebrows over his bent head. Charlie smiled and rolled her eyes.

"Another American beauty!" Pepito proclaimed as he straightened his back. "The East Coast apparently has the proper climate to nurture such sublimity." He looked solemnly at the two amused friends.

"Mr. Cardoza, do you have children?" inquired Charlie.

"Yes, I have a fourteen year old daughter, Rainbow. She is here with the other young people. Such a shy child-since her mother died she has been reclusive so I am glad that she is getting this chance to socialize."

"Yes, this is good for the kids," agreed Rose. "I have a twelve year old daughter and a fourteen year old son here."

"Really, your son is here?" said Pepito. "I must meet him. Meanwhile I will check on Rainbow. Such a shy child-she always likes to know where her parent is."

"Well, that got him off like a shot," laughed Charlie.

"It sure did," agreed Rose. "Do you think Maggie got scared at the thought of this mob and bolted for her room?"

"Why would you think that?" Charlie asked.

"Come on, Charlie, you must know that she's been having problems recently. I think Homer's gubernatorial campaign has terrified her."

"Come on! She's accustomed to being in the limelight. Her father's a politician. She loves it. She photographs beautifully-she's thin, and she's got those high cheekbones."

"Maybe," said Rose slowly, sounding unconvinced. "Where's Germaine?"

"Here, she's with the other kids."

"Good, Sydney'll have a friend to hang out with. Let's check on them. I want to look at Maggie's rec room. When we were here last summer it was for the pool party so I didn't get the chance to explore the house since she remodeled."

"First Cardoza, then you; fine!" Charlie threw up her hands in resignation. "Let's go check on the kids and you look at the house."

Charlie and Rose meandered through the large room.

"Charlie, there you are. Hi Rose, Merry Christmas," said Lennie thrusting a napkin of cold crayfish cakes into Charlie's hand, "here."

"Mrs. Gopilal?" A tall, dark black, middle-aged man held out his hand to Charlie. He wore a heavy, silk blend sweater with Harvard emblazoned across the chest. "I can see you don't remember me, Nathaniel Proudface. I was at your house last summer. My son attended your daughter's party."

"Oh, how do you do? I don't remember who your son is..." said Charlie.

"He's Hans Proudface. Look." He reached into his pocket and flashed a picture of a handsome, golden-skinned child with wavy brown hair. "We left your house and went straight to the airport. There was a near drowning I heard-that's why I remember the party so well. Anyway, Hans went to soccer camp in Germany."

"How nice, does he speak the language?" inquired Charlie.

"Quite well; my wife is German and I fly in various cousins, at intervals, so he can practice. Honey, come meet the Gopilals." He plucked a small, elegantly dressed blonde from a nearby group and said, "Magda, meet the Gopilals."

When introductions were out of the way, Charlie said, "So you're from Germany,"

"Not really," laughed the very American-sounding Magda. "My grandparents were. My husband has been looking for Hans' roots, so we recently found all these German relatives and they're ... blending, I guess you'd call it." She pulled an invisible thread off her sweater.

"Fascinating," murmured Charlie.

"I see you went to Harvard." Rose gestured with her chin to the identifying sweater. "My nephew's a keen squash player, he's at Columbia, and he says Harvard's always had the strongest squash team. Did you play when you were there?"

"Indeed not. I refused to learn the game for political reasons when I was in their law program. As a black man I took that stand against white elitism. I also always wore a three piece suit to highlight my radicalism and refusal to be typecast."

Charlie had the sensation of being at the Mad Hatter's tea party. She felt her eyes and brain glazing over. "How interesting," she murmured politely. "Please excuse us. Rose and I were on our way to check on the children."

"Nice meeting you," said Rose as she and Charlie walked away.

"Well!" breathed Charlie, "Did you ever-" She stopped when she realized that Rose was enraptured by the concertina player's rendition of Lady St. Clare.

"I haven't heard one of these since I was a child," exclaimed Rose.

"Come on!" said Charlie, impatiently tugging her.

"...the black ultraconservatives are addicted to onlyoneism..."

"...so we're two million over budget when this reject from Bimbos Anonymous announces that she's pulling out!"

"...that there's a school in Mt. Vernon that teaches Swahili?"

"Who the hell wants to learn Swahili? That's going to help somebody make money or pass a national examination?" came a prompt response.

"There's Mumtaz!" shouted Rose above the din. "She looks beautiful, as always. I must say hello to her."

"The matrilineal archetype..."

"Hi, Mumtaz," said Rose, interrupting the mighty flow and lightly brushing cheeks with the young woman. "You look stunning, Merry Christmas."

"Hello, Rose, Merry Christmas to you too," said Mumtaz. "Please meet Viscount Kensington. Marmaduke, this is my cousin's friend, Rose Inniss."

She turned to a ruddy, ginger-whiskered, thirtyish, white man with whom she had been enthusiastically conversing, as she sipped her omnipresent ponche de crème.

"Charmed, I'm sure," the man drawled and took Rose's hand.

"Let's go, Rose," urged Charlie frowning at Mumtaz's drink.

"See you later," said Rose.

"Toodle oo," sang the Viscount.

"Ta ta," caroled Mumtaz. She returned her attention to the Viscount. "…the matrifocal working class of the cosmopolitan Trinidadian society engendered a zeitgeist from which authentic kaiso or calypso-"

"For God's sake! She should be forced to spell all those words she uses," snorted Charlie in disgust. "Why, there's Cardoza! Pepito what are you doing here? Did you check on Rainbow already?"

"Why Rose, Charlie, we meet again! I can't get out of this room. Everyone I've met since coming to Westchester is here. And they all want to talk to me," he added ruefully.

"You must owe them money. Come, we'll check on the kids together. If anyone tries to stop us we'll say this is the bathroom brigade. Stop us at your peril," said Charlie.

Finally they reached the large entrance hall. Rose dabbed at her brow: "Phew! I thought we'd never get out of that crush. Now where's that rec room?"

"Behind the staircase, where the music's coming from," Charlie said, following the rousing sounds of Sal Soul's Little Drummer Boy. She snapped her fingers to the beat of the drums and moved with a spring in her step.

"Nice music," said Pepito looking with approval at Charlie's undulating backside. "What!" he said suddenly. His olive skin turned ashen and his face contorted.

"Holy smoke!" whispered Rose.

They all stared at a beautiful, olive-skinned, adolescent girl with whirling blonde hair. Closely sandwiched between Buddy and an unknown white teen-ager she was enthusiastically flinging out her arms and furiously gyrating her pelvis. The two boys were no slouches, but the girl in the middle had all the major moves.

"Wow! The rainbow coalition in action," burst out Charlie involuntarily.

"Truly a gorgeous mosaic .Wait till I get my multicultured boy," added Rose.

"Madre de Dios! I remove the meat from this sandwich. Now!" The little man reached between the dancing boys and yanked out his daughter. "Puta!" he hissed.

"Daddeee!" she protested. "We were just starting to have fun!"

"Exit stage left," said Charlie with a laugh. "I'm going to die."

The two women staggered out, slipped into the library next door and collapsed against the closed door in tears of laughter.

"Oops, sorry." Rose grabbed Charlie by the arm and pulled her out.

"What?" said Charlie.

"Just come," Rose hissed looking in the direction of the oxblood leather sofa, where in the dim light they saw an alarmed couple. The man was desperately helping the woman shove her breasts back under cover.

Charlie said as she hastily retreated with Rose. "I can't take anymore; this place is like a Roman orgy. You don't know where to turn. When are we going to eat? Food should get these crazy people back on track. Who was that in there anyway?"

"Whoever, but bet your bottom dollar they weren't married; at least to each other."

"That's obvious." Charlie started doing some Kegels contractions in preparation for her own upcoming extramarital moments.

"What's in here?" Rose pushed against some heavy double doors and poked in her head. "This must be the dining room. Oh..."

Little, dirty, reggae teaser.

But you doin' it to tease me.

Charlie joined her friend at the door. Mumtaz stood on top of the heavy oak table. Hands clasped behind her neck, legs spread wide and the red dress ruched up around her hips, as she gyrated between the platters of food, singing and winin' Trinidad style. The Viscount held her shoes and empty punch cup as he watched her with rapt attention, his whole body on the alert, some parts embarrassingly so.

"Let joy be quite refined," declaimed Rose, raising her champagne flute to the couple.

"I give up," said Charlie softly closing the door.

49

Resolution

"Oh Gawd, m' head!" Mumtaz groaned next morning. She slid into her chair at Charlie's breakfast table and cupped her head in her hands. She looked washed out in the bright winter sunlight flooding in through the beveled glass window. Charlie regarded her coldly and rang the bell. Lennie frowned at Charlie. She stared him down then he looked solicitously at Mumtaz across the yards of white linen tablecloth.

"Shall I mix you my famous hair of the dog potion with raw egg, Angostura and some other things; it'll have you up and running in no time," he said sympathetically.

"Oh Gawd!" ejaculated Mumtaz again, this time dramatically making retching motions. "No thanks, cuz."

"You rang, Mrs. Gopilal?" Evadne entered the room neatly uniformed in black and white."

"Yes, Evadne, please see what Miss Thani will have for breakfast."

"Half a grapefruit and dry toast, please," Mumtaz said weakly.

"And some aspirin," added Charlie.

"Yes'm." Evadne said.

"Did you take up a tray to Mrs. Allsop?"

"Yes'm. She said she doesn't want anything. She hasn't touched her food for the last few days."

"I know, Evadne, thank you."

When Evadne left the room Charlie said urgently, "Lennie, I'm worried about Lola, we've got to do something. She's got to stop pining away and nourishing this pipe dream of a reunion with her husband. It's just not going to happen."

"Charlie, leave the woman alone, she'll do the right thing in her own sweet time."

"Owwww! My poor head," moaned Mumtaz," squeezing her head in her hands and looking around for sympathy.

Lennie said to her, "Well, Cuz, you were warming up for Boxing Day with all that liquor. You ready to fete fuh so when you go home tomorrow."

"No!" Mumtaz pressed in her temples and looked truly wretched. "I don't want to see another nasty drink for a long time. I don't care how many open houses I'm invited to when I get home. I'll drink soursop punch and pretend its ponce de crème. Yecchhh".

"What's she talking about? What's this Boxing Day, open house bit?" asked Germaine.

Lennie replied, "Years ago in England, on the day after Christmas, Boxing Day; the Lord of the Manor gave boxes of goods to servants and deserving villagers. It's still a bank holiday in the British Commonwealth." Before Germaine could ask, he added. "That's a public holiday to you. We call them bank holidays because they are holidays on which the banks close too."

"Gosh, you people are so different," observed the American child.

Lennie said, "Back home, there's always lots of 'open house' parties on Boxing Day and New Year's Day. The party runs all day and most of the night and you drop in and leave any time you want to. There's a constant supply of food and so much rum." Lennie raised his hands in the air and began to dance in his seat.

Drink a rum an a ponche de crème

Drink a rum

It's Christmas mornin'

"Daddy, you're so funny with your old Caribbean things." She turned to her cousin. "Mumtaz, where'd you get the nerve to dance on that table? I would've been sooo afraid to do something like that-and embarrassed too," she added.

Mumtaz shot her a dirty look, but Germaine continued unperturbed. "I'm gonna try that one of these days. It was funny when we all walked in and there you were-"

"Germaine, your eggs are getting cold. Eat," commanded her mother.

Lennie laughed. "When're we going to Vermont, gang? Mumtaz, come back early, you'll enjoy skiing in snow with us instead of on water."

Evadne entered the room and said to Charlie, "Excuse me, Mrs. Gopilal. Mr. Allsop is here to see you. He's in the living-room."

"Leroy?" said Charlie, rising. She quickly dabbed her lips with her napkin and left the table. Mumtaz and Lennie exchanged glances.

As soon as Charlie entered the room, Leroy looking rumpled and tired with bloodshot eyes, barked "Charlie, where's my wife?"

"I beg your pardon, and happy holidays to you too?" rejoined Charlie.

"I know she's with you. Well, I want her!" His voice rasped and broke and he turned his back to Charlie. "I need my wife, where is she?" he repeated hoarsely fists clenched at his sides.

"Have a seat, Leroy," said Charlie, sitting next to the fireplace. "Would you care for coffee or tea?"

"Charlie," he said, standing over her with clenched fists. "Don't shit me. I've come for my wife. I know she's here. She's got nowhere else to go. She didn't take any money with her. I flew to her mother's home, and she's not there or with her sisters.

"You're quite the detective, " Charlie observed dryly. "Sit."

"Look, I'm running out of patience. Where's Lola?" He glared down at her.

"Sit, Leroy; I won't speak with you while you're standing menacing me."

"Fuck!" he said and threw himself into the chair across from her. He glared at her then hunched forward and looked at his work calloused hands. "I want my wife home. It's all shit without her. The kids and I visited my parents over the weekend. Mom was beside herself that I caused Lola to leave like that. She let me have it. God! I wish I could take back the things I said. I'm a prick! I don't deserve a woman like Lola." He buried his head in his hands and sobbed, shoulders shaking. "I love her so much!"

Charlie watched him speechless. This, she had not expected.

"I need that woman. This has nothing to do with the children. Do you know what it's like to come home to a house where there was once someone like Lola; baking, laughing, joking, just being there, trying to make me happy? Loving me."

"No, tell me," said Charlie softly.

"She sang love songs and little kiddie songs, as she did things around the house. But you wouldn't understand," he said bitterly. "You people aren't like that. She's a good, simple ol' country girl. All she ever wanted was what was best for me and the kids. I hurt her bad, real bad. If you could see the way she looked at me!" Again his voice broke.

Charlie listened in amazement. He truly loved Lola! The man was in pain.

"Charlie, I don't care what she's done. I don't care what happens. I love her, we'll face this together," he said hoarsely. "I've got to have her back. Nothing is worth anything without her-to hell with the lawsuits. She was playing outside her league with you vultures. I should've protected her. I'm so sorry. My God!" He punched his fist in his hand and dropped his head.

Charlie patted his shaking shoulders and passed him a box of tissues. Her living room was fast becoming the Alsopp Wailing Wall. "Wait here," she said softly.

Charlie knocked on Lola's door. "Lola, it's me, Charlie. Can I come in?"

"Yes," came a muffled reply from under mounds of bedclothes.

"Lola, there's a distraught man downstairs who loves you and wants you-"

Before Charlie could finish, Lola leapt out of bed. Wild-eyed she flew out the door in her nightgown, sobbing, "Baby, Baby, you came for me!"

"Lola!" Leroy dashed out of the living room as his wife, uncombed hair flying, ran down the stairs toward him. He rushed to her and they clutched each other sobbing, rocking and murmuring words of love and forgiveness.

"Sweetie, let me change into my clothes," Lola finally said.

"No, you're not leaving me again. I'll fetch them later. I want you back in our house, where you belong; let's go."

"Oh, Leroy, " she cooed, as face afire with happiness, she snuggled in deeper and he swept her up in his arms and headed for the door.

Charlie called to them, "Hey, Love birds, I know you've got your love to keep you warm and all that, but it's twenty degrees outside. Lola you'll catch your death of cold in that nightdress. Wait." She went to the hall closet, and handed Lola a long, hooded, fur-lined coat and a pair of fur-lined boots. "Put these on. You can always return them later."

Leroy set his wife down and helped her into the outerwear. Then Lola threw her arms around Charlie and cried. Charlie gently kissed her cheek.

"Goodbye, Love," she said misty-eyed. "You guys have a merry Christmas and be good to each other." She let them out and closed the door thoughtfully.

"Charlie what was that all about?" asked Mumtaz, when Charlie returned to the dining room.

"The damnedest thing, Lola has flown the coop-the lovebirds are reunited. She knew her man."

"I'm glad for the gal," said Lennie. "She was like a bull without its balls without that man."

"Thank you, Lennie, for a very graphic description," said Charlie.

Germaine giggled, and Mumtaz smiled broadly.

Charlie removed the tea cozy from the teapot and poured herself a hot cup of lemon tea. She took a sip then turned to Germaine. "Germaine, how's French with Therese coming along?"

"For God's sake Charlie, it's Christmas vacation, get off her back," said Lennie. "She doesn't always have to think about her studies. Let her have fun sometimes."

"Mrs. Gopilal," Therese, the au pair, entered as if on cue. "Your friend, Mrs. Farragut, is here with her daughter. She said Caitlin is to spend the day with Germaine."

"What!" yelled Germaine shooting up in her chair as if electrified. "I hate that kid; she's rude and snooty!"

"Calm down, darling," said Charlie soothingly. "Caitlin is coming into Jack and Jill and Matefi, the president, asked if you'd buddy up with her – you know; get to know her, be nice to her so that when she goes to activities she'd have a friend there."

"Why me? What did I do wrong?" implored the child.

"Come on, honey, you're kind of at a loose end right now; it might be a good match. You're smart, pretty, aggressive black girls, living in predominantly white neighborhoods. You're evenly matched. You might even grow to like each other," she said with a laugh. "And we couldn't inflict Caitlin on poor Tatty, the kid's just getting her strength back.

"Alright," said Germaine grudgingly as Monica bustled in, wearing a heavy, tailored black cape. Caitlin trailed her mother in a junior version of the cape.

"Charlie, darling, Lennie, Germaine, and you too, Beautiful Girl," Monica said, smiling in Mumtaz's direction, "Happy Holidays." Monica kissed Charlie and Lennie, blew kisses to the girls and deposited an elaborately bowed, two pound, gold box of Godiva chocolates on the table. "For my favorite people." She beamed at them.

"Seasons Greetings to you too," said Charlie. "Sit, please. Coffee or tea?"

"Nothing for me, Dear, thanks," said Monica complying.

"Your gift is under the tree, we'll give it to Caitlin later." Charlie smiled at Monica and blessed her beautifully pre-wrapped boxes of gourmet chocolates; emergency gifts for times like these. "Hi Caitlin, how was Christmas? Have a seat, meet Lennie's cousin, Mumtaz Thani."

Caitlin smiled at them. "Merry Christmas, everyone. Pleased to meet you," she said to Mumtaz then sat next to Germaine and promptly asked, "What are you getting?"

"Everything," replied Germaine. "What are you getting?"

"Everything plus" said Caitlin.

The girls studied each other silently.

"Germaine, honey, be nice to your guest. She could have been with an ambassador's daughter, but I'm letting *you* spend time with her. I'll pick her up at 5:30 I've got shopping to do. Charlie, what are you doing New Year's Eve?" asked Monica, rising gracefully.

"We haven't decided yet. Mumtaz what are you doing?"

"Nothing, Charlie. Right now I've got no one. That's why I'm going home. I wasted my time on a really wonderful, sensitive man last semester. I thought I loved him and he obviously liked me. We talked so much and studied together. He loves the Chaucerian period as much as I do. Well, he asked to borrow one of my skirts a few weeks ago," her voice broke.

"That's okay," said Monica. "Maybe he's one of those, what do you call them? Fetishists? You know, he wants to kiss it, maybe wear it around the dorm pretending you're in it reciting Chaucer to him. '*Whan that aprille*' and all the rest of that stuff."

Mumtaz clutched her head in fresh emotional pain. "Nooo. He wore it to class, the flaming fairy!" She looked truly wretched.

"Oh, well," said Charlie suppressing a smile, "there'll be others, you're young and beautiful."

"Bye all," said Monica departing with a smile, a swish of her cape and a trail of Herrera perfume.

"...and when we go to St. Croix on Friday I'm going to water ski. I only do it there because that's where I keep all my equipment-my boat, my skis, my tow-rope; I never use other people's stuff!" declared Caitlin.

"I started water skiing at Hilton Head last year. It was fun," said Germaine.

"Limited fun," sniffed Caitlin, "How can you enjoy it with other people's stuff? Are you going away on vacation this winter, Germaine?"

"I dunno. I don't want to go anywhere. I'm bored with vacations. I want to stay here in my big, new house with all the new stuff I'm getting in my big, new bed-room."

"I'm so glad you said that, Honey," said Charlie. "because I can't get away for a vacation this month. My restaurant application's being considered soon, so I have to run down to the Bahamas and spread baksheesh to the right government officials. "

"What's baksheesh, Mom?" asked Germaine.

"Bribery," supplied Mumtaz. "Omigod, m'head!" Her accent slipped from British to Trinidadian as she yelped in pain and massaged her temples.

"So I'll come with you," said Germaine.

"Sorry, you can't, you'll be back in school."

Germaine glared at her mother and folded her arms in front of her chest. Caitlin watched the developing situation with interest.

"Besides, even if I was silly enough to take you out of school, I'd have no time for you. When everything's finalized we'll go there on a family vacation. I might buy a condo and get you your own water-skiing equipment," Charlie said with a straight face.

"Way cool!" exclaimed Germaine, looking at Caitlin.

50

Home Again

Charlie deplaned to the glorious sensation of warm air playing on her body; melting the New York cold that had been chilling her insides. The sun's rays on her face were a benediction. She drank in the cloudless, impossibly clear blue sky-Roderick's sky and she tingled in anticipation.

Pale tourists, looking unnatural in this land of heat and light, milled around. Their pallor, like her marriage, belonged in New York. She smiled as she entered the customs area and elbowed her way to the front of the crowd awaiting their luggage at the carousel.

"Charlie!"

She looked up. "Roddy!" she flung herself into his arms like a teenager. "What are you doing in here? Don't tell me, you're connected. You have a cousin who's a custom's officer or a sister who's a red cap."

He laughed, "How come you're so beautiful and know so much." He tilted her chin up for another kiss. "Give me your claim checks and point out your bags to me."

"My hero," she said beaming at him.

Later, settled into Roderick's open moke, he put on a CD and said, "Listen to this, it's Gato Barbieri playing, "I Want You." I commissioned this song especially for you, of course."

"Of course." Charlie smiled at him. She tilted her straw hat down over her eyes, did some Kegels in anticipation and leaned back in the seat and relaxed. It was good to be back in strong sunlight with Roderick's extravagant silliness. Barbieri's sensuous, insistent music pounded her as she heard the words to the Marvin Gaye song in her mind and she looked at Roderick and wanted him.

"We'll get you checked into the Crystal Palace, and then you'll come stay at my place out on Cable Beach; I've arranged for your calls to be forwarded there. The 'phone will have a special ring to identify them. I know folks in high places." Roderick winked at her.

"Yes, Mr. James Bond, mon capitaine; now what about your sons?"

"If we see them we're lucky. They're out carousing with their cousins. They sleep at the homes of aunts who cook well. When the old man was that age..."

"The local beauties chased you, right?"

He rubbed the back of her neck affectionately. "Right; but none of them were as beautiful as you. But they did chase hard-like you."

"Go to hell," she laughed and swatted him with her Business Week magazine.

Charlie strutted through the hotel lobby, atingle in happy anticipation. Suddenly she stopped. Entering the hotel from the beach side was little Monifa, Germaine's friend, lumbering behind her was her mother, the big, yellow, bitch Heather. She hissed to Roderick, "Act as if you don't know me and meet me by the elevator."

"Why?" Roderick asked.

"I know those people. Shoo!"

"Can I stay here and take off my pants? That'll distract them," he murmured.

"Do that and I'll deball you."

Charlie checked in. On the elevator all her senses focused on Roderick. She touched him just to feel him there. Her neediness was disturbing; he had her in a daze. Silently she followed him to her room.

"Earth to Charlie, Earth to Charlie." Roderick paid the bellhop and looked at her questioningly as he closed the door.

"Sorry, I'm out of it. I guess I'm still kind of shell-shocked at having my New York life collide with my Bahamian life in the lobby. That was a close call. Then there's the excitement of you." She touched his face. "Do I really dare stay with you?"

"If you don't I'll stay here with you. Your friend's in the hotel, so do you really dare not?"

He held her in his arms and she smelt his faint odor of clean sweat, tempered with cologne and deodorant. She inhaled his scents luxuriously and closed her eyes to better savor him. She stored memories to treasure later. She trembled when he lowered his arms to her buttocks and pressed his body into hers. Her knees went weak and a tingling began in her loins.

"Oh Roderick," she breathed, nuzzling into his chest like a small animal burrowing into its mother.

"Hey, Charlie, we have to leave, I have to finish plans for some guys who are going back to Geneva this afternoon at two; after that I'm yours." He murmured and stroked her hair.

"What will I do while you're working?"

"Watch me, of course. Mop my fevered brow. Do what a woman's supposed to do. Ow!" he exclaimed as she pinched him hard on the butt. "Sorry, woman-of-my-fantasies. You can read, listen to music, walk on the beach-anything. But you cannot, and I repeat cannot, sample the goods." He ground his pelvis into her and laughed.

Her breathing quickened, but he gently pushed her off with a devilish smile. "Hey, it's ten thirty. Let's go. Time's a-moving"

Charlie regarded Roderick levelly. "You know, you really are a tease, but you're not going to do this to me anymore." She paused. "I want you right now." She flung herself at him and they struggled playfully, then their breathing quickened and they fell to the floor. Soon, Charlie was on top of him, pounding away in the act both wanted.

"Do you always get what you want?" Roderick looked up at her as she straddled him and held him inside her, while his hands on her hips kept her there.

"I'd say I make what I want happen. How about you?"

He smiled and motioned her off; she complied reluctantly with a victorious smile.

"We've got to go, give me your suitcase," he helped her back to her feet.

51

Mi Casa es su Casa

Roderick's two-bedroom, Spanish style house was in an isolated spot on a beach. They entered through a black, wrought iron door, which also accessed a pretty, little courtyard with a fountain.

"I love this courtyard," said Charlie taking in the gaily-cushioned, black, wrought iron furniture and big black pots of brilliant red hibiscus flowers. "You've even got a hammock." She walked toward it.

"For you later, Madame; come, let me put your stuff in the bedroom. Then I must get to work."

Sliding glass doors led to a living room whose back wall was covered by floor to ceiling bookcases crammed with books.

"Careful, I had the floors polished in honor of your coming," Roderick said.

"I noticed," Charlie replied taking careful steps in her high-heeled sandals, past the cushioned, natural-colored, rattan furniture. "I love these ethnic rugs you have on the floor. Especially the one I just stepped on that almost went whizzing out from under me."

Roderick put down the suitcase and grinned at her. "Shall I carry your luggage, or you?"

"Both," she turned and smiled at him.

He easily lifted her off her feet despite her protests and carried her to the bedroom where he deposited her on the bed then went back for the suitcase. She looked around approvingly. A white bedspread and mosquito net adorned a highly polished mahogany sleigh bed. On a matching bedside table, a miniature, ceramic, English cottage stood next to a neatly stacked pile of books. A blue and white cushioned papa san chair and footrest positioned between a shiny mahogany armoire and campaign chest completed the furnishings.

"Very nice, is it my influence?"

"Didn't you teach me everything I know?" He winked at her then opened an armoire drawer. "Here, I've cleared this drawer for you, do you want to unpack?"

"In a minute, is this a music box?" she asked, examining the ceramic cottage.

He chuckled, "Oh that, it's a house-warming gift from George. It's a condom-minium. See?" He removed the top. "He even furnished it." Roderick fished out a packet of Day-Glo condoms with French ticklers attached, and a deed to the cottage.

"You're a strange family." She shook her head. "How's Felicity doing?"

"She's good. I had dinner there last week. She sends her best. I have to get to work now. Later, my love; you can unpack." He kissed her firmly and left the room.

Later, Charlie found Roderick in the living room engrossed in his work. She watched his capable spatulate hands move deftly over the drawing board. Small Ben Franklin style bifocals sat on his nose. A wave of tenderness for him washed over her. They were all growing old. They would soon be past this type of thing. She marveled at the capriciousness of a fate that had brought them together and changed her life so radically. What was it he had said the first time they made love?

The grave's a fine and private place
But none I think do there embrace.

She'd found the poem and learned it by heart. She shuddered. She needed to touch him again, feel the texture of his skin, to suck on his skin and taste his saltiness. She wanted her arms around him. She had to have him, whatever the cost. He was life.

Roderick looked up when she entered the room. "Make yourself at home. Mi casa es su casa and all that. Snacks are in the fridge, and bene cakes on the table. My grandmother sent them for the kids but they're never here to eat them."

"Your grandmother's still alive?" she said in surprise.

"That she is, and going strong. In her youth they procreated early around here so she's not as old as you might expect. You'll get to meet her some day." He looked back down to his work.

Charlie tentatively bit into a sugary bene cake and carried it out to the courtyard with a stack of Architectural Digest and a local, award-winning book of poetry. She lowered herself into the hammock and stretched languorously. She was warm, comfortable and stress free; this was happiness. She snuggled deeply into the hammock and the reading material slid to the ground while she gazed mindlessly at the pale blue sky and billowy, silken clouds. She followed their drifting across the sky as breezes off the ocean imbued with the heady scent of nearby tropical flowers and aromatic lovage from Roderick's herb garden caressed her skin. She drifted into a sleep of contentment. Much later, she awoke with a start that almost caused her to fall out of the hammock.

"Careful, I don't fix broken bones, just broken hearts. Dirk picked up the plans, so now I'm at your service. Did I awaken you?" Roderick asked, steadying the hammock.

"No, for a moment I couldn't remember where I was so I was surprised to see you standing there."

"I was watching you sleep, thinking how beautiful you are. Come, there's someplace I want to show you. Are you up to it? You seem tired." He stroked her face tenderly then took off his glasses and stuck them into his shirt pocket. "It's a place I'm thinking of buying."

"Well then, I must see it."

They walked out holding hands, and Roderick locked the gate behind them.

52

A Family Affair

"What the fuck are they doing?" queried Abie.

"Oh, man! This stuff is kick-ass!" Buddy crowed. He and Abie watched in awe as they downloaded pornography off the Internet.

"Oh God! What's that!?"

"Son of a bitch! They're-

"Buddy!" Rose flung open the door.

"Oh shit!" said the boys in unison. Buddy hastily positioned himself in front of the printer which was spewing out pictures that could get him grounded at least until he went to college in four years.

"Buddy, you and I are going to talk, and don't you dare lie to me. Goodbye, Abie."

"Hello, Mrs. Inniss, I mean good-good-I mean-"

"Abie, go!" Rose pointed toward the stairs. "Now you!" she turned to Buddy. "What the hell were you thinking with? Obviously not the brain God gave you."

Abie ran out the door. "Bye, Mrs. Inniss."

She ignored him; she had other fish to fry. Abie flew down the stairs, tripped and fell and they heard his shrill cries followed by the slam of the front door.

Rose glared at Buddy, "Just what the hell's been going on?"

"What do you mean, Ma?" said Buddy, wondering which of his many sins had come to light.

"The hell you don't know what I mean! Why did you do it, God damn you!"

Buddy paled and wished that his Dad were there. His would be the voice of reason. Anything could happen now. He looked at his mother. Her chest

was rising and falling rapidly as if she had caught him doing something like not just lying on her new sofa but putting his feet up on it too, and wearing muddy boots! He quaked.

"Ma, what are you talking about?" whispered Buddy. He kept a wary eye on her while behind his back he surreptitiously gathered up the incriminating sheets from the printer and eased open the desk drawer.

"What are you doing?" barked Rose. She rushed to him and ripped the papers from behind his back. "Oh my God!" she said and smacked him full across the face. The blow rang out like a rifle shot and blood spurted from Buddy's nose.

"Ma!" he yelled, holding his face.

"More white behavior!" Rose punched him hard on his shoulder and he ran out into the corridor whimpering with her behind him landing blows wherever she could. Sydney ran out of her room and stared open-mouthed at the spectacle.

Buddy turned and tried to fend off his mother.

"Don't you dare lay your hands on me, boy!" she screeched, and rabbit punched him in the kidneys. The boy staggered and lay against the wall panting, as snot, blood and tears streamed down his face.

Sydney, with tears in her eyes, screamed, "Mommy!" to the wild-eyed woman.

"Don't Mommy me!" Rose yelled, chest heaving as she picked up a nearby vase and, not scrupulous about her aim, flung it behind her son. Flowers and water hit the floor as the vase grazed Buddy's head and shattered against the wall. He flew down the stairs.

"You walk out of this house tonight and you're never coming back in here," yelled Rose.

"Ma, what did I do?" pleaded Buddy.

"Esmeralda heard Jason laughing and boasting to some friends about his little cousin who got this white tramp pregnant. So of course she called me-the bitch! Now she's laughing at us! What have I done to deserve this? It's so-so-so;" she felt for words. "Low class!" she finally pronounced and then burst into noisy tears as she took off her shoe and flung that too behind her son.

"Ma, I'm sorry," yelled Buddy.

"He's sorry," she said to the wallpaper, and advanced down the stairs with Buddy retreating before her. "He behaves like some depraved rapper from the ghetto and he's 'sorry'. I knew those little white whores would get him! Now he's got a 'baby Momma!' He's the neighborhood, black ghetto kid – King of the projects by behavior! One kid's a national chess champion beating white people at their own game; the other kid's a homeboy and can use his penis as well as his sister uses her brain," she said bitterly.

"Ma-"

But Rose was on a roll. "He's made it so no decent black woman in Westchester will let her daughter date him. His sister probably can't have a black girl sleep over again; women don't let their daughters sleep in a house with a sexual predator."

"Ma, it wasn't like you think," pleaded Buddy.

"Right, her parents held you down and she raped you! You could have been a father at fourteen – Satan get away from me!" she begged as her eye lit on a heavy crystal statue and she resisted the temptation to fling this too at her son. "Have you ever seen anything so despicable!?" Rose raised her eyes to heaven and Buddy's heart sank. Sure enough, this energized her, for she screamed and started pulling out her hair then changed her mind and rushed at him to box his ears.

"Ow! Ma!"

"Mommy?" called Sydney in a timid voice from the top of the stairs.

"Baby, you go practice chess, and get used to not having a brother around because this ghetto boy wanna-be, is headed for military school."

"No, Mommy," pleaded Sydney "I want my brother at home."

"Ma, please. I won't do it again," sobbed Buddy, tears running down his face, snot running from his nose.

"Like I said, there's going to be an end to this. You're out of here and your room's taken. I'm making it into my workout room. I'll put in some nautilus, a stairclimber; there's space for a big medicine ball. That room's mine now, homey; you can cry like Peter and preach like Paul; military school will show you how to keep your little balls in your books. You will not stay around here and disgrace us all."

"Ma, please," whimpered Buddy. "I'm sorry."

"You should have thought of that when you were unzipping and putting things where they had no business going at your age. Just wait 'til your father gets home."

Upstairs a bedroom door closed softly and a child cried in her room.

53

Building Dreams

"What on earth …"" Charlie's voice trailed off. She stood with Roderick in front of a burnt-out mansion with weeds growing out of its cracked walls. The sweet stench of decaying guavas and mangos assailed them as they stared at the crumbled, blackened shell, in the middle of what was once a garden, on a hill above the beach. Donkey dung dotted the path they had taken and rot and fecundity filled the air. "It would cost a mint to restore this place, and for what? Even if you build a development you'd still be behind God's back way out here."

"I feel something on this spot. Maybe it's the ghosts of generations past who lived in this place. Whatever it is, I want to be a link in that chain, part of the concatenation."

Charlie shivered. "That was a white chain, Roderick. They probably raped your great grandmother right here on this spot."

"Charlie, we can't escape our history. Look at my green eye. Can I deny it any more than my brown one? I embrace it all and I want this. Also my love, we didn't have much slavery here. We mainly provided refuge to pirates and runaway slaves."

"Fine, she was raped by Bluebeard the pirate then. But, this is still so... isolated. You'll be lonely, you have no family living with you." She looked into the distance and saw only beach, trees and scrubland.

"Alone, does not necessarily mean lonely."

"True." "She looked around at the lush overgrown garden with flies buzzing on the fallen fruit. "No one can accuse you of wanting to live in a yogurt city."

"What's that?" he asked, amusement in his voice."

"What I'd imagine to be your kind of place, a city with 'active cultures', you know; museums, symphonies, bookstores with regular poetry readings, artsy shops..."

"Charlie, we Bahamians fly to that kind of stuff when we get the notion but we live here far from the madding crowd. I'll be a culture guerilla – attack, imbibe culture, then retreat until the next foray."

"You nut," she said affectionately.

He smiled at her and said, "Let's sit." He spread a blanket on the grass. "We've never talked about our families have we?"

"We've talked about everything else but that," she agreed, and sat on the blanket.

"How do you feel about our situation?" He sat on a rock and looked at her.

"I'm conflicted. Lennie's been unfaithful for a long time," she said slowly. "I used to love him. But life with him became one humiliation after another. The first time he cheated I felt as if the bottom had fallen out of my world. I loved him then. After a while he didn't even try to hide his affairs-I suppose it was his way of getting back at me because I'd made it in my field while he was still struggling to pass his boards."

"How did you handle that?"

"I retreated emotionally. Now my love for him has died and I just need to bury it ... except that ... recently I've found myself feeling sorry for him; and wanting to provide a stable home for my daughter."

"Why?"

"Guilt, I guess, and the fact that I didn't have the perfect family after my Dad died. I've always wanted to have one of those picture postcard families; I'm torn. Lennie threw away the right to exclusivity on my love years ago when he started cheating. Now he's discreet about his affairs, probably because he realizes I don't care anymore, and here I am having an affair myself. What kind of message are we sending our child? I don't know what to do," she said with a sigh."

He looked at her sympathetically.

"Maybe it's my fault. If I hadn't succeeded so dramatically he might've tried harder; who knows? If he'd been the major breadwinner it might've worked. I guess I emasculated him." She shrugged her shoulders and looked past Roderick to the crumbling building in the distance.

"Charlie, stop beating up on yourself. You're not responsible for your husband's failure or whatever it is in him that caused a woman like you to be a threat instead of an asset. Don't be ashamed of your success-you earned it."

She smiled at him. "Thanks, Roddy. Do you know I'd forgotten what it was like to love and be loved by a man before I met you? Isn't that crazy? Marriage is supposed to be about love. I can't even remember love in my marriage," she said wonderingly. "Hell, it's been so long since I've had feelings like this! You brought something wonderful into my life that wasn't there before and I am so thankful for it. She turned away and said in a low voice, "I don't believe I said that. I sound desperate." She sprang up and walked to the end of the clearing and looked down at the beach, "Why did I meet you! I don't like being this vulnerable."

He chewed on a blade of grass and watched her.

She continued, "You always do this to me-make me look at things I'd rather not examine; wish for things I was content to live without." She turned and faced him. "You brought me back to life and I hate what it's doing to me now."

"Is it that bad?" he asked softly. "I guess it's true, *April is the cruelest month.* It's painful coming back to life.

"Yes, it is." Her voice rose. "Before, I was content to just work and be Lennie's meal ticket because he's tall, good-looking and has the title 'doctor' attached to his name although God knows its not worth fuck-all anymore. But it all looked good from the outside and I liked that. Now, since you, I want...more..." Her voice broke and tears ran down her face. "I want you!" This last was a cry of anguish.

Roderick wordlessly handed her a clean white handkerchief.

"Freud said the two most important things in life are 'laborare et amare,' to work and to love," Roderick said softly. Is it so bad that you want both?"

"I don't mind working, but I don't want to love you. I don't!" she shouted fiercely, and paced with clenched fists. "I don't want to be this vulnerable. I want to be able to just fuck you and go home and forget you!" She now cried in earnest and dabbed her streaming eyes with the handkerchief. "I don't want to feel an emptiness in my life when you're not there. I don't want to want you when I can't have you. I don't want to feel as if piece of me is missing when I'm not with you. I want to be content with my life again, awful as it was."

He said nothing.

"Damn it! why did I ever meet you? I didn't want my life to be this complicated. I care about you too much!"

"Is that so bad?" he asked in a low voice.

"Yes! Can't you see I don't want to be this involved?" She cried in great heaving gasps and dropped to her knees on the grass. "I don't want to want you like this. I'm too old for it. I sound like a love-sick teenage hit record. I'm the mother of a teenager, I can't be behaving like one." Charlie took a deep breath and forced out the words, "Please ... hold me. I ... need ... you ...so much"

Instantly, he was by her side, on his knees, sheltering her in his arms. He hushed her like a child and rocked her as she clung to him silently. "Shhh. It's going to be all right. Let's go home. I love you, we can work this out."

Charlie was silent all the way back. Roderick drove with one hand and held her hand with the other.

They returned to the house and sat in the shaded courtyard. "I've got something you must hear," Roderick said, going into the house.

Soon Charlie heard beautiful music and birds in the nearby trees started to sing. "Roddy, it's beautiful. Where are the birds?" she asked, looking around.

"On the CD; it's Ketelby's "In a Monastery Garden." He sat next to her on the love seat, and threw his arm around her shoulder.

"How come you're not always trying to jump on my bones anymore?" Charlie asked lazily as she leaned against him.

"Do you want me to?"

"I don't know, but how come?"

"Charlie, that was getting to know you time; I'm too old to keep up that pace. All that fancy sex constantly would throw my back out."

"Do you think you have me wrapped up so tight that you don't have to try anymore? What happened to Tantrism, the Kama Sutra, Taoist sex practices?"

"Charlie," he said with a laugh. He squeezed her shoulder companionably and looked at her. "What we did last summer was getting-to-know-you sex. Same thing when I came to New York. Now I don't feel the need to constantly surprise and titillate."

"Oh, really."

"Yes, I'm comfortable with you now. I love you. Sure, we'll have great sex occasionally but it won't always be fireworks and virtuoso performances. I'll always satisfy you because I won't ejaculate and let you waste my vital essence every time; thank Taoism for that. But we're past the stage where I have to constantly seduce you, aren't we?"

"You're right, sweetheart. From now on we'll lie quietly in bed in our nightclothes and do it missionary style with little movement and no foreplay." She patted his knee.

"Not on your life, wench," he growled. "Let me throw you down in that hammock right now and convert your entire body into one big, throbbing, erogenous zone." He grabbed her and started touching her all over. "Nah, Let's go have lunch." He said abruptly and stood up and looked down at her.

Her eyes met his.

"Help, Ma!" he shouted and laughed as he ran into the house with her behind him.

54

An Expansion

A glorious purple and blue sunset dimming into evanescent shades of pink tinted the sky as Charlie and Roderick whizzed along the Cable Beach road headed for dinner.

"What will it be, Continental, Seafood, American, Bahamian?"

"Bahamian, please."

"Good girl, I've Bahamianized you." He rubbed the back of her neck and sang in a pleasant baritone.

Bess, you is my woman now, you is, you is!

An' you must laugh an' sing an' dance. . .

Feeling as if she were in a movie she joined his antic mood and belted out:

Porgy, I's yo' woman now, I is, I is!

An' I ain' never goin' nowhere 'less you shares de fun

Roderick looked at her in surprise and sang the duet through to the end. "I readily admit my prejudice, but you are magnificent. Where did you learn to sing like that?"

"In the Abyssinian Baptist church choir in Harlem."

"Is there anything you can't do?"

"I don't know yet. Stick around maybe we'll find out."

"A deal!" He said, squeezing her hand.

Charlie nuzzled her cheek against his neck then slipped her hand inside his shirt and stroked his chest. She felt his heartbeat quicken. "Down boy I'm not going any lower," she whispered.

He smiled and turned on the radio. Natalie Cole was singing "Darling Je Vous Aime Beaucoup." Charlie committed the moment to memory-the song, deepening tropical shadows, and Roderick. Softly she crooned along with Natalie.

Je ne sais pas what to do.

You know you've completely

Stolen my heart.

"Here we are." Roderick stopped, jumped out and came around to her side. They were in a commercial area, in front of an unimpressive, long, low, pink building. "They have the best food on the island." He offered in response to her look of skepticism. "Of course you won't find any tourists here."

"Of course." She smiled at him and tried to slide elegantly out of the high vehicle in her short, hourglass dress. Damn fashion! She strove not to do a burlesque revealing as he watched with amusement. Finally he shook his head, grabbed her under the arms and practically lifted her down.

"Thanks, I needed that," she said.

"My pleasure, I can't have all the passers by viewing my treasures, now can I?"

She swatted him across the butt. He laughed and grabbed the hand and wrapped it around his waist. "You can look, but you cannot touch," he admonished her, then guided her through the parking lot to the entrance of Goombay Grub.

Candles in glass globes at each table, provided the only light in the dim interior. A bead curtain separated the dining room from the little bar where several men were already drinking. Natalie Cole's version of Unforgettable blared from a jukebox in the corner.

"I like this," Charlie said following the waitress across a little dance floor.

"Here," the waitress said. She seated them and left them with menus.

"Okay, Roddy, what's good?" Charlie perused her menu.

Roderick put on his reading glasses and joined her. "Uumm. Are you watching your weight or can we have a calorie blast?"

She laughed. "I never diet. If I overeat I just cut back the next day and increase my exercise, so get what you want."

He squeezed her thigh in the dark. "Let me see. Hmm, good muscle tone, you're absolutely right." He moved his hand further up her skirt. "Let me feel the flesh. "

She pushed the hand away. "Let's eat. What are you, a satyr?"

"Woman, you're never satisfied. Earlier on you complained that there wasn't enough 'jumping on your bones' as you put it; now you're accusing me of satyriasis?" He gave a poor imitation of a man with hurt feelings.

"Have it your way, just order me some food," she said with a sigh.

He laughed and covertly patted her bottom. "See, I can't keep my hands off you. You're a witch."

"You'll change that 'w' to a 'b' if you don't feed me soon," she warned.

They ordered then relaxed and looked around them.

"Look at that waitress's butt," whispered Charlie as the heavy, light-skinned black woman adroitly negotiated her bulk between the closely spaced tables. "She must pig out on this starchy food."

"Shhh. If she hears you they'll polish our plates with spit in the kitchen, or she'll spit in our food, or maybe worse."

"How do you know that?"

"Because I grew up here and bussed in restaurants in my youth."

Charlie studied the other diners. They were all couples, except for one family party. El DeBarge sang from the jukebox.

Blind faith, makes me follow you.

I'd live in a cave, if you wanted to.

Just ask me and I'd marry you.

"Is this place for lovers only? All they've played is love songs."

"I told them we were coming," Roderick said solemnly.

Charlie looked thoughtful, "Sure. But you know what? Those soppy songs do get to the crux of things?"

"How so?" Roderick took off his glasses, and polished them with his napkin.

Just then their drinks arrived. "Your food coming now," the waitress assured them before sashaying off again.

Charlie sipped her Bahama Mama and continued. "That blind faith deal, for instance. What do you know about me, or I about you? Yet we say we love each other. How can we? You could be a former axe murderer for all I know."

Roderick reached for her hand and held it. "I know that I love you, Charlie," he said quietly. "Here, I got you a gift." He reached into his pocket and pulled out a flat rectangular box wrapped in shiny gold paper.

"Oh no, not here," she said looking around her and starting to put it in her bag.

Roderick smiled. "It's okay, you can open this one in public."

"If you're sure…" Cautiously she opened the shiny package and found a large gold compact. 'Charlie' was engraved in script, in a circle formed by tiny pearls.

"Open it," he urged softly.

"What will it do?" she asked suspiciously. "You sure a dildo won't leap out and smack me in the face?" She took the plunge. A lighted mirror was revealed. "What's this?" she said seeing an inscription. She read in the dim light:

Our two soules therefore, which are one,
Though I must goe, endure not yet
A breach, but an expansion,
Like gold to ayery thinnesse beate."

"Oh… thank you," she whispered. She felt loved. She clasped his hand and looked into his eyes as tears welled in her own eyes. "Roderick, what are we going to do?"

"What do you want to do?"

"Something is missing in my life without you. But I have responsibilities."

He stroked her face. "I know that. That's why we have to think about this, we're not youngsters anymore. I won't do anything to hurt you. Look, I know this is harder for you because of your daughter, and you're still married; so the ball's in your court. What do *you* want to do? I never thought I'd say this again to a woman, but I want to marry you. Shhh." He placed a finger to her lips. "You don't have to say anything now. I can wait 'til we can work out something."

"Like what, Roddy?" She held his hand fast with both of hers. "Liquidate my assets in America and move here?" She squeezed tightly as if she were drowning.

"Charlie, I never said that. We would both have to make changes. We could maintain residences here and in the U.S. Owners of many multi-national corporations live in these islands and manage their businesses from here-Howard Hughes is the most well-known. We could commute to a home base, like I said, we can work it out."

In the background Frank Sinatra was crooning to the diners that love was "*more comfortable, the second time around.*"

"Roderick, I love you. I want to be with you, but I also love my daughter, I have to make this as easy as possible for her. I don't know what to do. Whatever we do, we'll have to do it in the summer because of her. I can't mess up her school year," she said quietly with pain in her voice.

"Shh, I know. That's why nothing has to be done right now." He held both her hands and looked at her. "But remember Charlie, 'tomorrow is promised to no man,' so if I love you and you love me…" His voice trailed off.

"Lennie's a good father. She loves him!" A tear trickled down Charlie's cheek.

He caught the tear on his finger. "Shh. Let's sleep on it. Want to dance?" He stood and held out his arms to her.

"No one else is dancing," she protested.

"Since when have we followed the crowd? For shame, woman." He pulled her up. He walked her to the jukebox and made a selection while they waited for the Sinatra song to finish.

"What did you select?" Charlie asked.

"Wait and see."

He positioned the length of his body against hers. They fitted like a jigsaw puzzle and moved just enough for the sake of decency. Roderick's hands were around her waist holding her firmly against his body. Heady sexual feelings surged through Charlie, and she prayed not to have an orgasm right there on the floor and wind up creaming and screaming like a banshee in front of the other diners. She clung desperately to his Egoiste-scented neck and buried her face in his shoulder. "Are we exhibitionists or what?" she whispered.

"Listen to the music, love."

I'll take good care of you.

That's what a man's supposed to do

Then I'll be there for you all the time.

"Oh, Roderick," she groaned, "If only it was that simple." He moved his hands down to her buttocks, pressed her in even closer, then deliciously ground his pelvis into her. The pressure was now turned up high. "Oh God!" she breathed as she began to see things his way. She had to have this man permanently. She was weak with sexual excitement.

Come on, come on, come on

Listen to your heart."

the song implored as Charlie tried to concentrate on moving her feet occasionally in this alleged dance. She felt the pulse in her clitoris as it rhythmically rubbed against Roderick's crotch.

If you think I am gonna be good to you

If you think I have got what you need.

Sho' you right.

The song was insistent in its demands and so was Roderick's body.

If you think I am gonna make love to you

If you think I, I like what you do

Sho' you right.

She was dizzy when Roderick led her back to their table. The fat waitress showed up immediately with all of their courses on the tray at once. She defended this practice.

"Sir, I jes bring it all one time before we gets busy and you-all have to wait a long time to get de rest o' yuh food."

"Fair enough. What do you say, Charlie?"

"It looks good and smells good. Let's eat." She smiled at the waitress who looked happy that her tip was no longer compromised. "Umm, this turtle soup is good! My compliments to the chef."

"Thank you, Miss." The waitress swaggered off smiling, maneuvering her caboose of a backside through the now crowded dining room.

Roderick shook his head. "Her steatopygia's phenomenal."

"I keep telling you, speak English to me."

Roderick looked mischievous. "What is it my Love, do you suffer from hippopotomonstrosesquippedaliophobia?

"What the hell!"

He laughed. "I was just having fun with you. Hippopotomonstrosesquippedaliophobia means fear of long words and steatopygia's what you call a rumbling, tumbling backside. This excessive protuberance is common to the Khoikhoi and other peoples of arid parts of southern Africa. . And Charlie, if your butt ever gets that big, I'm sending both you and it off to a fat farm."

"Me and J. Lo both," she laughed. "If you ever lose your hair and your gut hangs over your pants, I don't know the long word for it but I'll be sending you for hair transplants and liposuction." She sipped her soup and looked at him with twinkling eyes.

He laughed. "Touché' Madame. Hey! Turtle soup has been rumored to possess aphrodisiac qualities-conch too. You'd better be careful."

She pretended to push the soup away. "I'd better not touch it. Remember you're getting old; you can't keep up with me. By the way, when will I meet your boys? How are they doing?"

"They're great. Occasionally they descend on me with cousins and friends, raid the fridge then move on after trying to borrow my car. I walk with the keys."

She laughed. "It must be fun to have big teenagers."

"Sometimes."

Suddenly the mood of the dining room changed. A calypso blared the popular Dollar Win'. A group of black teenagers, who'd just come in; took over the dance floor. A white boy in the group, with short, blonde dreadlocks, danced outrageously, doing a real West Indian wuk up. He looked as if he was masturbating against the fabric of his jeans through sheer hip movement. The group danced wildly and seductively and sang along:

"Cent. Five cent. Ten cent. Dollar!

Charlie watched incredulous at the brazen sexuality of their dancing.

So she want me wuk up me wais'

An' raise the tempo – o o.

The blonde boy made a jukebox selection looked in their direction and smiled.

"Let's dance." Roderick said.

"With that lot! No way!"

"My son just made a selection for us. Listen."

"That white boy is your son! "

Roderick smiled. "That black boy is my son. Come, say hello."

"Hi, Dad, they're playing your song," said the boy coming over. He looked Charlie up and down approvingly."Brian, come meet Dad's friend," he called across the room. "I'm Tristan." He shook her hand.

A dark, handsome, teenager with long-lashed, green eyes came over. He slapped Roderick on the back, shook Charlie's hand and said, "Hi, Mrs. Gopilal, I'm Brian; pleased to meet you."

Charlie looked at the handsome pair in surprise. The upper-class, English accent seemed at odds to her with this one's black skin and the other's kinky, blonde, dreadlocks. "I'm impressed."

"So are we. Dad made us take a hike because you were coming," Brian said. "But that's okay, Dad. Go on, enjoy yourself, but first give us some more lolly." He held out his hand and winked at Charlie. She caught his father's playful sexiness in the look.

Roderick laughed. "You got me." He handed a fifty-dollar bill to each of his sons. He turned to Charlie, "Let's boogey." He led her onto the dance floor.

"We goin do a little soka
We goin do a little grin'.
We goin do a little back-back
An' show dem youngsters how to win'.

Roderick whirled her around the floor. They twirled, wriggled, slammed into each other, shamelessly rubbed up against one another, and had an exhilaratingly good time.

Tonight the black man just feel to boogey woogey.
So come on, come on, hold on to yuh man.

Charlie was glad when the dance was over and she could sit and catch her breath. Roderick had been moving his pelvis against her in a sinuous motion that had set her blood to bubbling. She wanted out of there with him, fast.

"Phew. I'm not as young as I used to be. I thought I'd die out there," Charlie said.

Roderick mopped at his face with a large, white handkerchief. "What about me? This black man has had it. Let's go home. Are you finished? Want dessert?"

"Just some coffee, cappuccino if they have it," said Charlie counting on the regenerative powers of caffeine to kick-start her lover's motor if necessary. It had been a long day.

Roderick laughed, "Darling, you don't come 'over the hill' for cappuccino. But I'll get us some coffee." He beckoned the waitress and she soon brought over hot, strong coffee in thick white mugs. They drank it and left.

55

Canonization

"Stay in the car and leave the lights on," Charlie commanded when Roderick was halfway into the carport next to his house.

"Why?"

"Because." She slipped out and stood in front of the car, illuminated in its headlights. She undulated and slowly pulled her dress up her thighs. "Josephine Baker's back without the banana skirt – music please."

The luscious strains of the Modern Jazz Quartet playing Ravel's Bolero filled the air as Charlie tossed her dress, followed by her crimson and black Merry Widow and black satin panties onto the hood of the car. Naked, she vamped it up. She was Josephine Baker on stage. The whole world had a hard-on for her. Charlie licked her lips and bent forward cupping her breasts as if in offering. She ground her hips slowly and lasciviously; then shook her breasts and threw her head back and laughed. Let them beg!

Roderick leapt out of the car and rushed to her. "Into the house," he said huskily. But he held her there and kneaded her backside then unzipped his pants and urgently rubbed himself against her.

"Make me want you,"" she panted as heat and desire suffused her body. She clutched him tightly and blew into his ear.

They stumbled into the house. Roderick almost fell as he tried to stroke her clitoris, suck on her breast, and step out of his chinos at the same time. Desire and amusement warred, 'til they both burst out laughing at the ludicrous situation.

Charlie greedily sucked on Roderick's neck and chest savoring the taste of the finely textured skin. She helped him shuck his intrusive clothing as she nipped at his belly in her downward peregrination. She was pleased to note that her love and desire transcended the sight of him naked and erect in shoes and socks.

He closed his eyes and followed her body's contours with his hands. On his knees he kissed her navel exultantly as he gently inserted a finger into her anus and rubbed it in rhythm with his other hand that softly rolled her swollen clitoris and tickled her perineum. "Come" he stumbled to his feet and urgently tugged her toward his work area. "Lean over this." He stood rampant and pointed to a brown, leather ottoman.

Charlie awoke from her sexual daze enough to remember dire stories of men who had used any port in a storm and wound up in places where they had no business being. "Hey, I'm not an ancient Greek boy, I'm a black woman from Harlem. I don't do that."

He stroked her breast and bent and kissed it gently then straightened up and rumbled, "I'm a black man from the Bahamas," he rolled the now erect nipple around and squeezed the breast reassuringly. "And I don't do that either. Trust me, you won't be disappointed." He slapped her lightly on the buttocks. "Bend, woman!"

She reluctantly placed her belly on the cold leather of the ottoman. "I could always sue…" She felt his eyes on her, as she lay spread eagled in the moonlight.

"Now you'll see why the Victorians were big on ottomans," he said softly, as he gently stroked then kissed the area around her buttocks.

Charlie felt a frisson of delight. She'd finally found a man who would kiss her ass! She smiled in the midst of her excitement and savored the luxurious sensation of him moving slowly in and out of her. The leather warmed as she radiated heat. She felt him favoring the right side of her vagina; idly she wondered why he was off-center. Suddenly he was thrusting rapidly in an area where she had never felt sensation before. Her belly filled with heat. His movements quickened. She felt him filling her entire body. He plunged in and out making short guttural sounds .She accompanied him with birdlike cries in a rapidly ascending falsetto as she clutched at the rug for leverage. She was the morning sun inexorably rising over a raging sea. She grew ever more refulgent. God said "Now!" and she blazed brilliantly. She exploded in light as the waters beneath her roiled and spumed as she came sobbing, screaming and frothing in a frenzy. Her last coherent thought was that a man who could fuck like this should surely be canonized. Roderick collapsed panting onto her back and too exhausted to move they dozed off spooned together over the ottoman.

"You're doing okay for an old man on his last legs," she teased him when they roused themselves later. "I thought I'd have to use special techniques to get you going after all that dancing. I read a cute little poem this afternoon – one of your Metaphysical poets; this young lady is talking to her ancient lover and she says about his 'parts',

From their Ice shall be releast:
And soothed by my reviving hand,
In former warmth and vigor stand.

But you needed none of that. You're not getting older you're just getting better, pardon the cliché."

"Because I won't let you kill me. I used the Taoist semen retention technique of "Riding the Tiger" that I mentioned to you. I saved my ejaculate to promote health, higher spiritual functioning and also longevity which you threaten daily with your insatiable demands on my aging parts." His eyes twinkled.

"Aging? You! You had me going crazy. What did you do to me? You should patent it, Island Boy."

"I used another ancient Taoist technique called "Mule in the springtime"; Westerners call it stimulation of the Graffenberg area. I did that and made you ejaculate."

"Me ejaculate? How? Did you tinker with my chromosomes when I wasn't looking? Am I a man now?"

"No, my love," he said with amusement. "Like I said, I simply found your G spot and gave you a Graffenberg orgasm. You've heard of the famous G. spot that everyone was trying to find a few years ago. Didn't your tabloids run articles like, "Woman has G. spot orgasm and is wafted off to realms where she meets Shirley McClain and comes to understand the mysteries of life." The operative word there, of course, being 'comes'. And come you did my love, again and again and again." He smiled teasingly at her and got stiffly to his feet. He arched his back and rolled out the kinks.

"So, this is what Rose was talking about," Charlie said with awe and wonder.

"I've got better in store. Next time you're especially good we'll do 'The Dance of Shakti and Shiva.' It will open your 'inner flute' and let you experience an even higher level of sensation. I'll make you happy that you were born." He turned his mismatched satyr's eyes on her. "But first I'm going to take out a hefty insurance policy on my 'parts' as you call them. You almost wrecked them just now. Come, let's shower." He reached down to pull her up.

She caught the hand and kissed it reverently. "I'll always love you," she said looking at him in the moonbeams that flooded in through the skylight. She cupped his hand around her breast and held it there.

56

Afternoon Tea

"Happy New Year,"" Rose greeted Charlie and Germaine with hugs. "Nice coat, Germaine, you're becoming quite the young lady." She winked at Charlie. "Denka will take your coats," she added as a uniformed white maid hurried forward. "Germaine, the kids are in the family room."

"Later, Mom." Germaine trotted off to join the other teenagers.

"Charlie, you look terrific, your business trip in the sun agreed with you."

"Thanks, I hear Buddy's going away to school. And what happened to Evadne?"

"That lazy devil – she's the last of a bad lot! I'm never hiring a black maid again-too much attitude! Buddy dropped off the high honor roll, so he's gotta go."

"Poor kid," commiserated Charlie, "but I hear you."

"Grantley always says that you must listen to the children's 'phone conversations to keep informed. Well we did. We discovered he's too involved with girls. So it's off to Military School before things get more out of control."

"You do what you have to." They entered the living room where tea was being served to a background of cool jazz. "My God, Rose, what have you done? This is magnificent!" Charlie stared at the redecorated room.

Rose smiled modestly. "I'm trying English Country for a change."

"I love it," stated Charlie. She bushed at the sight of Rose's ottoman. Suppressing memories of her erotic escapades she sat on a Windsor chair next to a splendid silver tea service sitting on a burnished mahogany side table. She looked around her. "Where on earth did you find a hunting picture with black riders?"

"Myra's niece fixed it for me, you know the one who's studying art at Cooper Union? I gave her a few dollars and she gladly darkened their lightness."

"You, idiot!" Charlie laughed. "She's good, I saw her stuff recently in a gallery. I should buy while she's still affordable. I see she's in good company – Romare Bearden, Jacob Lawrence, Charles White, not bad! " Charlie eyed the artwork admiringly.

A tall, striking, stylishly dressed stranger swept into the room. Everyone looked at her curiously. Rose hugged the newcomer and introduced her to the gathering.

"This is Amina. She's an M.I.T. educated engineer. Her husband owns his own software company. They relocated from Silicon Valley. Amina meet Charlie, she's a millionairess entrepreneur married to a doctor. Maxi's an artist. Her husband is an advertising executive, they live in a huge house in Chappaqua with a swimming pool and tennis court. Phoebe's a psychologist and has a big house in Scarsdale. Josephine here's a lawyer; she…" The list of the guests and their credentials rolled on…

"I can't possibly remember all this;" Amina said with a laugh, "Just tell me their names. I'm so happy to be here. I had no idea there were so many of us in this area. I have a thirteen-year old daughter named Radiance. We hope to get to know all of you and your children." She beamed at them.

"Of course you'll join Jack and Jill?" said someone.

"I'm a legacy, I'll grandfather in. We didn't need it in California but I guess it's a good way for Radiance as a newcomer, to meet kids."

"What kind of name is 'Radiance'?" whispered the woman on Charlie's left. "Obviously M.I.T. didn't teach her how to name children sensibly."

"Maybe that wasn't an issue for a graduate who would one day be able to afford that four thousand dollar handbag," suggested Charlie softly. "Can you?"

Rose led Amina to Sophie. "Sophie's an architect, as I told you; remember? She owns her own company. Maybe you two can network."

Sophie smiled appraisingly and soon the two were deep in conversation.

"Rose, is Estelle back from Russia yet?" questioned Maxi.

"What a dreadful place for a Christmas vacation," someone observed.

"She's not on vacation," said Rose. "She went to adopt one of those orphaned children. I think she's getting a toddler."

"How can she mother a white child?" burst out a pale sandy-haired black woman. "She'll scare the poor, little, Russian thing. I'm sure it's never even seen a black person."

"Her black daughter's in college. She just remarried and replaced her former dark husband with a yellow man, so why shouldn't she have a white child and make all her dreams come true? Girlfriend now wants to do it the right way, the white way," observed a voluptuous woman reclining on the sofa.

Uproarious laughter greeted this. Suddenly there was a news flash. "An apartment building has collapsed on the corner of one hundred and sixteenth street and Amsterdam Avenue. There has been some loss of life. No names are being released as yet."

"No!" whispered Sophie turning pale.

"What is it?" asked Rose, as Sophie's cell 'phone rang.

The room was quiet and all eyes focused on Sophie as she answered the 'phone. "Yes, yes, Oh my God! I'm coming."

"Are you alright?" asked Amina?

Sophie said woodenly, "That building that collapsed was done by my company. I must go." She rose abruptly and was gone before anyone could think of anything to say.

"More tea anyone?" offered Rose to the sound of the distant closing of the door.

"I'll have some," said a woman holding up her cup. There were murmurs of agreement. Rose enhanced the returning conviviality with Bobby McFerrin's soothing C.D. of Mozart interpretations.

Charlie wished she could go home tonight and have Roderick waiting there to hear about her party. Why had she not married someone with whom she could share things, whose opinion she respected... a friend. She'd give up stock options to be Mrs. Roderick Baine with her wonderful husband waiting at home, to love her not necessarily make love to her; though that was beyond wonderful. She stole a glance at the ottoman and her heartbeat quickened.

Someone said, "I've always wondered, which you should pour into your cup first, the tea or the milk?" as she held her teacup out to Denka for a refill.

"Well," said Rose, "I've been told that if you're having tea with a duchess you pour in the tea first. But for a real, hearty, working-class brew in casual company it's the milk first. Different chemical reactions occur, depending on the order."

The woman frowned as Denka, the white maid poured in milk followed by tea.

"We laughed at Estelle's adopting a white baby," said Phoebe, the child psychologist. "But no one here can say they've had an easy time raising black children in white Westchester. My practice is bulging with black children suffering from the results of racism – often covert, but still damaging racism."

"I believe you," said Maxi fervently. "Estelle will have an even worse time with a white child. People will assume that she's the nanny and ignore her at school functions. The kid will probably become ashamed of her."

"She'll need radiation therapy on her melanin for it to work," observed Madge.

"Yeah, let Michael Jackson tell her how to do it," said someone.

"Come on!" said Charlie. "Whites are not all ignorant and uncouth. You're talking about low-class-first-generation-in-the-suburbs Whites, who just moved up from the Bronx. They still watch their p's and q's-that means don't speak to blacks in public because the neighbors might think you're one. Someplace like Angloville, where I live, is generally not first generation money. Those Whites can afford to be decent because they're not threatened by us."

"It's not just Whites, it's other blacks too when they're in white company? And God help us when they get power then they're like Uncle Clarence's spawn, I swear. They prove their impartiality to questions of color by cutting down other blacks and presenting their gizzards to the Whites on a platter; " said a serious, dark-skinned woman.

Maxi interjected, "Save us from Clarence. The poet Kamau Brathwaite must have had him in mind when he wrote of our people 'teaching their children to hate their blackness/ Down to its bitter root in the bone'."

"Speaking of politicians, have you heard that Outpost, that radical gay group is 'outing' Charles, Maggie's husband. They've put out posters proclaiming him 'Perfectly Queer'. What will this do to his election campaign?" said a Jamaican accented woman.

"How horrible," said Rose. "I hope that's not true, poor Maggie."

As if on cue Maggie entered looking flustered. "Rose, sorry to be so late."

Rose pecked her on the cheek. "Don't be silly. People who show up on time surprise me and throw me off because I don't expect it."

Marguerite colored and Maxi called out, "Maggie, come meet Amina; she's just moved here from the West Coast." She turned to Amina. "You wouldn't believe this woman's schedule. If my husband ever mentions going into politics, I'll rip his head off with my bare hands and throw it at him. This poor child has probably had six other appointments already today."

Marguerite pecked Maxi's cheek and beamed appreciatively. Denka brought a teacup, Rose poured, and conversation resumed.

"Did anyone see the news on channel nine last night?" asked a woman in a hideous Versace pantsuit.

"What specifically?" asked Rose. "I watch channel nine."

"The old Kenneth Clark study was recently replicated in several major cities-"

"The one where black children are told to choose the more attractive of two similar black and white dolls and they invariably choose the white one?" asked Phoebe.

"Exactly! With the same depressing results today as in the fifties, same thing in the Caribbean-Black kids choose the white doll," said the Versace woman.

"No! This madness can't have penetrated my homeland!" said a Jamaican.

"Recently, one of Andrea's white friends asked why she had all black dolls, and questioned whether she was an American," said a voice with a Southern drawl.

"You can't blame the child," said Phoebe. "Americans in her universe are mainly white. Foreigners, gangsters and maids, according to the media, are people of color -the Cosbys were the exception of course."

A tall, striking, dark woman, elegantly draped in a lilac chemise entered the room.

"Madeleine, I'm so glad you made it," Rose greeted her. "Where's Tiffany?"

"Your maid took her to wherever the other kids are."

"Good; sit, have some tea," said Rose.

"I wouldn't have missed this for anything. The understudy's playing my part today. Now that the play's moving to Broadway I'm getting a bit of a breather."

Rose beamed at her. "You're a Broadway star now! This is exciting."

"Exciting, yes, but hard work; I just woke up a few hours ago. Tiffany harangued me all the way here for being late and so 'stereotypically black,' as she puts it. These children! We expose them to white culture in their schools and they want to come home and beat us with it."

A pale, quiet woman said, "Getting back to our discussion, my Nancy recently had a dreadful experience that illustrates what we are up against."

"Here we go again," Charlie murmured to Maxi, "crying in their cups over whiteness. Why don't they just shut up and get out there and make some money?"

"Charlie, behave yourself!" Maxi playfully tapped her friend.

"... my daughter in a Westchester private school. She and a little white girl always competed for first place. Not competing really, because Nancy always came first. One day little Miss couldn't take it anymore, because my daughter had bested her yet again, so she says to her, 'you may be smarter but I'll go further because I'm white'."

"The little snot. She already knows that her color alone has empowered her," said an indignant voice.

"There's worse," piped up someone else. "My niece was the only one from her graduating class who made it into Harvard. The white kids all said she got in because she was black. Mind you, she'd been a John Hopkins CTY member made the national honor roll and was a merit scholar with a perfect SAT score. She felt so cheated!"

"That's so typical."

Maxi said, "Don't those jerks know that upper middle-class, black women are among the highest achievers in the country."

"That's true," said Madeleine thoughtfully. "But a lot of colleges have been taking disadvantaged African American kids with low scores and achievement levels. This makes it bad for our kids because when you lower the standard you devalue the prize for everyone, and our kids become academically suspect. It creates just the kind of unfair resentment described."

"Something had to be done to address the issue of unequal access; but can they think Toni Morrison, Shirley Chisholm, Anita Hill and countless others are all anomalies?" asked Madge.

"They'll get theirs from the Asians. You've heard of the new 'yellow peril'? The Scarsdale Jews are getting worried because so many Japanese have moved there and are snapping up the top academic honors in their schools. I heard one of them at a party excuse the new Jewish 'failure' by saying that a Japanese girl got some elected position in the class because she slept with most of the boys," said a woman in disgust.

"Vicious! I hope she doesn't have daughters because God always gets people like that!" exclaimed Madeleine. She sipped her tea. "This is excellent tea, Rose, Earl Grey?"

"Yes," replied Rose. "Madeleine, Where did you get that dress? It's beautiful."

"Thanks, I picked it up at Plumage in Chappaqua, they've a wonderful selection."

A red-haired woman, looked appraisingly at Madeleine's dress and said; "Why do you shop there, didn't they follow you around the store?"

"Maybe," replied Madeleine. "But I wouldn't have noticed. If I did I'd figure it was because I was well dressed, and looked like a serious buyer."

"You artists!" laughed her interrogator. "They were making sure that your bad blackness didn't steal the store. They didn't follow the white customers around did they?"

"I wouldn't know; I don't focus on things like that. I guess growing up in the Caribbean makes it hard for me to imagine that anyone could look at me and automatically perceive me in a negative light," Madeleine said thoughtfully. "If I started thinking that way I'd go crazy."

"What's it, a Judith Leiber? You could get this at Nordstrom and accompanied by the thorough ass-kissing you deserve when spending big bucks," said her interrogator.

Phoebe said, "You're fortunate Madeleine; you don't see what you don't want to and let it make you crazy. But if you had a son you'd have to pay attention, or this place would make him crazy or dead."

Amina said, "They predicted that by two thousand, seventy percent of African American males would be unavailable to black women because of death, incarceration, drug addiction, unemployment, insanity, homosexuality or interracial marriages. The witching hour's passed so I guess our daughters now have slim pickings."

"Who'll they marry?" asked a pale green-eyed woman helping herself to a cucumber sandwich off a nearby brass table. "I'm sorry to say this, but most black men are already obnoxious. Imagine how they'll be when they're truly an endangered species. God knows who to test, I couldn't be a part of the next generation that is going to have to deal with this new even worse breed." She sipped her pale gold sherry.

"I've often wanted to pack mine up and send him with his infantile whining and unreasonable demands back to his Momma, but I'm too old now to learn to use a vibrator," said someone else.

"Oh!" sputtered Marguerite, spilling tea onto Rose's embroidered pastel napkin. "Oh, clumsy me," she dabbed at her lap in a fluster.

Maxi jumped in. "Wait a minute, I can't let that pass. A black man is no different from any other man. Treat him nicely and he'll be nice to you. Spoil him and he'll behave like a spoiled brat. What is that little slogan you sometimes see on black boys' tee shirts? 'God don't make no junk?' I heartily endorse it. We black women, wives and mothers; we make the junk."

"Hear hear!" cheered Charlie. To her surprise several women took up the cheer.

Madeleine raised her sherry and proclaimed in her throaty voice with its musical accent. "Here's to my black man, Oswald. Long may he reign in my heart and in my bed."

"'Nuff said," said Rose with a laugh. "But really, considering the depressing statistics, who can our little darlings marry?"

"Little as we want to hear this, we have to steel ourselves to our daughters marrying outside the race," said a woman in black with creeping vitilago running up her silk covered neck to her piebald face. "I've already told my daughter she can't bring an African home to me. I won't have him stranding her in his country; barefoot, pregnant, miserable and a slave to her mother-in-law, while he gets to keep her kids when she's ready to pull out."

"They'd be doing you a favor," laughed Rose. "Can you imagine your African grandchild with one of those noses that you could drive a bus up?"

"Really, Rose," said Phoebe with a laugh, "you are out of order."

"I'm not. You couldn't put a child like that into Jack and Jill. Those kids would shun it as if it had a disability," shot back Rose.

"That takes care of the Africans," said Amina. "I also don't want any Arab son-in-law because my daughter is not being raised to be subservient to men."

"That works for me," said a woman in a Gaultier suit absently polishing her enamel Hermes bracelet with Rose's napkin. "I have a friend who married an Iranian," she continued. "They had the most beautiful, loving relationship. Then he learned to speak English-the things that came from his mouth! She divorced him. He learned nasty words like 'cook, clean, lazy bitch, work'. It was pitiful," she said.

"I don't want any Japanese," declared Maxi. "They're racist. You've heard what they say about us. They run bus tours through Harlem daily to show how poor black folks live. And women in that society don't have much power."

"Please, don't talk about the Japanese. We'll be here all day. That's a set of racist, little bastards. I got rid of my Sony TV and told my husband not to buy another Japanese car after that little jerk Kajiyama -that's the one you mean Maxi? shot off his mouth. He's one of their government officials. He jumped up and said that blacks are like prostitutes, we 'ruin the atmosphere' of neighborhoods we move into. Then he elaborated that bad money drives out good money the way that Blacks come in and drive out Whites in American neighborhoods."

The plaintive conversation irritated Charlie . "What is the point of this?" she said to Maxi in a low voice. "The man is off somewhere making money then relaxing with his geisha, his sushi and his sake; not knowing or caring that we exist."

"Hush," countered Maxi. "Listen. "

"...been said by Nakasone that blacks and other minorities lower the U.S. level of intelligence. Waktanabe said that U.S. blacks do not mind going into bankruptcy."

Charlie spread caviar on a toast point and bit into it. "Mothers, you heard it here first. Those Japanese boys won't be beating down your doors in the next few years to marry your darling daughters. So let's hear it for women learning to support themselves. Then Prince Charming, of any race, can come share their bountiful lives on their terms."

"Hey, what if he's Hispanic," came a cry.

"Tell him to get lost. They think they're better than we are. And they're just as bad as the Arabs with that macho stuff; we got the word machismo from them. Let them stay there and beat up on their own women," said a deep brown woman with braids.

A Latina-looking woman said dryly, "Thank you for so neatly tying up the Hispanic connection." She looked daggers at the speaker.

Rose sidetracked her. "No offence to you, Maxi, but if Buddy brings home a white daughter-in-law to me when there are so many beautiful, intelligent, young black women out there, both he and his white wife will be out in the cold. It just doesn't make sense. His father and I have both told him that we would consider such an act a betrayal of the race and a repudiation of us as black parents."

"You're being extreme. I'm a product of Mr. Charley and Black and there are worse things. We have culture in common with Whites and we want the same things," protested Maxi.

"You can't legislate love!" Charlie exclaimed, coming to her best friend's defense. "I hope Germaine marries within her race, but if she doesn't then I hope that whomever she chooses loves her, and will be good to her. I don't care what race they are."

"Good by whose standards? These men can court you with roses then become the devil's own backside once that ring goes on your finger. If some man introduced my daughter to the business end of a vacuum cleaner in the name of goodness, she wouldn't know what to do with it except maybe hit him with it," said Madeleine.

"Bravo!" said Charlie. "I hope Germaine would do the same if it's not good by her norms. Talking about Germaine, Rose, I'm going to check on her."

"Oh, Charlie, sit and don't be a worrywart," said Rose.

Charlie was already halfway to the door with Maxi behind her muttering that she too would check on her daughter.

"Since Tatty's started walking without support I worry that she might overdo it and collapse," said Maxi

"She won't," said Charlie. "Your Chun Do Sun Bup has kicked Encephalitis in the butt. It's like a miracle. This attack from the East seems to be doing the trick."

Maxi said fervently, "Thank God I discovered the East. Tatty's now off all meds, she's doing the Chi training and getting stronger every day."

"Good for her!" exclaimed Charlie. "I knew you'd find a cure. I wore my knees out praying for you two." She hugged her friend. As they approached the family room the noise level became deafening. They recognized Buddy's voice.

"...you know I was just a little kid and my Dad said to me, 'why don't you watch 'Leave it to Beaver?' I said 'Dad that can't be a kid's show'. He gives me this strange look and turns on the TV. There wasn't any picture at first and I heard this woman's voice saying 'Ward, I think you were a little hard on the Beaver last night'."

"Yuk sick!" said someone.

"The little devil," laughed Charlie. Maxi joined in, then they composed themselves and entered the room. The kids were having a loud, good time. Some played video games on the big screen, plasma TV hung on the wall, others shot pool, and a group was with Buddy at the computer, surfing the net and joking.

"Buddy, where are our girls?" Charlie shouted above the noise.

Buddy jumped. "Mrs. Gopilal, Mrs. Paine, you startled me. They're upstairs with Sydney. Please don't tell Mom, she'll make them come down here with us. She'll say they're messing up the room or something-you know how she is." He clasped his hands prayerfully and flashed her the million-kilowatt grin previously reserved for white girls.

"We won't say a word." They returned his smile and retreated to the tea party.

"Why do we put our children in these expensive private schools and live in these neighborhoods? Do we want them to assimilate? And what is assimilation to us?"

A Caribbean accented voice added, "We don't go to church with them. My children don't know about God because I refuse to take them to the poor side of town to attend a black church. I didn't grow up with this black church/white church thing in the Caribbean. But I do know we're not welcome in the white churches on our side of town. Of course they wouldn't put us out if we went, they'd pretend, because it was church. But it's the same folks that won't let us into their country clubs to play golf. So I guess we're not religious assimilates."

"That may be, but I still see us as Lorraine Hansberry's 'assimilated Negroes'."

"We've certainly got all the trappings," said Maxi. "Does this mean that we lost our black souls to gain the white world? And why can't a moneyed existence be Black?"

There was a momentary silence; then everyone exploded with answers.

"Blackness does not mean poverty -"

"I can appreciate both Fanon and Schopenhauer."

"That's sixties cant-"

"Rose, what are these?" asked Phoebe as Denka served a tray of pastries.

"Cornish Pasties, aren't they good? I love them with tea."

There were murmurs of approval as a Chopin etude played softly. Charlie said thoughtfully, "You know what assimilation means to me? It means that I've made it; that they can't touch me because I have enough money to protect my loved ones and myself from anything that the white world can dish out. I'm equal. That's the difference between us and some downtrodden woman in a ghetto. We have money and education as armor. We're like white chocolate –chocolate flavor but an acceptable 'white' exterior."

"Charlie, I think that's a bit simplistic. But often the truth is simple, so I won't argue," said Phoebe rising. "Rose, it's been lovely, but I've got to go. No, I won't touch that cake. We're going to the Boulé dinner tonight and I have to fit into my dress."

Many of the women were attending the dinner, so the tea-party broke up.

"I had the best time," Germaine told Charlie in the car. Sydney got great stuff for Christmas. She got a six-hundred dollar Kate Spade backpack, a five hundred dollar cell 'phone with internet access and all kinds of gizmos plus an eight-hundred dollar hand-carved chess set made of some weird wood and a matching thousand dollar chess table. It is so cool! "

"Rose got that chess stuff for herself and her house. It has nothing to do with Sydney."

"Why don't you develop a hobby that'll get me great, expensive stuff for Christmas that I like," asked Germaine in an aggrieved voice. "Then maybe I could have really super-cool stuff like my friends."

"I never said that you couldn't get a job." Charlie smiled at her daughter and patted the hand that Germaine snatched away.

57

The French Effect

"...Scientists are blaming the greenhouse effect for this unusually warm Spring-like day in Early March-" said the radio. Charlie switched it off and sang joyously.

Sweeeet love,

Hear me callin' out your name

Lennie and Germaine were in Trinidad for a week and Roderick was on his way to her. They'd have a glorious weekend in Lake Placid. All phone calls would be forwarded to the Lake Placid number and no one would be the wiser." *How sweet it is!"* Charlie sang then laughed and gunned her motor, the quicker to reach Kennedy airport and her lover-her wonderful, marvelous, virile lover. Who said there wasn't a God?

"Wow, you look fantastic!" Roderick said as he hugged her and spun her around.

She knew she looked good. Her dress hugged her curves the way her mother had prescribed: "tight enough to reveal that you're a woman, but loose enough to show that you're a lady." She was an elegant, ladylike sex object; Roderick's sex object-and in his honor she wore no panties.

"You like," she teased. "Don't handle the merchandise too much."

"Trollop! Let's get out of here." He grabbed his duffle bag.

"Sure, by the way, I love the way those jeans cling to your buns. Did I ever tell you that you have a magnificent ass?"

He gave his sexy grin. "Shall I drop trou so that you can get a better view?" He pretended to unbuckle his belt and Charlie walked off quickly.

"I don't know you," she said over her shoulder with a laugh.

He caught up with her and trousers still on and arms around each other they hurried to the parking lot. The unseasonably warm wind whipped their faces as they roared down the highway with the convertible top down. Charlie felt glamorous and carefree in her sunglasses and silk scarf tied around her hair like a 50s movie star.

"This weekend is going to be great," Roderick shouted above the wind. "I'll beat the pants off you on the ski slopes, then pull the pants off you in our little nest for two."

"Will you stop it," laughed Charlie, she slapped him playfully and did her Kegels in anticipation. "I'll get into an accident from thinking impure, exciting thoughts."

"Then we'll die together, locked in a passionate embrace. All true lovers will seek our ashes as earthly relics of a love sublime. "

"Idiot!" She smiled at him; then her cell phone rang. "Okay, fine. I'll be right there." she yelled into the 'phone then hung up. "Bad news, Roddy," she shouted above the wind. "Damn, I can't hear myself." She closed the automatic convertible top and continued, "There's trouble at my Fordham Road restaurant. I have to go there now. I'll drop you off at my house-"

"I don't want to be at your house if you're not there,"he protested.

"Please, It's only 'til I get this situation under control," she wheedled. "I don't want you hanging around a fast food place in a commercial section, and not a pretty one either; on a hot day-I'd feel guilty. You're on vacation."

"In other words, you want to administrate your empire alone and don't want unexplained men hanging around you and causing gossip among your staff."

"That works for me," she said with an apologetic smile. "I can't fool you, can I? Honey, I promise I won't be long." She touched his hand. " There's no one at the house, the staff has the weekend off and Therese, Germaine's au pair, is out of town."

"How can I refuse you anything?" He snaked his hand under her silky dress.

She playfully slapped the hand away. "Will you stop it! You'll make me get into an accident when I have an orgasm and press down on the gas pedal."

"You don't love me," Roderick clowned, in a little boy voice."

"Shhh, baby, I'll show you later," she stage whispered; "in Lake Placid, by the fireplace tonight. It's still cold up there."

"You're wrong. It's going to be hot, hot, hot!" he assured her, and gave her breast a quick squeeze. "Guess what goodies I've got in my Dr.

Feelgood bag for your sexual delectation? Guess what I'm going to teach you tonight?"

Charlie's uterus contracted with desire, and the car momentarily careened from left to right on the highway. Would she finally experience that Shakti/Shiva thing tonight with her sexual gourmet lover? She felt excited already. All too soon they reached Westchester. "This is what I love about Angloville-close enough to the city to keep you in touch with the real world, yet far enough to insulate you if that's what you want; almost like your Bahamas," Charlie said when they reached her town.

"What do *you* want, Charlie?" Roderick asked.

"Everything, of course. Don't we all?" She turned into her driveway.

"Hey, this is lovely," he exclaimed. "I never saw your place by daylight."

"Thank you." She drove into the gatehouse that had been converted into a garage. She closed the automatic garage door, popped the trunk, and slid out of the low car. "Will you need your bag to freshen up before I get back?"

"No," he walked toward her in the dim light. He closed the trunk. "I need you."

They were on each other like magnets. He stroked her back through the soft material and she moaned long and low as they both feverishly pushed aside each other's clothing. Roderick slipped on a condom and next thing Charlie knew she was perched on the back of her car, legs wrapped around Roderick's thighs with him deliciously pumping away. They screamed in release.

"Oh, God, Roderick. Suppose the neighbors hear, whatever will they think?" Charlie dropped her head to his shoulder, panting and giggling.

"That milady's getting laid like she's never been laid before. Isn't that true?" His glowing, mismatched eyes held the light, and they kissed again.

Charlie looked at the luminous dial of her watch. "Oh God, Roddy, I must go."

"After you've just come? Shame on you."

"You!" She tapped him on the bottom smartly. "You're awful. Yes, I've just come, but I should have 'come 'to my restaurant hours ago. I'll let you into the house. There's food in the fridge. Mi casa es su casa." She pecked him on the lips but he held her head and prolonged the kiss. Charlie gently disentangled herself. "We won't go there again," she said breathlessly and laughingly ran out into the sunlight.

"Spoilsport," he said following her outside. "Hey! This is truly beautiful."

"Thanks, there's a gazebo in the back, a pool with its winter cover on, a cabana, tennis court and rock garden. It's a lovely day, walk around a bit and then let yourself in. Here's the key." She pressed it into his hand, kissed him quickly on the lips and hurried back to the garage. She felt his hot eyes on her unfettered behind and this excited her all over again. "Tonight," she promised aloud to both herself and her lover...

Charlie roared onto Angloville Road and headed north to Zachy's Liquor store in Scarsdale. She bought Cristal champagne and avoided Touristy Lake Placid's prohibitive prices. It would be a nice surprise for her Roddy-nothing but the best for him.

Charlie looked at her watch when she reached her restaurant. Damn! They'd probably have to overnight at her house and head for Lake Placid tomorrow. Still, virtuoso sex, even at home in her guestroom was not to be sneered at. PC muscles aflutter she marched into her manager's office. You could never be too tight.

"Okay, Frank, what's up? It had better be good, I was on my way out of town." She had to break her concentration and do some work. Damn!

"Mrs. Gopilal, there's an urgent message for you to call someone named Therese at your house."

"Therese?! " said Charlie grabbing the phone and dialing. "What!" she shouted into the receiver. "You're joking. You dumb ass! Cochon! You're not even supposed to be there!" Charlie screeched. "I don't pay you to think, you stupid cow! He was telling the truth. Why the hell do you think he had my key! Give me that goddamn number." She wrote quickly then slammed down the phone.

"I hope everything's all right, Mrs. G.," said Frank.

"It's not!" she snapped striding to the door. "That silly bitch! "Handle the situation here. I have no time for it. If you can't deal, I'll find someone who can."

"Will do, Mrs. G., don't you worry, everything here will be just fine."

But she was already gone, roaring up to Westchester and cursing volubly as she unsuccessfully tried to get through to the number she'd been given; she gave up in disgust. The dumb foreign fuck-up had probably taken the number down wrong. "Shit! How dare she call the police! Damn!" Charlie smacked the steering wheel soundly and for the second time that day, almost ran off the road.

Charlie screeched into a parking space on Angloville Road in front of the Police Station. She calmed down at the reassuring sight of the pretty, orderly town, her town, with its clean, old-fashioned, red brick municipal building opposite the matching red brick library. This wasn't like going to a Bronx precinct to spring a Black or a Hispanic miscreant. Life was civilized here in her little, moneyed oasis.

Charlie slid out of her sports car, smoothed out her dress, threw up her head imperiously, like the owner of a two and a half million dollar house in Angloville should; and strode, Mischka bag in hand, into the neat police station. Fancy Roddy getting busted for trespassing on her property, did this mean that she would be marrying a jailbird? They would laugh about this later, but now was not the time. She assumed a stern mien and forged ahead.

"Yes, Ma'am, can I help you?" asked a pleasant young desk sergeant.

"Good afternoon, I'm Mrs. Gopilal. I'm here to pick up my houseguest who was mistakenly arrested for trespassing on my property."

The young policeman looked uncomfortable. "Yes Ma'am. I'm aware of the case. Have a seat, please."

Charlie sat on a wooden bench by the wall. Idly she glanced around the neat, clean, little room with its water cooler, candy machine dispensing nuts, gum and M&M's and an American flag propped up in a corner. In God We Trust, she mused. Luckily she had plenty of that in the bank and in her little Mischka wallet. This allowed her to sit here, dressed in silk and leather, and be treated politely by white people who were her financial inferiors. Liberty and justice for all who have money she thought smugly. She could easily make whatever bail was set. She concentrated on doing her Kegels so everything would be tight. Tonight could still be salvaged. She was lucky to be someplace civilized like Angloville. Put this situation in the Bronx and it could easily have become explosive. One-two-three-flutter. Two-two–three-flutter.

"Mrs. Gopilal?"

"Yes?" Damn, he'd interrupted her right in the middle of a series of flutters. Maybe she could finish the series while walking. It would be great for her concentration. She rose and approached the young man at the desk all the while concentrating on her PC muscle; three-two three-flutter, four-two-three-flutter...

"Sorry to keep you waiting. But the chief wants to speak to you himself. He's on his way. There's been a terrible misunderstanding."

"I know; you arrested my houseguest."

The young man avoided her eyes. She sat again and wished they'd get on with it. She was getting bored. Roderick was probably having the time of his life trading witticisms about wrongful arrest with the cops. She smiled at the thought of seeing him soon-better be ready, she switched to the slow squeezes-one, hold, two-three, two, hold, two-three...

A door to her right unlocked electronically and an urbane, older man in police uniform entered. "Mrs. Gopilal? I'm Philip Stewart, the Chief of Police here. I understand you're a new resident? Welcome to our village." He said warmly and thrust out his hand.

"Where is Mr. Baine?" she asked coldly, briefly touching the proffered hand.

"There's an unfortunate situation we must discuss first. Would you care for coffee?"

"Take me to him, now," she commanded.

A burly, young cop entered and asked, "Everything all right, sir?"

"Yes, Simmons, we'll be fine. I was just telling Mrs. Gopilal about the unfortunate situation with Mr. Black."

"Baine," Charlie hissed.

"Quite, quite," said the chief soothingly.

Simmons added. "Ma'am it's our duty here in Angloville to protect white-"

"Simmons!" roared his chief.

"Sorry, sir," the young man said, and blushed and lapsed into silence.

"Come." The chief pressed a button and opened the door. Charlie and Simmons followed him through it. "What Simmonds was trying to say, Mrs. Gopilal, is that we try to protect our villagers. You pay high taxes and heavy mortgages. You deserve the best, and we aim to give it to you." He opened a door and led them down a long corridor. They approached a room where indistinct, angry voices were raised. The voices became increasingly clear through the open door.

"Okay, even if the old biddy visiting next door said he was exposing himself you didn't have to do that. You dumb fuck, you can't do that here! This isn't Bedford Stuyvesant?

"The old girl was scared-we had to help her. How was she to know the coon was legit? He wasn't wearing a chauffeur's cap or pushing a lawn mower; so how the hell was *anybody* to know," a nearby voice said defensively.

Charlie's blood ran cold and she stiffened.

"Simmons, close that door," ordered the chief.

Simmons looked uncomfortably at Charlie and hastened away to obey. Charlie and the chief reached the end of the corridor where there was a room containing two jail cells and a painted-over window. Charlie gasped when she got close enough to make out a figure in one of the cells. He wore Roderick's clothes and had a pulpy mass where Roderick's face should have been. One eye was swollen shut, and a half closed brown eye gazed blankly around. Her knees went weak and she felt coldness in her entrails. She leaned against the cell and clutched the bars for support. She wanted to throw up. "My God, what did you do to him?" she whispered.

"There was a slight misunderstanding," replied the chief of police. He sweated visibly, and she smelled the fear on him.

Simmons hadn't reached the door yet and she still heard the loud voices.

"Schmidt, you cocksucking ass-hole! You got us all in deep shit now. That's no nigger in there; it's a fuckin' *Negro*. And this is not the mother-fuckin' eighty-seventh precinct in Brooklyn-its Angloville! You flaming ass-hole! That fuckin' rich, black broad's goin' t' have our asses. You should-"

"Hey, a nigga's a nigga. Hang on to your balls. I put the stun gun on the buck's big, black, dick. You shoulda seen him jump and yowl." He gave a big laugh. "That'll teach him to talk fancy and say he's a what? A archy teck or some bullshit so? I closed down that green eye real fast. No nigger ought t'have a green eye anyway. He looked like a fuckin' freak 'fore I rearranged his face."

Charlie's nausea was quickly replaced by rage. She refused to lose control. The chief nervously regarded the damning open door. Soon there was the thud of the door closing, but it was too late.

Charlie flipped out her cell phone. "Get the hell out of here," she said in a cold fury. "I'm calling my lawyer."

The chief silently stood at a distance until she was finished. "We can go in now," he said unlocking the door. They entered and the chief said courteously, "Sir, you can leave now, will you get up please?"

Roderick remained seated on the wooden bench that ran the length of the cell. His face was expressionless and he reeked of urine and feces.

Charlie whispered, "Roddy, please, get up, darling." Her voice broke, "For me..."

Still he sat there. The chief reached out a hand to to help him up.

"Get away from him!" Charlie cried sharply as Roderick shrank from the white man and cupped his hands protectively over his genitals.

The chief retreated. Charlie gently placed her lover's arm over her shoulder and pulled him up. Then, like some strange lumbering animal they made their slow progress down the hallway. A large, florid, blonde cop stepped out of a room in front of them and Roderick shuddered. He clutched Charlie tightly.

Someone shouted from within the room. "Get the fuck out, Schmidt. Next time ya have to drop a prisoner off at Sing Sing, don't stop by here. Just haul ya fuckin' lard ass back to Brooklyn. You got us a shitload o' trouble. Damn!"

The chief hurried past Charlie and Roderick. When he reached Schmidt he hissed, "Beat it ass-hole, and keep this fuckin' door shut." He slammed the door to the incriminating room then walked back to Charlie and Roderick, explaining as he came. "We ran a pedigree on him on the computer. Of course nothing came up, and we were just holding him until you got here to identify him. If you had called we would have released him on his own recognizance and given him a court date. But he had no I.D. on him-"

"It's a warm day. His jacket's in my car with his I.D.," Charlie said dully.

"This is all such an unfortunate misunderstanding. Your friend probably overreacted -"

"Where he comes from he's accustomed to being treated like a human being, a special human being." Charlie's voice quavered.

"The young woman at your house could not identify him. In fact she was quite adamant in maintaining that he was a prowler. I understand he was not the most cooperative ... sometimes police officers get carried away. They live with death and danger every day. They overreact ... Cops from other precincts don't know our ways. They try to be helpful-This is an expensive village. Everyone wants to protect its residents ... You understand." He threw up his hands conveying helpless despair at an imperfect world.

Charlie looked the chief dead in the eye. Eyes bright with unshed tears she swallowed and said softly, "This will not end here." They stared at each other.

The chief flushed. "Please come with me, we must finish the paperwork and return the contents of his pockets to him."

Later Charlie retraced her steps to the entrance of the station, this time half carrying, half dragging her befouled lover with her. She crooned to him as she had to Germaine when she was a baby. After what seemed an eternity she reached the exit door, an officer ran ahead and opened it for her. He visibly stiffened. Charlie strode to the door and dragged Roderick across the threshold into the balmy day. Lights blinded them as media people with cameras, outstretched microphones and notebooks swarmed them. Her lawyer, Walker had done his job.

Roderick's arm around her shoulder tightened, like that of a frightened child. He whimpered. Tears sprang to her eyes at this show of his vulnerability and need of her strength now. She steeled herself and held his reeking body closer.

A black Adonis in an Armani suit cut through the crowd and took her arm. "Here, Charlie, shall I get you some help with him? I'll set up a press interview in two hours, that gives you time to get him cleaned up and get the hospital report."

"Thanks, Henry, I can manage him. I'll get him to my car. You help by dealing with this pack. You're the best lawyer a woman ever had. "

"Charlie, please tell our viewers what happened in there?"

Charlie recognized Aviva Richardson, the stylish black anchorperson, holding the microphone. They were fellow members of The One Hundred Black Women, the political and philanthropic group of black women who quietly made a difference in the city. A flicker of recognition passed between them.

"Aviva, I'm sorry but I can't make a statement right now. As you can see, my friend and business associate is injured. He needs immediate help. Mr. Walker, my lawyer," she nodded toward him, "will give you all the information we can release at this time."

"Everyone get your shots now. I'll brief you on the situation later. We'll need some answers from the chief of police," said Walker.

There was another eruption of light and whirring of cameras as the media then the media with pounds of equipment swarmed past Charlie and Roderick into the police station in a feeding frenzy.

The sun was even warmer now and there was a soft breeze. Charlie sighed and carefully settled Roderick into the front seat of her car. She buckled him in, stroked his hair gently and crooned to him; she dared not kiss his painful-looking purple face. She slid into the driver's seat and took one last despairing look at her lover. Then her face crumpled, tears streamed from her eyes and she put her head down on the steering wheel and cried in great heaving sobs. Finally she wiped her face and turned on the ignition. The radio played,

And I say to myself

What a wonderful world-

She jabbed the button angrily and switched it off. In the sudden silence she backed up to a garbage can and with deadly accuracy flung the bottle of Cristal champagne into it. Sunlight blazed off the diamond bracelet on her slim brown wrist before she closed the convertible top and drove away.

No more music played.

58

Secrets

"Honey, we're home," Lennie walked into the library where Charlie sat reading and pecked her on the lips. "Mmmwah! It's good to be back home; we missed you."

Charlie cringed but kept up a front for Germaine who ran into the room behind her father and hugged her. "Mommy, listen to this." She pulled a miniature steel band pan from her duffle bag and beat out a few bars of a calypso."

"Wow, Honey!" said Charlie.

"I played the harp down there too. Granny has a friend that plays. She has a beautiful, concert grand, pedal harp with a real gold finish. Of course it has a crown. Granny took me to her house and invited a lot of her friends and all my cousins over, and I played for them. I practiced at her friend's house a few times after that. I have harp competitions coming up next month. I want to make all-state."

"Aren't you responsible!

"Uh huh. But Mom, Trinidad was the bomb! I went to so many fetes. I can dance the calypso, play the steel band pan, I met cute guys who thought I was cute too. I have to go back this summer. Chandra-"

"What about your sick grandmother?' Charlie interrupted with a laugh.

"She's cool, she says she started feeling better as soon as she saw me an' Daddy. I spent time with her too. We had tea together every afternoon in the garden by her new lily pond. It was cool. She allowed me to have a pool party last night and Chandra – remember her? Mumtaz's younger sister who's my age; she invited the coolest kids!"

"I see you had a great time, sorry I couldn't pick you up. I had this meeting I couldn't get out of. But how'd you like the limo I sent? Was it cool enough for you?"

"Mom, it was the best! When I came out of the baggage area and saw this old dude holding up a placard that said Germaine Gopilal, I was like to die! I said 'Daddy there's my fan club'?"

"You little monkey!" said her mother with a laugh.

"Gee, show your Mom what we got for her," said Lennie. "Your daughter's a chip off the old block-she's got her mother's commercial instincts. Do you know what she did? She sold her new graphite tennis racket to one of her cousins for twice what we paid for it. It was on sale in the pro shop there for four times the amount. What with the import duty and taxes, luxury good prices at home are astronomical."

"Mom, we got you the best minaudiere. I'll give it to you later; it's packed away in my suitcase. We got it at a duty free store in Port of Spain. When I get older I'm gonna borrow it, may I please? It's fierce!"

"I hope it doesn't bite," said Charlie, smiling from under the avalanche of words.

Germaine continued, "I didn't want to get it messed up with the food I had in my hand luggage. Granny sent me with the best food! I ate so much on the 'plane. Mom where's Therese. I've got to do my vacation homework tonight and that French subjunctive stuff makes me crazy!"

"Honey, Therese is no longer with us. We're interviewing a young, French Canadian woman who'll be available at the end of the week. The family she au pairs for is moving to Greece. We'll meet her on Saturday and see if we like her."

"Good, Therese was mean, and she smelt under all that perfume. I'll go online to a homework help site. I'd better go unpack. Mom, your minaudiere's to die for! Wait 'til you see it!" She bounded out of the room and up the stairs carrying her hand luggage and steel band pan and loudly humming the tune to that year's Trinidadian Road March.

"Is she a great kid or what?" said Lennie, with a proud smile.

"She is," agreed Charlie. "I enjoy the weekly mother-daughter outings we started last fall. She doesn't always want to come, but she's great company, she's so funny."

"My girl!" said Lennie and he made a self-congratulatory fist.

"Yes, Lennie; she's your girl, and she'll always be that. However, I'm not 'your girl' and I can't do this anymore."

"What are you talking about?" Lennie looked bemused.

"Us. I want you out of here. This charade is too much for me. I can't do it anymore."

"Are you crazy? Where is this coming from? What the hell is 'out of here?'"

"Look Lennie, I've come to my senses. I don't want this anymore. I don't want us anymore. This keeping up with the Joneses, this having everything, including you, for show has taken a toll on me. The emotional price is too high and I'm not paying anymore."

"I heard that Moonies are now in Westchester. They bought a place around here. You sure you're not in some kind of cult?" He looked at her suspiciously.

"No, Lennie," Charlie said tiredly. "It's very basic. I'm leaving you because I no longer love you and you definitely do not love me."

" Wait up! What shit are you talkin'? Of course I love you-"

"No, Lennie, you don't love me, you love yourself. I was the free ride that allowed you to indulge that immense self-love-excessive womanizing, nice cars, nice clothes. You never ever told yourself 'no'."

"And you were the good long-suffering wife, being taken advantage of-"

"I didn't say that, Lennie."

"You don't have to. Perhaps if you hadn't insisted on wearing the pants and working and behaving like a man things might've been different around here." He lowered himself into the chair where Leroy had sat that emotional day. He studied her.

"Lennie, you never loved me. I've seen love and it's not this. If you loved me you would've been happy with me for my success. You would never have seen me as a threat and have to hurt me with other women. The money would've been for *us!*"

"If you were a real woman you would never have had to wear the pants. You had to make the most money, work the hardest, buy the biggest house. You could've paid my damn salary if you wanted to. You certainly have enough money! How do you think that makes me feel?" He asked bitterly.

"Lennie, I made money because I'm good at what I do, and I work hard. It wasn't about belittling you-Jesus!"

"Right, you're so damn good. How could I ever forget that?"

"Lennie, whether or not I'm good, I'm looking at the big picture. My life is wrong. This is wrong. I've got a husband who sees dollar signs and doesn't see me. I belong to an organization for my child that doesn't care a rap about its members, just about their social status and financial standing. I have two friends who've lost practically everything in the last few weeks-"

"And you've got shit on the brain."

"Maybe I do, Lennie, but let's not fight. I want friends who want to see *me* rather than my house. I want a man to love *me* and not what I can provide. When all of this is gone," she waved at the expensively appointed room, "all we have is people. So it had better be the right people or they'll be gone too. To that end I'm leaving you. I'm taking Germaine out of Jack and Jill so we'll both no longer have to settle for being around the wrong people, and we may move out of the country."

"What the hell are you telling me?" said Lennie staring at her as if she had suddenly gone mad.

"That I've come to my senses. I have detailed information about your well-known infidelities. So don't even think that you can try to stop me legally. But let's try to stay friends; we've got Germaine to raise. We need to make arrangements. She and I might be moving to the Bahamas."

"The Bahamas! Now wait a minute, woman; are you crazy? You're not taking my child out of this country!"

"Medicine is not a lucrative field. I could make it worth your while..."

"Do you think I'd sell my child?"

"No, I just think you'd want her to be happy and looked after. She's a young woman now, are you going to discuss boys and periods with her? Do you plan to have your girlfriends give her romantic advice? Who'll be with her while you're out dating? You don't plan to give that up, do you? Marriage didn't stop you, so divorce surely won't. And can you afford her?"

Lennie lowered his head into his hands and sat quietly.

"Lennie, you had your chance," Charlie said. "I once saw this really banal saying on a mug, 'the best thing a father can do for his children is to love their mother,' It's true. If you had loved me this wouldn't have happened. We could've created a happy, two parent family for our child. We could've all been happy."

Lennie kept his head down. Finally he looked up and said: "I'm sorry. We'll do what's best for Germaine. You're right as usual and you win as usual. I can't afford her; the time, the money for all the things that she needs; I don't have the money to fight you. But I do love her." There were tears in his eyes. "Why the Bahamas? Can I see my little girl sometimes?"

Charlie sat down and told him about Roderick.

59

Contemplation

"Darling, don't send me away," Charlie cried.

"I'm not sending you away." Roderick kicked at a pebble on the beach. "This whole thing's beyond our control." He put his hands in his pockets and looked out to sea.

"It's not. We can still choose to be with each other," she held onto his arm and rested her face on his shoulder as they both looked out to sea. The sun was setting and there was a coolness blowing off the water. In the distance a fisherman's boat headed for shore.

"Roderick, hold me, I'm not strong enough for this," she said in a small voice.

"Charlie, you are." He held her and she clung to him tightly and buried her face in his chest. He grimaced. "Move your hand up a bit, Love, that spot's still tender. Your cab will soon be here we should head back to the house. You should let me drive you."

"I couldn't bear it. Please, let me do it this way."

They held hands and walked slowly back to the courtyard. Roderick unlocked the gate and let them into the cool, shaded, patio garden.

"Let's sit here," Charlie sank onto the love seat under the hibiscus covered pergola. Roderick sat next to her. She looked at her waiting bags by the gate and sighed.

"Say hello to Maxi for me," Roderick picked up her hand and studied it. "You have beautiful, strong hands."

"Roderick," she turned to him with tears rolling down her cheeks, "Will you really be okay?"

"As okay as I'll ever be. Let me put on some music." He touched her shoulder lightly then went into the house and returned accompanied by

Rodrigo's Aranjuez Concerto. "Remember that?" He sat next to her. "It's really a dirge, but I didn't tell you then. Maybe it was an omen."

She smiled, "A lifetime ago, the first time..." She gazed into the distance. "It was cruel of you not to take my calls. I've phoned you so many times."

"Charlie, I couldn't deal with you and this."

"I know, Sweetheart, I'm not blaming you, that's why I came-you need me. You're doing so much better than you were before. Do you remember right after the-the accident? Who'd believe that I'd ever let one of your erections go to waste?"

He winced and smiled. "That was something wasn't it-a four hour long, drug-induced erection. Suppose I could do that at will. I'd go into business providing solace for lonely ladies. I thought I'd pass out when I saw that needle and where it was going."

"What was that drug they pumped you up with to produce that beautiful monster?"

"Papavarin, it certainly did the trick. We both saw that the old equipment could still work. So don't you worry, I'm going to be alright.."

"Roddy, can it ever be like it was before, between us?" she asked wistfully.

"Love, everything changes, including you and me. You've been a brick, and I can never repay you."

"Don't say that, you don't have to-I love you." She touched his hand.

He held the hand briefly then rose and walked off to the garden gate; he looked out to sea. "Enjoy Disney World; I know Germaine will."

"I'm sure. She must have arrived there hours ago with Maxi and Tatiana. I can hardly believe I'll be having dinner with them later this evening? The world is so shrunken." She sighed and came and stood next to him, joining him looking out to sea.

"Charlie," he cupped her face gently in his hands and looked at her tenderly, "Forget about me and get on with your life."

"No," she moaned, placing her hands over his. "Roderick, darling," she whispered, "please, love me like before."

"I can't, I'm not the man I was before. I won't tie you to a sexual cripple who has to use drugs to get erections. I don't want your pity, or your Viagra. You don't want the sexual Bionic Man." He gently moved her hands and walked onto the beach."

She cried in earnest now and followed him, wobbling in the sand in her high heels. "I don't pity you, I love you and you've spoiled me for other men. I can't go back to Lennie after loving you. I didn't tell you before because you had so many of your own problems to deal with; but I left him."

He stared at her in surprise. "You did? "

"I put him out as soon as he returned from Trinidad. I couldn't live like that any longer-almost hating him, knowing that he didn't care about me. I told him about us."

"How did he take it?"

"The only way he could. He's not innocent; I have so much stuff on him. We both want to make it as easy as possible for Germaine so I subsidize his lifestyle and permit him unlimited access to her; once she's available, they can see each other."

"Let's take a walk. Here, give me your shoes." He took them from her, put his arm around her shoulder and they walked toward the water's edge. In the distance they could faintly hear the Aranjuez Concerto.

"Charlie, you understand that I could never live in America after what happened."

"I know, darling, and I'll regret it to the end of my days. But I could live here. You said that yourself. I could arrange things. Roderick, I've learned that people matter, not things or places. I want you. And I'll take you however and wherever I can get you-even if you have to take Viagra to function and I have to run my business from overseas."

"Charlie, it wouldn't work, and it's not your fault." He stopped walking and clenched his fists behind his back and looked out to sea.

"It is!" she clutched him. "Roddy, I'll never forgive myself for what happened to you. I know you haven't forgiven me. No, don't say anything; your body says it all."

"Charlie," he tried to shrug her off, but she held fast.

"I've been flying between New York and Nassau for the last six weeks and the only erection you ever got around me was brought on by that drug the doctor used to see if your penis still works. It works, so your problem's in your head and it's with me."

Subtle nuances of emotion played across Roderick's face. He turned and looked at her. "Charlie, give it time."

"I have, Roderick. But obviously you don't want me anymore, and it's my fault. I know it is." She said bitterly.

He pulled her to him and held her. "Charlie, Charlie, don't do this to yourself. Give me time to heal, okay?"

"You won't let me live in your world and you can't live in mine," she sniffled.

"Charlie," he tilted her face upward, "I love you, but I've got to get adjusted to my new state." He pecked her on the nose. "By the way, I like your new look. This haircut suits you." He stroked the newly bared back of her neck, and the natural curls.

"Thank you," she smiled through her tears.

"Now get on with your life. Who knows, maybe some day things will work out for us." He gently removed his arms from around her and held her hand as they walked back to the courtyard. "Enjoy Disney World with Germaine and Maxi, and what's her kid's name? Tatiana? You need a break, you've been under so much strain recently and it's my fault. I don't feel good about this either. We'll talk again when you get back to New York"

"Roderick, you will be up for the trial won't you?"

"Shhh," he placed a finger on her lips.

"Roderick!" tears spilled down her face, "You can't give up like this, you must come. You must fight-for you, for us! Don't do this-" She clutched him.

His face contorted with pain. He pushed her off him and suddenly lashed out. "Charlie! Don't you understand?!" He strode to the courtyard wall and smacked it resoundingly. "The white man has pissed on you for me, okay?" he shouted, his back to her, "as if you were his bitch," his voice broke. "He defended you like his own," he rasped. "The same way the plantation owners claimed slave women and fucked them at will or worse and beat off their men-"

"The same way John Donne, Bach and Frank Lloyd Wright among others, fucked your mind Roddy-"

"No! Your crackers meant me harm. They destroyed me, to protect you. Oh God, American woman, won't you leave me alone? Don't you understand! They've taken my manhood from me, I've nothing left to give you!" He sobbed and his shoulders shook as he clung to the wall. "I'm a useless eunuch," he whispered. "I can't even service my woman."

"No," she whispered. "Never say that, don't ever say that. We're more than animals and it's not about 'servicing' me." She went to him and gently placed her face on his back and held him. "Darling, you need help to get past this. But you can do it!" her voice grew stronger. "Black women have dealt with crap for centuries and damn it you can too! Roderick, listen to me," she raised her head and shouted. "You will get over this. You are more than a fully functioning penis! Move on for God's sake, be a man! "

"Says the woman who joyously came five times a night with the penis in question," he said bitterly. He shrugged her off and re-entered the courtyard.

She followed. "Roderick that's not what's keeping me with you. A vibrator, I'm told, can do it faster and better. I don't love a vibrator-I love *you*. I want to grow old with *you*. Remember all our plans? The eco-marvel house you're going to build for us, evenings we'll spend sitting together on our wraparound porch watching the sun set."

"Charlie, don't. It was all just a dream," he kept his back to her.

"No! It was my reality. I still want it. I want you. If I have to fly here once a week, take you by the hand and drag you to a therapist; and not just a sex therapist-I will. I want you."

"You're so determined," he said tiredly.

"Remember your poem?

The graves a fine and private place

But none I think do there embrace

Well that's what's approaching," she said.

"Charlie," he groaned.

"Do you think I want to live without you now that I've seen what love can be? This isn't about hot sex; any pimply teenager in the back seat of a car can have that. This is about love. I love you. I want to share my life, my love, my opinions with you. I want you there at the end of the day to rub my back, make me feel lovable, hold me against the dark; be there for me-not just fuck me."

"Can't argue with that since I can't do it."

"I want you there for lazy Sundays, when we stay in bed all day and watch the game, do the Crossword Puzzle and keep on our pajamas 'til Monday."

"Charlie," he said in a voice filled with pain."

"I want you there when Germaine leaves me in a few years and goes off to college. I want you there when I trade in my running shoes for a yoga mat and the funerals I attend are for my friends and not for the parents of my friends. I want my life to end with you," Her voice broke and tears ran down her face, mirroring the tears she saw in his eyes in the face that was finally turned to her.

They held each other in silence for a while then Roderick murmured into her hair, "Here's your cab." He gently held her away from him. "Enjoy Disney with Germaine and your friends." He paused. "I'll see you next week, Love; we'll start working with a therapist then. As the future Mrs. Baine, it's time you begin taking your responsibilities around here seriously."

"Roderick," she screamed. She rushed back to him and threw her arms around him.

He winced, but held her and smiled.

"So we're gonna do that getting old together thing?" said Charlie.

"Yes, we'll do it. We'll toddle together down cemetery lane.

Grow old along with me!

The best is yet to be.

and all that." He kissed her nose. "We'll sit on our veranda with our teeth in glasses and watch the sun set –"

"No, no, Roderick. We'll see it rise-every day. And you know what? You'll rise again too. I know it. The south will rise again!" She ground her hips into him. "I can feel it." She laughed.

He laughed too. "I bet you can; who knows? Maybe with your ministrations..." he kissed her forehead.

Roderick and Charlie were locked in a kiss when the cab arrived. The driver put the luggage in the trunk without a word then coughed loudly and returned to his cab.

Finally Roderick whispered, "Goodbye, Love," and edged her toward the cab.

Charlie floated into the cab on a sea of bliss. She sent up a silent prayer of thanks and beamed at her lover. "To the airport, please," she said to the driver and they pulled onto the Cable Beach road while Roderick stood outside the gate waving. She blew him a kiss and looked back until he was no longer visible. Then she settled down in the back seat, rhythmically flexed her muscles in a series of Kegels, and looked straight ahead.

Angela Lynch-Clare, a member of Harlem Writer's Guild, and the Westchester branch of the National Writer's Union, is a sex therapist living in Westchester County, NY. She has published short stories in Boonoonoonos, a Caribbean magazine and articles in the Westchester NY edition of The Journal News. She has three grown daughters and currently resides in Westchester NY with her husband and a variety of pets.